OUR SOMETIME SISTER

A NOVEL BY NORAH LABINER

COFFEE HOUSE PRESS
Minneapolis, Minnesota

Coffee House Press is supported in part by a grant provided by the Minnesota State Arts Board, through an appropriation by the Minnesota State Legislature, and in part by a grant from the National Endowment for the Arts. Significant support has also been provided by the McKnight Foundation; Lannan Foundation; Jerome Foundation; Target Stores, Dayton's, and Mervyn's by the Dayton Hudson Foundation; General Mills Foundation; St. Paul Companies; Butler Family Foundation; Honeywell Foundation; Star Tribune/Cowles Media Company; James R. Thorpe Foundation; Dain Bosworth Foundation; Pentair, Inc.; Beverly J. and John A. Rollwagen Fund of the Minneapolis Foundation; the law firm of Schwegman, Lundberg, Woessner & Kluth, P.A.; and many individual donors. To you and our many readers across the country, we send our thanks for your continuing support.

Coffee House Press books are available to the trade through our primary distributor, Consortium Book Sales & Distribution, 1045 Westgate Drive, Saint Paul, MN 55114. For personal orders, catalogs, or other information, write to: Coffee House Press, 27 N. 4th Street, Suite 400, Minneapolis, MN, 55401.

LIBRARY OF CONGRESS CIP DATA
Labiner, Norah, 1967—
    Our sometime sister : a novel / by Norah Labiner.
        p.   cm.
    ISBN 1-56689-072-1 (HC : alk. paper)
    1. Title
PS3562.A2328092   1998   97-43268
                                                    CIP

10   9   8   7   6   5   4   3   2   1
first printing / first edition

I long for the tiny world, when we were miniatures of ourselves, when the fishes were pink, and I can still—please don't make me, no, stop—recall the screams of delight in the summer that we cried among the garden at the sight of ants, big and sturdy, crawling deliriously over the peonies. How sweet.

—Frances Warren Lieb
from a letter to her sister
June 24, 1960

foreword

THIS BOOK WAS COMPLETED in March of 1994 on a portable typewriter. There to date exists only one complete copy of the manuscript. It is perhaps due to this material singularity that I cannot help but feel, at this time, that the novel is another *thing*, another of the nostalgic oddities, the unique if not useless tokens and trinkets I have been collecting, mooning over, sorting through and saving my entire life. *Our Sometime Sister* is itself, herself, the collection of all my saved scraps of the past; quite frankly, junk, odds, torn movie tickets, candy wrappers, marbles, patches of fabric, pencil stubs, class photos of children whose names have long escaped me. I find now, only now, there was an odd underlying logic to my relentless, okay, obsessive accumulation. It has added up to something. And what it has added up to is this poor heap of pages, inky, bruised and battered, difficult to read, but more than that, a difficult little world to inhabit. The sentences never lead to coherent narratives; plot, which should be causal, collapses into story; and the characters, worst of all, they never loved me, they were always leaving exactly when I needed them most. Don't worry, I'm not asking for your pity here. Well maybe I am. Maybe just a little. I want you to know that for me, sequence means far less than instance. There is an inexactitude to the way the days, hours, weeks follow each other. A moment of course is something quite different; it is an instance of memory: full, disastrously overwhelming in the complexity of detail we bring to it. Who can after all recall the days of the past, let alone last week, one from the next? Yet how simple it is to recall the instant when perhaps the afternoon began to slip away and even how at that moment the real was slipping impossibly out of reach, already into the past and what could one do but try to recapture it?

We can neither of us escape the inevitable; the things we collect will come back to haunt us. All that we have keeping us together, you and I, from start to finish, are words. What can I do but regret that I cannot show you baby pictures, spray on your wrists perfume, haul out the dress I wore on an October day ten years ago, that is, present you with the concrete remains of a world already slipping away into obscurity. Words, this is going to be difficult, fussy little things, short, guttural, romantic, sonorous, to replace all that is and was real. How difficult it is with words to separate the time, moments, years, the scent of oranges, sticky orange-scented kisses, the afternoons, all of them, one by one, and the words, yes, where would I be but for the words?

I know about this, about telling stories and how it is to tell a story aloud over a cup of coffee and maybe a cigarette or two while the afternoon slips away, to digress, to touch the knee of your companion for emphasis, perhaps have another cigarette and then resume as you stare out the window into the bleak winter afternoon; this is far different from the lonely prospect of setting a story down on paper. I don't have you here to ask questions, to tell me when things are confusing, upsetting, or flat out boring; that is when you would politely interrupt and rise asking, More coffee for you, Pearl? On paper words are lonely things. The more of them one strings together the further one strays from intention; something is always missing. I know this better now than ever before. I no longer have illusions about how romantic it might be to sequester myself away from the world in a cabin in the north woods and write a novel. I have just done this. I have just written a novel.

It is difficult for me to keep hold of a strict chronology in *Our Sometime Sister* because I am forever swept back into instance; the story proceeds more by circuitous association than linear progression. I began working on this book when I was nineteen. It was written during school breaks, by the sides of pools, on park benches, in library carrels, locked rooms late at night, and bright kitchens with the typewriter set on the table and the early morning sun shining in. I was earnest. Even better, I was honest. Perhaps I was little more than the amalgamation of all cliches. I didn't know a thing about writing a novel. I knew only enough to follow the paths of those who had gloriously gone before me; I read their works and feverishly lived by their rules and theories. In the beginning, you could say, I was full of righteous aesthetic ideals. I meant to portray in my novel something of what I understood about my generation; what I had learned in libraries and bars, the unspeakable logic of curling irons, lipstick, and girls' bathrooms, the language of graffiti, love letters, and suicide notes, the mysterious concept of triple existentialism by which so many of us abided. This book was meant to portray a group of friends and relations growing up in the late seventies and eighties with all the love, loss, and boredom this would necessarily entail. Perhaps the most important aesthetic ideal to which I firmly clung was the belief that there was no place for the author in the world of the story. The author created the characters, settings, scenes, and action, and then quietly excused him or herself from the pages; wasn't this how it was supposed to be? Wasn't this, quite simply, the meaning of *fiction?* There are only three notable instances I can recollect in which an author has successfully placed himself, intentionally cloaked, into his work: the man in the raincoat, M'Intosh, at the funeral in *Ulysses;* the butterfly collector in "Spring in Fialta"; and, of course, my sentimental favorite, the rude bar customer in Hugo Tappan's "How the War Ended." But these instances were about play, games, and placing oneself into the already created world as a spectator after the fact, not as part and point of the story itself.

This is the first question one gets after admitting to writing a novel: Is it about you? Oh, we are all sophisticated enough to understand the concept of *based on;* it is only that we want to know a little bit more about the background, the history, the parameters of truth and fiction. Are you in it? Did it happen to you? These were the questions asked of me by the first readers of the completed draft of my early novella. Are you Butternut? Some insisted there were distinct similarities between the precocious girl and myself at that age, not the least of which being we both attended boarding school and enjoyed tragedies overly much; perhaps my unlikely attendance at a boarding school makes me in general a bit less of an individual and more of a character. Do you identify with Rose? Some swore they could identify me in her sentimental love of flowery things, her obsession with time and regret. Where can I find you in this? Readers wanted to know and some even quite frankly asked aloud. Where is the writer in these pages? Will the real Pearl Christomo please stand up?

I must admit that I never really found myself in that original manuscript draft. There was no *one* character I created with the intention of representing myself and telling *my own story.* But still, reading over the drafts, I found myself in doubt; I began to understand my readers' sense of *lack.* The book was indeed missing something. But what was it? Let me attempt to explain; you know how people become nostalgic over certain moments in history? Think of how many times you've seen a teacher, parent, hairdresser, or waiter get damp and misty-eyed when he or she recalls where they were when they heard Kennedy had been shot, the space shuttle crashed, or Elvis died. The important thing is less the historic event than the personalization of the experience; the memory of the self, the capturing of the subjective experience in the context of something national, big, important; the self frozen against a moment of history. This is what was lacking from my novella. Not just history or place, but *personalization*. The first readers, those professors, waitresses, students, and coffee house radicals wanted to know one thing first and foremost: To whom does this story belong?

What was missing? I asked myself this again and again. I rewrote. I changed typewriter ribbons. I switched brands of coffee. I adopted rituals of writing and then did the exact reverse. What was missing? It was certainly not emotion; there was plenty of that. There was love, loss, and a bit of sex couched in the language of poetry for the romantic-minded but disfigured by lust and adultery for the cynical. There was enough dialogue to keep things rolling along, maybe a moral lesson to be learned, and finally a conspicuous lack of plot in keeping with the best tenets of triple existentialism. The first readers predicted what I had ominously begun to sense; in the process of detailing how my characters grew and how their lives changed with the words they spoke to each other, the lies they told, and the years that passed, I had carefully and exactly excised the center and had left, as it were, a cutout, an absence at the very heart of book. It was like one of those chalk drawings of a body at the scene of a crime, and it was in my own shape, hunched before a typewriter. I had no recourse. I changed my typewriter ribbon. I brewed another pot of coffee.

I lay down in the chalk outline and began to write myself into the book.

No writer wants to admit that he or she is at the center of their own novel. A memoirist will admit this without a blush and for an autobiographer it is de rigueur. But how can I explain to you that I, a real person, exist in alternating chapters alongside these fictional characters and events? I have been writing this in a cabin in the north woods for more than two months now. I have done little more than watch the ice frozen solid on Lake Superior and the snow fall daily; I am close to the places I once knew and have thought a great deal about what I wrote once in that kitchen, sunny with light, when I was inspired by the great words of the dead (or was it the dead words of the great?) and those who had trudged this lonely path before me. Who was to say they had been right? Who was to say that an author didn't belong in her novel; or that to a writer a novel was anything more than a lodging place, a habitable world in which to live after the cabin has been vacated, the key returned, and the spring rains set in? Writers are both shy people and infamous braggarts; after all, this is and is not our world. We want nothing more than to live among our characters, and we hate nothing so much as admitting this, even if only to ourselves.

I admit, *Our Sometime Sister* is not the novel I intended to write. To tell you the truth, I wanted to write something better—and I'm referring to more here than the endless run-on sentences, split infinitives, plagiarism disguised as intertextuality, typos (Joseph Cotten for example is consistently misspelled *Cotton*), the slippery albeit justified misuse of the present tense—these are merely symptoms of my failure. I wanted to impress you, in specific, reader, not the collective reader out there, but *you*. Because I like your contrary nature.

Because you are in the business of refusal, and so am I. You refuse to accept the limits of belief, story, dream, and history. Maps are useless to you. You want to get there, to find *it*, on your own. You're so undeniably headstrong, so fiercely original that you don't even want an antecedent for *it*. I can't, I won't keep any secrets from you. How could I? I confess to you that I failed, but I kept trying and I swear if you can make it past chapter ten it gets better, really. I'm not being coy. This is no joke; those will come later. I admit there were moments when I was not in control. Read chapter eighteen, you'll see what I mean. I fought the good fight. I lost. But that doesn't mean you have to give up on me. I thought you liked the underdog, I thought you had a spot in your heart and on your book-shelves for the well-intentioned loser. Forgive me; I let the past take over.

What I have to offer you in this expanded text of *Our Sometime Sister* is quite different than what I had originally intended when I was nineteen. It no longer embarrasses me to see myself so blatantly in these pages. But now, I am ashamed to admit, there is something else, something worse. I no longer worry so much about the book being artistically pure. It is finished. That sort of thing is for others to decide. I worry instead that you won't like it, and in not liking my book, you won't like me. Isn't that an ironic way to end a six year strug-gle? Here I sit watching the winds rise and snow drift, the pre-lude to yet another bleak winter storm. My bags are packed, my manuscript retyped and filed away, secured with a strong rubber band, pages numbered in a hopeless attempt at order, and I worry about that anonymous day in the future when you get home with your copy of the book from your public library or local book store. I worry that you will say in the lamplight as you shut the book, It was nice enough, but I don't see the point of all that business with the separate stories. If only that Pearl character could have been as endearing as Rose, brash as Theresa, hopeless as Aaron, or as sensitive as Butternut. In fact, you may not be able to entirely trust young Pearl, and I can commiserate with you. The moment she became a word, part of the story, she became someone else, no longer a ghost in my memory but a replacement of the memory. So this is the risk: I may not measure up to my fictional characters. What else is left for me to do now but offer myself up to you? There is a strange and free feeling now that it is over, now that all that is left is the explanation, like closing your eyes, coasting downhill and yelling, Hey, no hands, a moment before you actually let go of the handlebars.

This is, in the end, a novel about learning how to write a novel and how someone, particularly and specifically me, goes about it her whole life, collecting facts, images, memories, bits of wrapping paper, photographs, and sad little vignettes; storing and shoring up without knowing exactly what they will be used for later. I know that you are clever and like to figure things out on your own, so perhaps you will be disappointed that I have revealed the premise flat out, that I have ruined the certain mystery and suspense of opening a new book and wandering alone through the pages. If there is any mystery in this book, it is in how we ceaselessly manage to create ourselves through rags and scraps and forgotten things; recreate ourselves again and again in both the stories we tell and how we choose to tell them. So I apologize if I've told too much. You'll see that my prose style can be flowery and I tend to run to excess. You'll see that I'm awful at keeping secrets, my own, other people's, and I have a tendency to blurt them out at the most inopportune moments. And I apologize also to the real people, to those who although names have been changed, will no doubt find themselves in the pages of this book. You may in the end lose sense of who is real and who is not; I say this not to insult your intelligence, but because this was my own experience. In general I began to care far more for the fictional set of characters than I did for the real people from my own life. One can love them or hate them, these fictions, pale ghosts and chalk outlines of people I used to know, wished I was, or perhaps saw once in passing only to have the memory of an anonymous face imprinted indelibly, inexplicably, forever in my memory.

Is any of it true, you may warily begin to ask. I assure you that it is, or was. The real exists alongside the fictional. Some of it happened exactly the way I will tell you it did, while the rest never happened, not in any way, version, or form. I can assure you, in spite of my dreams, some of it never occurred at all. But to me, the strange aspect only begins now, to part with it all now, to say it is, in fact, over. To say that it all happened a long time ago. To say it is, for me, over, when for you, how lucky you are, how I envy you, how I have always envied you, it is only just about to begin. Please, turn the page.

Pearl Christomo
Chassell, Michigan
March 6, 1994

Pearl

IF I WERE TO MAKE A MOVIE OF MY LIFE I would start with a picture of how we were then. No stories, no background, no characters, no time. Start with this: me in the paisley dress I wore that day and him, sincere, his face obscured by the sun, or his hand shielding his eyes from its brightness on the last day of October. Of course, you lose something in a picture; the scent of pine and birch trees, peppermint candies, bitter crab apples, or the oranges we ate that afternoon and the sticky sweetness that clung to us long past evening, long past the time when even then it was already a memory. The crunching leaves, paths we walked, tall grasses, the paper bags which had held our lunches, crumpled, now seem to be carelessly blowing forever beyond our reaches. It is, of course, only a picture. He and I, his plaid shirt, my dress with its neat black buttons indiscreetly undone, unfastened, the shadows as the short afternoon passed into evening, the early disappearance of the sun.

Charlie Gumm and I did it whenever we wanted. All that summer and winter and into the spring we did it whenever we got the chance, the notion, the dare. We did it without passion or expertise. We did it the way we did our homework. We did it like Hester Prynne and Arthur Dimmesdale. We hugged our sin in private and gloated. We caught each other's eyes across the dining hall and exchanged knowing looks. We did it in the school laundry room, the girls' gymnasium, classrooms in the long dark hours of dusk. We did it until we were sore and bruised and sometimes bleeding and then we stopped and started again. We did it on the floor, standing up, on desks, in the rain, out in the grasses and wet dark earth, we did it, and each time it was wordless, unadorned, open-eyed; each time it was the same.

What is it about the past that makes me want to be magnanimous and evenhanded, to offer the story from all angles, place a remote camera on the moon and aim dreamily downward to study our images only to find the same scene played out again and again, but made tiny, more miniature and perfect with each telling? It's an old story, mine by way of his; please do not mistake compactness for completion, please do not say I did not warn you about the small obstacles in your path—clunky adverbs, fresh-faced boys, lies, misspellings, repetition, cafeteria food—small, I admit, by way of being large. Before I begin the story proper I need to know that I have your agreement; we'll never get anywhere, you and I, unless we both understand what the past means: *lies,* the first lie and the second and the third coming hard and fast on the heels of the former until, yes, until it becomes difficult to recall the instant, what someone or other used to call so assuredly, the *truth.* None of it ever happened the way they used to tell me it would. But still, you must admit, it isn't difficult to dream it and pretend that it did happen, to paint a picture in the mind and file it away as a memory. Instead of what? Dream? Fantasy, a fiction, worst of all, a lie?

Imagine this: winter blueness, you are a child, you fall asleep in the car returning home at night, Sunday, how all the days seem the same to you, infinite, wearying, endless, you have fallen asleep in the car returning from a place now long forgotten, home, you are carried in the arms of your father from the car through the chill of the night into the house which at first is cold and then the heat is turned up and you can smell the funny biting smell of it as you stumble, fall, are carried to your bed, the heat comes in waves, your bed is cold and as you recede back into sleep you hear voices from the hallway, the warmth, the scent of heat recedes and you can only feel it, and then sleep, and then nothing.

I remember this clearly, more clearly than I remember things in the recent past which should be familiar, things like any one word Charlie Gumm ever said to me separate from another. I recall sentences. I see his mouth moving forming words. Bright and damp, two spots of color burn high on his cheeks. There is no sound. Nor can I recall with exact certainty the shape of his mouth; this I know only in words. In words I would say he had a modest mouth and delicate neck, but no image comes to accompany those words. It is as though I know of these things without having experienced them myself. Still, how easy it is to remember being a child carried sleeping from the car into my house and the warmth of my awaiting bed.

The problem is this: there was a Charlie Gumm. You can find him. Maybe he's a doctor or dentist. Maybe you'll stumble with an abscessed molar into a waiting room in an unfamiliar city and think, *how ironic* when you see his name listed on the placard, "Charles Gumm, D.D.S." I cannot tell you with exact certainty what he might look like now; then, he was lanky and too tall. I imagine he has grown into his height, if not, he may tend to stoop, hunch his shoulders, or slump from the hip. His hair was light and fine. I don't deny this; everything about him was fine, except perhaps the most important thing—but there will be time for that later—later we'll get cozy and I'll whisper in your ear about how it was, how fine it all was to be sixteen and to have a boy like Charlie Gumm to do it with all the time and never get caught, never once get caught.

I believed afterward, for perhaps the space of a year or two, that I could have spent those afternoons with any of the boys I knew at that time. Red-cheeked, corduroyed, unanimously wide-eyed, inevitably broad-shouldered, those boys with their clean hands, high-top sneakers, their smatterings of freckles and puritanical good looks, line them up one after another and see if I can pick Charlie Gumm out of the crowd. I do not say this to insult either Dr. Gumm or that row of ghost boys, but to admit my vision has gone blurry and my dreams unreliable by way of sitting too close to the television.

Even though it has been almost ten years now, even though I might not recognize him from any stranger on the street, it was real. It did happen. If you still want proof I can supply you with letters, photographs, a copy of Hawthorne's *Young Goodman Brown and Other Stories* with his name in his loping handwriting signed on the title page right below the author's, a sweatshirt with a school insignia, gifts, charms, a pair of copper hoop earrings bought from a novelty store, but still they've held up, though tarnished green, better than my memory of him. It was real. It did happen. There was a boy named Charlie Gumm and a girl named Pearl Christomo and they met at school in September and once together they couldn't stop themselves; they found locked closets, hallways, dark and hidden places and they did it whenever they wanted. This all happened. I cannot say as much for the other, for my favorite memory of childhood, the night, the car, the heat; this did not happen, well, at least not to me.

I don't know to whom that memory belongs. Perhaps children in grade school pass these things around like the flu virus. Perhaps this glowing memory belongs to my childhood friend Mary Suzanne Regan, who lived in a house crowded with children. Her family was always coming from or on its way to church, observing the festival of a saint after whom one of her brothers or seven to ten of her cousins were named. Off they went on Sundays to see the grandparents, aunts, and great-uncles, always to return tired late in the evening. Perhaps Mary Sue needed to be carried from the wood-paneled station wagon to the bedroom she shared with her younger sister. Perhaps their father carried both girls, small, towheaded children, to their twin beds with the white dust ruffles and matching quilts, and she fell asleep and her sister fell asleep under the pink-checked blankets and the radiator hissed and the damp warmth began to smell tangy, of dust, of an apple core sweet and rotting in the wicker trash basket, of the old house, sleeping children, and then of nothing at all, but of sleep.

I know that this never happened to me. Until my mother married Martin Hamlin when I was fifteen, I never lived in a house. In the memory, in the way it occurs to me so vividly through feelings, smells, sounds, so close as to be real, there are no five flights of stairs to be climbed. And so you say to me, maybe this is not a memory, but a dream or a fantasy, a fiction, an ambiguity of the past, because, you must admit, it is so hard to remember things that have happened yesterday let alone such a long time ago. Perhaps you may begin to wonder, because you really know nothing about me yet, if it isn't all a lie. What can I do? I turn my hands, palms up, empty, nothing up my sleeves, no proof, no letters, no psychiatric verification that this is an authentic memory passed on to me through a braided rug during nap time in kindergarten by Mary Sue Regan out of compassion for my status as an only child or mistakenly over graham crackers and an inadvertently switched Dixie riddle cup of orange drink. One knows somehow, one learns to trust oneself about which images played against the inner eye are dream, which are memories and which, the lies, fall in between.

That dream comes back to me. I wonder if it could have happened. I've searched my memory for some hint, a clue. Could it have been one of my mother's boyfriends carrying me home after an evening at the movies? Other things, other details I recall specifically: a monkey doll in a tartan dress given to me by Louis, whom my mother dated on and off for two years; a diary from a fat man I saw only once; a rainbow-colored bikini bathing suit from Morty, the chiropractor. I remember the boxes of chocolates my mother received, ribboned and sometimes heart-shaped, from all of them on various Valentine's Days and birthdays. We poked our fingers into the candy to see what was inside, just puncturing the milk chocolate. We ate the jellies first, raspberry and strawberry, methodically working our way from the orange, lemon, and coconut creams to the nuts, leaving in our wake a battered box half-full of collapsed caramels, cordial cherries, mints, and nougats. My mother had long slim fingers with neat rounded nails, and she delicately made the incision into each candy before either approving or wrinkling her nose. She ate each chocolate cream in tiny particular bites, timing herself from commercial to movie to commercial on television.

This is, again, real. You must begin to trust me now. I implore you. We have only each other at this point, and I hope that you understand that I illustrate what is false only to prove that the rest is true. I'll supply you with the names and if you want you can look them up in various local phone books. I'm sure not everyone is dead and gone; ghosts will always find chains to rattle and houses to haunt. I have sometimes seen them. I am prone to vivid dreams. I have been known on occasion to lie; still we won't let flights of fancy come between our fundamental understanding. Ghosts thrive on fiction: the dreams, the lies, the past. Of course, there will be more time for this later, for speculation and prophesy both; you and I, we will have all the time in the world. You and I, how I like the sound of that, you and I, we have world enough and time to figure it all out together. We have each other now.

In the beginning I was a child. There were three of us, my mother and father and me. Mother was slim and youthful. Father was dour and severe. I was skinny. I was mournful, an oracular child who could guess with innocent and astonishing accuracy the astrological signs of my mother's friends. Libras were balanced. Capricorns were grounded. Aries, strong willed. My mother was a Virgo, and my father a Pisces. My own birthday was in the late hot days of June. My mother left my father, and then there were two of us, my mother and me, and we lived in an apartment on Lafayette Street in Flint, Michigan. The sky was blue, the snow was white, the grass was green.

I used to think of my mother as a sort of 1940s glamour girl, a more Semitic and scrawny version of Joan Crawford in *Grand Hotel* when John Barrymore calls her "funny face" or Katharine Hepburn as the wacky anthropologist in *Bringing Up Baby*. Silk stockings, champagne, screwball antics, Cuban heels, nameless good-looking ultimately worthy young men in white tuxedos bearing armloads of gladioli, gardenias, daisies, carnations, jaunty endearing flowers brought in fisted bundles and heaps, peonies and chrysanthemums signifying nothing more than a well-edited script. That is, they were not tokens of love. Whatever her world was in reality, in dreams, for me, it was about illusion: mules with puffs of white fur on the front, faux silk dressing gowns, and a princess phone with a gold rotary dial in her bedroom, just like in the movies.

I have no one to blame but myself for keeping these dreams alive, for enjoying the absurdity of them and painting a picture of our life together as something girlish, giddy, and unstoppable. It was after all not the movies and not even the forties. Even at this time, during my childhood in the seventies and early eighties I knew few children of divorced families who lived with one parent. My mother had friends and relatives who were divorced but they always seemed to remarry quickly; families were redrawn with more cousins, halves and steps all related by complicated family trees which began to look like flow charts when we were assigned to draw them in our fifth grade art class. My own drawing was simple: my father on his little branch, my mother on hers, and then two little lines, one jutting from each branch, connecting me to them. It was a dry, barren tree, but I made up for it with scrolling leaves, swinging monkeys, birds, apples, and even a bough with an oversized stalk of grapes suspended from it just like I had seen on Manishewitz wine bottles. The other children must have marveled not just at the baroque detail of my work, but at the amount of space I had for sheer ornament. While they were busy furiously working on lines, connections, whos and hows, scarring holes in the grainy paper with erasures, I was drawing flowers. On paper my life was simple, but when I was with my mother it was something else entirely; it was glamorous and carefree. Her words were even better, "chic," "panache," and "gaudy." She tossed her words like shoes, kicked them off and sent them skidding across the floor to land at a sexy and risqué angle, stiletto heel overturned and suggestive.

By the time my mother was twenty-two, some three years younger than my age now, she was divorced, smoked a pack of Camels a day, had a bachelor's degree in art education, and supported herself and her daughter by substitute teaching and with the aid of my father's timely child support checks. Still, she was determined that we would not go without life's small necessities. For her this meant a leg wax or facial, an occasional pair of Italian shoes, delicate and lace-edged slips and panties. For me, truly, it was luxury enough being with her. I'm not exaggerating. There were those winter days when she wasn't called in to work and let me stay home to watch soap operas with her. I adored my mother, the glamour of her, the odd way in which she was both careless and determined. My childhood necessities were normal things: buttered popcorn and matinee movies, overdue fines from the library paid out in dimes and quarters by my mother without complaint. There were sketch pads, colored markers, crayons, and poster paints. Early on there was a dismal attempt at ballet lessons. Although in my mind I could see myself keeping perfect time, moving fluidly from position one to a neat plié in unison with the other girls in their black leotards and pink tights lined up at the barre, my feet could never carry out the instructions; my arms jerked and knees buckled. I found all that was graceful about me limited to dreams. I could color anything with my drugstore watercolors. This is the first lie: the representation of reality in pretty colors. Pictures of the three of us, mother and father and Pearl, surrounded by important flowers, lilies, violets, roses.

I don't think I knew how to draw myself. I had no image from which to work; quite simply, while I could say that I had short dark hair and curious, almost fearful, eyes, I didn't know what I looked like. Other things were easy to draw. I spent hours on the carpet in front of the television drawing scenes from movies, but when I showed the pictures to my mother, I kept secret from her that she was always the princess, the heroine. I crayoned princes in royal blue and maize doublets foisting embarrassingly masculine swords ready to save her from the tower, ready to climb the ropes of her hair and spirit her up, up, and away. Dreams, lies, copies. Nothing more. I traced dresses from fashion magazines and memorized the names and seasons of flowers in garden catalogs mistakenly delivered to our mailbox. Lilacs, Marilyn Monroe and Cary Grant roses, apple blossoms, virgin lilies, night-blooming jasmine, pine for endurance, wisteria, delphinium: I drew them all with my set of thirty-six colored markers, my childs' newsprint Draw-Along sketch pad and the handy Encyclopaedia Brittanica volume twelve, *Fable–Functionalism,* opened to the heading, "Flowers, Garden Variety." I could recreate my skinny, high-strung mother as a princess using shades of scarlet and gold, dress her as Joan Crawford complete with a seasonal wedding bouquet, but I could never put together the features to create my own face. I have always wanted this, to draw a justified self-portrait, a representation of both sides of the mirror.

In real life my mother resembled a cross between Barbra Streisand and Sandi Duncan, minus the hips and glass eye, respectively. Judith Taubman Christomo was the sort of thin vivacious mother who introduced herself as my older sister and for the most part either got away with it or people were too polite to question her. Dreams were one thing, but those necessities of ours were something else entirely. Her sling-back heels, silky nightdresses, and padded brassieres were bought on clearance at JC Penney, Sears, the Goody Barn, and sometimes, although my mother wouldn't even admit this outright to her best friend, at Meijer's Thrifty Acres. I didn't know until much later that what I thought was silk was really nylon, what I thought was glamorous was cheap and gaudy, all imitation and paste. In real life we ate lo-cal frozen dinners or else just made ourselves popcorn and watched *Dallas* or *Flamingo Road.* We drank $3.99 red wine with our freezer-burned lasagna, read aloud the "Agony" column from *Cosmopolitan* magazine and commented ceaselessly on the breasts of other women. Growing up with her was like living in one of those television sitcoms where, due to circumstances beyond their control, two unlike characters are thrown together and find that, despite their differences, they get along quite well; except in our case we happened to be, no matter what my mother would tell you if she met you for the first time, mother and daughter.

At the time Martin Hamlin came into our lives my mother was thirty-five and I was fifteen. She was younger than most of the mothers of my friends. Mary Sue Regan's mother wore house-dresses and did charity work at her church. The Regans were Irish Catholic and had nine children. The two oldest were already married and Mary Sue was an aunt by the time she was twelve. The family lived in a yellow Victorian house with gingerbread latticework, a porch swing, and an upright piano in the living room. Their kitchen table was like something out of *The Waltons,* long and wooden with extra chairs because their sunny and always gregarious children often brought home dinner guests, myself included. Their life wasn't like the movies at all; it was just like television. They ate yankee pot roast and buttered mashed potatoes. They drank milk with dinner, and not little glasses, but hefty tumblers poured from a large glass pitcher. My mother and I had in our refrigerator a carton of skim milk hovering perpetually around the expiration date. We added it to our coffee, but it always went bad and had to be poured down the drain, clotted and bluish. The Regans drank whole milk, but it might as well have been heavy whipping cream for how rich it seemed when I was offered a glass of it to go along with some after-school treat, sugar cookies cut in the shapes of letters, celery lined with peanut butter, or, best of all, a slice of Mrs. Regan's prize-winning green apple pie.

It was during that year, when Mary Sue and I were sophomores in high school, that her mother died. Mrs. Regan woke in the night, went down to the kitchen for a drink, and a little later when her husband went downstairs to see why she hadn't returned to bed, he found her, the glass of milk empty on the drainboard, found her stretched out dead on the polished wood floor in her bathrobe, one hand on her heart and the other clutching a dish towel like the patron saint of good housekeeping. The funeral was open casket. Mrs. Regan's painted face was as pink and cheerful as it had been in real life. As I stood staring at her bright open eyes I got this image, like the coming attraction before a film, of her life in one long, dizzying, sped-up reel. I saw her as a jerky-elbowed young bride carrying a baby on one hip, doing laundry, wearing a gingham blouse and rolled dungarees, defrosting hams, walking her ordinary dog, baking chocolate chip cookies, changing diapers, decorating a birthday cake, knitting socks for our boys overseas, saying her prayers and lighting candles in church, wiping away the milk mustache on her youngest child, having an unexpected final child, getting old, and then dying at 4:27 A.M. on the clean oak floor of her very own kitchen

Mary Sue abandoned me for girls who smoked in the bathroom between classes, smearing ash and raspberry lip gloss on the pages of their spiral notebooks as they copied each other's algebra problems; but I didn't hold it against her. Of what use could I have been to Mary Sue? I was bookish and shy. My mother was thirty-five years old with auburn hair; her skirts were a bit too short and her high heels clicked and clacked in an almost poetic meter down the nighttime halls of my school on parent-teacher night. Mary Sue Regan had been faced with her own mortality. She had seen her mother's painted face staring out of a casket in her best Sunday dress. I figured Mary Sue had better live it up with the tough girls for a while, wear Jovan musk to cover the cigarette smoke, buy tight purple jeans and cowboy boots with fringes at the Eastland Mall, double pierce her ears and know by heart all the songs on the Billboard top ten list, because she had seen the future. She had seen it in herself and in the sudden domestic talents of her once heavy metal sister, Kay, who now wore aprons and bunny oven mitts, carrying wooden spoons and feather dusters from room to room in their still clean, well-waxed house. Mary Sue must have known it then, sensed that she was destined to knit and sew, to grow hybrid roses, live in a gingerbread house in a decent hard-working neighborhood in an anonymous city, to bear a bunch of freckled, big-headed babies all named after New Testament saints and abstemious maiden aunts.

Mary Sue Regan was in a race against time. People like me, and I count you, reader, in this grouping, people like us, we may be losers in just about every sense, but we always manage to sneak by. We trick fate. Time and place mean, sincerely, so little to us. We slip unnoticed, the last one, onto the overcrowded crosstown bus. We always manage to get a seat in the sold-out movie theater because we aren't too particular; small things satisfy us. No one notices us, and the ones who do don't envy what we have. I'll live my entire life this way, slipping by slightly unnoticed in hope and fear and dread of something more. I am certain this is why Charlie Gumm and I never got caught. When he was with me we were invisible. We could have shamelessly disrobed revealing our pale and awkward teenage bodies and done it right on a table in the dining hall during a fine dinner of chicken divan and spinach salad; we could have pushed our trays onto the floor breaking plates, saucers, and water goblets, done it on the bare wooden table and no one would have so much as dropped a fork or strayed for a moment from polite conversation. How else can you explain how careless we were and still how we never got caught? We became, finally, intentionally careless, daring someone to catch us, to pay attention, not for the thrill or the risk, but because the odds scared us, or me at least. The odds have to change, I thought, it was important that the odds change whether in my favor or not.

I knew, I had known all along that I wasn't like Judith Taubman Christomo; it was more than our apparent physical differences. I didn't share the bright, giddy way she had of winning people over or talking her way into and out of any problem. I guess in the world of old movies you could say I was like Joan Fontaine to her Katharine Hepburn; Kim Hunter to her Vivian Leigh; a melancholy Valli to plucky Barbara Stanwyck. I existed, a strange, pale child in the wake of her words, never quite understanding how I had ended up in her charge. It was only that I always forgot about *him.* He was a ghost. All fathers were ghosts to me, asides, afterthoughts, whose absence was more explicable than presence, like Frederic March in *Little Women* fighting in an endless and faraway war.

The first time I saw Mary Sue's father was at the funeral. Even though I had been friends with her since preschool, I couldn't remember meeting her father, seeing him at the dinner table, being driven to the mall by him. He was always at work in an anonymous office, insurance or was it accounting? He was a nondescript, tallish man in a black suit. He looked exactly like his wife. She had looked just like him. Maybe I really had met him before I just couldn't tell the difference between the two of them. Maybe if it hadn't been Mrs. Regan who died in the kitchen that night it would have been Mr. Regan instead. He stood at the funeral with his nine children and three grandchildren, all of them freckled, plain-faced, skinny, dressed in black, all of them wearing glasses. I swear to God, you couldn't tell one from the next.

My father was an intellectual. Sallow-skinned and insomniac, Anthony Christomo was something of a ghost, a late-night wanderer from room to room in the long shadows of a desk lamp. He was a depressed man and not above telling you about it; it is from him that I learned not to fall victim to the assumption that to be depressed is not to be happy. Believing this about him, that his moody silences were symptomatic of unhappiness, was not a genuine mistake on my mother's part or even simply an error in judgement; it was a token of the complete opposition of their characters. My mother would tell you, "I'm a glass half-full kind of person." My father would groan not so much at the sentiment expressed but at the phrasing employed. Their marriage lasted under two years, during which time I was conceived, born, named, and most probably developed my full personality.

Sometimes I think I can remember things, scenes, details, bits and pieces of what my life must have been like for the short time that my parents were together and I was with them, but then I become certain that any recollection of this time is an impossibility, a false memory, probably the result of too much television so that plots and dreams have been mixed up in my head; then there is a sudden brilliant clarity to it. It is so easy to remember. There are words and images. There is a little pink jacket, an ashtray glittering in the sun, shaped like a fish, the smell of Royall Lyme aftershave. How can this, these things, be lies? I have an exact sense of how it was when my mother was twenty-two, living in a one bedroom student apartment, the crib set up next to the black-and-white TV, stuffed animals crushed under stacks of overdue library books. She wore mini-dresses revealing her slim legs and a good deal of thigh. There are photographs. There was a card table in the kitchen that my parents must have used as a makeshift desk and dining area; newspapers, formula bottles, textbooks, stained coffee cups, overflowing ashtrays, high chair, and baby makes three.

In one particular photograph my mother is sitting at the table staring straight at the photographer, my father. She's leaning over a manual typewriter, a sheet of paper rolled in the carriage. My mother in this picture is having a hard time stay-ing awake; a clock in the background reads 3:45. I don't know if this is morning or afternoon. The grainy quality of the snap-shot doesn't give much away, but her large kohl-lined eyes are closing slightly. My father must have still been working on his doctorate in history; maybe my mother was typing a paper for him. He was eight years older than she, and was, I think, a teaching assistant in a course she had taken. The details of how they met, fell in love against the flat Ohio landscape, by all accounts, quickly, passionately, inexplicably, are sketchy. There are few photographs of my father because my mother didn't have patience for cameras and when asked to take pictures she snapped too soon, moved, or cut off heads, blurred faces by standing too close or impossibly far away.

Their divorce was much happier than their marriage; his checks were both generous and timely. She never complained about or begrudged me the one month a year I spent with him. All in all, they kept their distance from each other. I spent each July with him in his apartment near the campus of the University of Chicago where he taught history. His specialty was European intellectual history: the Enlightenment, the Reformation, but most specifically issues of religious intolerance, the ethical import of crimes and atrocities committed in the name of religion. He wrote a book, *The Prisoner's Dilemma;* you can probably find it in a used bookstore, or you could special order it from the publisher. I mean, it won't be out on some big display the way Martin Hamlin's books are, with promises of the things reading this book will do for you right next to a cardboard blow-up of the author himself, my stepfather, looking oddly both Rabbinical and jaunty.

My father's book will never change your life or teach you how to look like you lost ten pounds by being more assertive, make more friends and boost self-esteem, but his book might scare you and make you less secure about what you thought history was. My father had an infective paranoid streak, a belief in conspiracy theories, forces in the world always beyond the control of the individual, yourself, himself, included. Those summer nights, I remember my father sitting in the dark staring at the ringing telephone, both afraid to answer and afraid not to, ridden with guilt believing that someone on the other end of the line might realize he was there alone waiting for a call.

When I was eight, during my annual visit with my father, he took me to the Field Museum of Natural History. As we stood in front of the case displaying the chipped remains of a tiny Australopithecine female, I saw, I remember seeing both our reflections in the glass; we were identical. I am certain he saw this too. Pale-skinned and hollow-eyed, we wore the guilty expressions of a vampire and his little assistant hiding from the summer sun. As we stood in front of the skeleton, he gripped my small hand and read aloud the placard on the glass-fronted case. I lost myself in the words and images of palm fronds, coconuts, and mysterious little people. I nodded gravely and stored away this new information which was not about the family trees of my friends, divorces, marriages, legalities, but the kind of history with which my father always supplied me; it was of an impossibly faraway world, whether it was Imperial Russia, the Iron Age, or the Italy of the Medici. This was the world he could be counted on unfailingly to know about and have the endless patience to explain to me again and again, making it seem as though it had all happened yesterday and was just as necessary to life as popcorn, watercolors, and Ingrid Bergman movies on the late show.

There we were seeking refuge from the hot afternoon, from the blare of horns and clash of traffic on Michigan Avenue. There we were peacefully taking shelter in history when suddenly a troop of Brownies in their tan jumpers and orange berets came running toward us, quickly closed in, and clamored up to the case where they pressed their sticky fingers and faces against the glass. From the front of the crowd I heard a frantic girlish voice cry, "Troop 227, Troop 227, there's no mummy here, only bones!" From the depths of the huddle a whistle shrilled. The Brownies swarmed off, white anklets and penny loafers skidding across the dull parquet floor. One girl hung back, turned to my father and me, and said matter-of-factly, as though she felt personally responsible for the unseemly behavior of Troop 227, "We've come all the way from Des Plaines, and we want to see the mummies. You understand, don't you?" She smiled like a tiny cocktail party hostess before turning and skipping off, ponytail flying, to catch up with her compatriots.

I remember that moment. Even after all these years I remember the exact look of nervous terror on my father's face. Long after the girls disappeared and we couldn't hear their shoes scuffling down the quiet hallways or their echoing laughter, we stood in absolutely abrupt silence in the Hall of Human Beginnings frozen in jealous admiration of the neat composure of that child. I think we both wanted her to come back. She was, you see, although this is hard to explain, very much like my mother. It was only an air, an attitude, something about the way she flipped her ponytail and spoke, both solicitous and frank, in that overly adult manner. She meant so much more to us when she was retreating, almost, but not quite gone and we could still hear her footfalls as she abandoned us.

I suppose it shocked me. When I was with my father I lost all sense of my mother as real. How could she possibly live up to my memory of her, the almond smell of her talc and bath beads, her tapered fingers, the funny faces she made, the way she imitated all her friend's voices the same way, high and whining. When I was away from my mother for that one month, I indulged in being unlike her. I acted like my father; there was a novelty to it, acting like someone else, identifying my own image in his face. My father and I wandered museums, fruit markets, bookstores, and the halls of his history department with the same curious invisibility. We drank strong coffee, never complained about the heat, and sometimes did not speak for days. By the end of July I both longed for and dreaded my mother's chatty vibrancy, her love of all things popular, feminine, and overpriced. Maybe what I missed most was the way she could make time pass. When you were with her you might suddenly look down at your watch and realize the afternoon had slipped away. My father counted the hours as though waiting for the moment when they would finally run out, exhausting the clock. I return here to you reader, not just to end my paragraph with a question, but because I want your opinion. You are not just my reader, but my confidant, my silent collaborator, the sister I never had. How could any child have lived split between these two worlds, let alone learn to reconcile them?

There was a fundamental incompatibility between my parents that went deeper than their slightly mismatched astrological signs would imply. The disparity had something to do with not just faith, but relativity. Ask my father about religion and he wouldn't answer you straight-out. He talked about religion historically, empirically, politically, and ethically. Get specific, ask him about himself, and he would just shrug and say, "I was raised Catholic," as though disassociating himself from the whole messy business. If you asked my mother what she thought about her religion, Judaism, she would have squinted up one eye, done her best Popeye imitation and said, "I yam what I yam and that's all that I yam."

My mother raised me and for her there was no question of choice; she was Jewish and so was I. I attended for a pious and often painful six years a Hebrew school where I learned the language, conjugated endless irregular verbs and constructed workbook sentences like, "Please stranger help yourself to the fresh figs and apples from my garden," and old world proverbs, "When it is hot in the desert even dogs will sleep in the sand." We followed the seasons, year by year, eating dry chunks of carob on Sukkout and bitter herbs in the spring at Pesach. Even the moon was a strange artifact, full, bright, obscured, we celebrated its newness each month. I dressed in skirts and stockings for Shabbat which we observed every Saturday morning when there wasn't an early sale at the downtown Smith-Bridgeman's store.

From 4 to 6 P.M. on Tuesdays and Thursdays, from the age of six to twelve, I read Old Testament stories, learned prayers and songs. Mostly I stared dreamily at the walls with their posters of Haifa, that beautiful seaport town, the blue nightscape of cosmopolitan Tel Aviv, craggy Mount Masada, and next to that a poster for Y'ad V'shem, the holocaust memorial, showing in stark black and white a child staring through a barbed wire fence at Auschwitz and above the photo the legend, "Lest We Forget." We watched films documenting the training of a crack Israeli commando squad, the business of baking in a matzoh factory, witnessed happy brown children laughingly picking oranges while a narrator from the BBC extolled the virtues of kibbutz life. We took a break between the two hours, when, exhausted from the long school day, I looked forward, especially in winter, to the last hour of bleakness, the violet hour between five and six. While we drank our grape juice and chewed thoughtfully on raisin cookies, the students complained, talked, and argued about God or the Michigan-Michigan State football game. I hoped that my mother would remember to pick me up and I wouldn't have to go down the hall to the director's office and ask to use the phone.

I did all this and yet I never felt particularly Jewish. There were other children who did; they practiced bar mitzvah haftarahs with fervent belief, braces gleaming and spit flying. Something held me back; perhaps it was precocious cynicism. Those other children had *belief*. They bought the Bible whole cloth, believing that the stories were firm, nonfiction, historical, and happened in the fixed chronological order of page number. It was an order I could not trust. I liked best the pictures in the translated storybooks, beautiful Rachel with silver bracelets on her wrists and her sister Leah with the bad eyes, and the way Laban tricked Jacob out of marriage with the daughter he really wanted so that he had to settle for his second choice. Imagine how Leah must have felt about the bargain, being second; she had all those children, ten sons, and still Jacob waited and still he was devoted to Rachel. Who was this God? The character the stories never explained. Who was this God to punish Rachel for Jacob's preference? Rachel was kind to her cousin at the well and offered him figs and oranges from her basket. The afternoon was dusty and burning and it slipped away from them. I wanted to ask the teacher about who wrote this book. Did the writer know all the events, the answers and outcomes, the end, when he started the beginning?

I have since been told that the sense of alienation I used to feel in class bordering on paranoia, the lack of connection to other children, Jewish and Christian alike, is exactly what it feels like to be a Jew; so maybe those years of instruction paid off after all. Perhaps it has to do with my father who never talked about his religion, so that the things I learned about Catholicism were mostly from the movies on television around Christmastime like *The Robe* and *The Bells of Saint Mary's.* He never tried to make me accept his religion, but then maybe things seep into you anyway, gain power over you through their very absence in your life. You can't quite place what is missing and the absence seeps into your dreams; you don't know what was there—only that it's gone when you wake in the morning. I'm talking about more than Catholicism. I'm talking about love and sex and the things that drove me to Charlie Gumm. Can you imagine, now that you know me a little better, know the kind of girl I was, can you imagine me going around with a name like Pearl Gumm? Or even worse, Pearlie Gumm, the dentist's wife? See, this is just what I am talking about, there it is, see how dreams get beyond the reality of any recollection until remembrance itself cannot help but be a lie? Once you feel the lack, the emptiness, you can never again remember, recall anything with the same objective clarity. See, I said *wife.* I was only sixteen, who said anything about husbands and wives, let alone love? All we did was fuck. The dream of anything can overtake you at a moment's notice: the past, feverish boys and their dry biting kisses, a woman at a well in the afternoon heat, the glass of milk the moment just before Mrs. Regan placed it on the drainboard, a thousand blue roses tumbling down unexplained from the sky, the room you slept in as a child and the way the heat smelled when it was turned on the first cold day of autumn. You can't lock the door against yourself, forget what you are bound to remember, quell desire from a distance of years, deny your nightmares and believe that if they aren't there when you wake that they were never there at all.

My first memory is this: flat Ohio winter in our small apartment. We are sitting at the card table in the kitchen and my father is complaining about his lack of sleep. My mother, standing at the stove heating my oatmeal, interrupts him saying, "Why are you always so damned unhappy? Can't you just look on the bright side of things for once?" He is quiet and pauses, looks at her for a moment before saying anything. Then he says, and his voice changes like an actor stepping out of character to explain a scene to a member of the audience who has fallen asleep, he says quite firmly, "Who says I'm not happy?"

It was confusing, but like any child I fell into the routine of life. Maybe I tended more toward mood swings than other children, from brightly capricious, from showering my mother with affection when she returned home from work to snubbing her for days because of some injustice, real or imagined, a sock lost in the dryer, a comment about my hair she might have made carelessly to her best friend Sofie. We lived our life like this eleven months a year for almost fourteen years. I got older, of course, I got older, but I never expected things to change the way they finally did. I never expected that all the pleas I had made for a prince to save my mother, to save us all, had not really gone unheard whether by some God in charge of things or by my mother herself.

It was only much later, and I was older then, like I am now, drinking coffee, up late at night with nothing to do but think about it all, and how it happened so quickly, only later when I began to realize I had all along been drawing my mother's dreams, not my own. Children are highly sensitive to moods, innuendos, the subtleties of desire. It could have been in the bedtime stories she told me, her tone of voice when she spoke about men or my father. It could have been a dream of hers that drifted from her room across the hall into my bedroom in the summer when it was hot and the doors to the rooms were ajar and the windows wide open although the curtains barely moved in the dull city heat. It could have been carried on any wind or in any dream; it could have been any or all of these things and more now buried forever with time that made me believe there was a prince out there on his way, moving slowly but inexorably toward us, my mother and I, in our snug two-bedroom apartment, lace curtains, clean sheets on the beds, romance novels with pages bent back, flower boxes in the windows, on a quiet tree-lined street, oaks, elms, blossoming crab apples, blackbirds, dusk.

Butternut

THE WAY I FIGURE IT, people are either breaking into your life or out of it. If they use a door to get in, sometimes they need a window to get out. I think that's a rule or something. When we left class last Friday, Hamlet had just broken into Ophelia's room with his doublet unbraced and stockings ungartered. Mr. Sargent handed out the assignment sheets, and then, taking his time, sat back down behind his desk.

For Monday—in 500 words or more answer this question—Were Hamlet and Ophelia in love? And if so, how is love an aspect of the revenge tragedy? Support or refute, but please, elaborate on the themes of love and loss. Be careful not to shuffle off your mortal coil in the process.

I looked down at the sheet, read it again, and turned toward Emmie who sat next to me by the window. She was doodling birds and telephones into her notebook, but the only note I could see was this scrawl under the date, "Oh feel ya. Ophelia. Oh the feel of not to feel you." All around it were little flowers and hearts. Emmie looked at me over the top of her glasses, grinned, rolled her eyes and went back to drawing. When I looked that way and saw the crazy insistent banging of the bare lilac branches against the glass, I knew spring would come early this year.

I ran across campus in the rain from the girls' dorm to Eames Hall because I had slept right through the ringing bell of my alarm clock. More than anything I blame the weather. You should be able to wake in the morning and look out the window while you're still in bed and count on the weather. It was a gray sleepy morning without breakfast and without Emmie to walk to class with me.

Friday we quit at Act ii, scene i, but this morning when I slipped into my seat with my hair tangled and dripping into my shirt, I crossed the border back into Denmark to find that nothing had happened in between. It's still Act ii, Hamlet can't fix his stockings. Polonius is moaning about love while Ophelia eats candied apples and wipes her fingers on the good embroidery. Emmie is gone and her seat is empty next to me. She should be sitting with her legs crossed and her anklets turned down and sloppy over her loafers. At a little after eight Mr. Sargent comes into the room and slams the door. He does the Jerry Lewis thing where he tries to hang up his raincoat but it falls, and he can't quite get his umbrella to close right. Slowly, he looks around the room, but when he looks at the place where Emmie should be, I just keep staring at my notebook.

Emmie had leaned on the door and said good night, but it wasn't final. I mean, she didn't know then. She couldn't have known, and she leaned on the door with her sleepy grace and her wrist about to turn. As she said good night, she hesitated for a moment.

"Have you started that essay for Sargent's class yet?" she asked.

"No," I said.

"Are you sure you don't want to sleep in my room tonight? Come up after room check and all."

"I'm not really sleepy," I told her.

"When you read books sometimes," she asked, her eyes on the clock, its hands, its dial, "do you ever try to put in the characters who are left out?"

"How do you mean?"

"I mean," she said, "Have you ever wondered if maybe Ophelia had a younger sister—" She scratched her neck and from downstairs Ingrid paged the eleven o'clock room check announcement. Emmie turned her wrist on the doorknob and said good night in a slur, with the faintest hint of Noxema and White Linen. The door shut and I stared at the illuminated face of the clock. I missed her already.

Suppose Ophelia did have a younger sister. Would they have dressed alike? Worn the same crinolines, tangled lace, and embroidered slippers? Suppose that Ophelia had a younger, less attractive, well, less oracular sister who saw with a worn-down innocence all the intrigues of the Royal Court of Denmark in one tragic season. Maybe the girl even loved Hamlet. She loved how Hamlet and Ophelia were in love, yet hated that she would never be a part of their lives so wound and knotted around each other. If Ophelia had a younger sister would she and Horatio have taken turns telling the tale, reciting in a responsive chant the names of the victims? Or would she have danced from grave to grave tossing daisies and Queen Anne's lace, waiting for the bloom of summer's later more heady flowers?

When I was packing for school in September, I found a copy of *Hamlet* on my sister Rose's bookshelf. I knew that she hadn't even read it because the binding wasn't cracked, and when I opened it up there were no bent pages or coffee stains. On the cover where there is a picture of Hamlet and the pen and inky shadow of the ghost, she had drawn Ophelia standing off to the side with a wreath of Day-Glo orange flowers in her hair. I knew that Rose would never miss the book. The only writer she had ever liked was Poe and that too was a long time ago.

Rose used to shut herself away in her room for hours. It seemed like weeks went by without anyone in the family seeing her. She got her first deck of tarot cards in the third grade, the bicentennial. Everybody wore red, white, and blue. Ricey wore black and read fortunes. That didn't last long though. She was impatient with things given or gained too easily. She gave up out of boredom things she had only begun to get a taste of. I got her Poe books, the tarot deck and ouija board. I took what I could get and was content with what Ricey would cast off, toss my way.

She let objects, people, time, casually slip away from her because there was always more. There was an endless supply of places you could dream about, or run away to. It wasn't until later that I realized she was beautiful. I mean, I realized that different rules applied to her than to regular people. Beautiful people are careless and irreverent. They can say a million things without saying a word; it's all implied. The rest of us stammer and stutter and still can never say what we mean. But beautiful people, well, you have to assume that they live by different rules.

The problem when people start breaking in is that, inevitably, you know they are going to break out. It's the beautiful people who make the most noise when they go, leave dirty ashtrays, forget to flick off the lights. They make a mess for someone else to clean up. They always assume that someone will do the real-life things like that. It's the carelessness that gets to me, like they assume that you'll be there, that you can wait forever for them to decide.

Somehow I always knew that I had an oracular older sister, but there was one night in particular when I realized that she

37

was different from me because she was beautiful. Before that night she was just some dark-haired girl who came out of her room on rainy days and played paper dolls with me in the basement when my mother had a headache or just wanted me out of the way.

One night, and I think that I couldn't have been older than five or six, my parents had their friends, the Saltmarshes, over for dinner. We were sitting in the dining room and my father had put the extra leaf in the table. There were flowers; Mrs. Saltmarsh must have brought them. As it got later the street outside became very quiet. Only every so often the sound of a car or a bicycle wheeling by clattered on the pavement. The white curtains blew in the breeze from the window. I was sitting by my brother, Thermidor, and yes, that is his name although everybody calls him "Door" because he's so big, like oh you make a better door than a window. We were eating fruit salad and Ricey was nowhere to be seen. She hadn't been at dinner. Mrs. Saltmarsh was pregnant and whenever she laughed she put her hand on the curve of her stomach.

I heard these footsteps on the stairs really softly, and not one step after the other but one foot on a step, then both feet, then a pause, so that it took twice as long to make it down. It was like I couldn't remember Ricey, but I was waiting for her to be born. I wasn't waiting for her to get there, but to happen.

Ricey stood in the doorway leading from the living room to the dining room. She was wearing a white sheet patterned with little pink flowers tied toga style on her shoulder. She just stood there and stared at us with her tangled hair and wide green eyes and that white sheet until we were all silent, except for Mrs. Saltmarsh who giggled.

Ricey shut her eyes and intoned, "And we loved with a love that was more than love, I and my Annabel Lee."

She opened her eyes and with a simple gesture unpinned the sheet from her shoulder and stood there nine years old and naked in front of the dinner table. She bowed, kissed the inside of her wrist to us and turned dragging the sheet behind her as she went.

That's when I knew that the reason she could do anything she wanted was because she was beautiful. She could be as crazy and loving as she wanted. There were no rules and it wouldn't have mattered had there been any, because she wouldn't have understood. It wouldn't have made a difference. Ricey denied that any of it happened. She said that she had felt sick and had slept through that whole night. Three weeks later when Mrs. Saltmarsh lost her baby, Ricey's psychic powers were confirmed. My mother bought her the tarot deck and small glass bottle of vanilla perfume.

"Carina Rogers?" calls Mr. Sargent looking down at his attendance sheet.

"Here," she waves from across the room.

"Butternut Simon?"

My "here" is barely audible. I don't even look up because I wouldn't be able to handle the eye contact. He's looking at me trying to tell if I'm okay with the fact that Emmie is gone. Her father came Saturday afternoon while I was at the library and had her pack her things. He pulled her out of school right then and there. He said that it was planned long in advance because of his job transfer to Germany. But if that's true I don't know why no one told us. Mr. Sargent says "Butternut" with that sarcastic edge in his voice mixed with concern like after—well, like that morning when I was in the infirmary and he came to see me and said my name that same way like "Oh, Butternut," which is such a stupid name to have to say with any feeling. When he says it like that, I just look away.

If I'm never serious about anything, it's not my fault. It's that name. There was never any sense in trying to fight it or telling people to call me something else. I've had to live with that name because when I was born my mother looked down at her jaundiced newborn girl and said, "Well, she looks like Paul's prize squash." My dad laughed and asked, "The butternut squash that he won the ribbon for?" She said, "Yes, yes exactly, a butternut squash." The name stuck. It clung relentlessly through elementary school, found its way onto attendance sheets and report cards. It went through various junior high school abuses. I mean, no one has ever said that I was anything near beautiful, or even attractive as far as I remember. Butternut turned into Butterball or Butterbutt, the laughing stock of the luncroom. When I came here, I realized that it could be a sort of cool thing, I mean after I lost some weight and all. It became a name sort of like Khaki for Catherine or Fling for Ingrid on the field hockey team. It definitely has a sort of quirky coolness.

Today I'd like to concentrate on how the Shakespearian tragedy Hamlet *can be interpreted as a version of the Oedipus saga. We don't tend to approach a work of literature thinking that like spectators of Greek drama, we already know the story by heart. We like to be enlightened by the mystery, come to the climactic denouement in the pleasure of the text. But, in* Hamlet *as in all tragedy and perhaps even mystery novels, we always already know the outcome. So can anyone tell me why it is still moving to us?*

No one has ever called me by my real name except Aaron. He did it that morning in September right before I was about to go back to school. It was a few weeks after Ricey and I found out about our father's affair with Mrs. Saltmarsh, you know, Mrs. Amanda Saltmarsh who was over the night I realized that Ricey was beautiful. She had lost her baby and later (Did Ricey predict this too?) lost her husband. She was Aaron's mother, and my father slept with her. He didn't make any apologies. He sat us all down and actually said that he had "committed a transgression"; that's just like my father, to cheat on his wife and call it a transgression as though it was a crime against all of humanity and had nothing to do with real people. My mother was calm, practically vacant about the whole thing; she must have known about it all along. She just sat there with her hands pressed white-knuckled on the arms of her chair. Nobody even mentioned divorce.

It was September when it's so hot that you can sleep naked which is what I always do although sometimes it makes me feel very indulgent, especially if the sheets are white and clean. Aaron came into my room early without knocking and I sort of woke up as the door blew open, but sort of not, so that I thought it was a dream. I hadn't seen him more than twice that summer and then he breaks into my room grinning in the early morning sun with me naked in bed and dreaming of God knows what.

Sometime after I realized that Ricey was beautiful, it hit me Aaron was too. He asked me to get dressed because he wanted to take me to breakfast. I was tan and sleepy, but I wasn't Ricey. I knew I would never be what Ricey was to him. I was wearing khaki shorts and a t-shirt. He said, "Are you losing weight?" And I said no, which was a lie because, you know, I had been all summer. Somehow I hated that he noticed.

It was Sunday morning and we went to the Big Boy on Procne Street. It was crowded with families jammed together in booths in the nonsmoking section. The waitress, she was cute even though I can't quite picture her now. She might have had her hair cut in a short, boyish bob, or something like that. "What are you going to order?" I asked him.

"Pancakes," he said. "And maybe a side of bacon."

"You know, I'm not even that hungry," I said thinking about Rose who is soft and brown without being fat. No one would ever call her Butterball. They called her Ricey, and they called her on the phone, and they called her all the time. People couldn't help adoring her clumsiness.

"Why don't you order the waffles?" Aaron said and he pointed to the picture in the menu. It looked like a wedding cake with all these layers of strawberry and whipped cream.

"Just order it and I'll help you."

I gave him this look and he grinned. His long hair fell on his face, but I could still see how his eyes crinkled up in the corners when he laughed. He didn't laugh much that morning even though the sun was so nice and strong and weak at the same time. I like the summer because you can be pretty sure of the weather, the heat, I mean. You can wake up and know what you are in for. No other season is like that. The waitress brought our order. The waffles didn't look real. They looked like the picture, exactly like the picture. I couldn't even touch them. Aaron didn't notice and he started in on his pancakes.

"Jeez," he said with his head bent over his breakfast. "You're in what, tenth grade now? That seems so old. I mean you were always a little kid."

"Fifteen," I said. "Sixteen next March, but—"

"Look," he said interrupting me, waving his fork which had a chunk of syrup-sodden pancake speared in its tines. "Why are we trying to ignore everything and act like nothing happened. We both know what our parents did. It just makes me sick. But the strangest part is that it makes us practically family in a sick way. I never had a sister."

"And now you have two."

"How is she?" He asked trying to act casual, but he flushed as he quickly sipped his coffee. "Have you heard from her yet?"

"Not since she left. No letters. No nothing."

"I wrote her a love letter once. Did she tell you that? I think I was fourteen. I told her to doubt everything else in the world before she doubted me. It was pretty silly, but I never thought it was a joke the way she did. She thought it was all a joke."

"Even worse, she could have thought you were serious," I said.

He gave me a crooked grin. I thought about Rose as she was about to leave. Her things were packed as though she was going to go to school, to college, the way Aaron had gone and everybody had gone or would go. The girl who was supposed to be her roommate called us a few days later and asked bewilderedly, "Is this where Rose Simon lives? Is she there? Where is she?" Across from me Aaron's grin faded into a dreamy look and he leaned over and cut into my untouched waffle.

"Can I tell you something?" he asked. "I mean something really personal? I trust you Lilith," he said. So that's my name. There it is. It sort of shocked me. I was like, who? Who is he talking to? "Will you promise not to tell anyone?" he asked.

"Of course, I won't say a word," I told him, but I did end up telling two people. Somehow I didn't think that he would have minded.

"Right after I found out about them, about the affair, the first thing I did was go to her. She was acting really crazy. She said that she wanted to get out of the house. I knew some guy who was having a party, so we went over there. She got even worse. Everybody was so happy and drunk, and then there we were, depressed as hell. None of it seemed like it had to do with us anymore. I felt so old, older than everybody else there. It didn't make sense."

"You're not that much older than Ricey," I said.

"That's not what I mean. I said, I told her that we had to leave and she just followed me without saying a word."

"And?"

"And, we drove up to my parent's place by the lake. I was mad at her but just as mad at myself. We went inside, into my room, and it was so hot in there. The place had been shut up all summer. She opened a window. We were drinking a little, but it wasn't just that. She kept sneezing, but she said that it wasn't the dust. She said she had a cold, a summer cold."

I could imagine her standing by the window with her face still flushed pink from the party, maybe drunk, the skin around her nose raw and chapped. Probably without even turning out the light, she unbuttoned her flowered dress and stood by the window in her white bra and matching underwear. It was so hot and stuffy in that room. She took off all her clothes. The more drunk she got the more it became a matter of giving up rather than giving in; nothing in the world seemed certain anymore. It probably never before occurred to her that things could happen beyond and separate from her. She leaned half-naked at the window, just hidden by the dusty curtains. He had a sense of continuity about her body as though it was part of the night, and the night part of history, and history part of something greater than he would ever be able to understand or touch. She stood there drunk in the faint, dull late-summer night breeze.

"She was crying," he said. The tone of his voice changed when he told me that. He was no longer telling a story. He was explaining, justifying something. He said it twice—she was crying. He wanted to convince me that whatever had happened was not his fault.

"Things are so confusing. She was crying and I said to her, I remember saying, 'What's wrong?' Ricey said, 'This isn't even the beginning.'"

Aaron drew her back from the window. Ricey let herself be led, be moved from the window to the bed as though she was weightless. Of course, he didn't say that exactly. I pictured it. He said that things had happened that he hadn't meant to happen. He couldn't change that.

He stopped speaking and shook his head, blinked himself back from memory into the bacon and eggs bustle of Big Boy. As I looked at him, it sort of hit me, I mean hit me not just that he and Ricey were different from me, but that they were stupid. I mean, not just in an obvious way. Maybe dumb is a better word. They were dumb to the world and dumb to what they had. I looked at Aaron and didn't know what possibly could have been bad about the night they spent together when they had been in love for as long as I could remember. They must have been stupid to be so sad. They were alike; they were beautiful and no rules applied to them because they were too stupid to understand rules. They were careless and beautiful. He was careless to talk about love while the waitress rushed by with placemats and rolled napkins of silverware. He shouldn't have told me that he had loved her and she had been in tears, and yet they couldn't stop themselves.

And once only they slept together in his narrow bed without sheets with the window letting in the dull breeze of Indian summer. She had cried because she wasn't sure what else to do. Sometimes I think that beautiful people don't know what else to be; I mean they don't know what it's like not to be beautiful. The blueness flooded them and the night that continued from the outer edges of the Midwest to the last pages of history textbooks softened and let them sleep.

Once only they had slept together with the wide dark halls echoing full of ghosts. She had let her lace, her frills and flounces fall to the floor in a heap; her stockings and ribbons unroll in a soft tumble. She had put her finger to her lips and with a tilt of her head motioned for him not to speak. Once only they slept together under the heavy feather quilts on a servant's narrow bed in a bare, chill room in a winter frozen with something deeper than cold.

When Hamlet left her, kissed the pale of her sleeping shoulder, she slept on, dreamed on through the morning. When she awoke and into the day her singsong dirty rhymes clattered to the clumsy patter of her bare white feet on the cold stone floor. They left the bed unmade behind them. All the ribbons were still skillfully knotted, the bells, the bows, the twisted yards of lace.

Another aspect of tragedy we need to examine is not only how the workings of fate take their toll on the individual, but how the fall is precipitated by a fatal flaw. It could be physical, like Achilles' heel. It involves something that the hero has no control over. Events have been set in motion before the hero is born, before he has a chance to contest his fate. What might Hamlet's tragic, perhaps fatal, flaw be?

The readiness. Hamlet could never decide. The readiness to action was all. But wasn't Ophelia ready to stay the night and sleep through the morning in the hushed sanctuary of that bed? Sleep under those covers past winter and into spring? She was ready and she woke up alone.

Aaron tried to look happy. He smiled in a forced way and looked at my plate in front of him. When he realized that he had eaten half of my waffle, he pushed the plate back toward me.

Why doesn't Mr. Sargent ask what Ophelia's tragic flaw is? No one ever notices that while Hamlet only pretended to be crazy, something really drove Ophelia into madness and beyond that into death. Why didn't she just cut her losses, pack a bag, head for the nearest bus station picking the twigs from her hair, eating jelly hearts, counting he loves me, he loves me not on the ceramic beads of a rosary?

Ophelia's tragic flaw was maybe loving too well the flowery pretty things of this world. She tottered, white lace and embroidered stockings from this world, nettles, saffron, hyacinth, toward another. Words for another, better world? Celestial, empyrean, ethereal. She was ignored in life and loved in death. She had too many brothers, too full a grave. Her rhymes and songs and cold bare feet were slippered and stockinged in her grave because there was not world enough and—

Time is a crucial factor to the tragic hero because it cannot fail to work against him. Events have been set in motion even prior to his birth. He is placed in a position of making a decision about time, action, and his moral obligations. If we are all "pipes for fortune's fingers," what action can work against fate? In this respect we see Fortinbras as a dramatic foil to the prince. Is Fortinbras the real hero of the play? Doesn't he avenge his father's death? Lead his armies to success while Hamlet moans and intellectualizes his dilemma? Is it specifically Fortinbras's ability to take action that saves him from a tragic end? Or was Hamlet doomed from the beginning?

So there were Ricey and Aaron dreaming sleep, doing an Eve and Adam. As Aaron finished my breakfast and again swore me to secrecy, as Hamlet crept with his stockings down-gyved from

the history of that blanketed bed where they had slept just as
tangled, I wondered what it might be like to be in love. I
thought it was a secret that everyone else in the restaurant, as
they poured syrup and buttered toast, understood. I know that
I never loved Aaron, at least not the way that Ricey did. I supposed that if I was ever in love, I'd be lucky because beauty
wouldn't get in the way. Even the thought of those arms and
legs and I shivered in the warm September morning.

Less than a month passed from that night outside of Seven
Rivers in that old cabin to the day that Ricey left us. I thought
a lot about what Aaron had told me; about my mother and
father so far apart, about Ricey and Aaron coming together
with tears and uncertainty. Finally, I told Emmie Aaron's secret
because it had started to scare me, and I just wanted someone
to explain it to me. I wanted her to sit down like a geometry
tutor and explain his story step-by-step using a ruler and a
compass. I told Emmie because she shuffled her heels in a lazy
way when she walked. Emmie drank a lot, the same way Ricey
did, and once drunk on orange vodka she talked in her childish voice about how love was something like the space between
desire and regret. I don't know if there's anything special to
understand about Ricey and Aaron; but if there is, if it took
some special heat-warped, half-drunk sensitivity to understand their dumb beauty, I knew Emmie had it.

"Did you ever want a sister?" I asked her.

"No, not really," she said.

We were in the bathroom. She had her bare leg up on the
sink and was lathering it with soap. She was hungover from
the night before and as she soaped her leg, she paused to splash
water on her face. I blurted out the story as Aaron had told it.

"Wwweeell," she said drawing out the word to match the
gesture of the razor taking a long swipe up her round calf, "it's

sort of like a book, isn't it? It's romantic, but sad. It's also very, um, common. You know, real."

She gave me this look that said she too even at sixteen had had summer nights that she regretted out loud, but hugged the memory of in secret. I should have known then, I mean, I should have told her that I was jammed full of secrets, and couldn't stand any more. She rinsed her razor holding it under the stream of cold water.

"Did he tell you that he regretted sleeping with her?" asked Emmie.

"No, he didn't exactly say that, but it seemed like it was what he meant."

"Well then he lied. Think about it. Do you think either one of them really regrets it?"

She let the running water punctuate her question and again gave me her deep-eyed knowing look. Aaron had been lying that morning when he said that he regretted sleeping with Ricey. There were so many lies and he only wanted to protect himself. If Emmie had her own delicate regrets it wouldn't make me hate her, or think she was bad. She was only careless, as careless as the rest of the world, as careless as Hamlet was careful.

Maybe Hamlet and I are the only two careful people in the world—

in which Hamlet lives is a paranoid nightmare. There are ghosts asking for revenge, murderous uncles, unfaithful mothers, and spies at every corner. There has been much critical speculation about the subtle ways in which Hamlet tries to take action by appropriating the text of the play. He writes twelve lines of speech for the players, but we don't know exactly which lines they are. If we knew, we could—

know where Hamlet starts and Shakespeare ends. There are twelve lines and we will never know which they are. Maybe if I ever write a story, my tragedy, I'll have twelve lines which are true and the rest will be lies, have nothing to do with my life. No one will ever know who he was to Hecuba, or which the true lines are.

Mr. Sargent asked why, if we know the ending, is it still tragic? Doesn't just knowing that it will never change, that things have been set in motion . . . isn't that sort of tragedy in itself? We have always known what the outcome will be. We can't do anything to stop it. Gertrude won't put her cup down, and I can't teach Ophelia any new dirty jokes. They started before me, go beyond.

You can't stop the slow poison making its coagulating trickle through the king's veins. I couldn't stop his hands, Ricey and Aaron on that mattress, his hands, Emmie's wrist on the door.

On Tuesday afternoons when I have to go see Mrs. Sirin, the school therapist, she tries to make me remember his hands. Even that morning after it happened when I was in the infirmary, I couldn't remember. Mr. Sargent came to see me and he said my name and asked, "What happened?" I told him, "This isn't a book. I can't just flip back to page 52, to where the lights were out and I was in bed before he, flip to page 53, you know?"

Maybe I was wrong. Sometimes I think if I lived in a book it would be easier, or a play even because then I could just turn around in my seat, turn away from Mr. Sargent and toward the audience and clarify my stance to them. I could turn to them like an actor reading a script and say, here is the segment in which I tell about my own personal tragedy which is somehow never construed as important as the high tragedy of, say, *Hamlet.* I went to bed one night and woke up too early and too bruised to find that another page, a whole chapter had fluttered by and I couldn't remember reading it.

I can't turn because there is no audience, just Mr. Sargent droning on; just sleepy kids resting their faces on their hands.

Mrs. Sirin said, "Remember."

"I can't."

"Try again. Try harder this time."

My alarm was set. I wanted to wake up early and study for an Italian exam. When the door blew open at four, I remember, I looked at the clock by my bed with the foggy illuminated dial. One of my favorite poems has a line like that—the moon is an illuminated clock. The curtains were pulled and I couldn't see the moon, but I saw by the dial of the clock that it was late. The door blew open, then shut. The room was dark but the darkness felt charged and blue and maybe my eyes weren't focusing right because the dark blueness was hot and fast and moving in tiny particles. I knew that I wasn't alone. My heart was beating like crazy. I buried my face in the cotton of my pillow. I thought, I tried to think, you are safe here. You have to be safe somewhere. This is school. You are alone. I tried to conjugate Italian verbs, Essere, Avere, Fare, but my heart was beating and—

"Well, time is up for today anyway," said Mrs. Sirin tapping her pen on the table and breaking the silence.

Emmie waited for me in the hall outside the office. When I came out she grabbed my arm and giggled, "Any words of advice today? Any words to live by?" As we headed down the hall laughing neither of us had any idea how soon she would be gone. We didn't know that her father would wait the proper length of time after the scandal died down to take his daughter out of school. It was unsafe, he said. He poured the poison into my ears. Sometimes I can feel it, so I have to move slowly and avoid bright colors.

The door opened letting in the browngolden late summer light and Aaron squinted in the brightness and touched me on my sleeping shoulder. And I was so happy then. The illuminated clock. The timeless moon. The wind rustling the curtains. My heart beating like the spinning second hand. The clock. My heart. The night. It was so dark. He was so heavy. And my heart. I don't want to remember. His hands. Just that darkness. Just the door opening as he came into my room, and the window breaking as he left. Just that rhythm, that over and over rhythm, and the sharp pain and—

This fall, this abandon, gives us a better notion of what motivates Hamlet's desire, his zeal with respect to an act that he so longs to carry out that the whole world becomes for him a living reproach to the perpetual inadequacy of his own will—

Because maybe I had a stupid name, I never believed that names were real, or anything else was real, except maybe books. If Ophelia had a younger sister would she have been a spy for Gertrude? Would the queen have given her chocolates in exchange for secrets heard down echoing halls at night?

They were my secrets that night. I had been screaming without knowing it, bleeding without feeling it, and maybe everyone who touches you leaves a mark on your soul as well as your skin. All the girls came out of their rooms, sleepy and staring. It was like they were all beautiful but I had never seen any of their faces before. There were so many girls and they were all staring at me. They were all so strange and beautiful.

I kept trying to conjugate the Italian subjunctive, il conjunc-
tivo, very slowly and carefully, abbia, stia.

Emmie had her arm around my shoulder. She was talking
low and smoothing my hair. I thought, I have to go to class
tomorrow. What will the weather be like? What will I wear?
They were wiping the blood from my face with gauze. It
was soft like voices, like white dresses, like all the sleepy, beautiful row after row of plain-faced, brilliant, unremembered,
unknown girls—

*In both Greek and Shakespearian tragedy the element of audience
involvement contradicts our own ideas about the quiet of the theater. An Elizabethan audience seeing* Hamlet *would have reacted
the way you might at* The Rocky Horror Picture Show. *The
audience knew the stories and the outcomes previous to the enact-
ment. Enjoyment came not from the revelation of the mystery, but
from the assurance of the ritual repetition. Things did not change.
Oedipus always comes to the same problem at the crossroads both
physically and—*

I can find the symbolism in *Hamlet,* but what about this
world? No, there is no symbolism, nothing but sleeping and
waking and wondering about the weather. Love, marriage,
divorce; people are raped, bruised, and beaten. What are their
fatal flaws? You still wake in the morning, wash with cold
water and look out the window. You switch off the illuminated
moon of your clock. You have to go on, and it doesn't make
any difference to anybody what you carry or what you've
done. So they think that you are old or young, or distance
means miles and experience means age, and desire begins static at one point, peaks, and ends just as abruptly.

No, I'm screaming it. *No,* I'm announcing it to all the beautiful careless irreverent beauties of this world. *No,* I'm saying

that age isn't going to help. The things time will heal are just countered by the things it will destroy.

Mrs. Sirin rapped her neat nails on the desk as I stood in the doorway to go and meet Emmie. She asked me, "Do you feel better, more resolved about the whole thing yet?"

"Yes," I said. What else could I tell her? The truth?

She smiled and said, "That's good because when you are older you will understand the world better. Sixteen is very young. You will see that what happened to you is very small. It will pass and one day when you understand life better, it will seem, this small incident, very trivial."

"Understand life," I said. "But I've read *Hamlet.* What else is there to learn?" And I shut the door behind me as I left.

What is there to learn? You become the jilted lover of your mother, the ghost of your father, the loving jilter of another, and even if you can sneak in twelve lines of your own no one will have the sense to figure out which they are. Wheels have been set in motion. If Ophelia had a younger sister would she have been illiterate, drawn flowers, traced stars on the frosted-over glass of the windowpanes?

I was tired and dizzy that morning when Mr. Sargent came to see me in the infirmary. The nurse had given me orange juice and a handful of pills. Blurry around the edges, he walked in the door smelling like libraries and tobacco. He said, "Oh, Butternut," full of concern and pity. I kept having to bite my lip to keep from crying. He wanted me to cry. I saw his swimming face and his tweedy concern; he asked me to tell him what happened. I burst into tears, not movie tears but those horrible loud, stuffed up noisy ones.

"Tell me everything that happened," he said.

Instead of the dark room and the fists hitting my face, I told him about Aaron and Ricey. I blurted out that they had slept together on a humid August night and that there weren't even sheets on the bed. I was between fifteen and sixteen on a September morning and there was this horrific wedding cake of a waffle in front of me, and I went freezing numb in the middle of the restaurant. I wanted to know why everyone, everything else was beautiful and I could never be. I just kept sobbing to Mr. Sargent that there hadn't even been sheets on the bed.

I told him that in some ways Ricey was the most trite and conventional girl. My voice went on without me. Ricey my sometimes chocolate bar, matinee movie, rolled-Levis sister, my sometimes siren sister. My stupid sister and her stupid sometime, one time, all the time lover clinging through the night and into the morning and beyond that into memory on a bed that didn't even have sheets.

When I stopped crying, I looked up to see that Mr. Sargent had taken off his glasses. He was rubbing his eyes. I made him promise not to tell anyone. He promised, but he has probably told somebody by now. I mean, people are like that about secrets.

And Hamlet responds, but to his mother, not the king, "I know not seems."

Sometimes you have to say "no" to mean "yes," just to trick fate out of another victim. If I say that I couldn't have cared less about my father sleeping with somebody else's mother, that I expected it, that it never meant anything, maybe I'm lying. If I say that Ricey leaving me doesn't matter maybe I'm just upset because I never had anything I wanted more than I needed. I don't know, I always just wanted.

Mr. Sargent with his dry rambling voice has taught me about iambs, dactyls, and anapests; the rare and hidden trickery of phrasal tmesis. He has taught me about tragedy, romance, and meter. I've learned to conjugate, decline, divide, hypothesize, rationalize, estimate, and obfuscate. But he forgot one thing; he never taught me how not to yearn. They taught us everything else, why not teach us how to stop wanting?

When I climbed into their bed, into the space where they had been, it was too late. They were already gone. Everyone was gone and that was when Fortinbras came in with his armies to see what was left. I like to think about Ophelia and Hamlet before the fall; the curled hair on their pillow, the fears that disrupted their sleep. I like to think because there isn't anything else I know how to do.

So good-bye Fortinbras, and good night. Sleep Horatio in dreams whose limits and dimensions you'll never understand. Good night to all the kings and counselors, lords and ladies. Good night to the sleeping, the dead, and those close to dying. Poor Hamlet loved Ophelia's grave more than her bed. I always knew there was something very stupid about beautiful people. Good night to the grave living and the flowery dead. Good-bye and I toss you a wreath of all your favorites, full overblown roses, sickly sweet lilies, peonies with heads so full and lush that they droop over their own thin stems. I toss you fat heady flowers because you never understood the more delicate ones. You crushed them under your boots and slippers at the footfalls of each patterned saraband. You crushed what was nascent.

I don't want to hear anymore that I'm too young or too something else, because maybe people don't know what it feels like to be young and hot. And it feels like forever with Emmie walking and her heels shuffling in her black loafers and her anklets turned down and sloppy. Young and hot. How can people go around being so careless, just running down other people's lives like some bus out of control? You don't know if maybe somebody's father died, or if somebody is in pain, or if they just feel raw inside and their arms and legs don't feel like they belong to the same body. I don't think this because I'm young and don't know anything about the world. I think there are only so many things you can know, and everything after that becomes some version—just some same shirt in a different color. The things that change are the people.

I don't want to hear that I'm too young or too shy, or too aloof and it will all pass. The passing doesn't bother me. I just can't stand hearing the words when I know that there must be something better that people are ignoring. Look, I know all this for myself. I'm set with it. I'm always going to be alright because I understand this, but it's for Ricey, you know? I'd like to tell her that sometimes it hurts for no reason, and that's not something you can explain in a postcard with a pretty picture on it or in polite conversation over dinner.

Bad things happen to people. I know that good things must too. It just hasn't seemed that way in a while. It's like if we could all just make it through this winter, we might have a chance. It's not for me; it's for Ricey and Emmie and people who still think there's something about this world that's right and matters. It would all be so good if we could be good and goodness would heal and save . . . and then there were his hands and fists. I don't know. I don't recall what there was because something in me went straight up. I mean, rose above the whole scene, the bed, the room. I wasn't watching. I wasn't anywhere but some place good and that wouldn't be this world. Better than good, and the waitress whose face I've searched my memory for put the strawberry waffles down in front of me. It looked just like it did on the menu. Aaron grinned at me and shook the hair from his eyes. There is something in me that is so good and pure, that it flies above the everyday and every scene and moment.

And I know my father would kill me to hear me say it, but I believe in Jesus. I fly above the bed and his fists are hitting some other girl and it's her blood on the sheets, her mouth and her hands. I'm above it like a prayer you might say softly, your frozen breath on a cold midwestern day, even better a picture in a child's pop-up book, there when you open the page and gone when you shut it. Jesus must be like that, like a light that doesn't go out, or a color that mixes every range in the spectrum and you can't say this is blue or this is purple, this is twilight gray or mauve. So you say to yourself, to your hushed prayer self, this is Jesus.

In the midst of the crazy moments of broken glass, the sleepy girls, the blood turning brown quickly, the policemen milling around, I was calm. I sat in an office chair and a policeman, who had ink on his knuckles, said tell me what happened. I'm giggling like crazy because I want to tell him that Jesus is serving me waffles at an I-Hop in Kentucky and some old men who must be the apostles are eating pecan rolls with cinnamon butter. There is a humming in the air like flies but it is only their laughter. I think everyone must be laughing because this is not what I ordered. Everyone is laughing in a warm buzzing way, because they know what I really wanted.

I didn't tell the police officer anything about Jesus or souls, about how Ricey is gone, Emmie is gone, Aaron is gone, and I'm gone now too because something in me flew out of my body and went and lost itself into the January night whose blueness could hide all the sins in the world.

Mr. Sargent is handing out essay questions and assignment sheets. He says in his dry, monotonous tone, "Let's talk about the ending. Let's talk about the implications of piling the bodies on the stage."

If I could answer him, if I could lean forward and say a word and not care that everyone might look, start looking again, I'd tell him that spring must have been very beautiful at Elsinore with all the columbines, the long purples, the nettles in bloom. When the rains came and the stream overflowed, children might have played with the jetsam washed ashore, a ragged hem of satin, a girl's lace garter, a long white scarf winding through the green water like a shroud. My hands are shaking and I don't look up at him. No one is answering his question. I try to steady my hand and write in my notebook, Spring at Elsinore must have been very beautiful for those who survived.

Pearl

My mother met Martin Hamlin at the stroke of midnight, New Year's Eve, kissed him in the cascade of balloons, confetti, and crepe paper streamers which poured down from the ceiling to the dance floor below at the "Coming Alive in '85" singles party at the downtown Hyatt Regency Hotel. The way she told it, she knew it was love the moment she saw him, his face suddenly aglow in the blue glare of the giant video screens showing the glittering ball drop in far-off Times Square. He was dancing with another woman, but my mother was determined not to let something as trivial as a redhead in a sequined dress stop her from meeting up with, as she later phrased it, "my destiny." At the stroke of midnight as the lounge band belted out a woozy "Auld Lang Syne," my mother pushed through the crowd to kiss the stranger's illuminated face, bright blue, glowing, just like in the movies. She found herself standing under the awning of the hotel with Martin Hamlin in the freezing January rain while a teenage valet with gold epaulets pocketed his twenty-dollar tip and drove a shimmering Mercedes sedan up to the curb. Later she couldn't be sure whether she had fallen in love exactly at first sight or when the valet held an umbrella for her as she climbed into the car to realize the windows were tinted black, and she had the odd sense, for the first time in her life, of being able to see out at the world without the world looking back.

I was asleep in front of the television when she came home that night. The fuss of the new year, even then, at fifteen, did nothing but depress me. The highlight of my evening was not watching Dick Clark drop the glittering disco ball, but awaiting my mother's return and hearing the story of her night. I toasted to 1985 drinking Vernor's ginger ale with a line of maraschino cherries speared on a cocktail sword. The television revelers chanted and screamed in the cold. When I woke the Creature Feature late movie was just starting. It was then that my mother came dancing in.

She entered in midsentence and without so much as removing her faux fur coat, waltzed around the room clutching her rhinestone-studded pocketbook in one hand and a take-out bag from Angelo's Coney Island in the other. She threw herself down on the couch next to me and lowered her voice, worry creeping into it. "Big breasts. Probably not real, but big. Do you think that's why he was with her? Because he likes big breasts? What am I saying? I mean, who doesn't?"

"What?"

She paused, letting her eyes rest on the television.

"You should have seen the girl he was with. You should have seen the hips on her, and this hair, red, no, orange, it was orange hair. That green dress, that hair. She looked, I swear to God, like a Christmas tree—"

For the moment the thrill of her victory over the anonymous redhead was diminished and my mother opened her coat to stare down dismally at her breasts, small and high against the fabric of her party dress.

"Who?" I asked just as I had been taught in my public school English classes. "What? When? Where? And most importantly, why?"

"Martin Hamlin," said my mother shrugging out of her coat.

"Martin Hamlin? What's a Martin Hamlin?"

"Don't be such a smart-ass," she said. "Martin Hamlin is the man I'm going to marry."

"Jesus Judy," I said. "Not again."

"Again? You make me sound like Liz Taylor. All we did was have coffee. Look," she held up the take-out bag. "I brought you a milk shake, it's vanilla. It's not like I slept with him."

The man on the television had just found the body snatcher pods in the basement.

"He drives a black Benz."

I punched my straw into the shake and kept my eyes on the television.

"He's been on *Donahue,*" she said.

"Donahue?"

She nodded, pleased with herself, and leaned over and sipped from my straw.

"What's wrong with him? Has he had a sex change or something?"

"He's a writer," she said.

"Like Tony?"

"No, not like Tony. Nothing like Anthony. And I'll tell you that even the mention of that bastard, of your dear father, who, did he call you tonight, on New Year's Eve? No, oh, how unusual, how unexpected. Even the mention of him does not burst my bubble tonight, honey."

"So what does he write, this Martin Hamlet?"

"He's got a Ph.D. He helps people work out their relationships. Love, commitment, self-esteem, things like that."

"Jesus."

"He writes self-help, *self-improvement* books, and he's very successful at it."

"Jesus, Martha, Mary, and the girls at the tomb."

"Who taught you to talk like that? I don't talk like that," she said leaning back against the cushions. Her dress had spaghetti straps and her shoulders were revealed, narrow, white, and bare.

"You're in love," I said disdainfully.

"Jesus Pearlie," she said digging into the bag and pulling out a carton of soggy french fries. "Happy New Year's to you too."

Sofie Kornwald, my mother's best friend, counted herself in on the romance from the start. While lingering with Martin Hamlin over coffee and a shared banana split, pineapple topping, hot fudge, strawberries, and one spoon, at Angelo's Coney Island, my mother briefly excused herself, slipped away to the lady's room and called Sofie from the pay phone.

"She told me, and I quote, 'I have just met my second husband,'" said Sofie. "I, of course, was out with Elliot, but she left the message on my machine."

It was a bright cold Saturday afternoon and Sofie had arrived on our doorstep perspiring from a low-impact workout at Lady's Swim and Trim. She shifted her grocery bag from arm to arm while humming a show tune. I think it was "Hello Dolly."

"What's the occasion?" My mother asked as Sofie thrust the bag upon her.

"As if you don't know?" She said. "We're celebrating your two week anniversary. Two weeks of the New Year. Two weeks of a new man in your life. I've got Nova lox, and—" She peered into the bag. "Let's see—assorted goodies—that cream cheese you like, you know, with the dill?"

My mother smiled. "This is so sweet of you—"

"How did you get in?" I asked. "You didn't ring."

"The nice man on three, with the mustache," she winked at my mother. "He let me up and carried the bag too. Such a sweetie—"

Sofie broke off and removed her coat displaying for us her new exercise gear. Turning in a circle she gave us an all-angles view of her pink spandex pants, shiny orange leotard with plunging neckline and matching orange Reeboks. "But enough about me already," she said. "I want to hear about your date last night. So tell me—and I want details—have you two finally done it?"

"Sofie," laughed my mother. She was setting the brunch on the table. "You are just too much."

Sofie stood in our kitchen like Venus de Milo with arms elbow deep in her oversized purse. She pulled out a Ziploc baggie of coffee beans, her own "special blend." She stashed and stuffed all the mysteries of the universe in that tote of hers. I tried to keep a running list of things I had seen produced from its burgundy leatherette depths: taupe nylons, a mini-bottle of ketchup, cellophaned packs of Virginia Slims, butter rum Life Savers in econo-rolls, a daily astrological guide, liquid paper, twine, and a Day-Glo whistle for either her personal safety or attracting the dogs of attractive men.

"It's been two weeks, and you haven't told me. If you had done it, you would've told me, right?"

She punctuated her question by pressing down emphatically on the grinder so that the beans swirled into furious motion.

"What? Does he have some kind of problem?"

"No," said my mother. "He has no problems."

"You don't have to be ashamed to admit it if he does. Lots of men do."

"Oh really—" My mother looked at me and crossed her eyes. Sofie really cracked her up. "Any you'd care to mention?"

"Well, for instance—Walter. Walter did."

"Oh, news flash."

"How would you know about Walter?"

"Sofie," I interrupted. "Even I could tell. There was something funny—"

"He had a girl butt," said my mother.

"What?" said Sofie. "What does that mean? Why do you two always gang up on me? That's not fair, you know."

"So have your own kid," said my mother.

"Don't think I haven't considered it, but after all that trouble with Walter—I've been thinking about going to one of those, you know, sperm banks."

"I'm losing my appetite," I said.

"Don't be so immature," said Sofie.

"Pearl's got a point," my mother said opening one of the plastic deli containers. "There is something vaguely unkosher about mixing lox with sperm."

"Semen," said Sofie archly. "The correct word is *semen.*"

The coffee was dripping into the pot, dark and sweet.

"Do me a favor, Pearlie," said my mother. "Get the cups and spoons."

To get to the cabinet with the dishes I had to pass Sofie. We had this narrow little kitchen; all the apartments in the building were laid out the same way, a narrow strip with the stove, sink and fridge on one side, cabinets above and below, and the counter on the other side also serving to divide the kitchen from the living room. Sofie didn't budge from her spot next to Mr. Coffee so I had to squeeze between her spandexed girth and the sink to get to the upper shelves. She didn't notice that I was struggling to get by. It reminded me of a cartoon I had seen about those little birds who fly into crocodiles' mouths and clean their teeth while the big reptile notices nothing peculiar.

Sofie Kornwald, self-proclaimed seductress and every man's fantasy, pronounced the coffee was ready and moved her soft bulk from the kitchen to the table in the living room where my mother had nicely set out the bagels, cream cheese, lox, fresh cigarettes, and a bunch of bruised, overripe bananas. I poured the coffee into three cups.

Sofie liked to describe herself as voluptuous and in the broken Yiddish into which she often lapsed, zaftig. When they used to sit together constructing personal ads which they would never place, Sofie's started, "Sensual Capricorn SJF i.s.o. fate, destiny . . . or a doctor—" My mother said that when they went to bars together men just fell, quite literally tumbled over each other for the honor of lighting Sofie's cigarette. I never really picked up on her magnetism. I figured that maybe it only worked on men, or it was some chemical thing. She was always doing things like leaning over counters and tables, standing in doorways so you had to bump up against her to get past. When you brushed against her, she gave off the clinging scent of cloves and sweat.

"Does anyone need Sweet'n Low," asked Sofie as I set down the cups. "Because I have some in my purse."

"Just black for me today," said my mother.

"Another late night for Judy?" Asked Sofie, her voice rich with innuendo.

"Oh, before I forget," said my mother. "I've got something for both of you." She rose and hurried to her bedroom.

"You think maybe she's got some naked Polaroids of him?" Sofie asked me.

I stirred milk into my coffee.

"The latest," my mother said returning with two paperbacks. She handed us each a copy of the book. "This one is really important. It's about learning how to love yourself first, you know, before you can let someone else love you. It's all about trust."

"And self-esteem," said Sofie.

"Of course," my mother nodded.

"Tell me again about the car," said Sofie.

"Tell me again why he's here," I asked.

"What's wrong with Flint?" said Sofie.

"You should feel the leather. The seats are like—"

"You must have a guardian angel," sighed Sofie wearily. "I swear to God, you must." She leaned forward letting her breasts rest on the table.

"It was fate," said my mother almost apologetically. "It was the moment I've been waiting my whole life for. I just *knew.*"

"You can't argue with fate, right? He could have been any-one. He could have been a janitor or some bum off the street —but you hit pay dirt. Has Rudi done your cards lately?"

My mother nodded. She glowed. *"The Lovers."*

"Me," said Sofie. "I just keep getting *The Fool.* What do you suppose that means?"

"What did Rudi say?"

"She said it meant I would meet a younger man."

"What's he really doing here?" I insisted.

"You act like this is some kind of cultural wasteland," said Sofie. "You act as if a man like Martin Hamlin wouldn't hold his seminars here."

"Don't start this again," said my mother. "He's on a limited engagement. One month here. And I don't want to think about anything beyond that."

"There's theater here," said Sofie. "Last summer, for your birthday, don't you remember? When we saw William Shatner in whatsit, *The Plaything* over at the Star Theater? He can sure act, that Captain Kirk," she sipped her coffee and held the cup like people on TV do, by the sides, not the handle.

"Sure, he'd rather just stay in New York, but he has this mission. He has to help people and if that means going on the road giving his seminars across the country—"

"Stop," I said. "You're breaking my heart."

"Don't be so rude to your mother," said Sofie.

"Where does he go next?"

"I'm not listening," said my mother.

I flipped over the copy of the book she had just given me. I was amassing a collection, the complete works of Martin Hamlin. I stacked them under my bed where I didn't have to be confronted with the penetrating eyes of his picture. The book was called *Love Me Alone*. The gospel according to Martin Hamlin. He looked like some crazy Old Testament patriarch; his hair and beard were pure white just like Moses after he saw the burning bush. He glowed with an authoritative light. A certain wisdom burned in his eyes. There was the hint of a curl to his lip, a jauntiness to the proud tilt of his head. His skin was seamless and soft, a child's skin, not an old man's. I toyed with the idea of asking my mother if he had had a face-lift or maybe sold his soul to the devil.

Sofie eyed me suspiciously. "Have you met him yet?"

"No," I said.

"Then why don't you like him?"

"Who says I don't like him?"

"You act," she opened her purse and began emptying its contents: reading glasses, bite-sized Snickers bar, premoistened towelettes, ah, her Bic lighter, "like you don't like him."

"She doesn't like anyone," said my mother.

"Are you keeping something from me? You are, I can just tell, you are," moaned Sofie. "What is it? Did you elope? Are you trying to keep it out of the tabloids?"

"So-fee, I've told you everything," implored my mother grabbing Sofie's hand.

"Is Martin Hamlin famous enough to be in the tabloids?" I asked incredulously.

"Of course," said Sofie. "He's like that juice guy. He's got a, you know, cult following."

"Are you sure you don't have him confused with someone else? Like Marvin Hamlish? Or Harry Hamlin? Marvin Hagler, maybe?"

"You're a real card," said Sofie. "A whole goddamn deck of them. What are you trying to do, make your mother cry? You know what your problem is? I read about it, read it right here," she held up her copy of *Love Me Alone*. You've got a reverse gender Oedipal syndrome," she said flipping through the pages of the book as though searching for proof.

My mother took two cigarettes, one from each pack, a Camel and a Virginia Slim, and lit them, one at a time. "I didn't know," she said handing a cigarette to Sofie, "that you had read any of Martin's books."

Sofie inhaled and kept it in for a while. "I happened to browse through it at a bookstore—"

"What bookstore?" Asked my mother suspiciously.

"Just over at Eastland Mall. So sue me, I was getting a prescription filled at Perry's and I thought I would—"

"—sneak a look at his picture," concluded my mother.

"He's cute," said Sofie. "Mature."

"He's much younger than he looks."

"I like the hair. It makes him look smart."

"He is smart," exhaled my mother. "Very."

"It makes him look like Donahue."

"He's been on *Donahue*. I told you that, didn't I?"

"Sure, *that* you've told me a million times, but what I want to know is have you slept with him yet? Sexual compatibility is the cornerstone—"

"There's a child in the room," I said. "In case you haven't noticed."

Sofie snorted. My mother laughed.

"Some child," said Sofie. "Keep your mouth shut and maybe you'll learn something."

"If there is anything to be learned here, it's from Sofie," my mother said. "This woman," my mother continued. "She puts spells on men. They can't resist her. If someone could bottle her sex appeal they would make a for—"

"If that's so true then why don't I have a Martin Hamlin?"

"You have Elliot," said my mother. "You're crazy about Elliot. You always say how no man has ever paid such attention to—"

"Where's my Martin Hamlin?" mourned Sofie.

"It was fate," repeated my mother.

"So what's my fate? The Elliots, the Walters of the world? The realtors and chiropractors? Is that *my fate?*" She moaned into her hands.

The smoke was getting thick.

"Two witches," I said.

Sofie exhaled like a femme fatale.

"Did she just call me a bitch?"

"A witch," said my mother.

"She needs professional help. Maybe you should have a talk with Martin Hamlin about her."

"She gets it," said my mother, "from her father. Not me. She gets it all from him."

I shut the door to my room, but I could still hear them out there trading secrets. Our apartment was like that, sound carried from room to room, conversations, the television, my mother's blow-dryer, phone calls. I turned on my radio to WTAC, Flint's rock station, and opened my Algebra II book, but my heart wasn't in it. I was thinking about fate and about what my mother would tell Sofie after I left the room about sleeping with Martin Hamlin, or if she would keep it secret from both of us, or maybe if she was telling the truth and she hadn't done anything with him because he had some mysterious male problem. Maybe she had already had sex with him, and they had done it the night they met. Maybe they had gone to his hotel room. Maybe it was in that car she always bragged about; people in movies were always drinking champagne and doing it in cars. People in the movies.

I leaned on the windowsill and peered through my lace curtains at the street below. The paperboy was coming up to the building through the slush of the sidewalk delivering the afternoon journal. The full winter sun was receding; there was just an edge of darkness, the deepening blue along the little streets and avenues. I could see lights on in the houses across the street and two blackbirds sitting on a chimney. That was the nursery rhyme that used to lull me to sleep, wasn't it? Four and twenty blackbirds, baked in her sweet pies. I watched the birds out there in the smoky afternoon until they disappeared into the darkness. Good night, sweet ladies. Good night Queen of Hearts.

My biggest mistake was keeping quiet about Martin Hamlin. Perhaps this affair was more mysterious than her time with Morty, the chiropractor, or Howard who sold restaurant equipment, but I did believe that first and foremost Martin Hamlin was a luxury, a limited engagement in our lives. He was in town for a month to conduct one of his self-help seminars; soon he would go away and take with him the phone calls, late nights, the perfume that replaced cologne on my mother's bedside table. It's always a mistake to bet against time. One short month, it was nothing, a succession of days until he took his traveling therapy circus on the road, on to the promises of other cities, more help to be done, other needy divorcees enamored with black cars and the lure of predestined love.

He was true to his word. Martin Hamlin moved on to Detroit and his "limited engagements," but it was far from the last of him. His phone calls persisted and then there were his weekend visits, although he never came to our home. His gifts were displayed around our apartment. A framed photo smiled benevolently down at us when we made our breakfast in the kitchen nook. My mother always met him someplace else, for drinks, for dinner, but she never once stayed out all night. Should I have been playing the neglected child? Done something to dissuade her continuing relationship with him? I know what I did. I was fifteen. I kept my mouth shut, and I watched and I listened, because even though I generally did not put much faith in what Sofie said, I thought I might learn something.

The whole thing troubled me. Even before I met him. It was just the *idea* of him. And her. If he was Martin the great Hamlin, the Martin Hamlin and you always said his first name in one long breath with his last name, and he could have his choice of any woman, why did he pick my mother, a thirty-five-year-old divorcee, a sometime substitute teacher who liked nothing better than to stay home watching soap operas, dreaming, I always suspected, of other lives. There must have been so many women who came to his seminars looking for salvation, the lonely wives, the needy, the self-help circuit groupies, the talk show guests whom he had psychoanalyzed and cured with the light touch of his pure hand on their respective feverish brows in the space of an hour, why did he have to come here, to the end of the road? Flint, here, of all places and single my mother, Jittery Judy, out of the crowd?

"I want you to meet Martin Hamlin," my mother said dropping her shopping bags onto the carpet.

"When?"

"Tomorrow, dinner tomorrow."

"Valentine's Day? Don't you want to be alone?"

"Don't be silly," she said absently.

She thrust a shopping bag at me. I didn't want to take it. Her eyes were bright and expectant. It was late evening. Snow was falling outside illuminated by the streetlights. Snow speckled her disheveled brown curls. I did not know if it was the cold or the thrill of shopping which caused the flush on her damp face. The bags she carried were from expensive stores that we went to only for clearance sales. My mother hated sales and found some secret shame in heading to the clearance racks with their disarray of forgotten fabrics, fading and already out of fashion. I think it was as much about me as it was about herself; she imagined that my dreams must have been the same as hers. But I could have cared less for her fashion magazines; it was only her faith in those glossy pictures that drew me in.

There are some people with money who love sales, who refuse to buy unless they are getting a deal; my mother was nothing like this. She fingered expensive dresses longingly. You could see it in her eyes, a crazy desire to have, to own, to be able to walk right up to the counter and tell the salesgirl, "charge it," with a throwaway nonchalance. She wanted to be able to spend more than necessary; she wanted to ask the sales-girl to mark up the price. Even before she met Martin Hamlin she left extravagant tips at restaurants, gave money to panhandlers, stuffed my hands full of change for the gumball machines at the grocery store, and later when she wasn't looking I put the change back in her pocketbook so that she never had to worry about not having enough to give.

I reached into the bag.

It was a green dress.

"Guess how much I paid," she said covering the price.

I tried to guess low to please her with the grandness of her purchase.

"More," she said beaming.

"Fifty dollars."

"Higher," she said tossing me the dress and then proclaiming before I could guess again, "Seventy-two dollars and eight cents."

"That's a lot of money," I said.

She nodded. "It gets even better."

She pulled a black strapless dress out of another bag.

"Glamorous."

"I know," she said. "Isn't it? But I know what you must be thinking. You're thinking just what I thought when I saw it. It's tough to carry off strapless."

From the depths of her bag she pulled a black lace bustier and held it against herself. "This should help, hunh?"

She did something then that seemed odd even for my slightly exhibitionist and certainly shameless mother. She began to undress right there in the living room with the blinds open and everything. That's when I knew that no matter what she had said to Sofie or how she protested, that she was sleeping with him. I just didn't understand why she had denied it. There was something about the way she moved, how she carelessly pulled her dress over her head, flicked the front catch on her sheer bra, something about the way her wrist turned and the gold watch he had given her caught the light. Maybe it was naive of me to believe they hadn't been sleeping together all along, from that first night on, but I never truly had a sense of it, and of perhaps, more importantly, my mother wanting me to know about it, until that moment.

"Don't be such a circus freak, Judy," I said as I let down the blinds.

I kept my back to her and peered through two slats of the blinds out onto the darkened street below as though I expected to see a crowd of gawking onlookers or at least one lone figure, like Harry Lime in *The Third Man* when Joseph Cotten finds him in the shadows staring up at the lighted windows. My mother's nudity was not so much embarrassing to me as it was an odd and indecipherable omen of things to come into our lives; but then at fifteen I was constantly finding omens thrown in my path. A black cat, a naked mother, my fortune read in tarot cards by my mother's shampoo and set girl, a pocket size copy of *The Parallax View* on sale at the checkout rack in the grocery store the very day I studied the theory in astronomy class, an overturned salt shaker: I had no trouble finding symbolism, only interpreting it.

I turned from the view of the empty street to find that my mother had not yet dressed. She stood before me, hands on her hips, naked on the shag carpet. Her black dress was draped neatly, full length across an armchair.

"Now you, Pearl Rose Christomo, I want your opinion. Tell me the honest to God truth. Do you think I should get my breasts done?"

She arched her back. She faced me from front and side, and then struck some sort of swimsuit model pose, arms uplifted, hands clasped behind her head.

"Why didn't you name me *Rose* first and then *Pearl* second? It has a better rhythm that way."

"You're avoiding the issue," she said.

"Names mean everything. You get your whole identity from your name."

"Well then what does *Judy* say about me?"

"It says," I paused. I threw myself on the sofa, back turned to her, where she stood still naked, but now bent from the waist over her shopping bags and purchases. And I looked at her then, naked, when she didn't think I was looking, and I found her breasts strangely unfamiliar to me; they were curiously shaped and delicate. "Your name says *Judy:* cheerful, effervescent, friendly, shameless, naked, slutty—"

"You can stop anytime you want *Rose Pearl.*"

"The two names," I went on. "They just don't even go together. There should be some kind of syllabic variation. *Rosa Pearl.*"

"Too, you know, ethnic."

"Okay. *Pearline Rose.*"

"White trash."

"*Minnie Pearl.*"

"You'll spend your whole life searching for Grandpa Jones."

I craned over the sofa. She was pulling on a pair of lacy black underwear.

"Do you know about the holy underwear?" I asked her.

"With holes?"

"No. H-O-L-Y. Mormons wear them," I said. "I read all about it in *Cosmopolitan.* They never take them off."

The bustier closed up the front in an elaborate series of hooks, catches, snaps, and latches. My mother had to hold it against her body with her elbow so that she could use both hands to do the fastening.

"I guess it must be easier to take off," she laughed, struggling with a catch.

"What's Martin Hamlin's opinion of breasts?" I asked.

"Mine or in general?"

"Yours, I guess."

"You know what he says? He says I'm perfect. He says 'Judith, you are as perfect as Eve in the garden.'"

"Is that a good thing or a bad thing?"

She laughed. "You know how it is. Men will say anything. You know how men are."

"No," I said. "I don't."

"Men," she said.

"Men," I repeated.

"I just worry about getting married again after all this time, after all these years."

"Married, for real?"

"There goes the surprise, I guess. I, we, we were going to tell you tomorrow, but I couldn't wait. Can you believe it? He really asked me. I was certain from the first moment I saw him, wasn't I?"

"You know I won't wear that dress to dinner. It's hideous."

She was laced and tightly fastened so that her small breasts bobbed up, pushed to the limit over the top of her corset.

"So don't," she said. "We'll go out tomorrow morning and buy you something else, anything you want. It's a gift, from Martin Hamlin."

"I look awful in green."

She nodded.

"I mean, you know that. I look like Frankenstein in this pukey shade of green."

"I'm sorry," she said. "I forgot. You have your father's skin, that sallow Italian bastard."

I tried on the green dress. We sat there for a while like that, me in my dress and she in the black gown, on the night before Valentine's Day, the night before I would meet my future step-father, and we watched the eleven o'clock news and part of the *Tonight Show* until we both fell asleep. Around three my mother woke me. "You should go to bed," she said. And then, or was I dreaming? In a sleepy voice she whispered, "How do they bathe? The Mormons, I mean? How do they wash?" I don't recall whether I answered her even though in the article I had read it said that they always kept the underwear around one leg, when they showered or bathed or even had sex. I don't think I answered her that night. I just stumbled off to my room and fell asleep without changing into my pajamas. The next day I felt pretty guilty about returning a seventy-two dol-lar dress that I had slept in, but my mother shrugged and said that that was the way we were going to live from now on.

We met Martin Hamlin at the Fan Dancer, on the top floor of the Genessee Tower Bank Building, Flint's claim to a sky-scraper. The restaurant slowly revolved and perhaps because I watched a lot of television, I was jaded and this fact did not thrill me as much as it did my mother. It had snowed all day and I couldn't help hoping that Martin Hamlin would call and cancel. I should have known better; weather would never stop him. The snow fell and fell, blue against the winter skyline, falling against the luminous swirls of smoke chugging all night from countless late shifts at GM Bus and Truck, AC Spark Plugs, those big mysterious factories that we could see as blurry dots from our revolving vantage point. I should have been dizzy. I should have been the happiest girl in the world.

My mother spent the day in the beauty saloon and had emerged, to my amazement, although Martin Hamlin seemed unfazed by this, a blonde with neat marcelled curls; she had jumped back two generations, gone from the heavy eyebrowed Joan Crawford forties look to some sort of mutant Mary Pickford, a pale and powdered silent screen star. Her dress was tight, and the two half-moons of her breasts glowed alabaster white against the stiff dark taffeta.

We sat at a table by the window and they both with intuitive grace ignored me throughout the course of the meal. I studiously ignored them back and concentrated intently on my broccoli florets, rice, and lake trout as though they were my sincere companions. *Your hair,* he said. *Your suit,* she laughed delicately and he lighted her cigarette for her. They spoke in objects and images. It was difficult for me to follow their conversation and I am not sure if this was because of the fleet of tuxedoed waiters moving flawlessly from table to table who distracted me or whether my mother and Martin Hamlin were speaking in some kind of indecipherable lover's code. *Yes, of course,* she said. He nodded in tacit agreement. After dinner he ordered coffee and the dessert cart was wheeled to our table. No one spoke of marriage. I tried to sneak looks at him, caught glimpses of his face against the backdrop of the blue night. My mother leaned back in her chair with a look of sleepy contentment and turned from us halfway in her seat to watch the piano player in the center of the room. She seemed suddenly quite oblivious of Martin Hamlin and me.

"So," he said turning to me as though for the first time he realized I was there. "I'm going to marry your mother. I must ask," he went on with white-haired and deep-voiced magnanimity, "for your acceptance."

"Sure," I said. "Sure."

Martin the magician, I expected him to produce from deep inner pockets of his neatly cut jacket bouquets of silk flowers, cooing pigeons, a line of midget clowns jumping one after the next from his hip while he laughed and laughed, as surprised as his audience. My mother was no help to me. I raised my eyebrows. I coughed. I tried to get her attention, but she was swaying her head to the piano strains of "As Time Goes By" and watching an elderly couple display in tango form the fruit of Arthur Murray dance lessons.

"It's no simple thing to marry a woman," he said. "When my grandfather married my mother do you think either of them could have imagined their true name would be lost forever in the clutter of history?"

"Your grandfather married your mother?" I asked intrigued.

"No," he said, his level gaze burning upon me. "My grandfather married my grandmother."

"Oh, I thought you said—"

"It must have been the music," he said offering me the gift of his forgiveness. "It's quite loud, isn't it?"

"Hamlin isn't your real last name?"

"No," he said. "The original patronym was bowdlerized, and it was more than a matter of simple misspelling. It was an act of emotional terrorism, the intentional misrepresentation of a culture, a lifeway. I have my real name, and I have it," he gestured, drew an "X" over either his heart or his narrow Italian lapel, "here, on the inside."

"Hamlin is a mistaken name?"

"No, Hamlin is the name I chose. I renamed myself. This has become a cornerstone of my philosophy of self-identity.

The old name is lost," he gestured upward with a hand and I was certain that pigeons would appear, rise up and circle above us, descend and pick scraps from our table. "I chose my own name and in doing so become my own man."

"Martin Hamlin."

"It's poetic," he said. "Two dactyls."

This was the first time that I would not completely trust what Martin Hamlin told me. I couldn't remember a dactyl from a trochee. He smiled at me. There was no malice in it, no challenge. He looked over at my mother and smiled. He sat bestowing his smile on the world, and this was not a cheap smile, not a salesman's or solicitor's toothy grimace; it was a holyman's smile. There was a heavy-lidded quality to his eyes, and the corners of his lips curled ever so slightly. It was a smile bestowing grace, a look of pure agape, forgiving and benevolent, a smile so carefully paternal that it was devoid of romance, lust, or desire. And wasn't that the most seductive smile of them all?

He watched as the waiter set a goblet of sherbet in front of me.

"You know," he said. "You don't look at all like your mother."

The busboy came by and refilled the coffee cups.

My mother held the small silver ashtray in the palm of her hand, smoked like Lauren Bacall and stared out the window.

"You must look like your father," he said.

I paused, spoon still in the frozen and delicate depths of my dessert. "Yes," I said. "That's what people tell me."

"Girls," he said and then coughed, correcting himself. "Young women have strong feelings for their fathers. It is, of course, entirely natural. They look to them for both emotional and physical protection. They think of them as invincible. What they often fail to understand is that fathers are simply men, and that,

perhaps, in the course of time, as life is a complicated path to follow, others may just as successfully, if not more so, play that role.
Yes," he said. He set down his coffee cup. He spread his palms
up on the table in some sort of symbolic gesture of honesty.
"Father is a role, one of many, that a man may chose to play.
Having a child, this does not necessarily make one a father, let
alone a good father."

"What did she," I tilted my head toward my oblivious
mother, "tell you about my father?"

He tipped the silver creamer into the china cup. The smile
spread warmly, benevolently across his seamless creamy face.
"I'm certain, Pearl, that your father was, is, a special person for
you. No one is asking you to think or feel otherwise."

"I don't know what she's told you," I repeated. "But you
don't know him. He's not like *that.*"

"Like what?" He asked quizzically.

Pick a card, any card.

"My father," I blurted, "is an intellectual."

No sooner had I said this than I was burning with embarrassment. I wanted to reach bare-fisted into my dish of apri-
cot ice and smear it all over my face. What game was this?
Cheat? Go Fish? Old Maid? He smiled shuffling the deck,
all pity, all bemusement over a precocious fifteen-year-old girl
in an ill-fitting party dress. His game was Hearts. He held
a suite of queens, diamonds, clubs, hearts, spades. The queen
of tarts. I was blushing red, but I looked up and met his
gaze, eye to eye. For me the battle had begun. Blackbirds,
blackbirds baked in her sweet pies. I spooned up what he
served fork by knife. I was that stupid. I was that naive. It was
nothing to him, a shell game, all words and the illusion of
sophistication, all style and grace. I would never learn to beat
him at this game; the best I would do is break even, cut my

losses, and get as fast and far as I could from him. Blackbird, blackbird fly away home. I met his gaze. I spooned up my melting ice.

"Before I tell you anything else about myself," he said. "You should know that I have what is called a *photographic memory.* Your mother has told me what a *smart* man Anthony is—" he broke off, "surely this is no contest, but the fact remains that I remember everything, and believe me, there is no small advantage to this."

My mother smiled and covered a yawn with her delicate fist.

"If you remember one thing about tonight," said Martin Hamlin reaching into the depths of his jacket to produce not a bouquet of flowers, not a deck of cards or duet of lovebirds, but his thick wallet from which he extracted his Gold Card. "Remember this. Life, like good conversation, is a give and take. The surest way to succeed, to make everyone, all parties involved happy, is for everyone to give a little. Compromise, my dear Pearl, is perhaps the most underrated of arts."

That night I slept fitfully. The phone rang in the early hours of the morning and I lay in my bed hearing my mother's voice through the thin walls and knowing it was Martin Hamlin wishing her good night or good morning. She answered on the first ring. The dawn was pinkish. I could smell my mother cooking in the kitchen but I didn't get up, not just yet. I stayed in bed for a while smelling the oniony warmth and the light steam in the air, knowing she was there. It came back to me. Fate. I swear I heard the birds calling it. And I knew then that I would never accept it. I would fight and struggle against it. My fate. It was bound up inextricably with hers. Fate gave my mother and Sofie something to look forward to, a destiny by which to count the hours and shape their dreams. I thought about fifteen and how even though everybody said fifteen was a lousy age, and it probably was, it was my age, and it was all I had, and I would never again be fifteen in my bed and have my mother in the kitchen cooking an omelet and brewing dark, sweet coffee as dawn broke. I knew that my mother would marry Martin Hamlin and soon it would all be different. He was her fate and perhaps that made him my fate once removed. She waited her entire life for fate to come knocking and when he did he wore an Italian suit and smooth leather loafers and gave her a precise gold watch so that she would never again lose track of time. It was seven in the morning. She was brewing coffee and making breakfast. It was Sunday. Martin Hamlin. My mother would marry him. Martin Hamlin. He rode that Mercedes sedan like some black stallion on the cover of a Harlequin Romance and the lonely ladies cried out *fate, fate, fate,* like the birds singing in the cold and they couldn't help swooning for him, all towers, all bowers, and rose, roses, roses in the dull midwestern winter. Martin Hamlin. He was to be our fate. Martin Hamlin. I knew he would be my stepfather. Martin Hamlin. I never forgave my mother for falling in love with him. I never forgave her for not knowing better. Checkmate, said Martin Hamlin, as he took my queen.

Aaron

As Aaron Saltmarsh stood in front of Hart's Jewelry Store, he turned away from the raw January wind to face the display window. Pulling his collar up against the snow which was beginning to fall in the late afternoon twilight, he saw the necklace behind the glass. If he had had more decorum and less desire, he might not have placed his suede gloved hands against the windowpane to peer more closely at the necklace. The blue lapis stones were set in silver, wrought into ornate twists, florets, and curls strung on an antique chain; it lay against the jeweler's robed backdrop of dark velvet against which other gems and jewels shone far more brightly.

The store was warm and scented thickly with both polish and perfume. The wind blew the door shut, slamming it behind him, causing the young woman sitting behind the counter reading a book to look up with a sudden start. She smiled then, discreetly, and placing a marker at her page, shut her book. Her eyes dropped for a moment to her wrist where the face of her watch was turned inward.

"May I help you?" She asked muffling the end of the question as she covered her mouth to stifle a yawn.

Aaron Saltmarsh removed his overcoat. He brushed the snow from it, folded and draped it over his arm. This is the face I see before me, he thought, and thought too, what do I look like to her? Her face, narrow at the chin and wide at the forehead so that her eyes were far set and peculiar, was like one of the heart-shaped pendants on display, sweetheart diamonds, lockets for a teenage keepsake. Her eyes were brown with pale spare lashes and her hair reddish brown and in perhaps the matter of an hour he would remember neither of these details, but knew also there was something about her he would never forget. Her book shut, she left it on the polished glass of the counter under which against rich black velvet lay gold rings, wedding bands, diamond-studded, emerald-chipped, sapphirine, glistening with the nacre of whole fat pearls. Aaron extracted his handkerchief and politely wiped his nose. How do I look to her? He carried himself according to his thoughts, mysterious, dark, and regal.

Aaron Saltmarsh had been married for six months and still thought sometimes that none of it had ever happened, that the marriage ceremony in June, that the bride and the wedding and the dense overbearing pink roses had been the things of a dream. When he closed his eyes at a stoplight, behind his desk, pushing a cart at the grocery store, he thought he might open them and be someplace else entirely. Is this desire a dream or a wish? He did not fall. You could not call it a fall. He saw the salesgirl, her hair parted on the side, her curious wide eyes, the black turtleneck that she wore and how, as he peered down into her case of baubles, tokens, and toys, she distractedly pulled the turtleneck up over her bottom lip and chewed the fabric a moment before setting it straight again. Was this a fall? And what was a fall anyway? If he closed his eyes right then and swirled into the oil and resin of her perfume, perfume like Leslie wore in delicate dots sprayed on her wrists, her nape, between her small soft breasts, if he closed his eyes it would all have been a dream and he would exist only now.

"Could I see the necklace in the front window case?" He asked her.

She nodded, bent her head reaching into a drawer.

"Keys," she said face tilted up toward him brightly, a jangling key ring in the shape of a diamond reading "Hearts from Hart's" worn ringed on one of her slim fingers.

He felt against the pocket of his coat, slung over his arm, for his keys. She was at the window, unlocked the case, held it, the necklace, and in the light he wasn't disappointed, and he was glad too that he had waited, had not settled for something less specific and more useful. The girl held it against her black turtleneck to show him how a dark color would set off the brightness of the blue stones, the fine high polish of the antique silver. Yes, he said. I'll take it.

"Does she have blue eyes?" The girl asked, holding the necklace against the palm of her hand as though weighing it, weighing the moment before deciding the exact worth of either a stone of lapis lazuli or a minute of time.

"Who?" He asked. A reflex. Yes, a reflex, to always answer *who* even when suddenly the next second you know who exactly. The girl meant Leslie, but he said *who.*

She smiled, eyes turned downward on the task of setting the necklace just so against a richly lined case. Her mouth was small, pointed, sharp. This he will not remember, but delicate too, and lightly lipsticked. To think is not to fall, is it? To fall is to fall is to fall.

"Your girlfriend—" she looked at his hand, ringless. "Or your wife," she said. "If she has blue or green eyes, this will be—" she paused. "Utterly fantastic on her."

Her eyes? Leslie's eyes. They were brown. I have raccoon eyes, she told him sometimes in the mirror brushing on mascara, drawing dark on the lids and lower lashes.

Aaron reached into his wallet for his credit card. The girl stared down wistfully at the necklace before snapping the case shut.

"You know," she said. "I don't mind telling you. I wish I had the coloring to wear something like that. Silver looks so good on these pale types—" she tapped her finger against the cover of her novel emblazoned with a picture of a Gothic heroine, tangled black curls, heaving bosom, a horse, a cape, a rainy night, a ripped gown. The girl laughed. "I'm sorry," she said. "I guess I'm just daydreaming." Outside the snow fell and fell, illuminated by the streetlights, spiralling downward. Her face. How will I remember it? How will I remember her from the next one? Or the last one? He signed the receipt, put on his coat, took the bag from her, she turned her forearm and looked at her watch worn on the inside of her wrist, she sighed and shivered as the door slammed letting in the gust of cold night air.

I am married, he thought, how odd. I think in words. Her face is gone already and the perfume, when I smell it again, resin, clove, violets, it will remind me of something but I will not remember it or her or now. And Leslie must be home by now, in the bathroom washing her hair, steaming the mirrors. His footsteps crunched with authority on the pavement, the snow, new and fine, fell away beneath him. Her face is being replaced, already, with another, and I can see Leslie now, because it is past six and she will be washing her hair which is straight and brown and goes limp if not cared for daily and washed in the evening with astringent shampoo, grapefruit and lemon. Her arms are strong and when she works the lather through, I see this, I see her in the mirror, the muscles on her forearms raised slightly, damply, she shuts her eyes from the bite of the shampoo and the apartment smells of her and her straight brown hair and her skin, wet, soapy, nutbrown and dotted, speckled across the shoulders, breasts, and forehead with a spatter of freckles.

"Aaron?" called Leslie Saltmarsh at the sound of the door opening in the next room. "Aaron," she said, "is that you?"

"Yes." He dropped his keys on the table and felt for the package in his pocket.

Leslie came out of the bathroom, a towel wrapped turban style around her head. She wore a plaid flannel bathrobe. Her feet were bare. He found himself, still in his overcoat, hair damp with snow, hands gloved, staring down at her feet, counting her toes, each one strange to him, new, curled and flushed pink from her hot bathwater.

This will happen. Her robe will fall away. This is not falling because this is how it should be and who it should be so this is alright then and not a fall. Her robe falls away and I remember this body even though it seems new to me because I forget when I am not certain to remember, because I forget until I remember. She said something about the cold and snow and then later, how long was it? Much later in their bed and the lights off and the snow falling dizzyingly against the window, she said sleepily what a wonderful birthday and then he remembered and said wait, don't go anywhere. Where would I go? she said and stretched out naked under the eiderdown quilt and against the flannel sheets and the high points of her breasts brushed against the fabric and she yawned and called again to him already in the next room searching through the pockets of his drying overcoat, Where would I go?

"Happy birthday," Aaron said returning to the dark bedroom.

Leslie accepted the package. "You shouldn't have," she said.

"See if you like it first."

"I know I'll love it," she said. "I already love it."

She snapped the lid open and the blueness of the stones caught the light from the open doorway. She reached over, turned on the lamp.

"Oh," she said. "How wonderful. How did you ever, where did you ever find it?"

"I saw it," her husband said, "and I thought immediately of you."

Her robe had long ago fallen away. He could not recall the face of the salesgirl; by now she could have been any stranger on the street. On the cover of the book there had been a pale, dark-haired woman, and the girl, he remembered had said wistfully that she would suit the necklace, one should be pale to wear blue and silver. A rainstorm, a tangle of curls, the heady summer scent of roses, her robe fallen away, the fine high tips of her breasts against the quilt, a January quiet, how strange, how strange, to think of roses in the winter, hips, thighs, grapefruit and lemon, the muscles of her arms, and he turned out the lamp and he shut the door.

"But the light," she admonished. "I want to see the necklace in the mirror."

He fastened it against her bare neck. Her robe had sometime ago fallen away and this was alright because they were married and she was his wife and the blue stones were cold to the touch and she shivered all along her skin and sang, her voice like her body, athletic, competent, cheerful, happy birthday to me. The snow fell, stopped, and in the early hours of the morning began to fall again so he wondered if, in fact, it had fallen all night while he slept and dreamed and woke sometimes without opening his eyes to reach out and feel her there and the warm softness of her breasts against the blankets and the sharp tang of grapefruit and the memory of roses in the dead of winter while he woke and slept and dreamed.

For six months Aaron Saltmarsh had been faithful to his wife. He had not cheated, if cheating was an action, but he could not, sometimes, stop himself from thinking when he saw other women about improper things. He wanted not to fall to temptation. He had been married in June, the month of brides and weddings and roses, in Temple Adath Shalom with six bridesmaids in lavender tea-length gowns and six groomsmen in black. He wanted not to cheat because he understood what a promise meant, and that once you broke one promise nothing would stop you from cheating again, in some other way, perhaps you would take what was not yours, steal, murder, dishonor your family. And then there was Leslie herself, who had changed for him.

Together they had entered the rabbi's study in the months before their wedding and she had begun the conversion process. She had cast off a part of herself. Aaron knew this was part of the promise; he knew also that it was not for God that she did it, but for him. God made little sense to her; she was athletic with strong calves and freckles and a bounding walk as though always just coming from or going to a tennis court. A God made little sense but a husband was someone with whom you could drink coffee and sleep late and dream and wake to touch there sleeping naked beside you before you fell asleep again to the sound of the swirling snow. Snow was real. Promises weren't real in terms of object but you had to picture them as real which was why, he sometimes thought, they put it down on a piece of paper and you sign it so that it becomes a real thing and not just the idea of a promise; so law was real too, in a sense. And the necklace had cost a lot of money and that was real enough, but how could you know if a God was real if you couldn't feel the weight of him naked in the dark next to you? The rain, a horse, a cape tangled in the thorns of a rosebush.

Aaron Saltmarsh woke before his wife the morning after her twenty-sixth birthday. Her bare freckled shoulder was uncovered and her face turned away from him and toward the one large window in their bedroom. The date was January seventh. How do I know this? he thought rubbing his eyes at the brightness of the cold morning.

Leslie woke, he was certain, though at first she said nothing, but then rolled over, breasts unabashedly bare in the sun.

"The dream I had," she said, "I dreamed that I was married to Aaron Saltmarsh and it was my birthday and he gave me this fabulous necklace—"

"Ha, ha."

"I'm going to call Gina and Heather, right now, and gloat."

She grinned and shook her head from side to side so that her straight hair, cut blunt to the chin, covered her face and then swayed back into place. It was Saturday. Before it had been Friday and when her robe had fallen away he had felt for awhile safe from the fear. He was certain, at least, of his own good intentions. He had never wanted to hurt anyone or any of them and they had all once had faces and dreams and smells and words and after a while, well, it falls away, it all falls away. Leslie stood at the window, naked, her back to him, she turned, naked, wearing only the necklace which in this light, he could clearly see, was far too rich for her freckled skin, narrow hips, the boyish cut of her hair and raccoon eyes, frank and sometimes pleading. She rested a hand against the necklace.

"It's perfect," she said.

"It's exactly you," Aaron said and turned away but she didn't notice and sang her way into the bathroom, and he heard water running, a flush, the television in the large main room of the apartment, the smell of coffee and Leslie calling out to him, reading his horoscope from the newspaper.

"Read it again," he said coming into the kitchen.

There was coffee on the table and snow outside. Today I will not fall. The toast was brown, the jam was strawberry, neither of them could stand grape, cherry, or peach. She held three eggs in her hands and pretended to juggle singing a circus song while he read the newspaper. Could your horoscope tell you the truth? Would it tell you the day it would happen? Would it explain in detail how your life could change if only you stopped living now and started living from remembering and you couldn't remember Leslie and her breasts under the blanket and her ten toes like pink shells and how she tried to make up for her lack of what she considered glamour with tomboyish frankness. And if he could remember marrying her, did he remember why? Flowers. Yes. June. His mother and his stepfather. Leslie pretending to pitch the bouquet to her bridesmaids like a fastball. Here's the windup and the girls, their hands, reached up toward the light for the flowers which might or might not have been roses and lilacs and violets.

Monday January ninth was the date on the calendar on Aaron Saltmarsh's desk. His head was bent down toward his papers, and he read on for a while about a certain client who alleged that a certain editor at a local newspaper had slandered his client on a certain day of a certain month which was not January ninth. How a mind can turn at any moment. How in a moment I can remember my whole life up to this point even though it took twenty-eight years which meant planets and motion and unendurable stretches of time. He was twenty-eight and Leslie was twenty-six and they were both lawyers. They had met two years before when she had clerked at his law firm. She was still in law school then and awkward around the office, and she peeked her head into his office sometimes while he was writing or on the phone and she stuck just her head in with her tan freckled face and mouthed the words *lunch?* or *coffee?* And he nodded or held up a hand to mean, *just a minute,* and she waited coltish, moving gradually but slowly, in increments, her body into the doorway and her skirt hit always at the same point right above the knee but this was alright because she was more athletic than sexy or so all the secretaries had decided and she carried herself with a neat prep school grace. They began to get together after work sometimes to play racquetball and drink sparkling water in clear bottles that she gripped loosely around the neck like beer, he thought, not like water at all and not like a woman but like a kid sister.

Slightly drunk in a downtown restaurant once after work, she had reached across the table and brushed her fingers against the crenelated ridges of the scar on his forehead which was to him there when he thought about it and surprised him when other people noticed it so that sitting in his office on January ninth lost in a memory instead of studying the details of the case of his client he touched the scar instinctively over his right eyebrow and lower along the eye almost to the cheekbone. Leslie had been drunk that night on wine spritzers or maybe gin and tonic, which in her sorority fashion she called *gin, tonic, and lime* and she had said to him, "The scar makes you look mysterious." Had he been drunk? It was dark in the restaurant. She had touched his face. He took her hand from his forehead, held it then, still ringless in the dim light and kissed the fine tips of each extended finger. It was romantic to kiss her fingers in the dark restaurant on a windy late summer evening when she was going back to school soon and it would be nice too to be separated from her and to miss her and to miss kissing her and the fluid grace of her muscular drunken arms reaching across the table and maybe that was why he asked her to marry him, but maybe that wasn't it at all. He asked her and at first she said *yes* right away and then drunk, giddy, and embarrassed she said *no* and then she had said *no that's not right at all, ask again, Aaron.* Aaron, ask again. He did. *I want to get it right,* she said. He asked again. *Yes,* she said. *Oh, yes.* Just like a girl in a movie. He held her wrist still encircled by his hand. The waitress cleared away the plates and the glasses and the silver. She brought coffee and they sat for a long time without saying a word. The phone rang in his office, it was January ninth and his secretary said Aaron, line two. Do you want to take the call or should I take a message? He said yes, thank you, Debbie I'll take the call.

Always when you try to remember something you may end up forgetting. You can forget your whole life like that, you can feel like a person without a past. Each day Aaron Saltmarsh woke, turned to find his wife sleeping, in some various position, sometimes on her stomach, other times on her side, sometimes naked but often in a T-shirt although he had bought her a drawer of the lingerie which sometimes she took out, piece by piece, and tried on, or wore for a while until the robe fell away, and she said that she wasn't really a lingerie type and he accepted this maybe because she had changed for him and now was not Protestant—or was it Methodist? Or were they the same? But was now Jewish and had an entirely different god although she dressed in the same tasteful earth tones and short skirts, wool in the winter, and walked with the same easy stride of a girl athlete and let the sun sometimes rest full and warm on her bare breasts in their bed without the slightest bit of shame.

In February he met a girl. Could he say that? Did he meet her? It was an encounter really, not a meeting. A meeting implies an appointment like the meetings he and Leslie had had with the rabbi in his study and how before the ceremony he had signed the ornately scrolled bridal contract. His pen had never faltered. So it was simply, at first, an encounter. The girl worked in a coffee shop in a strip mall by Aaron's law office, Reginald, Malech, and Royce. He walked into the coffee shop and wiped the slush from his shoes. There was a girl behind the counter talking on a portable phone and tapping her free hand against the counter absentmindedly.

"Because I told her not to, that's why," the girl was saying. "Because I asked her not to and she should respect that, you know?"

"Excuse me—" said Aaron.

She looked at him, nodded, covered the receiver of the phone with her free hand and whispered, "one second, okay?"

He nodded back as though there was some secret understanding between them. As the person on the other end of the line presumably spoke, the girl nodded gravely, breaking in every few seconds with "I know" or "but she did it, not me."

"Now what can I get you?" The girl asked breaking off the conversation abruptly and pushing down the antenna of the phone.

He ordered a cappuccino with low-fat milk and she smiled, nodding again.

"Do I know you?" He asked. "You're acting like I know you."

"I don't know you from the next guy," she said smartly and propped her elbows on the counter. Sometimes when someone looked at him, like this, like she was doing now, with her brown eyes and eyebrows arched high so that she looked quizzical and pondering, when she looked at him he tried very hard to keep all the parts and pieces of himself stuck together as though arms or legs might fall off if he didn't concentrate on wholeness. She leaned on her elbows. Her hair was caught in one tight braid down the back, thick and roped, she shrugged her shoulders at his questioning gaze and the rope of her hair swung against her back. He knew that he had signed the document, the Ketubah, rolled into a scroll, and that he had written out his name and that Leslie had lobbed the bouquet to the waiting bridesmaids like a volleyball and their arms and hands had shot up toward the light to catch the ribboned flowers.

"Nivla," he said pointing to her name tag. "Does it mean something? You know, one of those African names?"

"It's my father's name. But spelled backward. Spell it backward." she urged him.

"Alvin," he said after a moment's deliberation.

"My parents wanted a boy," she said flatly.

She wore a cardigan sweater bulky and bright, the kind college girls bought at import stores. His parents, had they wanted a boy? They had him and named him Aaron Jacob Saltmarsh, and his father had been Jacob Saltmarsh until he died when Aaron was ten and then, well, he had become nothing at all. The plane had crashed. There had been a storm, turbulence, a cape, a horse. Nivla leaned on her elbows over the counter. Two women carrying shopping bags came to wait behind him. Aaron moved aside and watched as Nivla reached into the refrigerated case to extract two bran muffins and chilled bottles of mineral water flavored with orange. She smiled and joked with the women. Pressing her long fingers against the cash register, she quickly rang up their orders, made change while he watched.

"It's too bad," he said after the two women seated themselves in the interior of the coffee shop.

"What is?" Asked Nivla brushing crumbs from the counter with a white towel.

"That they didn't have a boy."

She paused, did not say anything, turned to make his coffee but then, bemused, turned back about to speak, but said nothing.

"Everyone should get what they want," he said in explanation, palms open and upward.

"I don't know about that," she said and handed him his cappuccino onto which she had sprayed a whirl of whipped cream and sprinkled curled twists of shaved chocolate.

This is how it happens. This is how it will happen. She propped her elbows on the counter, pushed up the sleeves of her sweater, the rope of her hair swayed and swung, fell against her back and the jangle of beads, bright, glassy, sounded with her movements and rested in between the space where her breasts weren't. I did not expect this, and this is when it happens, when I do not expect it at all. And if I give way for an instant, just to look, just to think, after all it is February and what can I do in February but think about Februaries past? The girl, Nivla, wore no makeup, her fingers were tapered, she smiled in a crooked smirk and her hair was a braid and breasts were hidden under her bulky sweater but a bright tangle of beads rested between them.

Aaron called Leslie from Nivla's apartment and told her that he was working late. It seemed like a lie to him, because it was a lie, but she yawned over the phone and said that she had gone home from work early anyway and had just washed her hair and taken Motrin, she lowered her voice to a confidential tone even though she was alone in the apartment which must have been humid and scented of bathwater and straight hair just washed and now drying under the towel wrapped turban style around her head as she talked on the phone to him and told him that she had awful cramps and was going to bed early. While Aaron used the phone, Nivla sat on her narrow single bed unwrapping the foil from the day-old pastries that she had brought home from work.

It was a part of the city where students lived, run-down, shabby in the winter and dirty in summer although then with the respite of weedy flowers and thriving unmowed lawns which now were simply unshoveled walkways that when he and Nivla had made their way through to get to her building, she had almost slipped and he had taken her arm firmly and helped her along the narrow icy path littered with beer bottles and fast food wrappers.

Already it had begun. There was no trash like this where he and Leslie lived. Each decision, each step, moved him downward. It had begun. She sat on her bed and removed her sweater under which she wore a T-shirt, the string of beads was heavy enough to draw a demarcation between her breasts. It was an efficiency apartment, a narrow bed, a bathroom, a tiny kitchen. Unmade, the bed was littered with books and clothes, a pair of green stockings tangled into the blankets. A fat yellow cat carefully licked her paw from where she rested on a cluttered desk. When he looked out the window, Aaron could see into similar windows of other tiny apartments. Nivla turned out the lights so no one could see in. Her world is small, he thought, she occupies so little space. Maybe just once and then I will be free from the fear of the first time, of the first fall, and I will know not to do it again and I will not have to do it again. In the dark Nivla recited from memory a poem she had written for a class. Did her face feel like it looked? She smelled like vanilla, cinnamon, and coffee grounds.

Aaron Saltmarsh bought his wife Leslie a puppy for their seven-month anniversary. It was a mutt from the Humane Society, a mix of springer spaniel and border collie. Does she know? It is not hard to keep a secret and it becomes, why had he not thought this before, another contract. He must have had a contract with Nivla although not on paper. She was sometimes condescending to him because he did not say clever things. She was clever and said things which may or may not have gone beyond him more because he did not listen than because he did not understand. She wrote poetry and her mouth sometimes tasted of blueberries and her hair sometimes she wore unbraided, all curls, poetry is not a luxury she said to him, it is a necessity, yes, yes, he said. Her earrings were heavy as coins.

Leslie sat at the kitchen table, Saturday morning, gloomy gray of February.

"Aaron," she called to him in the bathroom where he was shaving.

"Hmm?" His head emerged, face half-lathered.

She turned toward him in her chair, from the waist, let her brown hair fall across her face and held up the magazine she was reading. "It's your girlfriend," she sang out.

"Not again," he said. "I'll be done in a second."

Together they sat at their kitchen table and Leslie spread the pages of the magazine apart and pushed the picture toward him.

"'Theresa Boughton emerges from seclusion to tell her side.' I could be jealous of *all your women,*" Leslie said, "if only I wasn't so proud of being the one who finally got you."

Finally. Yes, he thought, staring down at the picture together with Leslie. Because time is now and not then, because I knew this girl not as a picture but as a person, without this picture I would not recall exactly her face.

"I thought she had long hair," said Leslie. "I guess short is *in* now." She ran a hand through her own short hair with glamorous exaggeration.

"I guess she cut it," Aaron said.

From this picture I can remember snow, a cape, a horse. No that is another picture entirely. From this picture I can remember that faces do not change. The woman in the picture stared out at them, bored, jaded, through narrow blue eyes.

"It gives me the shivers to look at her," said Leslie. "Even in a picture it looks like she can really see us. Those eyes—" Leslie broke off with a nervous shake of her head. The coffee was ready. She went and got them cups. Well that was all in the past and that was gone and finally he was here with Leslie, his wife, and his dog, McDougal, and the coffee which she brought to him while he read the article about Theresa Boughton who had as a child, a girl, sworn that she loved him though it might not have been love, but jealousy, or spite, but now she was a picture in a magazine because she was an actress making a bold new film that showed her to be, said the article, at the height of her beauty and ability.

"Those eyes," said Leslie reading over his shoulder, "follow you right off the page."

There had been snow, blood, the certain cold of blue eyes, a silence which was difficult to remember, but he would know it forever simply because he would never hear it again, not like he had heard it on that day.

Things will happen. March first was the date on the calendar on Aaron's desk. The party of the first part hearby states that the statement of the party of the second part is an untruth. He leaned his head on his hand. How had it happened? Nivla had said only the night before, I did it for the experience, a married man and all. He said nothing. She stumbled a bit although she was usually good with words. Just this morning at breakfast Leslie said out of nowhere, over her toast with strawberry jam, you're not going to try to get in touch with her are you? *Who?* He asked before he had thought about what she meant and before he could answer he knew that she meant Theresa Boughton, but then when someone asks you always answer *who* even before you think. No, he had told her. You don't have to worry about that. And she didn't, not about Theresa Boughton, and he rubbed a finger along the narrow ridge of the scar which in the beginning Leslie had told him once slightly drunk, made him look mysterious. She had giggled, you look like a pirate, she had said and reached her long tan arm across the table. Nivla had been pragmatic, no scenes, no drama at all. And when he had driven home he remembered nothing of what she said and only momentarily recalled her thin stalklike neck and the childish way she drowsily rested her head against him in the dark of her uncurtained apartment. If he sent her flowers, would that be right? Would her life then seem like one of her poems? A Gothic heroine, the cape, a snowy night, a bouquet of winter flowers brought by a delivery boy down the path, up the steps, through the grim and trashy squalor to her door behind which she might be sitting at her desk staring out the window, her braid falling against her back, her beads between her breasts, her mouth tasting like blueberries and coffee, disturbed, she will be, but happy, when she answers the door to find flowers.

Aaron picked up the telephone.

"Debbie," he said, "do you remember what florist we use?"

"You'll never guess what," said Leslie when he came home from work that night.

"What?" He said.

"Gina saw your girlfriend on the *Today Show* this morning. At least I think it was the *Today Show*. She's really making the rounds."

"How did Gina say it went?"

Leslie grinned, "Gina said she was just cold, very cold. And skinny. Gina thought she was probably anorexic or something."

"It was a long time ago," he said.

"Tell the truth," she said leaning on the open door of the refrigerator. "Did you sleep with her."

"No," he said. "I didn't."

Did I? No, he was fairly certain that he had not. He had not slept with Theresa Boughton although that was a long time ago. If Leslie, his wife, turned from the refrigerator before making her decision to order out Thai food and asked him, did you sleep with Nivla Strauss, what would he say? Would he say *yes* or *no?* Maybe he would say without thinking when and if she ever asked, *who?* She did not ask that and he had not slept with Theresa Boughton although it did feel strange to know someone who was in magazines and on the morning news. It made him feel, to see her face, and her hair cropped short but still light blonde, as though no time had passed at all.

"Let's order out Thai," said Leslie.

Aaron looked at his watch. By now Nivla had probably received the flowers and perhaps felt like a girl on the cover of a romance novel, perhaps she had unbraided her hair and was writing mournful poetry of love and loss and revolution.

The light from the large outer room shone under the bedroom door and through the curtained window he could see the night, foggy, in like a lion, out like a lamb people had been saying all day. Leslie was awake, working on a brief, he could reach out to the spot where she should be, but she was not, and the dog was snoring at the end of the bed. Had things been set in motion? Was it different than he expected, not a fall but a gradual crumbling away of the path beneath him so that day by day he might be oblivious to the change?

How to think of it? How to remember it? Theresa raising the hockey stick, the snow, the cold morning, he could not see himself, he saw her laughing, the cold flush of color on her cheeks and Theresa spitting out her laughter, saying *If it's Ricey you want, hell, you idiots deserve each other.* Was it Ricey that he wanted? Leslie had said with pleasure and awe, *all your women.* Had there been so many of them? It was hard to remember faces. Would it have been different if he had not kissed the fine tips of Leslie's extended fingers when she was slightly drunk in that downtown restaurant? It is hard to imagine that things are not set, that outcomes might have been different. But he was young and it had all been a long time ago. There had been snow. Snow was Theresa. And rain? Rain was Ricey. And Leslie was in the next room. And the dog was sleeping at the end of the bed. And Nivla wrote poetry with flowers in a jar used as a vase on her cluttered desk and there were others but he couldn't think of them now, but to fall was to fall was to fall and if your path crumbled away beneath each steady footfall, who could judge you? Who could say it was your fault?

He sprawled out alone on the king-size bed. Nivla's parents had wanted a boy, he remembered that. His own mother had had a second child, stillborn, a girl. Later when his father died his mother came into her own, everybody said. She lost weight, colored her hair. She remodeled the house. How old had she been? She remarried, then divorced, then married again. She had an affair with a married man and in a strange confessional mood told her son about it one late night in the kitchen, newly painted. The affair. Had she fallen and was this a thing in the blood? In the blood? Did you slip on it, on the blood, on your way down?

If Leslie had come in from the other room to find her husband, awake, eyes open in the darkness, and if she had asked him, Did you sleep with Ricey, not Theresa or Nivla, but Ricey, what would he have said? He would have said, yes, that he had done it to spite his mother who had cheated not just on his stepfather, but on his dead father and so he, a son, had cheated back, he had thought then, but now it all seemed foolish because it had been a long time ago, and maybe things might have been different but that is, of course, difficult to imagine.

How had she looked that day? It was August, hot and dry or maybe September the end of a summer where every night on the news there were stories about spontaneous roadside fires caused by sparks, errant cigarettes, dead dull heat. He wore, he saw himself, whole, a collection of parts, he wore a lightweight summer suit because he spent that summer working at his uncle's law office running errands, xeroxing endlessly, picking up lunch. I walked the path, I walked the steps, up to her, where she sat on her front porch with her little sister. Butternut, they called her, or Lilith, Lilith, she drummed her fingers against a bag of potting soil, there were roots, yes, and plants and leaves and pots, trowels all around them on the porch and her arms were grimy up to the elbows and when she saw him she waved and held up both hands to show him the dirt on her fingers, wrists, and forearms. Ricey wore a summer hat, skin burnt redbrown the way pale brunettes burnt but when pale, yes, that was it, they could wear blue and silver. She turned her face upward and squinted in the evening light as I came up the walk. Her eyes were pink rimmed. Her sister tapped her grubby hands on the wood railing of the porch and then stopped and stared down at them like a pair of claws and examined the dirt crusted beneath her ragged fingernails.

The dog slept, gave hesitant whines from sleep, from dream. The tea kettle in the kitchen whistled. Leslie had the television on low because sometimes, she said, the quiet scared her. Butternut sat on the railing of the porch, rubbed a grubby hand across her cheek and stared dismally at cars as they drove past. Ricey came through the door carrying a sweater. She stopped. He played the image over. She came through the door. She stopped. She touched his arm. She came through the door. She smelled like dirt and leaves and flowers. It might rain, her little sister said. Ricey came through the door and into the evening darkness to touch his arm and Aaron reached to where Leslie should be, where she slept sometimes on her stomach or on her side with the blanket around the fine high points of her soft small breasts and the light shone under the door, and Leslie was not in bed at all and if he slept and if he woke and she was suddenly there he might believe that she had been there all along.

In March Aaron Saltmarsh thought he saw the spring. The path was slush under his feet, mud and rain, a Saturday afternoon and Leslie had gone shopping with her girlfriends, Gina and Heather, who grinned at him like a couple of high school girls when they came over to the apartment and after they left he always asked Leslie, what did you tell them about me, and then she grinned too. He spent the morning at the office, left for lunch, drove, parked his car, walked across the parking lot through the slush to the door of the Burger Barge where he hardly every went, he told himself, but it was okay to go there once in while.

"May I take your order, please?" Said the girl behind the register in the polyester uniform.

He ordered a bacon double cheeseburger, large fries, vanilla milk shake, and a large coke.

"If you order it different, like if you say bacon double cheeseburger, *curly* fries and *jumbo* coke and then you say the shake after, it's a Barge Bargain Meal. And," she added lowering her voice, "it'll cost less."

"Really," he said, pulling out his wallet in which thick rolls of cash lay snugly curled.

"Not that I'm saying, you're, you know, cheap or anything. I was just trying to help out."

She is anonymous, not later, but now, even now standing in front of me, she is anonymous and when I walk out the door there will be less of her to remember, a uniform, the cap under which her hair must be pinned and the plain, wide face and the young eyes which seem forgettable, unformed, but not, no, not innocent.

"I appreciate the gesture," he said standing aside to wait for his order.

There were no other customers at the counter and the girl leaned on the register looking bored.

"Ever try our Breakfast Burrito?" she asked.

"No," he said.

"How about the Cap'n Fish Fillet?"

"Sorry, no."

She shrugged and stared down at her chubby hands, the nails of which were painted bright pink. When his order came up, she held onto the tray for a moment before letting him have it.

"You shouldn't eat this crap," she said. "Not a guy like you."

"What does that mean?" He asked taking the plastic tray onto which he loaded little packets of ketchup, salt, and mustard.

"I mean, nothing, it just looks like you take care of your body and all."

"Oh," he said. "Thank you."

"My name's Linda," she said. "What's yours?"

"Ron," he said.

"I can get off work early, Ron," she said, eyes narrowed, waiting for his response.

"I'd like that," he said.

Aaron Saltmarsh had few memories of his first stepfather, Leonard Pomeroy. When he was eleven he acquired at school, perhaps simply a mistake of remembering his name on the part of teacher, the nickname Ron. The name tentatively took hold. He was Ronny on the softball diamond and when he raised his hand in math class Mr. Williams with the mustache said, "Good answer, Ron." When his stepfather, Leonard Pomeroy, had found out about this he had taken Aaron into his study, newly remodeled by Aaron's mother, and told him about the importance of names. Leonard Pomeroy, was his face different from the next husband? He spoke questioningly to Aaron, who felt ashamed, who felt like he was slipping down a cindered path bit by bit, who felt that betrayal was in his blood. "Ronny," Leonard Pomeroy had said. "It's like the name you'd give a dog. Aaron, now that is the name of a great man. The name of the brother of Moses." Where was Leonard Pomeroy now with his deep eyes and promises of greatness? Aaron glanced at the girl on the seat beside him, she removed her cap and shook free her bright tangled hair, she dug into her purse, found a lipstick and tilting her chin toward the rearview mirror painted her lips pink. He could not help but realize that her face was, even now, slipping away into indistinction. And that she thought he was Ron and that maybe Ron was slipping and not Aaron, and maybe the sooner we realize that we are all slipping, falling, tottering on the edge, the slippery slope, maybe the better off we all will be.

Leslie called Aaron at work. Her secretary put the call through to his secretary.

"Can you meet me for dinner tonight?" she asked.

"You know I've got a meeting," he said doodling a naked woman onto the legal pad in front of him.

Linda had no face, no body, nothing he could remember.

"It's important," she said.

"What's wrong?" he asked. He drew a telephone in the woman's hand. Leslie had been sick lately, raccoon eyes ringed, brown skin dull, mooning her eyes to him, but saying nothing. It was not like Leslie to say nothing. "Is everything okay? Are you okay?"

"Oh God," she blurted out. "I wasn't sure. I know I shouldn't tell you this way. I've been to the doctor—"

"And?"

There was a pause. He asked *and* the way he asked *who*. It was not hard to figure out. Or was it? It would be bad to guess and be wrong. The teacher with the mustache would say, "that's not quite it, Ron."

"I'm pregnant," she said. "Just a little bit."

Since he would have guessed correctly he was a little upset at not guessing at all, but he told her how happy he was and not to worry, because really, as long as she was healthy and took care of herself, what was there to worry about?

After he hung up, he dialed again, to his secretary.

"Debbie," he said. "Can you get a hold of that florist for me?"

He ordered a dozen long-stemmed American Beauty roses and picked them up later that afternoon. They seemed vengeful in their box, a miniature coffin, too blood red and brutal for his own taste but they suited the occasion. At his wedding there had been pink roses and lilacs and violets and it had been June and even in March, June can seem like a long time ago.

"Your wife is a lucky woman," said the florist wrapping the box.

"Yes," said Aaron. "She is."

When Aaron Saltmarsh arrived that evening at Linda's door, he paused, looked up and down her hallway, but as usual, he saw no other signs of life. The dark hallway. No one but me here. He had his own key. Linda was lying on her stomach on the sofa, folded out into a bed. She was still wearing her

Burger Barge uniform. Her face, again, I forgot it until now, and even now, as I see it, there is nothing there at all, nothing to remember except her pink lipstick. There was a game show on the television.

"I've been missing you all day," she said changing the channel with the remote control.

"What a day," he said sitting next to her on the sofa bed.

"Get comfortable," she said.

"I can't stay long." He loosened his tie. She turned on her side and helped him. Her arms were round. She looked him straight in the face. What does she see? Does she see my face or something else entirely?

"Hey," she said. "So when will you tell me where you got that freaky scar?" She touched the jagged line above his eyebrow and down around his eye, almost to the cheekbone.

Is it still there? I forgot about it and so thought, yes, well, no, maybe it was gone finally.

"From a girl," he said.

"Oh," said Linda knowingly. "The jealous type."

The snow, the blood, Theresa's laughter in the cold morning, the only sound in all that silence which he would never hear again but would remember only because it could not, would not happen again, the silence of snow heavy on birch boughs and the frozen lake and the blood, but mostly, since he closed his eyes, there was sound and smell and cold and silence and her laughter.

Jealous, was that right? Do you see her then? Theresa? No, not Theresa, the other one? Linda? No, not Linda. Oh, Nivla. No, no, no. Then, the wife, Leslie? No. Oh, yes, he troubled himself to remember because it was such a long time ago and dreams had gotten in the way and sleep had gotten in the way and you can do a lot of things in this life and even change a god if you feel like it but it's hard to fight that feeling of falling, let alone the fall itself, which could come at any time, which had come so long ago. It was Ricey then. She had come through the door. And it had rained later and there had been darkness, and she had been embarrassed and covered her breasts with one hand and her face with the other. We should have shame, shouldn't we? She had let her hair, long and dark, cover her face, hair and face wet with rain, covered herself with shame and embarrassment and guilt yet they could not, did not, not then, not now, not in time or dream or moment, stop themselves. The rain on the roof sounded tinny and hollow. She smelled of rain and dirt and leaves and flowers. He had closed his eyes and so had she.

Aaron touched the scar. Linda lay naked beside him. It had some time ago begun to rain but he could not place the moment exactly. There are things, not just faces, not just jewels, or minutes, there are things that can never be reclaimed and to justify it with a bargain, a contract, will not save it, to say it happened a long time ago, this will not save it. He found the remote control near Linda's sleeping body and clicked off the television. The sound was gone for a moment and then he heard the rain and realized it must have, some time ago, begun to rain and he reached out to Linda and felt her, round-hipped against the heavy blankets, her stomach, thighs. Linda was asleep on his arm leaving a pink smear of lipstick in a streak from his skin to the pillow on which her head rested. She had only hours before gotten off work at the Burger Barge and her skin smelled curiously of sweat, french fries, and cologne.

Was he falling, slipping not as he feared on blood or heredity from his mother's sins, but on grease? Hadn't he tried to get clean? Hadn't he tried to bend? Hadn't he even once or twice used Leslie's astringent shampoo, grapefruit and lemon, to burn with bitterness all that was too rich, too lavish, too indulgent in his spirit? Linda shifted and he pushed a spray of her bright brown hair stiff with gel away from his face. This cheapness, this grease and polyester, it only endeared her more to him. He had a weakness for tragic girls and fat girls and naked girls and girls like his wife Leslie who might at any moment reach out to you across a table with drunken grace. These girls, they had no shame and with no shame, really, there was no fault, no fall, no grease, no blood. Yes, he knew it now, the way was firm beneath his feet. Linda moved and mumbled something through her wet, open mouth.

He slept and woke to find that sometime earlier the rain had turned to snow. Linda lay sleeping fitfully next to him. The blanket had fallen away from her body and her bare breasts nodded heavy and sad in the half-light. He sat up and began to feel around on the floor for his clothes. There were roses freezing in the backseat of his car. He picked up his watch from the table and looked at the time. It was late, almost seven, the roads would be bad. As he pulled on his socks he knew he had to hurry. Aaron Saltmarsh had a wife to get home to.

Pearl

WHAT FOLLOWS NEXT MAY NOT BE CLEAR TO YOU. It is not, in fact, entirely clear to me. I struggle with the chronology of events. It is difficult to recall the days, one from the next. In April my mother married Martin Hamlin as the cards had promised week after week at Mr. Tom's salon where she went for her cuts and color treatments. She changed from brunette to blonde and finally, by the time of the wedding, was a frisky redhead.

And then. I think it is best to begin with the words: and then. We moved. This is simple to say in a line. We packed up and moved. We were like the contestants who win the big showcase on *The Price is Right;* we abandoned everything we owned and never went one moment without. Martin Hamlin, daddy, can I call him that now? He replaced our former lives, our past, our television, my mother's rayon lingerie with Chinese silk, our milk with cream, our cologne with perfume. Martin Hamlin transformed my mother and me into the real thing; gone was what we had spent our lives being. That was imitation. This was real.

What stands in my mind is the house. I see it like this. We, my mother and I, are driving up to the house. It is April in Bloomfield Hills. We follow Martin Hamlin's directions and drive on past the sprawl of strip malls, bagel bakeries, health clubs, diet centers, Chinese Restaurants, video stores, beyond subdivisions with names like "Piney Woods," "Heathcliff Heights," and "Greenery Acres" until, yes, finally we find the house. Secluded, it is set off by wooded grounds, trees, grass, flowers. The house looms before us. "Jesus help us," I say. My mother laughs and starts singing the theme to *The Jeffersons*, "Hey, hey, we're movin' on up, deluxe style." A black cat wearing a silver bell sits at the beginning of the long winding driveway, seems to contemplate crossing our path and then catching sight of a starling fluttering her wings, runs the other way, bell jangling in pursuit.

I am reminded of ninth grade English class. Mr. Rueben with his polyester pants and thick Brooklynese accent reading *Hamlet* aloud. The house. Elsinore. That beetles o'er its base. The house will trap you, make you a prisoner to appetite, luxury, a victim of your unchecked desires. The house had no columns, vistas, or porticoes, no turrets, grape arbors, or hidden passageways behind bookshelves or under stairs. It was less like the mansion in a Dracula movie than the house of a Colombian drug lord in an episode of *Miami Vice*. It was his epithalamium to her, a big boxy wedding cake, better than any tin of chocolates no matter how many raspberry creams or white chocolate truffles were wrapped and foiled inside. Bite, this house could eat you, by bite.

The day we arrived at the house the sunlight was splotchy, stippled, casting long shadows, sun over cloud, cloud over sun. We got out of the car. Our footsteps sogged through the new spring grass. The crocuses, hidden in shadow, were illuminated briefly, suddenly, by patches of light. There were rows of purple iris, tulip, and white daffodil. My mother opened the front door, caught her breath and gasped at the expanse of whiteness waiting to be filled.

"I'm in love," she cried, opening her arms to the empty room.

Martin Hamlin emerged from the stark brightness. "In love? Again? Am I jilted so quickly?" He asked raising his eyebrows.

He and my mother laughed in that indecipherable way like a couple in a coffee commercial reminiscing about old times. He took her hand and led her from room to room. At first I could hear her calling my name. She was saying, Pearl, oh, Pearlie you've got to see this—a music room, piano, library— and then her voice trailed away, and it was only his name that I heard her calling ever more faintly. I found my way into the kitchen and stood before a wall of windows. Behind the house, beyond the manicured lawn, there was a lake, murky and swollen with spring rains. The green gray expanse of the lake and the neighboring houses, not half as monstrous as ours, lay before me through the uncurtained windows. Little docks dotted the shoreline with pontoon and motorboats tethered, bobbing to them. In the summer children would splash and wear those stupid inflatable arm rings to save themselves from drowning. How funny, I thought, standing there on the tile floor with the pattern of aqua and teal shapes matching geometric patterns cut in the windowpanes. How normal this will all one day seem. I will forget Flint, forget I lived before entering this house. I heard a playful shriek of protest from upstairs. Martin Hamlin and my mother had found the master bedroom. Their laughter became less general. In sunlight the water was green, but as the sun passed behind a cloud, the water turned gray. The house belonged to Martin and my mother and me. The king, the queen, and the reluctant dauphin. My mother was delirious; it was going to be just as it had once been, three of us, like in the beginning.

So why wasn't I happy? That's the question, I suppose, we can all ask ourselves when we look back on fifteen. And we all know that the answer is unworded, impossible to voice. There was no reason to be happy and no reason not to be. You found a place, a name, a seat in the front, back, or middle of the classroom and stuck to it. What had I to fear from Martin Hamlin? After all, he did marry my mother. He didn't run off with his cart and pony show and leave her sobbing by the roadside or, worse yet, pregnant with his heir. All he asked of me was that I be willing to compromise, to bend in my obstinate ways so that we could all be happy together, three peas in a postmodern pod. And even I had to admit that it was a reasonable enough request. Perhaps it was simply that something about Martin Hamlin provoked my relentlessly paranoid side, brought to rise in me the ghost of Anthony Christomo.

It seemed odd that my mother had once, if only for a short time, loved Anthony Christomo, and following a line of crazy extended logic; if she could love him and abandon him, and I was like him, well then . . . perhaps she might just as easily forget about me. But I feared not so much the loss of attention from my mother as the loss of the Judy to whom I had grown accustomed; this new Judith bore a resemblance to the old, but she took everything the old Judy did one step beyond. Growing up, we had poured over mail-order catalogs dreaming about ordering this and that; the new Judy picked up the phone and, reeling off the digits of Martin's Gold Card, had our dream junk: silk blouses, a bushel of Maine apples, sandals, a breadmaker, FedExed and sitting politely on our doorstep within two days. The old Judy lamented in the spring how the winter had worn and washed her olive complexion; the new Judy lay naked in the bed of a tanning salon slathered with cocoa butter wearing only eye goggles.

If no two people were more at odds than my mother and Anthony Christomo, no two people were more alike than she and Martin Hamlin. First they fell in love, New Year's Eve, and then they got engaged, Valentine's Day, until at the burning height of their desire and passion, when they could no longer contain their unfettered lust, they gave in to each other with reckless and heady abandon; oh, Marty-Mart-Martinest, oh Judith, cash, check, or charge, how they shopped with tumescent fervor! Once certain of their mutual love, once the ring, gold, an inevitable big rocky diamond, was ringed on her slim tan finger and the key to her heart worn on his watch chain, hanging, tick tock tick, tolling the hours, there was no further discussion about anything as vulgar as sex. It was china patterns, stemware, Finnish crystal and Egyptian cotton. Even Sofie never again asked or insinuated (at least in my presence) about sex. Instead she brought over catalogs that she and my mother poured over along with copies of *Bride's* magazine. My mother spoke strange new words: trousseau, valise, peignoir, portmanteau, Beaujolais Nouveau. They tripped off her tongue. When couples are in love the world is French. Sofie said wistfully that maybe soon she and Elliot would tie the knot. My mother clasped her hands, oh, it would be wonderful, we can all get together, the four of us, we'll keep in touch. We'll still have our Saturdays. Oh course, said Sofie, and they were almost in tears until Sofie happened to turn the page of the Macy's Spring Preview catalog and they saw the Braun dual-spigot six-cup cappuccino maker. Call these the halcyon days. Call this, the engagement, the salad-dressing days. When he called her on the phone, I heard their tense and combined silence as they waited for me to hang up after my mother picked up the extension in her bedroom. I didn't spy on them. What interest could their secret love words and credit card limits hold for me? I was a strange creature. I had no desire. I had, quite simply, no want or need for anything beyond my elaborate dreams of escape, no fight, no will, no ability to stop or start the events taking place around me. I moved sideways, clung to walls, scuttled in my shell.

Martin Hamlin and my mother were so certain of each other, of tastes, expenses, and styles, they suddenly turned to me, or turned on me, whichever seems the most fitting to you. They wanted to win me over to their side. But believe me, I could have cared less for his gifts: a charm bracelet with the heads of presidents in silhouette, a black velvet beret from Paris, a silver picture frame, a clear glass paperweight with a delicate hand-blown rose suspended inside. Gifts are wonderful things, are they not? I wish I could give them to you, reader. I'd wrap your wrists in those Kennedy, Roosevelt, and Lincoln charms, put your picture in the frame, help you arrange your hair under the band of the velvet chapeau. I'd give all these things and more in exchange for an hour of sleep. We are getting to the many-chambered heart of things. When I arrived at Elsinore with my mother and found my stepfather waiting in the white expanse of empty rooms, it was spring, the bitter perfume of new flowers, moist warmth of the ground, the colors of evening all afternoon, and the swollen waters rising. My arms were loaded with bracelets and my mother's fingers were coated with rings. Our jewels weighted us down and we would have sunk to the bottom of the lake had not our gowns, the yards and yards of light silk fabric, buoyed us up to the surface like seaweed princesses.

But, oh, we are in the thick of it now. There has been an o'er hasty wedding, echoing sounds at night, a house so new, pristine, so frosted and creamy that I am tempted to slice it with a knife to find the rings baked into the center. The scent of vanilla and buttercream, I am sure, wafts up the stairs, strangling me, nightly keeping me far from sleep. Slice it, spoon it up fork by knife, until stuffed full of sweets, the full moon leaves me empty.

It was May and I was void of desire. I remained nightly wakeful, wandering on bare feet past their door, firmly shut, down the stairs to the kitchen for apples and honey, then down to the basement where I watched the big screen TV until dawn. Maybe I did sleep, yes, of course, I did, sometimes around dawn for a few hesitant hours until the sun was full in the sky and the birds singing woke me. Oh, Anthony, my father was a ghostly apparition to me during those lonely hours. He was a guide. He was with me sitting on the leather sofa in the basement watching *The Love Connection* and *The Facts of Life*. He was at my side prodding me, keeping me from nodding off, telling me which *Facts* girl was the best actress because of how she emoted or that the plot was a thinly veiled adaptation of the Cupid and Psyche myth. Hadn't my curse those summers as a child been not my own sleeplessness but to be a witness to his? If I woke in the night and found myself in his guest room, if I stumbled out into the hall and followed the light I would find him awake at his desk in the long shadows of his reading lamp, pen poised, his book open. His eyes dark ringed. The father. He said, he whispered low as though there was someone else around to hear, oh, there was just us. He said, well Pearlie, renting a room tonight in the insomnia lodge? I sucked on my thumb and curled up on the floor at his feet. The father. The mother. The child. Why didn't I have more of my mother's brightness? Her ruthless and regal ability to adapt, to get by daily, instead of inheriting my father's nightly affliction? The repeat collection of his features played out on my face a mirror, his eyes, see them staring? His nose, his mouth, too soft and round for a man, his ears, brow, jaw, and teeth chewing my breakfast cereal. My father is a ghost and I am the spittin' image of him. What does that make me? The ghost of my own father? My mother is cheerful these honeymooning days. She glides on an air of perfume and cuts bouquets of new green flowers before the bloom is on them. My stepfather admits he wants only the best for me; he has, my mother exclaims breathlessly, her eyes damp and arms heavy under the weight of the hyacinth, the lilac and apple blossoms, always wanted a daughter. And still I cannot sleep. And I have no desire. I am briefly aware of the time, the tick tock tick of it, I cannot think without hearing the telltale beating of the heartless minutes.

I want to return to the events in question. Let me tell you, in tenses that vary from now to then, past and on and on, what happened to get us up to the point where I am living in the house, sleepless, and cannot in good conscience celebrate my mother's nuptial festivities. It is difficult for me to go back. I haven't carelessly omitted important things such as what my mother's wedding dress looked like or the total of the caterer's bill; I haven't left out these details and jumped ahead simply to confuse you. You know reader, don't you, that I have always wanted the best for you. It is always easier to remember the emotion than the event, the sense of what it was like at the tick tock rock bottom than the feel of the water during the descent. But for you, I'll buck up and make a genuine concerted effort to explain the linear and coherent progression of events. I'll wear the beret and jangle the silvery guillotined presidents on my wrist. Call me a raconteur, bard, an honest-to-goodness troubadour wearing the colors of heresy on my jacquard sleeves, I don't mind. Let me tell you what happened and how it was that I began to feel so desperate and alone, so like my father, just when my prospects should have been at their best, just when I was closer than ever to living the way I had always dreamed, like a girl in a movie.

The Courtship: January, February, March
When my mother is with him she is bright and giddy, always waiting for him to leave so that she may have the pleasure of his return. I am not strictly jealous. She and Sofie used to go out every Friday night, but when she returned, if I was sleeping, she came into my bedroom, she turned on the lamp, sat on the bed fussing with the covers around me and telling me about whom she had seen and what she had done that night, about the dresses women had worn, their hair, what she might do with her own hair, the perfumes, funny things and jokes that she always wanted to remember so that she could tell me later, but she always forgot, she was sorry but she couldn't help forgetting the punchlines. When she comes home from a date with Martin Hamlin, it is late. I hear her in the next room, the kick of her shoes against the closet as she tosses them off. She smokes cigarettes long awake alone.

Truly, I am happy for my mother. She deserves good things. All mothers do, do they not? I think I have failed her, and I want only to be good, but I do not quite know what actions being good might entail. They are going to be married, and they want to include me in the things they do. They plan activities around me. I could care less for the weekend trips to amusement parks. I throw up on the boat to Boblo Island; I get lost in a crowd of Campfire Girls many years younger than myself at Cedar Point and I have to go to the information desk and have them recite my name over the loudspeaker. And then there is that mall in Edmonton with its indoor ice rink, garish arcades for children smelling dismally of sweaty little boys, bright with neon, exploding with sounds, a pizza parlor in Windsor where I watch a dancing bear who delights the other patrons but sickens me because I have this image of someone, a girl like myself in a bear costume sweating, dancing, playing a fake ukulele while grinning parents snap keepsake photos. I should have been the happiest girl in the world.

Mother says my hair is unruly, nails ragged, bitten down and grubby, that I dress in inky, mournful colors wrong for the season. When I tell her my stories and the things that have happened during the day—and is it my fault that my stories revolve always around injustices I see daily? I tell her how I saw Mary Sue and her new friends with their hard-sprayed hair and tight jeans tip over the lunch tray of Lisa Miller, a fat girl whom we have all known since second grade at least. I tell my mother how they walked by her and it was such a simple gesture, a mere flick of a braceleted wrist and how they laughed when her hot lunch splattered across the floor, tater tots and ketchup, and how they fake apologized while punching each other in the ribs. Worst of all, I tell her how angry it made me and how I sat and did nothing, just watched, unable to act. My mother says, these things happen, it's how kids are. But I am indignant, it's not fair, I say, not right that they think just because they have ratty hair and padded bras they can get away with anything. My mother says, I'm tired of your negative attitude. You can't see the forest for the trees.

Is this what I have become at the ripe old age of fifteen, tree blind?

The past is being erased, even now, even as we speak. It all changes when she meets him. It is less that she no longer needs me, but because she needs to see the world the way he does, not as dark and inaccessible, but gaudy and worth every dime you pay out for it.

The Wedding: April
We are pleased to announce the wedding of Ms. Judith Elaine
Taubman Christomo of Flint, Michigan, to Mr. Martin Ham-
lin of New Yawk City, New York. The ceremony was held
April 21, a brilliant Sunday morning at eleven with services
performed by Rabbi Irving Sheflin in the Henry Ford Room
of the Hyatt Regency Hotel, Flint, Michigan. A brunch fol-
lowed in the Pontiac Room. Bridesmaids were Ms. Sofie
Kornwald, Mrs. Shelly Price (née Taubman) of Boca Raton,
Florida, the maid of honor was young Pearl Rose Christomo.
The bridesmaids were a charming sight in ash rose empire
gowns with bouquets of white roses, baby's breath, and pink tea
roses. Groomsmen in attendance were Mr. Nelson Lippman of
East Orange, New Jersey, Mr. Alexander Berkowitz of Shaker
Heights, Ohio, and Mr. Mitchell Price of Boca Raton, Florida.
The happy couple plan to take up residence in a new home in
Bloomfield Hills, Michigan.

When my mother married Martin Hamlin, April 21, 1985, she
wore a tailored suit sewn with tiny, almost imperceptible seed
pearls and a jaunty hat with a veil pinned to it, just like she
had seen in a picture in *Modern Bride* magazine. The ceremony was held at the Hyatt Regency to commemorate their
fortuitous meeting months prior. They had labored over this
issue: should the wedding be held properly in a synagogue?
But spring was the season for weddings and the two temples
in Flint and every place they called in Detroit had been
booked months in advance. The couple took this as a sign
from God, I suppose. So they set up the huppah and the folding chairs, wrapped the wineglass in linen and brought in a
Rabbi friend of Martin Hamlin's all the way from East

Orange, New Jersey, and married in the Henry Ford Room of the hotel. Oh, there were flowers, champagne, and a plentiful banquet table. No detail went unattended. This was the wedding my mother had not had the first time around. This time there was not only a photographer but a videotape crew and a soundman. My aunt Shelly, my mother's younger sister came in from Florida, tan with creamy frosted hair, air kissing her big sister whom she had not spoken to in two years, since they had had that fight about the antique rocker after my grandfather had died. Shelly ended up with the rocker, somehow, but old grudges were forgotten and the rose bridesmaid's dress looked so good against Shelly's brown skin and the empire cut was far more flattering on her than Sofie. Well, not in Sofie's opinion, of course, she thought it looked great, and she did bear a certain resemblance, her hair done in ringlets, to the heroine on the cover of a romance novel, bosom heaving over her gown and a white rose clenched between her teeth. My Uncle Paul, the middle child between Shelly and Judy, sent his regrets but the invitation had come so unexpectedly and he was scheduled to perform an angioplasty that very day. My mother was angry with him. On Sunday, she said suspiciously over the phone to Sofie, who gets heart surgery on a Sunday? Martin Hamlin's guests were men indistinguishable from each other, stone-jawed, gray-haired. They wore watches on chains and the high polish of their black leather shoes could blind a poor girl like me so innocent of the bright world.

My mother was superstitious about Martin seeing her before the ceremony so suites had been rented in the hotel for the wedding party. This way, from midnight before to the morning of the ceremony, my mother was safe from the specular gaze of Martin Hamlin. That morning my mother and

I dressed together. The air in the room was perfumed, hair-sprayed, cigarette-smoked.

"I'm going to throw up," my mother said decisively as we stood together in front of the large bathroom mirror. "Do you think it will be alright?"

"Yes," I said.

I didn't like seeing myself under those harsh cosmetic bulbs. In the mirror I tried to look at her and avoid my green tinged reflection. My mother fingered through a tray loaded with her bottles and potions. She pulled out one lipstick, frowned, pulled out another, daubed it on a tissue, paused and handed me her choice, wildberry plum.

"I keep thinking about that guy Shelly used to date. Or remember Philip, the one Betsy married the first time? He was a real loser, everyone was afraid to tell her and hurt her feelings. You'd tell me, I mean, if you thought it wasn't right? Or if you thought that Martin—"

She broke off. She couldn't say the name Martin Hamlin and the word "loser" in the same breath.

"Judy," I said setting down the lipstick. It was far too red. "Judy, let me tell you something I learned from *Donahue:* losers attract losers."

"Really—?"

"Yes."

"So I'm not a desperate old maid?"

"No, no, no," I said.

Martin Hamlin was many things, but he was not a loser. If anything his problem was the opposite. He was a winner.

"I'm going to marry Martin Hamlin," she said. "I'm going to be Judy, Judith Elaine Taubman Christomo Hamlin. How do I look? How does Judith Elaine Taubman Christomo Hamlin look?"

"Beautiful," I said and I meant it.

Her dress reminded me of Greta Garbo in *Grand Hotel* when she's waiting for John Barrymore to meet her but he never shows up because he's been killed by Wallace Beery.

She studied her nails, her hands, her face carefully in the mirror, rubbed a fingertip along the sharp line of her cheekbone, her bronze skin. Her hands drifted to her neck, a rope of fat sea pearls, the buttons of the jacket, and rested cupped against her breasts which were hidden, imperceptible under the neat cut of her jacket.

"Beautiful," she said smiling at her reflection. "When I was pregnant I was actually a whole cup size bigger."

"Don't start," I said.

"I know," she sighed. "It was just that I felt, until I really ballooned out, I felt so sexy. Like that was how I should be. Anyway, what difference did it make, Tony never knew the difference."

I was silent. I wanted her to go on. She rarely spoke about my father and when she did it always to say what was wrong with him, Anthony, that Italian bastard. It was never to remember or tell me what had happened. Perhaps that bothered me too, on her second wedding day I still did not know the story of her first marriage.

"It's stupid, but I'd kill just to be like that again, just for today."

She didn't say anything else about my father and then the photographer's assistant knocked on the door and told us, fifteen minutes ladies. My mother put on her hat, adjusted it, the veil against her crimped red hair. She looked at her gold watch.

"Hey wait," she said touching my arm. "Give Judith Elaine Taubman Christomo her last cigarette."

She smoked slowly while I stood leaning against the door holding our bouquets of pink and white roses sprigged with baby's breath. I don't think that she so much wanted to smoke at that moment, but she wanted to make all the guests, her sister, her cousins, friends, photographers and florists, the out-of-town men in shiny shoes and pink-gowned bridesmaids, the caterers and groomsmen, wait for her grand entrance, and no one, not one of us, would deny her that.

In the candid shots the photographer caught me at odd moments, brooding over an empty punch glass, helplessly holding a slice of wedding cake while some young business associate of Martin Hamlin wrapped an arm around my waist. Martin Hamlin had slipped the diamond ring on my mother's finger. He had broken the glass and kissed her to the delight of the audience. The ushers led the way down the hallways, mazy and plushly carpeted, to the banquet room. The placecards for the table seatings listed each guest's name and the "name" of the table—each table after the theme of "jewels"—ruby, emerald, sapphire and the head table was diamond. Isn't it funny, laughed the man with his bourbon breath and his glass sloshing overfull of Israeli champagne, that you are a jewel too, a pearl. Each chocolate-covered strawberry from the dessert table ticked away like a second. I saw my mother in the bathroom smoking, surrounded by women, the perfume in the air smoky and thick, warm as roses. The glassy eye of the salmon laid out whole on a silver tray stared at me mournfully. My mother smiled, I swear, it was not my imagination, knowingly at me from across the room as the man whispered heavily into my ear. I watched my swirling reflection broken into waves in the champagne punch speckled with cherries, the cross sections of floating oranges and lemons say the bells of St. Helen's. Here comes the candle to light you to bed. Here comes the chopper to chop off your head.

The Honeymoon:
It could have been anywhere: Boca, the Riviera, Cancun, New Orleans, Hawaii, the High Sierras, or the outback of Australia. It could and should have been anywhere, but Mr. and Mrs. Martin Hamlin chose to delay their postnuptial celebration until a later, as yet unspecified date. There were other matters to be attended to; Mr. Hamlin had a previous engagement which unfortunately could not be delayed and immediately after the banquet boarded a plane for Iowa where he was leading a two week seminar on stress management for which some seventy-five participants had paid well in advance, check or credit card only, please. Mrs. Hamlin, née Christomo, once Taubman, and before that just plain old knobby-kneed, flat-chested and frisky Judy girl, ahem, Mrs. Judith Taubman has employment obligations of which she would not be clear until the date of May the first. The daughter of Mrs. Hamlin from her previous marriage (a youthful mistake, a forgotten escapade), Miss Pearl Rose Christomo is a sophomore in high school. A bright student, no doubt engaged in numerous extra-curricular activities and teenage involvements (cotillions, fundraisers, hairstyle parties), Miss Pearl will take her exams a month early and finish out the year by completing supplemental assignments so that she will be right on par with her new classmates when she begins the new school year 1985-86 at Andover High School in Birmingham, Michigan. What a lucky young Miss, our Pearl Rose Christomo is! She is embarking on a new life rich with promise! The world is Pearl's oyster.

So you see, my mother and her new husband did not move in together immediately after the wedding. They had not, even as the movies would have fashioned it, one night together before he rushed off, dazzled and dazed from her kisses, to catch his plane bound for Iowa. After the reception they bid each other a practical good-bye before the teary eyes of their guests; for the guests, wedding-drunk and romantic, it might as well have been Ingrid Bergman parting with Humphrey Bogart. But it didn't really seem to bother my mother, this sudden separation from her new husband. After the wedding we returned to our apartment and nothing was different except her red hair and the new rock on her finger. It was as though we had been in a play and the months before had been rehearsal; now things would return to normal.

It was then that she sat me down and explained the wedding present. I'll admit that at first I liked the idea. I had always wanted to live in a house, you know, one like Mary Sue's with an attic and maybe a dog and a porch where you could sit in the evening and drink lemonade or at least some powdered lemonade-flavored drink mix and catch fireflies in jars, a house where there would be a wooden table in the kitchen just like *The Waltons* or maybe it was *Little House on the Prairie* and smoke coming out of the chimney and ma sewing a quilt and pa out in the fields baling hay. I imagine the house all done up in a red bow waiting for us to come and unwrap it. So, you see, she said to me, we have a lot of packing to do before Martin comes home. Home. Which home? His? Ours? The mysterious new house? I don't think that she meant any place in particular, just that wherever she was, that would be his home, wherever her Samsonite luggage was stowed, he would berth his at its side. Ma and Pa. And me.

The Trousseau: Ill-aspected

My mother did not want us to take any more of the past with us than was necessary. We packed sans mercy. We packed dishes, silverware, utensils, and curtains. The lace curtains from my bedroom, we packed them away even though I wanted to keep them. But that was foolish wasn't it? You will never again have the window you had in childhood. My mother packed her old clothes: shoes that had been reheeled, purses, gloves, A-line skirts, V-neck sweaters, party dresses, sensible blouses with bows at the collar, corduroy blazers with wide lapels, denim skirts, a velour vest, cowboy boots, scarves, socks, a cropped-length ski jacket, three bathing suits, bras size 34 A, panties with stretched elastic, kneesocks, tennis shoes, flannel nightgowns and T-shirts inscribed with clever sayings. We took these bags of clothing to the Goodwill store and called the Salvation Army guys to come by with their truck for the furniture and boxes of housewares. We offered our neighbors the chance to take whatever they wanted. The mustache man whom Sofie loved to buzz whether we were home or not, to let her in, took my clock radio, for his little niece, he said. He was a nice guy all in all. I found myself wishing my mother had married him.

The counterdesire of my mother's need to spend was her just-as-compulsive need to give. I half expected her to take the refuse, the leftover clutter of our lives, a toaster oven too embarrassingly grimy to give away, chipped cups, lone and mismatched socks, bras with safety-pinned straps and boot-cut Wrangler jeans—to take all this and heap it on the curb outside the building with a cheerfully drawn sign, "Please find a home for these items!" It was impossible that what we lived with one day, what we so needed to survive, was garbage the next day. I suppose it's more than nostalgic and sentimental, it's just plain stupid to have an allegiance to objects, but I couldn't help remembering when my mother and I went to buy the curtains for my bedroom. It was a Hanukkah present and she said that I was old enough, I must have been ten or eleven, to pick out my own curtains because I should start thinking about my own taste and personal style. We went to the JC Penney After-Christmas White Sale. And I saw them there—cream-colored, netted lace, patterned with flower pots. Those, questioned my mother with incredulity, are they okay? I asked. I was a child. I adored her, I wanted things to be okay always. Sure, she said, whatever you want . . . they just seem a little, well, old-ladyish, you know, fussy. We bought the curtains and compromised on a new set of sheets with pink circus tigers, blue fish, and yellow elephants. You see, even before we met Martin Hamlin we knew how to compromise. I don't know what made him think from the start that I was stubborn; sometimes I think he poured the poison of dissent in my ear. I mean, all those nights when my mother wanted to watch something on television, say a murder mystery with Angela Lansbury and I wanted to watch something else, like *Diary of a Teenage Hitchhiker* with Charlene Tilton, then we might compromise by turning back and forth between the stations during the commercials. Switching channels, that's the soul of compromise.

I watched while she folded up my curtains, the sheets, the towels, washcloths, and linens. It was only toward the end, the last days, when she unplugged the television with a final and decisive flick of her wrist that the nausea crept into me and rested somewhere deep inside and I would not lose it for a long time, not until a bright day in October when the birds were flying overhead and I was unimaginably far from my mother and stepfather. But how could I have known this? In fact, you should pretend I never told you. My mother unplugged the television and by degrees, little by little, the sickness overcame me. Let's leave it at that; let's not imagine that October awaits and with its arrival a boy (because isn't there always a boy?) and the bright genuinely genuine way he will pronounce my name full in the sun. Pretend that you never knew, you were innocent, you sat on the floor listening to my mother speak. I think, yes, she is speaking still.

"Has it ever occurred to you," my mother said setting the television on top of a box packed full of my dolls, "that you watch too much television?"

"It's educational."

I sat on the floor fiddling with a roll of strapping tape.

"What's so educational about beer commercials and Mel Gibson movies?"

"You love Mel Gibson movies."

"No," she said, hands on her hips, "I love Mel Gibson's butt, not his movies. There is a difference."

"Doesn't it bother you to talk like that, being married and all?"

"Pearl," she adopted a compassionate soap opera tone. "This is new to both of us, but it's not going to be like television. I'm not going to wear white gloves and bake meatloaf and stop talking about Mel Gibson's buns just because I'm Mrs. Martin Hamlin. I'm still *Judy.*"

"Mel Gibson is going to play Hamlet," I said.

"Well I'm sure they'll jazz things up a little, you know, add a car chase, some guns, a body count," she said absently as she surveyed the room looking for things she might have missed. She spotted the wall clock above the door.

"Last night I was watching *In Search of—*"

She pulled a chair over to the door and climbed on it, screwdriver in hand. "With Spock?" she asked.

"Yeah," I said. "With Leonard Nimoy. Anyway the show was all about Jesus, you know, in search of the historical Jesus and Spock walked the same path Jesus was supposed to have walked the day they crucified him, the Via Dolorosa. That's what he called it, the way of sadness. He went from—"

"They always show that kind of crap this time of year. Around Easter those TV people must start thinking, oh, it's time for Jesus and those damn Daytona Beach spring break specials."

She was working at the clock with the screwdriver. Her back was to me. I wanted to win her over. Not so much for the sake of television, but because it was important to me at that moment that my mother and I agree on something; I knew we would leave soon and everything would be different, that our rooms would no longer be so close and we would not sleep with the doors open and talk to each other, yelling across the hall.

"They reenacted everything," I went on, "did you know that the Marys at the tomb were the first—"

"*The Marys,*" she laughed tilting her head, "that sounds like a Motown group." She sneezed twice and laughed again, hard and brittle.

"That's the best part. That's when Jesus was resurrected and the women were the first ones he appeared to and then all the men were pissed off and didn't believe—"

"You see what I mean about television?" She asked turning toward me, clock in hand, triumphant. "It's all brainwashing, all these Christmas movies and singing nuns. Is that what I sent you to Hebrew school for? So that you could rot your brain with Rudolph the Reindeer and the Holy Ghost?"

"Two words, Judy, *Honor Roll.*"

She shrugged. "That, my dear, is purely genetic."

"You know, you can learn not just from what they show," I fumbled trying to explain what I loved about television, "but from how they slant things. Or what they leave out. It's all intentional. Even in the monster movies—"

The telephone, miraculously still plugged into its jack, rang. My mother could be very glamorous in ordinary situations. She wiped her hands on her jeans, tossed her bright red curls, and, even at that moment when I was frustrated with her for not understanding what I was trying to explain, I watched how, as she lifted the phone, she ran one hand through her disheveled short curls and cradling the phone against her shoulder removed her gold hoop earring from her right earlobe before saying with a newlywed's musical lilt, "Helllooo?" After a moment of nods and whispers, she held one hand lightly over the receiver and mouthed with grinning exaggeration, "Martin Hamlin."

The Wedding Gift: 2247 Cyprus Avenue, Bloomfield Hills, Michigan, 42248
There are certain landscapes which alter personalities, bring out the worst, or I suppose, the best in a person. The day we arrived was overcast, sun over cloud, cloud over sun, a black cat, rice and strewn rose petals under the feet of the bride, the groom, and their own personal biographer following behind, forming words, scattering flowers, inking her pen.

Mary Clare

WHEN MY SISTER THERESA was seventeen years old she dated a thin, delicate boy named Winston. She dated him not because he was in college and it was exciting how many miles he would drive each weekend to see her, but because he was an artist. He had dyed black hair combed stiffly back off his forehead, smoked foreign cigarettes from an enameled case and wrote her bitter love poems.

Winston wore black trousers and white dress shirts with neat pointed collars. His wrists were fine and trembled under the rolled cuffs of his secondhand shirt. Unlike Theresa, he was not thrilling or loud. He spoke in an exhausted breathy way as though at any moment he might lose both the will and energy to continue.

He always carried with him a leatherbound notebook with his name, Winston H. Delacourt, written across the cover in gold script. In that notebook he kept a series of poems he was writing called "The Cowboy Pages." Most of the poems were about terrible and sad things. A cowboy traveled through the world in pursuit of love but all he found was tragedy: famine, flood, plague, drought. At least ten of the poems focused on natural disaster. The individual poems in the set had titles like "Outrage" and "At What Cost Loneliness?" He thought that desperate words required desperate punctuation, and Theresa agreed with him.

Theresa wanted to be an actress. She used to talk about herself in third person as though her life was that of a girl she was watching in a movie. She hated that we didn't live in a big city or even a small town, but in a middle-sized city, in a middle-sized state. Seven Rivers, Michigan seemed like it was smack in the middle of the world. Theresa read a lot of fashion magazines, and I knew the things she wanted were big and glittery. Winston Delacourt must have seemed glamorous to her with his French cigarettes, morbid charm, and art talk which made little sense to the rest of us.

Winston started coming around in the fall right after my birthday. I was twelve and Theresa was seventeen. "Seventeen," my mother told us, "is a special age for the Wittenberg women." She referred to us, the three of us, by her maiden name even though officially, in school, at work, and in public we went by my father's name, "Boughton." "It's not that it's a prettier name," my mother said in explanation, "it's just that I'm used to it." Even when I was little my father had been gone a long time, and when I think about it now, it does make sense, about the name. We, Theresa, my mother, and I, had no connection left to him except the name. I can't remember anything about him, nothing except the fake things, the memories they must have told me, but nothing real, nothing for myself.

That fall when Theresa was seventeen and I was twelve my mother had a new full-time job as a secretary in a heat-treating factory that tempered steel for the big auto plants down around Detroit and Flint. Between working, the commute up to Niles, and her new boyfriend, my mother was hardly ever around. I know that Theresa blamed her for what happened that year, for telling her about being seventeen and then leaving us on our own. I don't blame my mother though. I don't even blame my father for leaving. People just do what they have to, I guess. That's one of the things my mother taught me—*judge not, lest ye be judged.* She believed in it so much that she embroidered it into a sampler, framed it, and hung it over the bathtub. It's been there for as long as I can remember, right next to the photo of my mother in the white dress, ribboned summer hat, and buckle shoes of her first communion.

My mother met my father when she was seventeen. He used to pump gas at his father's service station. She said she nearly fell down dead at the sight of him. Usually, she was just plain sentimental, but when it came to him, sometimes she lost herself and recalled without so much as blushing the way she used to watch him from across the street when he was at work or how later, when things were going from bad to worse, he still sang Theresa to sleep at night before he left the house for a bar or another woman.

Theresa was born when my mother was twenty, and well, by the time I came around he was long gone. My mother looks young but I don't think she ever feels young, not really. She sighs a lot, rests her face in her hands and stares out the window; sometimes she seems as far away from me as Theresa does. At least back then Theresa and I had each other. Now I wait for the mail, check for letters, hope for days when my mother's mood brightens and she asks me to go to the garden store with her, or the mall, sometimes we even go to the movies.

The thing is, I'm seventeen now and things seem pretty much the same as they always have. I think about Theresa when she was seventeen and I wonder. I look in the mirror and at photographs and wonder if I look or sound like her, if without knowing it, I move through a room the way she used to. And then it's like I wake out of the dream and know that I'm more like my mother than Theresa. We prefer to stay in the background, witness rather than act, to reserve judgments and opinions. If I was like Theresa, bright, loud, cracking her grape bubble gum and calling to older boys driving home from school—if I was like that being seventeen might feel different. There's a skinny, nervous second chair violinist who tries to walk me home after band practice, and once he even asked me to go to the planetarium with him. I said no. Mother says to give things time.

Sometimes I wish I had more opinions; not that I wish I was more like my older sister, it's just mostly I feel empty and aimless. I never thought about her *want* as aimless, because it could be satisfied so easily with things or people or food. Maybe I'm wrong. It's difficult to say, I was always too young. She talked to me, but she never really confided. I learned the important things accidentally when she was on the phone or didn't know I was in the next room. She told most of her secrets to her girlfriend, Rose. I think Rose fit in well at our house where my mother and I instinctively stood back and let Theresa rule. Theresa could mimic anyone and even when she was much younger I remember her putting on shows for the three of us; for a while we were her willing audience. For a while we were all the audience she needed, but like I say, things change and people change and I don't begrudge anyone their wants; God knows we each have enough of our own.

I associate, rightly or wrongly, my sister with Rapunzel and other princesses from the storybooks I used to check out of the Seven Rivers Public Library on Saturday mornings. *Snow White and Rose Red,* that was in my child's mind, a book about Theresa and Rose. The Princesses on the cover, flowers woven in their hair, one blonde, one dark, both lost in an enchanted forest. I remember how the book described them—*flaxen and raven.* Me, I wore my hair cut short. I was never the kind of girl to think about hair or fuss over it. But Theresa and Rose, they loved to do each other's hair. They even bought this old home beauty shop mirror type thing at a garage sale. It had lightbulbs all around and a magnifying mirror. They put curlers in their hair and painted their nails, their lips, their faces like movie stars with Rose's mother's Avon makeup.

They loved perfume, eye shadow, and sticky lip gloss, but hair was always far more important. They read up on the latest styles, treatments, and hints in fashion magazines and did each other's hair in front of the flickering bulbs of the cheap mirror. Secretly, they clipped away at split ends and fly-aways with my mother's good sewing shears. They french-braided, they pig-tailed, home-permed, deep-conditioned; whenever I could I was their accomplice. I was coerced into stealing a can of Rose's father's beer so they could rinse their hair in it and bring out, as promised one beauty column clipped out and pinned to Theresa's bulletin board, "the hidden fire and luster of any hair color."

I don't think that Theresa did any of those beauty experiments to get boys' attention. She had enough of that. It really seemed like she was searching for this image of herself. I know it probably sounds foolish; younger sisters often sound foolish, but if you could have seen her then you would understand. She was five-foot-eight, wore her hair almost to her waist and some nights let me brush it for her after she washed it. Her eyebrows were as light and pale as her hair, her nose long and narrow, but not quite sharp; her mouth was probably too wide for her face. She looked a lot like our mother, but I suppose, if there was something provocative and brash about our father that drew my mother to him when she was a girl, then Theresa probably had a lot of him in her—if not in looks then in spirit.

Theresa dated lots of boys. My mother didn't really approve of it, but since Theresa had been fourteen, she let her go out as long as she knew something about the boy or his parents. Theresa never stuck to one boy for very long; *boring, small*

town, bourgeois, pedestrian, she complained late at night across
the kitchen table after whomever, Stuart or Chip or Billy, had
dropped her off. I can only say that of those small-town boys
who bored her, she never seemed to tire of a certain one,
Aaron, and he in turn never seemed to tire of Rose; and this,
I think, is where the real trouble started. It's not that Theresa
was greedy or jealous of what her friend had. She just wanted
things to be equal. Theresa had to have exactly whatever Rose
had; I guess it just seemed fair to her.

Aaron was the one who introduced Winston to Theresa in
the first place. I guess Aaron met him in some class down at
school in Ann Arbor. Aaron made a big deal about going away
to college, but when the weekend rolled around he always
seemed to be back in Seven Rivers. I used to think that he was
a show-off, and that's why he brought Winston home for the
weekend that first time. When I think about it now, I don't
know if that was the real reason. I have to think about it some
more before I decide.

Aaron brought Winston over to Rose's house one Friday
afternoon in October. Rose lived a few streets from us in a big
yellow house with a stained glass windowpane on the front
door. Her mother didn't work back then. She does now
because all her children are gone, I guess. She works at a
preschool and sometimes I see her in the library park with a
bunch of little five-year-olds. All the kids go crazy running
around from the swings to the jungle gym, across the monkey bars, down the slide, and then back around to the tire
swings in an endless circle; and then maybe I was returning
some book to the library or something and I would see Mrs.
Simon standing on the wood chips in the middle of those
running shrieking kids, just standing still looking as lost and
helpless as an orphan. Butternut, Rose's little sister, used to

say that her mother's nerves were shot to the moon—that's why she looked so spacey. Butternut was always saying things like that.

The day Aaron brought Winston over was bright and cold. Someone down the street was burning leaves and it was all you could smell everywhere. Even in the Simon's living room which always smelled like furniture polish and dried flowers, you could smell the autumn creeping in. Theresa sat in a rocking chair with her back to the window reading from the script of the senior class play. She was wearing a short kilt and there were bits of dried leaves clinging to her tights.

"And who are you?" she read from the script.

"I'm the East Wind," Rose answered, giggling.

Theresa rolled her eyes. "Don't laugh. This stuff is serious."

Rose tried again and managed to keep a straight face, but her voice sounded as though she might start cracking up at any second. They were reading from Hugh Denmark's *The Plaything* and Theresa wanted the lead part, the youngest sister who ends up marrying the enchanted pig. Theresa wanted the lead part in every play she tried out for, but this time it was different. She loved Hugh Denmark more than any movie star whose picture she had taped to her wall.

She had one whole shelf in her room devoted to Hugh Denmark and his books. This seemed a little strange to me because she wasn't so big on books, not like she was on movies. We saw nearly every movie that came to the Capitol downtown. Mostly she liked dark foreign men who were always smoking or looking into the camera right at you through a cloud of smoke. I never saw his picture, but I always figured this writer, this Hugh Denmark must be handsome and tragic and all things, that, like I said, Theresa found attractive. She made this shelf into a sort of shrine of weird stuff she had collected—

colored birthday candles stuck in lumps of bright Play-Doh, plastic fiesta beads we won at the county fair and the two remaining Barbie dolls she had that didn't have any parts broken off and still had all their hair. She would never explain to me what the scene was supposed to mean, only that I wasn't allowed to touch it. The most I got out of her about it was that it was some scene from one his books, or something like that.

"And who are you?" Theresa read again.

"Winston Delacourt," said a voice from the doorway.

"She wasn't asking. She was reading," Aaron said as he walked in and threw himself on the sofa.

Winston remained in the doorway. His white shirt was buttoned at the collar. His trousers were a couple of inches too short, and his bare ankles showed pale above his black penny loafers

"Well come in already," said Aaron with great effort. He was lying on his back on the sofa with his arms under his head. "Sit over there," he ordered pointing across the room.

I was standing in the doorway from the dining room to the living room. Actually, I was standing with the door open just a little bit, watching.

"What's going on now?" asked Butternut without looking up. She was doing her math homework at the kitchen table.

"Aaron brought a thin boy. He looks like a vampire."

Winston looked from Theresa to Ricey and back to Aaron before he finally sat down in an armchair next to Theresa. She laughed and tossed her script on the floor in front of him.

"I'm Theresa," she said.

"Are you trying out for a play?" Winston asked blushing nervously. "I'm sorry, that was a stupid question. Aaron told me about you, that you're always in the class play. You were in *The Crucible* last spring, and that other one, you know," he gestured with a shake of his bony wrist.

"Oh yes, that one," she nodded. "Do you act too?" she asked with the polite condescension of a star to a fan.

"Oh no, no, nothing like that. Although I have read that play," he smiled knowingly at Theresa's papers at his feet. "It's a pretty awful adaptation of Denmark's original novel. I find Mr. Denmark, Hugh, highly misunderstood by the public and the critics alike. I should try my hand at revising that play myself. I'm something of a writer too, you know."

"Excuse me," said Aaron. "But didn't somebody famous and, well, talented already write the play?"

"Don't listen to him," said Theresa leaning forward toward Winston and tapping two fingers on the side of her head, "he plays football." She leaned closer. "I've thought the very same thing about the play. I mean you have this perfectly beautiful lead character, this princess and all, and she has almost the same amount of lines as the sorceress, the woodsman, and the pig, not to mention the narrator. Don't you think she should have more lines?"

Winston smiled, gave a dry sputtering cough and asked, "Does anyone mind if I smoke?"

"Of course not," said Theresa.

Winston took out his case, tapped a cigarette a couple of times against it, and lit up.

"He's smoking now," I told Butternut. "From a case and everything."

"Your sister is such a slut," sighed Butternut. "A real fast number, a real libertine."

"Libertine?"

"It's my word for today."

"But she's not a slut."

"Maybe," conceded Butternut resting her round face on her hand. "Maybe not yet, but definitely a libertine."

"More lines, better lines," said Winston taking a drag of his cigarette. His wrist shook the slightest bit as he smoked.

"I have an idea about the costumes too," Theresa said. "Something fluttery at the beginning, but glittery at the end."

"That's just great, Theresa," said Aaron sitting up. "Exactly how many costume changes do you picture for this part that you haven't even gotten yet. I mean what if someone better than you tried out, hunh? What then?"

"Better?" asked Theresa with melting innocence.

"Yeah, like what if Ricey tried out for the part? I bet she'd get it if she wanted it."

"Don't you have some place else to be?" Theresa said.

"In fact, yes. Rice and I were just going to the kitchen, weren't we?"

Rose, who was sitting in a love seat by the window, looked up sleepily and nodded with the sun in her hair. She stood and then stopped, turned back, picked up a candy glass dish with a couple of old starlight mints in it and handed it to Winston, who was busy tamping the ash from his cigarette into the sharp cuff of his trousers.

I skidded back from the dining room to the kitchen and into the chair next to Butternut.

"What's up Nutter-Butter?" Aaron asked raising his hand for a high five.

"Somebody is smoking," she said ignoring his hand.

"Tell me about it."

Rose stood at the sink watering a fern hanging over the windowsill. "Why did you bring him?" she asked. She fingered through the plant's leaves plucking stray dry shoots and tendrils. She was sucking on a mint. "Sweets for the sweet," she said tossing a handful of mints, and I think there were actually some lemon sours too, through the air to me and Butternut. They landed right in the middle of Butternut's math homework.

"Why? I don't know? I thought he was funny. I thought maybe Theresa would like him." Aaron pushed the candy with the eraser end of a pencil across Butternut's careful math equations.

"He's a freak is what he is."

"Somebody is smoking," repeated Butternut looking across the table at me.

"C'mon Ricey," said Aaron leaning off his chair and pulling on Rose's sleeve. "Walk up to the 7-11 with me for a slurpee—" he spread his arms magnanimously, took in the whole kitchen in a big, but steady, sweeping gesture. "I'll buy." And then seeing that she remained skeptical, unmoved, he added. "I'll buy you whatever you want."

"I can't believe you brought him here. I'll never get rid of him. How can I even leave? It's my house and you expect me to just leave them here alone?"

"What's the worst that could happen? They might start breaking things in the throes of method acting? Let's split," he said getting up from his chair. "And leave the artistes to—"

"Someone is smoking."

Aaron looked from me to Butternut.

"People are just like that. Someone is always smoking when they shouldn't be," Butternut said with an irresolute air as she got up and headed to the living room.

"Precious, isn't she?" Aaron grinned.

Butternut's feet were bare, and she deliberately made squeaky noises as she stomped across the floor. She ignored Theresa and stopped in front of Winston's chair. He smiled and looked amusedly at Theresa with whom he seemed suddenly very close and confident.

"Why hello little girl, what's your name?" he asked opening his eyes very wide.

Butternut pointed a finger in Winston's face. He gave a nervous smile.

"I mind very much that you are smoking," she said.

Winston looked around at Theresa again, but she was already collecting her papers from the floor.

"Butternut has spoken," Theresa said and flashed just briefly a narrow-eyed and intimate smile. "Anyway, it's time me and Mary Clare got home. Mommy dearest is big on *punctuality* . . . Aaron, give us a ride home?"

While Theresa pulled on her jacket, Aaron made a great pretense about whether he wanted to drive her home, but decided, yes, and threw his arm around her shoulder with exaggerated friendliness.

"Want me to carry your books or something?" he asked.

She rolled her eyes.

Butternut, who had been standing close to Winston while he stubbed out his cigarette, turned disgustedly away from the rest of us. "A bunch of libertines," she muttered, "careless, thoughtless, libertines."

I called good-bye to her as we left, but I don't think she heard because Aaron was repeating a joke he had heard at a frat party to Theresa, who was laughing.

That night Theresa crawled into my bed with her hair smelling like smoke. Her hands and feet were cold.

"Hey," she said poking me in the side.

"Whaa?"

"Do you want to hear the frog prince story?"

"Mmhun."

"What did you think of that guy today, that Winston?"

She didn't give me a chance to answer, but rolled onto her back with her hand under her head. "He's pretty froggy himself, don't you think?" She squirmed on her side toward me. "Mary Clare, you're lucky you have sister like me, a girl who thinks. You're not going to be a girl scout, a bookworm forever—" she touched my head lightly. "I'll talk to mom. I'll get her to let you grow out your hair." She left her hand on my head for a moment. I could feel her thinking, sleepless next to me in the dark.

After Theresa got the part of the youngest princess, Winston drove down from Ann Arbor every Friday. He had spoken to the drama teacher at Theresa's school and had gotten himself a sort of apprenticeship. He was getting college credit for an independent study, but he called himself a scriptwriter. He drove a battered gray car whose clean inside smelled like cigarettes. He stayed about fifteen miles away at his Aunt's house Friday night, spent Saturday coaching Theresa and in the dark winter evening drove off again in the gray direction from which he had come.

We always met at Rose's house. Theresa used to say it was because there was more room in the Simon's big living room for her to block out her movements, but I knew that it was because she was embarrassed of showing Winston our small house. She especially didn't want him to meet our mother or her new boyfriend, Ted Torvald, who was double-jointed and used to bend his fingers in odd directions to make me laugh. Theresa was not amused. She loved to sit on the Simon's velvet love seat and spread her long blonde hair over the armrest like a movie star. Our house, our whole world was hopelessly too small for her needs.

It was probably because my mother was so distracted with Ted that she didn't notice the change coming over Theresa. I noticed, but I stuck to her advice, watch and learn. It started with her clothes. She stopped wearing her pleated skirts and the blouses my mother bought her at JC Penney in exchange for outfits of all black that she bought at thrift stores with Winston. She double-pierced one ear and went without any earring at all in the other. Theresa rarely even washed her hair anymore, but left it straight and lanky, crookedly parted down the middle. She said that it looked more European that way. She exhaled with casual flair a drag from one of Winston's cigarettes and said—*from the moment I saw him I knew if I could ever have him, I could never keep him*— which I always figured was a line from a movie but I never did figure out which one.

All that winter the afternoons were dark, the evenings bleak and cold. The windows frosted over, but it was nice and warm inside Rose's house. Theresa and Rose huddled together, pulling on each other's hair, fussing with tiny braids and barrettes. Butternut always seemed to have more homework than anyone I knew, and so, those nights I spent my time waiting alone in the living room for Winston. I liked him, how he came in out of the winter night, smelling cold and musty, humming with self-importance. When I heard Winston's car pull into the drive, I ran to the window and watched as he crunched through the snow up the front walk with his jaw grimly set. His gloves were black with the fingers cut out of them. I opened the door at his light, hesitant knock. Standing at the hallway mirror, he unwound his long gray scarf which covered his delicate neck. I waited a little way behind him watching.

"Hey sister Mary Clare," he said wiping away the wet, melted snow from his cheeks with Rose's mother's scarf which was hanging on the rack, "do you like art?"

"Art?" I asked. Sometimes he wore a black beret. I thought that must have made him an artist.

"Art, like in poems, or acting, like when your sister is in a play. Do you like to watch her?"

I nodded.

Winston turned away from the mirror and looked at me. He bent down and rested one hand on my shoulder and with the other pulled off his shoes one at a time.

"If you are lucky, Mary Clare," he said straining with a lace, "you'll grow up to be like your sister. If you are extremely lucky."

Winston straightened up, wiped his hands on the sash of the hall curtains and passed through the hallway into the bright doorway of the kitchen. Outside snow was falling softly. It looked like it must have been falling like that all over the world. I started to carve my name into the icy pane of the front window but it was too long, and I left off in the middle.

In the kitchen Theresa and Rose were reciting the script from memory while washing the dinner dishes. Aaron and

Butternut were the audience. He was drying while she sat at the table slurping a bowl of chocolate pudding and tapping her feet under the table trying to make as much noise as possible.

"And I have traversed this world three times. Thrice through the gloamy mists, thrice 'cross the lonely sky," said Theresa. Little flecks of glitter shined on her cheeks and made it look as though she had been crying.

Rose turned from the sink to look at Winston entering the room and still wiping with a circular motion she asked, "And what was your sin? And for whom do you search?"

Theresa put her hands together. At first it was as if she was praying, but she opened her hands and pantomimed a book. "I have read from the book," she said. "I am searching for he whom the others have abandoned."

Winston clapped slowly. "Bravo! It's going to work," he said as though it was at that moment that he finally became aware of his own talent. "It's really going to work."

Theresa crossed the room and took his hand. "Come with me, darling," she said in a fake English accent. He smiled with his thin lips pressed together and let her lead him into the living room. Butternut grabbed my arm in imitation of Theresa pulling Winston, but we slid on the slippery wood and fell laughing on the floor in the hallway. Aaron and Rose stayed behind in the kitchen. I heard her light laughter. When I got up and peeked back into the kitchen, he was standing behind her with his hands around her waist. Her head rested against his chest. They did not speak.

You know things as a kid that you don't admit, or maybe you just take in without understanding. Theresa was my sister, of course, but sometimes, and definitely at that moment, I doubted her. She could laugh with Winston, playfully search his pockets for cigarettes and matches, and then when we were alone together at night, she talked again about Aaron. And I recall that moment so clearly, how I stood in the doorway, and how Butternut was calling my name, and I stood there and Rose and Aaron didn't know it, and then I turned and walked back into the living room. I know I was the youngest but I felt very old then, like I knew something that didn't have any words to it. That sounds stupid I guess, but that's how I felt and I never forgot, although I'm sure I forgot a lot of things, feeling that way.

When we watched Theresa rehearse, Butternut brought a notebook and a pencil. She sat there next to me squinting seriously as though she was really in a theater, but she hardly ever wrote anything down. Sometimes she doodled pictures of Winston. She made his head a big balloon compared to his stick figure body and wrote captions of him saying things like, "to pee or not to pee?" and "I luv my mutha." That one really cracked her up.

"Delacourt," said Aaron coming into the room and hurling himself onto the sofa. "Why the hell are you messing around with the script? Do you really think that you can write better than that Denmark guy? He's famous. I mean, what the hell are you trying to prove?"

Aaron picked up Theresa's script which was on the floor and began flipping through it. The pages were scarred with notes and inked over with red corrections.

"Like here, page 12. What the hell is a 'gloam'? That's not a word. It's just stupid."

"Do you know what is wrong with you, Aaron Saltmarsh," said Winston with great relish. "You are a fool, not a great fool, or a monumental fool, but a fool none the less."

At first I thought Aaron was going to punch Winston. I could tell Butternut wanted him to. She was leaning forward nearly tipping off the love seat on which we were both sitting.

Instead of getting mad Aaron just started laughing really loud and fake.

"HA HA HA, Buddy, I could laugh till I puke," he said.

"Laugh now," said Winston, "but I am going to prove you incorrect. I am going to show Mr. Hugh Denmark my work on his play. I am certain he will laud and extol my—"

"What?" Theresa interrupted spinning around in the center of the room at the mention of the playwright. "How? He won't see you. Even if it was true, if people had seen him around here—he won't see you. It isn't possible, is it?"

All eight eyes were focused on Winston as he sat thin and still in that chair moving only to finger the gold engraving on his book which he held close to his chest.

"I am certain that if I can find Mr. Denmark, he will make time for me," Winston uttered softly, more to himself, it seemed, than to his audience.

One night Theresa told me the story of the dancing princesses who ran through secret passageways on their satin slippers with no candles or light. She let her just-washed wet hair dangle down toward me. I wanted to tell her that I knew how she could escape—just wait until her hair was long enough and she could climb the braid out the window. The story ended when the princesses lost their magic slippers, but I wanted them to be able to run away, to be invisible forever. Her voice was sleepy. If I fell asleep before she was finished it was as though the story had no end.

Theresa's love of Aaron didn't stop her from getting closer to Winston. One night when my mother was out bowling with

Ted, Theresa brought Winston over to our house. I saw Theresa and Winston sitting close in the living room. He was reading from "The Cowboy Pages." She sprawled across the sofa, her legs on his lap. Abruptly, she sat up, leaned over, and kissed him long and hard on the mouth. Winston paused, touched the hair off Theresa's forehead, gave that dry cough and continued to recite his poem exactly where he had left off.

The play was scheduled as part of the spring festival at the high school. As the date approached Theresa got anxious and distracted. She slept even less than usual. In February rehearsals were canceled for three weeks when the drama teacher was out sick with a viral infection. Winston wouldn't comment on Hugh Denmark. He just smiled knowingly, *wait and see.*

"He's just buying time," Aaron told Theresa. "There's no way he could ever get a hold of that guy. He just wants to impress you."

"What's so wrong with trying to impress a girl?" Theresa asked and graced Aaron with her best fairy-tale smile.

"Too bad he has to try," Aaron said in return.

I didn't mind watching Theresa rehearse, especially in the winter when there was nothing else to do. The Simons used to keep their thermostat turned up much higher than we did at our house, and Mrs. Simon always let us have hot chocolate with the kind of colored marshmallows that my mother would never buy. In the spring things were different. Butternut and I were bored with their play. We wanted to go outside, but the first of the spring rains kept us trapped impatiently indoors.

"I'm bored," Butternut said in a robot voice. She kept repeating it mechanically every two seconds. "Bored . . . bored . . . bored."

"What do you want to do?" I asked her.

"Something fun."

"Do you want my book?"

She lifted the cover of my library book, read the title and dropped it with a grimace.

"Nancy Druid the girl defective. Puh-leeze. I'll find us some more suitable reading material," she said getting up from the table.

When she came back she had something hidden under her sweatshirt, a book, and the four square corners made it look like she was wearing armor. She grinned and pulled the book out of her shirt.

"Eat your heart out Mistah Hugh Denmark."

She held Winston's book in her arms.

"Put it back. Put it back before he sees it's gone."

"He'll never even know. Theresa's got on her itsy-bitsy costume and he's about to pass out."

She sat back down next to me, took a deep breath and opened the cover. She held the book upright and close to her face so that I couldn't see the pages.

"Read it to me."

"Okay, but keep quiet," she said pushing her glasses up higher on her nose. "Okay. This one is called "'Unravished Stillness.'"

"What? What does that mean?"

Butternut shrugged and flipped through the pages until she came to some loose papers in the back. She wouldn't read them out loud to me, but her fingers followed the lines down the page.

"Oh gross. You don't want to hear this stuff."

"Yes I do."

"Look, I'll tell you about it, okay? The cowboy guy's horse dies. He just stands there in the hot sun watching the body decay. He watches the worms eat the body and describes it in conspicuous detail. The cowboy also happens to be eating an ice-cream cone at the time."

"What kind?"

"Superman."

"Gross," I agreed with her.

Butternut closed the book.

"That stuff about the worms was so nasty," she said.

"It was kind of sad," I said to her.

She shook her head and said that it reminded her of that horrible song kids in school sang.

Winston pulled his car into our driveway on the rainy Saturday morning the weekend before the play was scheduled to be performed. He gave the horn one short nervous honk while he waited.

"That boy is so odd," my mother said as she zipped up my raincoat for me.

"Mother," said Theresa, "he's an ar-tiste. He's supposed to be that way."

Theresa had told her that we were going downtown to the Capitol Theater to see a double feature matinee of some Disney movies. I'm good at keeping secrets, and I didn't say a word about where we were really going.

"It was almost too simple," said Winston. "It was like a gift dropped right from heaven into my lap."

"You didn't just look in the phone book, did you?" Theresa asked as she brushed the rain from my jacket.

"Almost," he said turning the key in the ignition. "Mr. Denmark, ahem, Hugh, is teaching a course in contemporary drama at Wayne State. Fate, it would seem, is on our side."

It was a two-and-a-half hour ride down to Detroit. I was sitting in the front seat between them, and Theresa in her happiness kept leaning over me to give him quick kisses on his cheek. We drove with the rain beating against the windshield. Theresa fiddled with the radio dial. She turned the volume up way louder than the windshield wipers. Winston turned it down. "I have to think," he said. A few minutes later she found another song she liked on the crackling Detroit rock station and turned it back up.

"I wish I could have brought Butternut," I whispered to Theresa.

"Butternut," she said loudly, giving a short laugh. "That girl is nothing but trouble."

"But she won't believe I've seen him," I insisted.

"Well, we'll just have to bring something back for her. His autograph or something." Theresa was smoking. She had her window rolled down partway and the rain hit me in light flecks.

"Oh God no!" interrupted Winston with alarm.

Theresa was so happy that she could have cared less what Winston said. She leaned down and whispered in my ear, "We'll sneak into his bathroom and steal his toothbrush, or his little finger. That's something Butternut would really like."

"We need proof," I said.

"Proof," she repeated turning her face from me to stare out the window at the grimy Detroit skyline.

"Theresa, Theresa," I said tugging on her sleeve, "I've never met a famous person before."

Winston seemed amused by this.

"They are just like regular people. Except more so." He chuckled and looked over at Theresa for approval, but she was busy tossing her cigarette out the window. I turned around in my seat and watched the cigarette butt, still glowing and orange spiraling back into traffic until I couldn't see it anymore.

"I see you found your way in," said the old man sitting by the fireplace.

We three stood there in front of him. I wanted to ask Theresa where Hugh Denmark was because the little troll in front of us certainly didn't look famous. I thought he must be Mr. Denmark's butler or something; he was nothing like the dark men, actors, and movie stars Theresa talked about to Rose for hours on the phone. I wished Butternut was there because she always knew what to do when other people didn't. She could always think of something funny or smart to say.

"Sit down," said the man.

I didn't know where we were. It wasn't the city or the country—a small house, near other small houses, but there was a gloomy lake and trees right out the window. He was sitting in the middle of a large, mostly bare room. There were no chairs except the straight-backed one on which he sat and a cold black leather sofa by the uncurtained window. The room was chill and damp. Theresa was the first to sit. She just plopped herself down right at his feet. Winston followed her, carefully pulling the fabric of his worn trousers around his knees.

"I don't suppose I was terribly hard to unearth," said the man. "But now that you've found me, what is it that you want?"

Winston was frozen, but Theresa tilted her head, face rain-damp, pointed to some papers near the kindling pile and asked, "Could you read us something? Something new?"

Winston nodded ferociously. He glowed, really, like he loved Theresa so much at that moment for even *thinking* about asking that, let alone saying it aloud.

"Is that why you came here?" he asked. "For a story?"

It was Winston who answered. He pulled out his own manuscript and held it out to his idol, but Mr. Denmark just motioned for him to leave it with the papers heaped on the kindling basket. Winston gingerly dropped the bundle of papers which, in his oddly romantic way, he had bound together with one of Theresa's hair ribbons.

Theresa who had been silent suddenly got on her knees in front of Mr. Denmark, bowed her head and began reciting lines from his play.

"We have traveled far, from the house of the sun to the house of the moon," she said.

"Charming," said Mr. Denmark bemused. "An actress, a little actress."

He leaned forward and raising her still bowed head, turned her face up to his and kissed her forehead. Winston's jaw dropped and I could hear his breath go raspy and harsh in his throat.

"How lovely your visit has been," Mr. Denmark said grasping Theresa's shoulders and pushing her away at an arm's length. "But you must leave. I'm quite spent."

"Maybe, ahem, sir, we could return?" asked Winston blushing.

Hugh Denmark frowned. He looked at me, I saw it, I am certain I saw him look at me and then sadly look at Theresa.

"Sometime," he said, and his voice was as cold and damp as the room. "We may meet again."

My mother wanted to do something special for Theresa on the opening night of the play. She bought a crepe paper streamer that was supposed to say "Congratulations" across it, but when we opened it up it said "Congratulations, it's a girl!" in pink letters. We hung it up over the mantle anyway. She also said we could have a pajama party which really meant that Rose and Butternut could spend the night as long as we promised to keep the noise down because my mother had to go to work on Saturday morning. I heard Theresa talking to Rose about her own plans as she packed a bag to take to the auditorium.

"Are you nervous?" Ricey asked her. "I know I would be nervous." She was sitting on the end of Theresa's bed.

Theresa held a little jar of gold glitter in one hand and shook it up and down.

"Not really," she said. "I mean, not about the play."

"About something else."

Theresa nodded.

"Tell," said Rose flopping onto her stomach and propping her chin on her hands.

"It's a big surprise," said Theresa mysteriously. "But I'll tell you this—I feel like anything could happen tonight."

"Does this have something to do with Winston, hunh?"

"I refuse to—" Theresa dropped her vial of glitter into her bag. "Say anything now on the grounds that it may incriminate me later."

"Impressive," grinned Rose.

"Laugh now," said Theresa.

Fifteen minutes to curtain time my mother pushed the camera into my hands and told me to go backstage and take a picture of Theresa. It was important that I got back there before the play started. My mother was crazy about "before and after" pictures. She especially liked the ones of dieters, fat and thin. She liked to see that people had the will and ability to change. She wanted two pictures of Theresa, before and after.

It was noisy and crowded backstage. The drama teacher, Mr. Katz, was wearing a jacket and a black turtleneck. I looked and saw Winston leaning against a wall by a cord of rope and rows of light switches, he too was wearing a jacket and a black turtleneck. The black of Winston's jacket was worn to a dusky green. He was smoking and watching the chaos with a grim satisfaction.

"So just who exactly was in charge of the stupid props?" Theresa angrily asked a tall boy.

"I just do sets," he said defensively.

"For chrissakes," said Theresa turning to Mr. Katz. "Nobody bothered to get the book. The big stupid book in the first scene."

She pointed to the set of Act I which featured the library of the castle and the podium, empty, on which the king's book of prophesies was supposed to sit. Mr. Katz tried to calm Theresa. He called her a star and urged her not to strain her vocal chords. She was furious, but she tried to keep her face composed so that she didn't ruin her makeup. Her face was white with streaks of pink across her cheekbones and bright blue around her eyes. She was wearing her princess crown, a circlet of silk flowers.

"It can't be any old book," she said, as a girl dressed as a fairy handed her a geometry textbook. "It has to look—it has to—where's Winston?" asked Theresa shoving the book back at the girl.

"Winston," she called over to him.

Winston watched her through the crowd that had gathered.

I don't remember him having it before, but as if out of nowhere he produced and handed her the leatherbound notebook with the gold name emblazoned on the cover. She hugged it to her chest with both arms. Her dress was yellow chiffon and floated a little when she moved. Bits of glitter in her hair and on her stockings sparkled and caught the light. And that is how I took a picture of her. I ran back out into the audience and slid into my seat just as the houselights were dimmed.

Winston brought out flowers after the final act. Theresa stepped forward from the line of the cast and gave a deep curtsy. She looked as though all the things in the play really had happened to her, as though she really had lost her love, crossed the world from the sun to the moon and finally cut off her own little finger for the final rung of the ladder up the glass mountain. Aaron sat between Rose and Butternut during the play. He grimaced when Winston came out of the wings and onto the stage with the big bouquet of yellow daffodils that matched Theresa's dress almost exactly.

I was clapping and watching Theresa up on the stage. Everyone stood up, but when I sat back down again, Aaron was gone. Butternut shot me a knowing look over the empty seat between us. But Butternut didn't see the old man in the back row. I noticed him as we were filing out of the brightly lighted auditorium. He was wearing a slouchy hat like a gangster in a movie. He looked just like Hugh Denmark.

Theresa didn't invite Rose to the cast party. My mother kept trying to cheer her up as we walked home. She said that it was all the excitement that had made Theresa forget. Rose nodded, but she walked alongside my mother without saying a word. The ground was damp, and the evening was cool and smelled like rain. Butternut and I ran on ahead.

"Are you guys still awake?" asked Rose tapping on the door of my room.

Butternut and I were in my bed telling ghost stories. She

always told the same one, but changed the words she used to tell it. She called it "The Monkey's Paw."

"We're up," said Butternut.

I reached over and turned on the lamp. Rose covered her eyes at the brightness.

"No, turn that thing off. Come to Theresa's room with me."

"Why? Are you scared?" asked Butternut.

"Shouldn't she be home yet?" I said looking at the clock. It was after two.

"Parties, they can last all night," said Rose in an older sister voice. She collected our pillows into her arms.

We sat in Theresa's room with Rose. Butternut told another version of "The Monkey's Paw." She changed it so that this time it was about a monkey who had a man's hand. Rose looked at the clock. I remember falling asleep with the three of us in the bed, and Rose shaking me saying she heard Theresa coming up the stairs. It was Butternut's idea to play a joke on Theresa for making us wait so long. Rose shoved our pillows at us, and Butternut and I hid in the closet, pulling the door shut just as Theresa walked into the room. We left the door open just the slightest bit so we could look out.

Theresa had let down her hair. She smelled like smoke and the outside. She began undressing in the dark.

"Ricey," she whispered.

Rose didn't answer. Theresa pulled her dress over her head and stood naked in the middle of the room.

"Theresa," said Rose sitting up in bed, "where's your underwear?"

"Guess what I did," Theresa asked in a throaty voice. She pulled her nightgown over her head. "No, don't guess. I don't even want you to guess. No, okay, guess."

"You lost your underwear?"

"That's not all I lost," she laughed a little too loudly, covered her mouth and fell on her side on the bed still giggling.

"No. You didn't."

"Yes I did." She whispered to the audience. "I told you I was going to."

"Tell me everything," said Rose.

Butternut nudged me in the side with her elbow. A loose sleeve from one of Theresa's sweaters was draped on her head. I put one finger over my mouth. She nodded. It was getting very warm in the closet. I was trying so hard to be quiet that I thought I might forget to breathe.

"We were walking home from the party. I don't know what time it was, but it was late and sort of raining."

"Where did you go?" Asked Rose.

"You just wouldn't have believed that party. You know that Jenny girl, from the chorus? The one with the red hair? She told me that—"

"What happened?" Rose interrupted.

"Oh right, well, we go back toward school, out by the softball diamond. I could see into the windows of Mrs. Dunlop's classroom. I thought I could see those color mobiles that the tard kids make hanging in the windows," she giggled low and thrilling.

"Were you drunk?"

"I wasn't drunk or anything," said Theresa.

"So I mean, what did you do?"

I was beginning to wonder if Rose had forgotten that we were in the closet. I didn't know if I wanted to hear more, but I couldn't make myself leave.

"Do you suppose someone will find my underwear and stuff, and they'll post it on the lost and found board like lost mittens?"

"Everything?"

"Enough. I mean, enough to count."

"And?"

"I don't know. It was funny."

"Theresa," asked Rose, "it was Winston, wasn't it. You were out there with Winston, right?"

"I can't tell you," she said.

"Did he make you promise not to?"

"No, I made him promise, but Ricey, I did it for you."

"For me?"

"Not to ruin it for you." She rolled onto her back and sat up next to Rose. "For you," she said tugging on a strand of Rose's hair. "I was thinking about how I wouldn't want to ruin it when it's your turn. Because we share everything, we have to— clothes, books, boys, beds. There wasn't even a bed," she said.

"You're sick," said Rose.

"I'm hungry is what I am."

Theresa opened the drawer of her nightstand and pulled out a bag of M&M's.

"And who are you?" She asked in a stage whisper as she started down at the candy in her hand.

"Was it Winston?" Rose asked again.

Theresa ignored her. "I'm the sun and I'm the moon. I'm the sleeping and the waking."

"Was it," Rose paused as if she hated having to ask, "was it Aaron?"

"You know, for a while it was so thrilling. It was like I was really talking to the sun and the moon and all that garbage. I didn't have to think even because the words were written out. I thought I would just float away."

"Didn't it hurt?"

"Hurt?" She poured another handful of candy. "You thought I meant *that?* I mean the play and the costumes, all those colored lights. Do you even know what its like not to be real? Can you imagine? The other thing was alright, but not, but nothing like the play." She munched on the candy.

It was quiet, and I strained to hear them whispering. Butternut, who had been anxiously shifting her weight, standing on one leg and then the other, suddenly lost her balance, tipped over and fell right out of the closet. The door swung open wide.

"What a low-down dirty trick," cried Theresa. "Get the hell out of here you spies." She grabbed us each hard by the arm, shoved us into the hallway and slammed the door hard behind us. I was afraid that my mother would wake up. Butternut put her ear up against the door and tried to listen some more but I pulled her away.

"Jeez," said Butternut as we crawled under the covers of my bed. "Did you see her? I mean did you see how she looked? She looked positively debauched."

"Look," I said sitting up in bed. "You know just because you know what a word means doesn't mean you can use it any way you want. You have to use it like the dictionary says. You can't just go saying 'debauched this' and 'debauched that' whenever you want. Don't you understand that? It's not like it's your own personal word."

Before she could answer I turned on my side away from her in the dark.

Butternut woke early the next morning and clattered around my room trying to wake me, but I pretended to be asleep. I don't know what time it was when she left, but I finally got up around noon and went downstairs. I heard a car honking in the driveway. Theresa was in the kitchen standing on a chair reaching for a jar of peanut butter on a high shelf.

"Are you hungry?" she asked ignoring the noise outside.

"No," I said.

"Are you sure? Do you want half a sandwich or something?" I knew it was Winston outside.

"Can I go talk to him?" I asked.

"Be my guest," she said popping two pieces of bread into the toaster. "But make sure you get rid of him."

Winston was standing half in and half out of his car. The front door was open and he leaned on one knee on the front seat while hitting the horn over and over. He didn't come up to the house or call her name. He stopped when he saw me come out and stared at me as though he had never seen me before.

"What do you want?" he asked harshly. His voice was thin and breathless. He didn't wait for an answer. "She's not coming out is she? And you think the joke is on me? That's what you think, don't you?" He was shaking now and smacked both palms on the roof of his car. He suddenly turned around toward me and leaned down so that his face was right in mine. He was white pale and I had never noticed that his eyes were blue. I didn't know a lot of things about Winston, like where he lived and where he put his drab clothes at night. He leaned into my face and grabbed me by the shoulders.

"The joke's on you. What do you think about that, little girl? Do you see what you have to look forward to? You get to grow up like her. You get to look like her and sound like her and be like her. I had a choice, but you don't. You have nothing." He pushed me away. "I bet you just can't wait," he said. He turned and got back in his car. I just stood there shocked, and all I could see were his ankles. They were frail and thin. They were the saddest part about him.

"Hey," said Theresa, "will you get me a glass of milk?"

She was eating her sandwich. When she finished she put bread in the toaster for another and grinned at me like the conspirators we were.

"You know, for what it's worth, I think we've seen the last of Winston H. Delacourt. I hope that he learned something," she said and held a handful of her hair up to the bright spring light, studying it for split ends.

Butternut called me on the phone that afternoon. "Hello? Hello?" she repeated questioningly into the receiver.

"What?" I asked.

"Aaron is over here. He and Ricey are shooting baskets in the driveway. They're acting the same as always. Like nothing happened. It couldn't have been Aaron. It had to be Winston."

"No," I admitted to her even though I didn't want to. "He was here. It wasn't him."

"Oh," said Butternut in a flat, confused way. "But it had to be some—"

"Forget it," I said. "Forget you heard anything about it."

As I was about to hang up I heard her singing at the other end of the line, "The worms crawl in, the worms crawl out, they eeeaaattt your guts and spit them out. The worms—"

Theresa moved away right after she graduated from high school. I always knew our world was too small for her. My mother and Ted got married this past summer. They invited Theresa, but she didn't show up. Maybe she never got the invitation, or it went to the wrong address. I asked my mother to invite Winston too, but she said they had to keep the list to immediate family; she said he was probably living in Paris, France by now. Paris, I've never been there, but I can imagine that it would be a good place for Winston. I still wonder a lot about him, not just where is he and what's he doing, but was he right. I still wonder if I will end up just like Theresa.

It wasn't a big wedding, but the bride wore white and there were flowers everywhere. My mother got drunk and danced all night until even the band was too tired to go on. Ted gave me a piece of wedding cake wrapped in a linen napkin and shouted over the music, "sleep with this under your pillow. You'll dream of the man you're going to marry." But I ate it in the car on the way home.

When I tell people who don't know already, they can't believe that Theresa Boughton is my sister. They think that if you have a sister who is in the movies you shouldn't live in a place like Seven Rivers. She sends me postcards of palm trees and cowboys. Just today I saw her picture in a magazine. She's stretched out on her hip on a striped beach towel wearing a bikini. Nearby there are pails, shovels, an inflatable starfish float, somebody's perfect blonde baby in swim trunks. It looks like the summers we spent together on Lake Michigan as children. Theresa smiles shielding her eyes from the sun. She has long since cut her hair.

Pearl

MORNING, PERCALE SHEETS, LIGHTBULB SUN, Act III, scene i, the hospital corners of their wedding-bedded bliss just abandoned, I follow the sound of their hushed voices. Hush, of course, has nothing to do with their tones. It gives the scene a more ominous atmosphere, implies secrets, poetry, and the thrilling repeat reference to my mother's second-best wedding bed. In truth, they loudly wake in the morning, talking, laughing, listening to radio call-in shows, swapping jokes about how many Martin Hamlins would it take to. I am the hushed one. I navigate steps, clip corners, cling to walls, and always still find myself face-to-face with the face of the king who is not in his counting house, but basking in the bright light of his kitchen where pots and pans gleam suspended from racks; painted Italian tile, formica, stainless steel, lowfat recipes, testimonials from the healed in the form of wish-you-were-here postcards magneted to the fridge door. Judith and Martin are at home in their kitchen among their kin and cutlery and coffee. I enter stage right.

"Pearl," says Martin Hamlin. "Why don't you come with us to the gym?"

This is the scene into which I step. My host, Moses Hamlin, in a designer sweatsuit, jogging in place, monitors the rate of his inexhaustible heart on a device strapped to his wrist. My mother drinks Evian from a clear plastic bottle. In secret she has begun to wash her hair in bottled water; but this does not affect the scene, the moment, the hour, or the morning which was in fact like so many others. Her blue leotard matches exactly her eyes. This will not be a problem, I hope, for the wardrobe department. I see the tableau vivant, the slice of life, the marital blister, the days and nights of something I am afraid to acknowledge let alone *understand,* strike that, write instead, *endorse,* like a check, or *autograph* like a book, *sign* like a letter, *stamp* a passport. I exit, stage right, walking backward like a crab scuttling, cute, but suspicious. The audience explodes with laughter.

I wait in silence at the top of the stairs.

"If she had any friends," he says. "I would say she was running with the wrong crowd."

Pause.

"But she doesn't have any friends," he says.

"Give it time," sighs my mother. "This is all new to her."

"Yes, of course," he continues. "It's a period of adjustment, but we have to be careful not to set a precedent, not to allow her to believe that antisocial behavior is acceptable."

"Do you remember being fifteen?"

"Of course," he laughs. "I—"

"—Remember everything!" They recite in unison.

"Perhaps we should—" he says.

The sound of rubber-soled shoes on the tile. A zipping gym bag. The faucet on and then off.

"Where are my ankle weights?" My mother asks.

I stand in the shadows out of the bright morning light. I press myself against the wall, keep an ear to the air.

"Ask her again," he says. "Exercise is the best way to work out aggression."

"Who said anything about aggression?"

"It's obvious," he says. "If you know the signs."

"Like what?"

"Feelings of rage, aggression, guilt, and jealousy are consuming her. My God," he says. "Just look at her. She looks like the walking dead."

I can hear nothing else because the man who comes in three days a week to clean the carpets and buff the wood floors starts in with his industrial strength vacuum. It drowns out their voices. I see from my window moments later their car, a new red BMW speed out and down the winding stone drive. The man works on the floors all morning and when he leaves I miss him.

I lost my sense of time when I moved into that house. I couldn't find any clocks. Verbs refused to match me as a subject. I might cry at the sight of the letters "ed" whether tacked on a verb or simply used as a first name. I had nothing in the past to mourn and yet I could not stop wearing black. It was disappearing. The past disappeared. Here's a good one: the dreidel of time tipped in its spin to land on niente. Nothing. The absence of. The clocks I found all rang different times, chimed the hours of far-off time zones in which Martin Hamlin had people he needed to contact. One night my wristwatch fell into the bathtub and stopped. I did however gain a sense of timing. The punchline is obvious: One, but only if the lightbulb really wants to be changed. See previous page for joke.

My mother gave me a notepad on which I was supposed to write down plans for decorating my room. My bed was narrow. My sheets were white. The sky was the limit. She said this was my chance (and when would a girl get another chance like this?) to have my dream room. It would be just like living in the Barbie townhouse where all the furniture was pink plastic or winning the *Tiger Beat* teen crash pad competition. Mail us a photograph of your room, enter to win a totally paid for room makeover. Second prize a date with a hunky teen heart-throb in worn Levis and torn T-shirt snarling at the camera. The paper was blank. I wrote at the top of the pad: calendar, because I wanted to be able to keep track of the days and I wasn't about to trust a clock. The hands moved too quickly too often. This was early June. Or so the clockmakers would have us believe.

I did not consider, even at this time, the possibility that my plans to spend July with my father were in jeopardy. It was all that I looked forward to, the one fixed point in the unendurable maze of days, hours measured out against the accurate time grid of *TV Guide*. Surely this new marriage was a contract between my mother and her Martin; it would not affect my visit with my father. After all, hadn't Anthony been more than polite about the wedding? Was not my mother, herself, Judy the judgmental, touched by his wedding gift: a tree planted in honor of the connubial couple in the Ben Gurion National Forest in Israel? And Tony, absented, politely, discreetly, he did not, I think, haunt my mother, but only me, the inheritor of his fears, his late-night afflictions, his paranoid dreams. I wrote on the notepad: *1. crack the code, 2. hide the letters, 3. scale the walls.*

Let me tell you, I never really went over the edge the way my mother later and my stepfather at the time both insisted I did. I liked the idea that they thought I was bonkers. I just liked saying the word *bonkers*. So maybe I played it up for them, but the thing is, maybe I didn't. I was mean-spirited and difficult. I moved slowly and avoided bright colors. I was sweet and mild. Sometimes I had grand ideas and complete visions, dreams so vivid they became as real as lies. I suppose nothing in my life made me more aware of myself as a person separate from my mother than that house did. Tell me about your childhood? My mother went out, and she told me about parties, work, bars, men, and all the ladies with their scarves, mascara, tipping high heels, and perfume of aerosol hairspray, she told me, dictated the story, and the world seemed right that way. I never had a dog. The world was glittering outside the walls of our apartment. I was a good girl once. When we lived in Flint I walked to the library, the art museum, ate french fries with chubby girls in the food court of the mall. Walking those shady streets lined with elms, oaks, bittersweet, scrappy pines splinted for safe growth, weepy willows under which in the future, in all futures, I would sell him and he would sell me, marigolds, daffodils, simple city flowers lined my way and I had mobility or was it nobility? Seeing the houses of kids I knew, whispering the secret names my mother and I had given neighborhood residents. There was the Squirrel Lady down the block who every December designed a big red rodent in her front window out of Christmas tree lights; the Cookie Lady handed out Fig Newtons and lemon creams to little boys and girls if only they had the courage to knock on her door and ask; Old man Hillary owned a vacant lot where wild raspberries grew and one summer we found a garter snake and we ran screaming with fear and laughter. Gardener snake, we shrieked, we ran, guarder snake, we fell, I do not know who *we* were exactly, a troop of children playing kick the can, we skinned our knees, drank Hawaiian Punch, and ran, as best as I can recall spring summer winter fall screaming down those streets, ran faster and faster and nobody could catch us. I bought frozen cokes for fifty cents at the 7-11. I read romance books in the adult reading room at the library. I sold Girl

Scout cookies door-to-door-to-door, thin mints, lemon creams, peanut butter smarties, shortbread, pecan dandies and the enigmatic two-tone Hydrox. From house to house in the spring, the snow, the rain. Understand that place means absolutely nothing to me. It is not the place, the home sweet home of it that I want, but the fact of how it was at the exact moment and the nauseating, bitter awful fact that once there was a *we,* a thousand of us, a legion of screaming children armed with cans, bottles, slurpees, mint wafers, Fritos, sack lunches, merit badges, plastic bats, squirt guns, Bubble Yum laced with spider eggs, silly string, mumps, and worse and better, and I have absolutely no recollection of one grimy freckled face out of this teaming horde of us. I cannot not, of course, even be sure that I was a member of this barefoot, tennis shoe, salty-fingered militia. I was small. There was a world. It surrounded me. I fought the good fight. I adored sugar, television, and kitty cats. I was, as you can see, a good girl.

The new house trapped me. I longed for the old ways, and there weren't even any old ways to long for. I knew only what I did not want, and so began to draw the space around myself, to create the blank, rather than fill it in. We were miles from the nearest convenience store and farther from a library or movie theater. And this is where it always happened in the horror movies—out here where no one could hear you scream for help. I could not think at the time of places outside those walls as anything but destinations of escape. Was this an *edge* of sorts? And did I tip and totter? I admit begrudgingly I lost a certain valuable sense of spatial relations. I was prone to tripping over furniture, the tasseled ends of Oriental rugs, my own pale feet; I proved to be a poor spy indeed, my clumsy footfalls, teetering, step by step, preceded my appearance ghostly in every room I intended to haunt.

Piece by piece my mother and Martin Hamlin were filling the house. There were floor lamps, sectional sofas, glass-topped tables and slingback chairs. They chose black leather furniture with hints of red, and white accessories for accent. Rooms bustled with chrome and industrial cleanliness. One day I found my mother standing in the spacious living room packed full of lemony leathery silvery chairs, tables, bricker-denicknacks. She looked lost. She looked like she had seen an invisible ghost. The walls, she said. The walls.

They ordered gilt-framed reproductions of their favorite paintings from an art dealer in Birmingham. They brought home catalogs, oohed and ahhed as though they were the first to see the impressionists in some salon in Paris. But it was more than the art itself that excited them; it was their aesthetic complicity. It won them over anew to each other. They marveled deliriously at the similarity of their taste. Was this what love was, not sex, not desire, but endless shopping for pictures that matched the lies, memories, and dreams in your head and hoping someone else would dream these same pictures? To the stark white walls of Elsinore came the impressionists, the fauves, the postimpressionists, and a smattering of tasteful cubists. And it wasn't that I didn't like the paintings, it was that I began to think of myself as part of the collection, those paintings, those nudes with blooming fruity breasts, those dolls that came alive the moment you turned away; we were the night gallery, the hopeless prisoners who sent out letters in bottles.

The pictures, instead of cheering up the ominous atmosphere, served to add a weird distorted quality to the rooms. At night after the king and queen went to bed I followed the bright spots of color from room to room, a blue Chagall bridegroom flying in the dining room, red-orange Cezanne apples in the kitchen over the much longed-for six-cup cappuccino machine, the touching maternal solicitude of a Cassatt in my bathroom. This nightly tour led me back to my room which although fairly large seemed suddenly freakishly proportioned, the carnival-esque reflection of a room in a house of mirrors; Van Gogh's *Bedroom at Arles* tilted crazily above my bed. I could have shot out every mirror like Rita Hayworth in *The Lady from Shanghai*—only to find I was aiming at myself all along. I closed my eyes to it.

At the urging of my mother I sent picture postcards to girls back in Flint, but their responses suggested that they had for-gotten me as readily as I had them. There were funny stories of parties and summer jobs, new boyfriends, driver's permits, of exams coming up soon so sorry gotta run I'll write again real soon and then nothing. That world of teen parties, prac-tical jokes in chemistry lab and spitballs shot across the room with lights darkened during eerie films about space dust and the wonders of the Gum Nebula was impossibly far away. I began writing despairing letters to my father. I wrote late at night staring up at the familiar face of a Modigliani girl or Van Gogh's bedroom no less lonely for being so damn bright. Perhaps I wrote to my father because I sensed my wakefulness had been aroused by his ghost in me. I knew how he wandered at night. This, I learned, is the secret to letter writing: to find someone who will read your letters at the same hour you wrote them so that the true sentiment (for words are influenced by our perceptions of the quality of light) will not be miscon-strued. I was certain daylight would ruin my meaning, reduce my despair to sentimental mush.

My father answered my letters, purposefully, I am certain, with cryptic postcards. Anyone who picked up the mail from the box could read his card, but who other than me, his only daughter, could make sense of his clear spidery print on the back of a tiny replica of Michaelangelo's *Pieta?* "As in all generations, men experience themselves as lost and cry out in anguish for restoration. XOXO, Anthony (father)." He did that, you know, really put *father* in parentheses. His careful paranoia made sense to me; he was just being practical and thorough. He probably thought Anthony was a common enough name and that maybe I knew someone else named Anthony. It made complete sense to me. Only to my father did I reveal my secret name for the house. Wasn't I just as trapped with my mother and stepfather as Hamlet had been? And who could say, hidden behind those walls, whether Hamlet was mad or not? Who could say it wasn't just the time of the month, the pollen count, his thwarted desire, something in his genes, a new pair of boots that pinched his toes, his blood; who could say whether he was mad all the time or only when he ran out of his medication?

The postcards from my father frustrated my mother. She had promised after the wedding when she received the card and the tree certificate that she bore Anthony Christomo no grudge. She said perhaps it had all been for the best in the end and that fate was not just one moment, that moment of balloons, confetti, and spilled champagne when she found Martin Hamlin, but all the moments, good and bad, leading up to it. And maybe, she actually mused, if she hadn't married Anthony Christomo when she did she never would have met Martin Hamlin years later. She tolerated the postcards although she found them leaning toward some subversive agenda she was certain Anthony must bear against Martin

Hamlin. She also said that I didn't wash my hair nearly as frequently as I should.

It was the letter I received that finally infuriated her. She could at least sneak reads of the postcards and understand their cryptic nature if not the exact meaning of the messages themselves. The letter was another matter. It was sealed shut. It promised secrets, words, messages meant, she was sure, to turn me against her. She asked if she could read it and said that no matter what she had said about him in the past, she had never denied what an interesting writer Anthony was, how his style was so "old-fashioned," so "haunting" and that Martin Hamlin was awakening in her a true appreciation for what one could do with words and language, how sentences fit together like keys in gloves or locks in hands and clocks ticked all the time. She babbled on cheerfully and in the middle of the stream of words extended her hand to me, there in the foyer, as I held the letter fresh from the mailman and unopened. When I refused to let her break the seal she called me sneaky and secretive and even intimated that someone might have switched babies on her at the hospital. The letter was five pages typed single-spaced. There were coffee stains on the edges of pages two and three, and a mustard thumbprint on page four. I don't know if my mother went so far as to actually search my room for the letter, but I hid it daily in a new place and when I left the room I carried the letter with me folded small and hidden in the pages of a book.

It was in this manner, tucked away in a sunny corner of the bookless library that Martin Hamlin found me one afternoon. I had chosen the library because neither of them ever entered that room.

"Well, here you are," said Martin Hamlin.

I secreted my letter away into the pages of my Regency Romance.

"I've been so busy lately," he said with rich apology. "Have I been neglecting my paternal obligations?"

I searched his face for traces of sarcasm and found none.

"It's funny how time slips away when there is so much to do, so much that is so pleasant."

I was silent.

"I've been researching the new book, planning the next tour series, and then there's the house to furnish and my bride—"

He broke off with a sigh and sat down beside me on the leather sofa.

"How are you Pearl?" He asked in that tone that implied, see, no one else thought to ask you this, no one but me.

"I've been better."

"An odd choice of expression," he said. "Myself, you know, I don't think I have ever been better, or rather, more content."

"I'm sure things will seem more normal," I chose my words carefully, "when I get back into the routine."

"Exactly," he said. "That's the spirit."

"When I get to Chicago," I said. "You know, that's how we do things, Judy and Tony and me. I see him every June."

"I see," he said thoughtfully. He rubbed his beard.

"It's almost July."

"Yes," he said. "It is."

"And I should probably get my ticket."

He continued rubbing his beard. He turned and looked toward the large picture window. A pontoon boat was lazily making its way, cutting a swath through the green water.

"Let me tell you something my grandfather once said to me. I was a child and he was an old man. He said, 'Marty, reserving judgments is a matter of infinite hope.'"

"He said that?"

"He said it in Yiddish, but it's a fairly accurate translation."

"It sounds familiar," I said.

"All wise sayings sound familiar. It's proof of their time-tested truth. He told me not everyone had the advantages that I had. We didn't have a lot of money, but we had a good family, a proud name, and strong intellects among us, all scholars and teachers."

"I thought you said your family name was lost?"

"What?" he said. "No, it was only mistranslated on the papers. Later we restored it and adopted the original. Hamlin, it was the name of my grandfather's village in Austria."

"I must have been confused."

He nodded. "Perhaps," he said. "But my point is, this is your home, and we love you, your mother and I. We want the best for you. And we believe it would be a good thing if you postponed the visit, just briefly, and if we all agree to talk more to each other."

"Talk?"

"About what you think and want for your future. Don't you ever just want to open up and tell someone how you feel?"

"No."

"Pearl," he coaxed. "That's not true. We both know about that letter you've been carrying around for days. It's not real. It's an illusion, only a symbol of communication. It's not real. With me, sitting here, you can discuss everything, anything, in person."

"How can you say it's not real?" I asked.

"Letters are constructions," he wooed me. The sun streamed in. "When we speak together like this, two living beings, only then is there true dialogue."

"Just the same," I said, "I promised my father."

"Make a promise to me," he said. "Simply that you will consider my offer and what it means."

"Which is?"

"Think of me as your father. Stay here with us."

"Can I ask you a question. I mean, since we are dialoguing and all?"

"Of course," he said. "Anything."

"This should be your honeymoon. Why do you want me around?"

"Such low self-esteem," he chucked. "Such poor self-image."

"Really," I insisted.

"Maybe some day we can help each other."

"How?"

He smiled, wide, sagacious, sweet. "Who can predict the future? For now it would be more than enough if we just made a pact to do more of this, just talk together, honestly."

"You really like talking to me?" I said. "You like hearing what I have to say? You know that really boosts my sense of self-worth. Martin, I think you've healed me."

He laughed. "What a funny little mind you have."

"Is it more funny or more little?"

"Pearl," he said. "It's good to see you venting your hostility. You're a clever girl. I never thought anything less of you. You must realize that something isn't right? You yourself said that you weren't doing well."

"No, I said that I have been better."

"There is no need to remind me of what you said."

I heard the distant *whirr* of the floor waxer. I opened my book in hopes Martin would take the hint and leave me alone, but instead the letter fluttered out and we both stared at it like a strange bird resting white and injured on the oriental rug.

"Here," he said. He reached down, picked up the envelope, held it delicately by an edge and extended it toward me. "I believe this is yours."

I took it from him.

"You see," he said. "You can trust me. I don't want to read your letter. I don't want to take anything that isn't mine."

"Then what do you want?"

"I want you to learn what being a family is about. I want you to let me read the letter if I ask. I want what is mine to be yours and what is yours," he paused, reached into his vest, found his gold chain and studied the face of his watch before snapping the lid fast, "to be mine."

I held the letter. He smiled.

"But now, time has, proverbially, sailed away. I have to meet your mother. We have an appointment," he raised his eyebrows charmed at his own humor, "to meet a man about some drapes."

He left me and the sun passed briefly behind a cloud. I was certain it would not return, but only moments later when I looked out the window I saw children playing on the boats and splashing in the water. The sun had returned immediately.

The letter was the last thing my mother and stepfather needed to be worried about. It offered no escape plans, parental kidnapping plots, poison recipes, or promises to steal me across state lines while my unsuspecting guardians were color coordinating their outfits. His letter was an essay on the art of human endurance. He wrote about how the Conversos during the Spanish Inquisition had to practice their religion in secret and that just because we are now in the twentieth century, we should not think we are immune to this kind of spiritual censorship. I read the letter looking for clues; surely, he must have meant this to somehow apply to my situation. Part of it I can quote from memory: "[B]ecause the threat of punishment (physically) is diminished, the incentive to hold fast to one's beliefs is (a remarkable foible of human nature) also diminished. It is far more easy to forsake one's beliefs through lack of pressure (and, in fact, excess leisure) than the extreme duress of coercion." I am not sure exactly what these words on faith and moral belief had to do with my happiness; it seemed like a lofty comparison, but it also made me feel, each time I read the letter, like it was my personal duty to be unhappy for the sake of history, for the sake of all the unhappy ones who had gone before me, the Conversos, the prisoners, for Hamlet himself, trapped in Els-inore, who couldn't tell a hawk from a handsaw.

The letter arrived at the end of June. I counted off the days until July on the blocky squares of the calendar my mother had bought me. The theme of the calendar was "Fun Facts." There were pictures and collage style photographs of lizards, giant paper clips, *Guinness Book* record holders, a couple engaged in the world's longest kiss, a dog smartly wearing a man's hat and smoking a cigar, a little girl with waves of static electricity making her pigtails stand on end. For each day there was a "fun fact," a trivial absurdity which oddly had nothing to do with the particular day to which it was attached. June 22, *There are four chambers in the human heart.* June 23, *Peppermint was the first Life Saver flavor.* June 24, *Mark Twain was the first novelist to present a typed manuscript to his publisher.* June 25, *All the Great Lakes flow into Lake Ontario.*

She bought me the calendar, a desk and matching chair, bottles of oils, lotions, almond talc, witch hazel, lemon oatmeal shampoo, and facial mud. When she returned from shopping, when she came into my room without knocking and dropped her packages breathlessly on the floor, it was so like the past that for a moment I forgot about his presence and that he had paid for it all. I sat with her and smelled the talc and powders and let her dab cinnamon oil on my wrists. She bought me a radio that a salesman had assured her would pick up stations as far away as St. Louis and New York City. She bought me a stack of popular magazines, summer issues full of photo layouts, girls in bikinis, beach balls and frisbees whizzing through the air, sunscreen ads, tips on how to lighten hair and free samples of coconut-scented tanning lotion. We'll take a trip to the beach, she said, just like we used to and we'll pack some sandwiches and fruit and spend the a day at Bluebell Beach and work on our tans.

Some days were like that; my mother was bright and attentive, full of ideas and plans. Other days I heard her voice coming at me from around corners. She was scolding the floor guy, *Ahmed, please, did you really think I wouldn't notice these scuff marks? What the hell do you think we pay you for?* This was the woman I hid from and spied on and listened to, my ear always at the wall. I heard them call each other endearing names and talk upholstery, maids, lactose intolerance, about his blood pressure and her hair color, her nails and his creamy skin. I never heard what I was waiting for; my travel plans and the bus, train, or plane ticket I longed for. All the things they gave me, the gifts, the trinkets, the clothes, the ridiculous factoid calendar (June 26, *Don Larson pitched a perfect game for the New York Yankees in the 1956 World Series)*, the white writing desk, the jogging suit, all this accumulation of junk when so much had been cast off just to get us into this house, and they couldn't or wouldn't give me the one thing I needed. They gave and smiled and smiled. They said, go out, have fun, meet people your own age. They said, honey, there are no locks on the doors to our hearts, you are free to come and go, get some sun, see a film, dye your hair, eat onion rings at the mall food court like you used to with Mary Sue and her little sister. They said words. There were so many words and you could smile and say them one after the other. They swore they knew all about me. No locks. Back and forth, the doors to their ample and many-chambered hearts swung wide like a western bar at high noon. How did one go about getting a ticket, setting forth, not taking a pleasure trip but leaving a life behind. How did one begin the journey away from Elsinore, a prison of one's own fears, nighttime sounds and paranoid delusions, the dreams, the creaking floors, the past. It was like the moment in the movies when the police commissioner calls and says to the baby-sitter, get out of the house. We have traced the call and it's coming from inside the house.

It occurred to me that the only way for me to get my ticket, my passport out, was to play along with their game, abide by their rules; I would glow with self-esteem, shop with abandon, shine with exfoliation, eat with healthy appetite and converse with blank-faced sincerity. Play the play. I woke the morning of June 27 (June 27, *King Camp Gilette invented the safety razor*), washed my hair with lemon shampoo and conditioned with Nile basin mud that promised health, gloss, and sincerity. I passed over the outfit I had worn for two weeks straight (black, black, black) for an outfit my mother had picked out (light blue denim miniskirt, white T-shirt with satin violets sewn to the collar). Speak the speech, trippingly off your tongue.

"You're up early this morning," said Martin Hamlin good naturedly over the top of his *New York Times*.

I sat across from him at the kitchen table.

"Do you want a grapefruit?" He asked.

I sensed he was testing me. I felt my resolve crumbling already. I fingered the itchy violet flowers at my neck. Was it good or bad to want a grapefruit? Did it symbolize moral decay, or hedonistic temptation? Was a grapefruit safe from spurious or biblical connotations?

"Yes, please," I said. "Grapefruit. By all means."

"Louise, one grapefruit for the lady," he said.

There was apparently a maid named Louise in the kitchen. I had never seen her before. She set a halved grapefruit dotted with a cherry on a plate in front of me.

"Thank you Louise," said Martin Hamlin.

"Thank you Louise," I echoed.

She nodded. She had light brown hair pulled back in one thick barrette and was pretty in a strapping and sanitary way. It occurred to me that she was sleeping with the gardener, but then I wasn't sure if we had a gardener so maybe it was the floor cleaner man whom she met on the sly in one of the spacious guest bedrooms.

"We're having some people over tonight," said Martin Hamlin.

"I'll try to stay out of the way," I said.

He laughed the way old men laugh at small trained dogs who dance upright. I thought he was going to pinch my cheek.

"Pearl, you're invited. You may actually happen to enjoy it. Your mother and I have joined a book club." He set down his newspaper, folded the section neatly in half and then over again before pushing it aside. "You used to speak so highly of intellectual pursuits."

I dug my spoon into the grapefruit and nodded vigorously.

"What are you reading? Or, I mean, discussing?" I asked.

My mother came in wearing a slim black dress. Her legs were bare and tan, silver bracelets on her wrists jangled.

"Good morning Louise," she said. "Just coffee for me today."

I saw her eyes travel quickly over the girl taking in her thick calves and arms which strained the sleeves of her plain blouse.

My mother's gaze rested briefly on Louise's large shapeless chest before she looked away and smiled at her husband.

"Just coffee?" he asked. "You should eat a little something."

"You can't down biscuits and gravy and still get into a dress like this," she said smoothing the dress over her hips as she sat down with us.

"No argument here," he said.

"Now look at this," my mother said propping her elbows on the table and resting her face in her cupped hands. "The sun is shining, the birds are singing, and my family is all together. This is nice, really nice for a change. So what are you two talking about?" she asked expectantly.

"Henry James," said Martin Hamlin answering, I suppose, both our questions at once.

"Oh, he's wonderful," said my mother in her fascinated hostess voice.

"Our group is reading *The Turn of the Screw,*" said Martin.

"And it was just wonderful," repeated my mother taking her mug of decaf from Louise with an acknowledging nod. "Although I've heard it loses a lot in translation."

I looked at Martin Hamlin. He wore his magician's grin. The ear hears only what the mind wants to. He rose from his chair and kissed my mother on the cheek. My mother reminded him to buy wine for the party. I looked at Louise. Her knife was raised over the cutting board. It came down again and again. She was slicing grapefruit in half. One of the round yellow fruits rolled off the wooden cutting board and onto the tile floor, bounced twice and landed at the feet of Martin Hamlin like a little guillotined head.

"Three strikes and you're out," he called picking up the grapefruit and lobbing it over the table to me.

My mother clasped her hands over her mouth in laughter.

I watched the trajectory of the yellow orb, saw it come slowly toward me and allowed it to hit me in the forehead.

There was no escape. One day. Two days. Three. What would it matter. I think my mother had this idea, part of her grand sense of fate, and idea about the three of us being happy together forever and ever, of making up for lost time. I could explain why my mother wanted me to stay, but I couldn't figure out Martin Hamlin. Maybe it was the challenge of the situation as much as anything else; you know, how he had healed so many and could not heal his own surrogate child, because, you know, he had assured me many times, that was how he thought of me.

July 1 *(Reykjavik, Iceland, is the world's northernmost national capital)*. The sunny bright light hitting the lake, the flowers, the bees, the green grass, the shadow of the gardener in his slouchy fishing hat. At night I wander opening cabinets and doors. The liquor bottles, sealed, stores of food, cans, jars. I hear footsteps. I stand outside their bedroom door. It is July 1. July 2 *(The word "and" appears 46,227 times in the Bible)*. July 3 *(Gibraltar is the only place in Europe where monkeys live free)*. Kids jump off docks. I crack open my window and suddenly there is Martin Hamlin in a linen suit, neat, uncreased, like his skin, and he tells me not to open the windows because it throws the air filtration and air conditioning systems out of whack. What air? I ask. July 4 *(Sydney Poitier was the first black man to win an Oscar)*. I have not seen my stepfather recently. July 5 *(The queen is removed from the deck in Old Maid)*. And he is not here. Louise looks at me over the lettuce she is washing and says, Jesus, you scared me, Pearl, sneaking up on me like that. No, oh, Mr. Hamlin is out of town. Ohio, I think, for a few days. I make my way through the house room by room. There are chairs and sofas, some rooms echo empty with light, I stop in front of pictures on walls in bare rooms. My mother is in her bedroom. She is sitting at her dressing table wearing a sheer silk nightgown full in the sun.

"Pearl," she said, catching my reflection in her mirror and turning, waving me into the room. Her voice sounded bright and familiar. Her tone promised secret confidences.

"What time is it?" I asked sitting behind her on the king-size bed.

"About eleven."

"What day is it?"

"Wednesday," she said. She was daubing powder on her face with a sable brush. She didn't turn around.

"Wednesday," I said. "That's 'Anything Can Happen Day.'"

"You want to talk about it, about the visit, don't you?"

"Haven't you heard the latest," I said. "There isn't going to be any visit."

"Martin and I are planning a trip. We thought we could drive out west, just the three of us. Maybe see those president's heads."

"No," I said. "I'd prefer not to."

"Always stubborn. You don't get that from me."

"What exactly do I get from you, mother?" I asked.

"Look," she said turning around in her chair toward me. "Either your father is some self-centered jerk who for some reason you idolize even though he never calls, who sees you once a year out of his goddamn Catholic guilt—or your father is the man who bought us this house, who has never been anything but kind—" she broke off and turned again to face herself in the mirror.

"Why do you hate him so much?" I asked. "I mean what did he do? Did he cheat on you?"

"No," she said.

"My whole life you've said—"

"Your whole life isn't such a long time."

"My whole life you've hated him. 'That cheap bastard,' 'that Italian bastard'—"

"Okay," she said. Her voice was measured. "Martin says we should talk more, be more open. What do you want to know?"

"Everything."

She smiled. "That's too much," she said.

"How much can you spare? Tell it, tell me what happened."

"I'm not good at this kind of thing," she said. "Rehashing all the old crap."

"Tell me about, I don't know, meeting him."

She turned again from the mirror toward me. "I told you how we met," she said and her voice softened.

"In a class."

"He was teaching this European history class," there were pauses between her words. "I was a senior. It must have been a requirement because it was the only history class I ever took. My girlfriend, Shirl and I, we wrote notes about him. It was just a joke. We were bored, that's all. I ended up doing badly on the midterm."

"On purpose?"

"See," she said. "You do get something from your mother. I guess it might have been on purpose. He was, I don't know, unapproachable. That made him mysterious, not like the boys I knew. He used to sweat all through class standing up there at the podium. I was twenty, and I had never seen anything like it. Right through his shirt. I went to see him in his office. His shirt was soaked right through and he wasn't embarrassed or anything."

"And?"

"Shirl liked him, and I did too. We both did. It was silly—"

"You had a bet didn't you? You had a competition for him, for my father?"

"You make it sound so dramatic. He was, like I said, very foreign, so dark and quiet. He had this way of talking about history, about the world. He was so serious like he knew—" she broke off and gave a forced brittle laugh. "Anyway, to make a short story shorter, I won. Obviously."

"Well marrying him must not have been part of the bet—"

"No," she said. "It wasn't."

"Were you pregnant?"

"It wasn't like that, Pearl," she said. "He wasn't like that. There are things that I can't, that no one can explain. You just have to live through them, that's all."

"You mean love. You're saying that you were in love with him."

"I don't mean that. I mean it just wasn't meant to be. Whatever it was, it doesn't matter now. It was a long time ago."

"What changed your mind?"

"Okay," she said. She inhaled. Her fingers trailed over her makeup tray, the lipsticks, the powders. She seemed to be involuntarily searching for cigarettes, but there were none. Martin Hamlin was helping her kick the habit through hypnotic tapes which played, rewound, and played again nightly while she slept. "Okay. It was sudden. It was all a whim from beginning to end. I just, you know, I changed my mind, like you said."

"I don't understand," I said. "How you can just change your mind about being in love."

"You've seen too many movies," she said. "Stop thinking about it that way, stop thinking about love like it's some magic potion. I stopped thinking about it like that. I had to. It's hard work, and, I don't know, it can just disappear. That's all that happened."

"Things happen—"

"Things don't stop happening," she interrupted. "It wasn't something that I thought about. I know this isn't what you want to hear. You want to hear something big that will explain everything, but it wasn't like that. I wasn't keeping any secrets from you. That's not why I don't talk about it. I don't talk about it because it's the past and the past is crap."

I was silent.

"Look," she said, "I'll tell you what happened. One night I wanted to go out. He didn't want to or we couldn't afford a sitter for you, it was something like that. So he said, Judy, why don't you just go out with Shirley. He knew how much I liked to get out sometimes and see what people were wearing and talking about. So he said, you go out and I'll watch Pearlie. So Shirl and I went out. She still had the hots for him, you know. I had just had a baby and I was fat, but he looked better than he ever had. I'll be the first to admit that—"

She faced herself in the mirror. I watched her like she was an aging screen star giving the performance of her life.

"Nothing happened, if that's what you're thinking. Nothing ever has to happen. Shirl and I, we just went to some bar and I met some guy who was just out of the army and we talked. His name was—Brad, I think, and then Shirl and I left and we went to a party. I met some other guy, Fred or Ted, who can remember anymore? Brad and Fred, that sounds about right. Anyway, Shirl got drunk and passed out. She lost her keys somewhere. I stayed up all night talking to Fred, just talking—"

"But you were married."

"And I stayed out all night, and I didn't even call to let Tony know I was okay. I stayed out all night. You want to call me a bad mother? Fine. A bad wife? A whore? I stayed out all night and when I came home Tony was putting your little jacket on you. He was going to take you to the park."

"What did you say?"

"I told him the truth. I never lied to him. I told him how I stayed out all night talking about stupid things with some stupid guy I didn't even know and that it felt good, really good, to talk about stupid things every once in a while and not always talk about, or, or, listen to him talk about, lecture, about Jesus and death and whatever. And you know what? Anthony, he wasn't even mad. He just said he understood how it was. I guess it was true too. I guess he did understand and that just made things that much worse. I hated him. Okay? Is that what you wanted to hear? It just came over me all of sudden and then, I don't know, there was no turning back. I knew it would never be the same again. I hated him for standing there and being so accepting and understanding. And you were wearing your little pink jacket and this matching hat. He was always right, you know? I wanted him to yell, to break something, to be furious, to call me a whore—"

"I don't understand," I said. "I can't—"

"And you were there the whole time, wearing your jacket, just waiting to go to the park. You didn't cry or anything. You were always such a good baby."

I sat on her unmade bed. I watched her bare bronze shoulders.

"Jesus, Pearlie," she said. "Do you think I'm stupid? I never regretted it, never. It just hit me that I had to make a decision. I didn't want to live that way, just accepting, not fighting or trying to fight or change. That's how he was, is, so, so, passive. If my husband told me he had been out all night with another woman I would have wanted revenge. I would have gone out and found the bitch and killed her."

"You know he never says anything, not one bad word about you."

"He loved me," she said simply. "I just wanted something more."

"Is that why you left him?"

"Not right then. I thought about it, about where I would go, about you. That's when I went and had my cards read for the very first time. Shirl's aunt did it, read our cards and our palms in her living room. She told me that true love would one day come, but I would have to wait a long time for it. That's what Shirl's Aunt Irene said. She said I would marry a man who was a better father than a husband."

"Wasn't he a good husband though? You said that he understood—"

"Don't be so naive," she said. "Honestly, Pearl, sometimes you seem so young for your age. The things a woman wants from a husband are not the same things a child needs from a father."

"That's not what it says in Martin Hamlin's books. He says women try to recreate in marriage their relationship with their own father."

"I love Martin Hamlin," my mother said. "When Irene read my palm and my cards and then turned over my teacup and read my leaves, it was fifteen years before I met him, but it might as well have been a day. I love him, but I'll be the first to admit," she spoke more to herself in the mirror than to me behind her, "he doesn't really know a thing about women. It's not his fault. No man does. Really, how could a man know what it's like?"

I didn't answer.

"I don't regret any of it," she said. "And, in fact, I'm actually glad we're talking about it all, clearing the air. Maybe I should have told you about it all before, maybe Martin is right and we should all be more open with each other. It just seems so long ago, that's all."

She lay her hands across the satin fabric of the dressing table. Fingers spread, she studied them for a moment before picking up a bottle of nail polish and shaking it distractedly.

"There's something else," she said. "As long as we are being open and all. Something on a more positive note—"

"Are you pregnant?"

"No," she said. "Not yet, anyway."

She opened the bottle of polish, pulled out the little brush, and then seemed to think better of it and put it back in the bottle. "I'm finally going through with it," she said.

"It?"

She nodded, eyes brightly emphatic and reached into a bottom drawer of the table. She pulled out a spiral bound book and opened it on the table in front of her. It was just like the kind of book they show you at the beauty salon with all the different hairstyles in it, except this book was all breasts, headless female torsos, neck to waist, with only the size and measurement typed beneath each picture.

"Page 4," she said. "That one, the top right, number 11, I think it is."

I stood and studied the pictures over her shoulder.

"What do you think?" she asked. "Big, but not too, you know, obvious."

"This is drastic," I said. "I don't think you should do it."

"Oh God, Pearl, don't start with me. I've made up my mind. I know what I want."

Beneath the dusting of powder her face deepened in color. She looked in the mirror and said to either herself or me still standing behind her, "This is for me, no matter what you think, I'm not doing this to please him. This one is for me and no one else. This is not for Martin or Anthony. This one thing is for Judy. I've never had anything in my life like this—something—"

"Like what?"

"I don't know, something, something I just *wanted* more than I needed."

"You had Brad and Fred."

"I should have known you would find a way to twist things. You always have to make everything so ugly and mean."

"I'm sorry," I said. "I shouldn't have said that."

"That was a long time ago," she said. "I didn't know what I wanted."

"You wanted a husband."

"I needed a husband. I deserved one."

"You wanted a house. You wanted a maid. All those things you used to talk about wanting when we didn't have them, you have all those things now. You wanted a nice car—"

"Pearl, you don't understand."

"You wanted drapes. You wanted, do you remember? How much you wanted a goddamn set of Faberware pots and a chafing dish. You wanted and you got—" I couldn't go on. I had to go on. "Tell me one goddamn thing, Judy, that you wanted in your life that you haven't gotten."

Her face was tight and strained.

"Don't be like this," she said. "Please, don't do this—"

I couldn't stop myself.

"It's stupid, your whole life, I can't stand it," I said and grabbed at her book.

"No," she screamed and catching me hard by the wrist pulled me next to her in front of the mirror.

"Do you understand," she said lowering her voice. "Do you understand that there would have been easier things in the world than having a daughter like you? Look at yourself."

She pushed me up close to the mirror.

I looked.

"Sometimes I see you and I think it's him. I swear to God, I think I'm seeing a goddamn ghost."

"That's not my fault—"

"I don't give a damn about fault. When I was fifteen I got called stupid names like Minny Mouse or hey, string bean. I've had to work hard with what I've got. And so now I get the chance, finally. I want new breasts. So what? Really, so goddamn what. Does it hurt you? Does it hurt anyone? And if it doesn't, what the hell do you care?"

Why didn't I just give up then? I have to admit there was a certain hard logic to what she said. Why did I care? I should have left the room right then, left her with her book of headless women and the sympathetic eyes of a naked fruity-breasted Gauguin beauty watching from her place over the bed. I knew I would never change my mother's mind.

"Fine," I said. "Get yourself siliconed up, if that makes you happy. Everyone deserves to be happy, right? Sure. But why stop there? When does it stop, Judy? When will getting what you want, what you've always wanted, be enough?"

"You'll learn," she said. "It never stops. You'll see. It just doesn't ever stop."

She covered her face with her hands. I think she was crying.

"You're just like Tony. Hopeless," she said through her hands. "It wasn't easy. You both—the two of you—sucked the life right out of me."

A shadow passed over her, darkened her hands over her face, her bare bronzed shoulders, and for a moment I thought a cloud had covered the sun. Then, of course, I realized that the window was behind her and the shadow of the sun would have been thrown on me, not her, and I turned to see Martin Hamlin standing in the doorway, his jacket off and shirtsleeves rolled. My mother uncovered her face and sobbed with abandon. Her breasts under her thin silk gown nodded sadly in accusal. I pushed past my stepfather and ran from the room.

Thermidor

AFTER THE WAR EVERYONE STARTED DRINKING MORE. Tony, the wine salesman, says "plum wine" holding his empty glass up for a refill. Willy drinks Southern Comfort and Coke, heavy on ice to cut the sticky sweetness. The couple at the end of the bar, he drinks gin and tonic and she, whiskey sours. Me, I drink coffee and wait. I know I am destined for better things. There are still some nights when I am afraid to sleep.

I do not believe the things I hear sometimes. Not just the stories I read in the newspaper, but the things I overhear as I pour their drinks. If all you did was listen to Nate and his girls, you'd think the war had never happened. They never faltered, never stopped ordering those fruit-laced drinks dyed pink with grenadine, garnished with paper umbrellas. Even in this cold weather Nate goes shirtless wearing only a leather bow tie under his white jacket. The girls change every night. While I am totaling up the cash receipts, he calls.

"This is Nate," he says. "Stay open. I'm coming by."

I wait for him. I know the rules. I follow the rules and this is why I am trusted with closing, the cash receipts, with waiting on Nate so long past closing time. Hiroshi, the owner, trusts me because I keep myself to myself. The waitresses return from the dressing room changed out of their kimonos. Jenny and Kana wave good night from the doorway. Tracy sits at a table rubbing her feet, waiting for her boyfriend to come and pick her up. We do what Nate says, maybe because he seems untouched by the world. He never calls me by my name. Ted, he says, or Tom, but usually he just says, get us some drinks.

By the time Nate gets here the regulars have gone home. It makes sense. It's Christmas Eve at the Purple Flower Sushi Bar, turn right on Paris Street, lower level by the parking ramp. It's easy to miss and hard to find unless you know what you are looking for. We forgot about Christmas until the last minute. It was only this afternoon that Seichi, the dishwasher, and I pulled the fake white tree out of the storeroom and watched the girls decorate it with cheap silver bulbs and tinsel. Tracy was laughing. She dropped an ornament and it shattered on the tile floor of the entryway.

There is only one couple left at the bar. Tracy's boyfriend comes in and they sit together at the black lucite bar. I can tell that they feel like members of a secret club, drinking after hours. They order Saporos, and Tracy nudges him with her elbow, reminds him to save the tall silver can for her son. He, the boyfriend, looks at the can. He'd rather have a Pabst. He declines the glass I offer him. Once Tracy stuck her head and then her body, half-dressed out of the changing room and called my name laughing and showed me her new bra, leopard skin, before slamming the door shut behind her. I heard the girls laughing behind the door.

The other couple at the bar is drunk. They make jokes about how empty the place is. Tracy tries to be friendly. She says, "It's Christmas Eve, you know?" Nate comes in with two girls. They both look as damaged and trashy as usual. He treats them like queens and himself a king. The three of them are already drunk. Everyone is drunk. I have stopped believing what I read in the newspapers. Time stops. There is no one left in the world who isn't drunk and it is Christmas Eve. Like I said, like I told the police later when they came around asking questions, that's when he came in.

He is a small old man. I figure it is my fault because I didn't lock the door behind Jenny and Kana. So I let him come in. He sits at the only remaining seat at the small bar. He unwinds his long scarf from his face, dusts the snow from his bald head. Nate is already laughing at him. One of the girls has her paper umbrella stuck behind her ear and she giggles uncertainly, following Nate's lead. The dark couple does not seem to notice.

"A menu," says the old man. He has an English accent.

"The kitchen is closed," I say.

"Soup," he says ignoring what I have told him. "I would like some hot soup and bread. Doesn't that sound lovely? French bread, perhaps? And tea?" He says rubbing his hands together.

I nod.

The tea is easy. Even the soup is not hard to do. We have no bread. We have rice, pots and vats and bags of rice. Akira, the sushi chef, sometimes sits back in the stockroom on a fifty pound bag of rice smoking a cigar waiting for his bookie to call. I figure you can get used to anything if you have to do it long enough. I figure if the war had lasted we all would have gotten used to it. We have no bread, not even a loaf stashed away, hidden among the crates of carrots, onions, leeks, and lemons.

I pour the tea through the filter two maybe three times until the color changes from dirty to deep brown. I have the sudden desire to instead serve the old man ice cream, the bitter green tea ice cream that the girls scoop into martini glasses and douse with Midori liqueur. I don't know. I suppose I thought he seemed sad, old, and alone on Christmas Eve like that.

I ladle the soup out of the vat into a smaller pan and heat in on the stove. Sometimes I do this for Nate when he comes in late, after the cooks have gone home. Nate always asks for whole fat shrimp simmered in his eggflower soup. I get the shrimp out of the freezer and drop them into the pot. It is a far cry from freedom for any of us. Me, I'm destined for better things. How could I have had time to regret anything? I never did have time, not until later, not until now.

No doubt some of you will blame me. I serve him his tea and I say "wait" while I go back to the kitchen for the soup. When I come back he is gone. I feel his loss keenly. I ache for his return. The snow falls and falls. The dark-haired couple at the bar laugh in a frantic drunken way. Floating like a sodden lily in the dregs of his tea bowl is a fifty dollar bill.

"He said, that funny little man, keep the change," says one of Nate's girls. She gives me a quick confused smile. Nate tugs on her sequined sleeve, and she kisses him full and sloppy on the mouth.

I wish I could have given him bread. Maybe that doesn't make sense to any of you. Maybe you don't understand why this writing, why all writing should be kept secret. It had to do with him and me and Nate's girls and how sad they always looked, especially that night as they stumbled out the back door into the snow on their high heels. In the deserted parking lot my car won't start. I walk home alone through the quiet Christmas Eve and find block after block of darkened houses and in the snow lining my path are candles burning in wax paper sacks. In the high wind of the storm some of the bags have tipped over. The candles burn on unattended, small fires making pools of light in the snow. Keep it secret, I whisper aloud, alone. The war is not over. Keep it to yourself.

Pearl

I MADE MY WAY BAREFOOT through the darkness down the stairs to the kitchen. There, sitting in the pearly spotlight, under the dim glow of the track lighting, was Martin Hamlin at the table in his bathrobe eating a bowl of cereal. He was staring out at his lake through the patterned windowpanes. I tried to back out of the room.

"I heard you," he said. "I heard you take each stair one step at a time."

I didn't move.

"Surely you must be hungry," he said. "There is pizza in the refrigerator. Have something and sit down here with me."

He didn't say another word or turn or look at me. He waited by sounds. The opening of the refrigerator door. The brief pause of light. The knife separating the cold pizza into slices. My feet on the tile floor. The plate on the table. Each sound went beyond itself, multiplied, amplified by his patience.

"It is an easy enough thing," he intoned richly, rolling words around on his tongue like chocolate stars. "To say that you don't like something. It is even easy to admit that while you do not like something, you allow that others might. It is far more difficult to turn your understanding inward and question the basis of your fears."

I took a bite of my pizza. Cold cheese and red sauce. Some ancient communion, the blood and body. A symbol could go as far, and then, yes, further than it was forced. The father.

The past. Elsinore. Hawks and handsaws. Springes to catch woodcocks. Here sat the dazzling new king at his prie-dieu. He poured more skim milk into his bowl and stirred the cereal carefully, from sides to center.

"Pearl," he said, "do you know what it is that I am asking when I ask you to stay here with us?"

"What does it matter?" I said. I stared at the lights on the docks shining green in the darkness. "I have no place else to go."

"Your place is here with us," he said. "Stay and learn to be happy."

"People can do that?"

"Of course," he said magnanimously. "Don't you understand what it is that I do? I don't just write words or help people work out their problems, or as some of the grateful say *heal.* I give them something no one else can, the power to change their lives and more importantly, their minds."

"Brainwashing?"

"Since I was a child," he said, "I have been, there is no other way to say it, *blessed.* I have had the talent, an ability to move people to change, the gift, if you will, to bring about compromise."

He was glowing young and ancient, impossibly ageless.

"Have you heard the expression," he raised his cereal spoon aloft for emphasis. It cast a silvery light, suddenly less a piece of flatware than a divining rod. "A card fallen is a card played?"

I shook my head, no.

"It means we don't always have a choice. We work with the hand we are dealt. A misdeal, a fallen card, these are things, years, relationships that we cannot reclaim."

"Your point being—?"

"You won't have again the hand you were dealt as a child."

"Is that what you two think I want?"

"This has nothing to do with your mother. This is between us."

"That's not what I want."

"Oh, it's no use denying it," he lulled me and his voice rose and fell in waves. "We all want some brand of the past. But perhaps you are ready now, now that you know what it is you don't want—"

"Ready for what?"

"To deal, of course."

"How do you do it? I mean, make people compromise?"

"The trick," he said. "is to listen to more than the words. Here what is unspeakable, unspoken."

"You must be a mind reader."

"No, no, simply a word reader. There is in everyone, not only those who come to me, but everyone, an exact level, a fraction of a percent that each person is willing to settle for, to compromise on dreams, desires, even addictions. It has much to do with the interplay of past and present, what one will take today if allowed to pay for it sometime in the future."

"Everyone has a price?" I asked wearily like the jaded movie-goer I was.

"Call it price," he said. "I'm not bothered by that particular cliche. Our wants are not concrete things. We do not know what else to do with them except transfer them into terms we can understand: objects, tokens, specific and measurable amounts of goods that carry redeemable cash value."

In silence together we watched the lights.

"There is something that you want," he said. "And you made your mother cry this afternoon. You made her feel old and ashamed of her own wants. You should have come to me," he said. "If there is something that you want so much we could have discussed it, perhaps worked out an arrangement."

"A compromise?"

"A deal," he said. "You want to see your father."

"Yes," I said, but hesitated.

"How will you persuade me? What will you offer in exchange for your," he smiled, "letters of transit?"

"I don't have anything."

"Deal," he commanded. "What's your truest coin? What's the trump card?"

I didn't know what to answer.

He sighed.

"Why didn't you come to me first?" he asked.

"I went to my mother."

"Your mother," he repeated. "You went to her because, perhaps, you thought you had a better chance of getting what you wanted?"

"Maybe."

"You had her ear? Her confidence?"

"Once," I said. "I did."

"Your mother," he said. "Of course, this is hypothetical, but could you use her? Offer to make me a deal I can't refuse. Could you, is it in your power to turn her against me? Use the cards you have to make a deal with me."

"She's crazy about you."

"Perhaps," he said. "But maybe there are things that you don't know. Or things that I don't know. How young you are," he broke off. He was not a man prone to sudden movements. His tone was modulated and even, but at that moment he stopped with something akin to abrupt sadness. "I am telling you this only for your own good, despite what you may think of me now or come to think of me in the future. You must learn, and to learn, one must one allow oneself to be *taught*."

I remembered the sharp lines of my mother's powdered face. *Martin Hamlin,* she said and faced herself in the mirror, *doesn't know a thing about women.* There was no bride's glow on her face. Martin Hamlin doesn't know. The unmade bed. Other children had called her names. She had grown only to want, an unspecified, endless desire. While he was away on business. Her bare shoulders and the sheer taupe silk of her dressing gown. He stood in the doorway and the sun passed behind a cloud.

"You will never get anywhere in this life if you do not first learn how to bluff."

"To lie?" I asked.

"Lie is too deliberate a word. Let's say, pretend."

"Yes," I said. "I can deal. I think I could turn my mother against you if you don't give me that train ticket."

"That's right," he said. "That's an exchange. But, I don't want to simply barter like savages. We are, after all, reasonable people. Why should I accept the promise of an orange in exchange for an apple, that is, if I prefer apples to oranges."

"What more is there? What more can I give?"

"Let me ask you this," he said. "Why do you think I have so often asked you to stay?"

"So we can be a family, like you said. For my mother."

"This," he said, "has so little to do with your mother."

"Then why?"

"Would you believe me, Pearl, if I said it was because I knew it was exactly what you didn't want? How long would it take, how much would it take—"

"What would I settle for?" I finished.

"Yes," he said. "It's always less than one expects. I see in you someone destined to have a difficult life, an impossible life; that is, unless you can learn—"

"I don't know much about card games."

"There is something more than the cards themselves and how the hand we are dealt falls; it is how we play them."

"You don't understand," I said. "I don't want to know about cards. That's not what I want to learn."

The look of abrupt sadness returned to his face.

"It's too late," he said, "for all of us. Even for you."

"No," I said. I wasn't sure what I was denying, but I know I had to fight against it.

"It begins without one even knowing—"

"And *it* never stops?"

"One could say that, yes, I suppose that is what one could say."

"*It*—?"

"Your mother and I, we are going to take a trip."

"She told me."

"When you made your mother cry today you made her feel old, but more than that. You reminded her—"

"Of my father."

He dismissed that with a wave of his hand. "Of time."

It was only then that I realized what he wanted me to bet. It was all opposites. Oh, Elsinore, had only I known that all your hallways were lined with mirrors, convex, two-way, cracked, cursed, and tinted rosepink, I might have proceeded with more caution. I wouldn't have gone barefoot. I wouldn't have left those trails of bread crumbs. Why hadn't I known what he wanted from me? I was a fool, a child. Why had I believed what he had said? I had only thought in terms of objects, the money, the gold and silver coins he lobbed at us. What he wanted was invisible. He had pushed and prodded with sincere talk, with grapefruit and velvet berets. A birthright is an invisible thing. I knew I would leave that house, and it would not be an easy passage. I would learn these things despite myself: to lie, to bluff, to steal, run as far, as fast as I could. All I knew about cards was that you could make houses out of them until they fell, collapsed in on each other, hearts, spades, clubs, and diamonds. In the movies when you couldn't see your reflection in the mirror it was too late to save yourself, you were already a vampire. A birthright was easily enough traded, because of its apparent lack, for something more real like a slice of pizza, a ticket, a bowl of pottage, a handful of magic beans.

"Here's my offer," I said. "Let me visit my father and I'll stay there with him. I won't come back here. You can take your trip. You can be free of me."

"No," he said. "That won't do. Your mother doesn't think your father is a good influence on you. It would only buy time that would be wasted later. Do you know the one—"

And I realized with dismay and, yes, amazement, that Martin Hamlin was going to tell a joke.

"—about the agnostic dyslexic insomniac?"

I shook my head.

"He was up all night," he paused. He waited. "—trying to prove the existence of a dog."

Nothing about his manner betrayed humor.

"Don't worry," he said. "You will see him. He is, after all, your father. No one can change that. It's in the deal, is it not? You will see him," he said, and reaching into the pocket of his bathrobe, produced a train ticket in its red, white, and blue Amtrak sleeve.

"For how long?"

"The summer," he said.

"And then what?"

"I myself," he said, "attended a boarding school back east. A similar experience may prove beneficial for you."

"Does my mother know about this?"

"It's out of concern for you and your education. You have to think about the future. How strange it is, to see time and time again, children who think of nothing but the present."

"I don't—"

"How I envy you," he said. "How I envy youth and all the things you have to look forward to."

"Will I come back here?"

"Most likely we will take a long trip," he went on. "Your mother has been denied so much in life. It pains me to see how much she has gone without experiencing. She should see something of the world before she has another child and her time is otherwise consumed."

"What if there is no baby?"

"Don't you know," he said, "it's what the fortune-teller pre-dicted. She said that Judith would bear a son."

"Can I ask you one last thing?"

"Of course," he said and pushed the ticket across the table to me. I looked at it. I feared it.

"Why my mother?"

"What?" He was only briefly taken aback then he caught himself in the safety net of his grace and fluidity. "Why do you ask that?"

"You must have known, met, so many women going all over the country the way you do."

He smiled, not at me, not at the lights, but at the specter of the past, the dancing ghosts, fallen cards, the magic lantern shows and naked ladies sawed in half while the crowds held their collective breath in awe.

"It's a fair question," he said.

"Was it like she says? Was it fate?"

I knew he would not tell me the truth. That was part of the game.

"It was," he said, "her face. Her look at that exact moment, the stroke of midnight, I believe, that said there was nothing and no one in the world she wanted more than me."

"It was love," I said. "The look on her face was love. She fell in love with you at first sight."

"Love and fate," he said. "These are not words with which I am comfortable."

I didn't remind him that these were the words that filled the pages of his books, the words that his readers and followers doled out their coins for; this was the exchange he offered them first and foremost, their silver for his words of hope and fate and romance.

"I don't believe I had ever seen a woman with a face like hers. She wore a veritable mask of desire."

"That sounds awful," I said.

"Maybe it was. I didn't say it was otherwise."

The ticket lay untouched between us.

"Did I answer your question?"

"I guess," I said.

"What would you do now if I offered you one last option?"

"I'd listen."

"You understand, now, how it is? What is at stake?"

"Yes," I nodded uncertainly.

"Stay," he said. "Live here as we live. Be my daughter, and I'll give you anything you want. Anything, in exchange for you returning to me the ticket."

I propped my head on my hands. Which cup was the coin under? Now that my exit had been offered to me, now that I could conceive of it as a tangible reality and not a dream, was it half so promising? Was I already growing empty with this dubious success and in need of something a little more to satisfy me? He wanted me to play and it was for this reason alone that he had offered the ticket. There was no kin or kindness to it. He wanted to spark me with the thrill of a small success so that I would bet again for more, taste the suspicious pleasure of a winning hand; but I don't suppose he counted on my timid nature. Maybe he had counted on my having my mother's skill at taking chances, beating odds, risking her coins against the promise of future riches. I knew he would think I was a fool for not just playing it safe, but for not playing at all, not testing him and taking him to task on the outrageous limits of his offer.

There were two options really. There are always two options. One or the other. I could stay with my mother and live as a constant thorn in his side. He would be my teacher, my father, my mentor. I would forsake other fathers and give myself to him to be taught, formed, and fashioned. We would act as though this conversation had never happened and year by brittle year, I would chip away at my mother's resolve, hint at his flaws in secret, stoke her relentless need for more than what she already had. I could grow old doing this to spite him, just to win the game. One day she would want more than he could give her.

And if I left this place? I relinquished my childhood and my mother and turned them both over to him. I might, of course, in the future, be many things to my mother: a girlfriend, a confidant, a sister, a visitor in her house, but never again her child.

"There's nothing," I said. "There isn't anything I want."

"Don't be rash," he said.

"Nothing."

"You are so young—" he began, "and stubborn—"

I started to interrupt him, to tell him again, a third time, how I wanted nothing and nothing could replace my endless empty lack of want. But he did not wait. He continued speaking, and silenced me.

"When I look in the mirror," he said, "I am surprised to see an old man looking back."

Knock, knock. Who's there? Lazarus. Oh, you again?

He rose from the table, put his cereal bowl in the sink and tightening the sash of his robe, said, as he stood in the doorway of the kitchen, "Just remember me when you are far from here, and how I tried to help you. I'm a generous man. I don't forget, but neither am I vengeful." He left the kitchen and I heard his slippered feet all the way up the stairs and down the hallway to the bedroom where my mother lay sleeping.

After he left I stayed in the kitchen and ate another piece of pizza, less out of hunger than a certain emptiness he had awakened inside me. I looked at the ticket. I expected it to disappear in a puff of smoke, but it didn't. I touched it and it was real enough. He was persuasive, that was the odd thing. It wasn't all tricks and twenty-five cent carnival treats. He had a way of drawing out words like *want* and *need* so that it gave you a split second to imagine diamonds and emeralds. He roped words like strings of pearls and coaxed out the truth, not from your words, but from how the birds flying above cast ominous shadows. I knew then that he had been in the kitchen waiting for me. I believe he would have waited all night and perhaps all the following nights until I came to him, until I was ready to deal.

I finished my pizza and washed my plate and his bowl and spoon. When Louise arrived in the morning there would be no sign that we had been there and perhaps that would mean that none of it really happened. I went down to the basement, turned on the big screen TV and watched *Splendor in the Grass* on the channel fifty late movie you know, the original one, with Warren Beatty and Natalie Wood. When the morning news came on I turned off the television, went upstairs and started packing.

Winston

I KEEP THINKING ABOUT THE DEAD GIRL so long in the water that her face when you might have looked at it would be nothing, a bloated fleshless ghost staring back like a mirror to show you, to remind you in all your thoughts and dreams that this is what it comes down to, that we are all nothing. Two weeks gone in the rising waters of the Detroit River and she was found, for virgin crants empty sodden cartons of cigarettes, candy wrappers, and briny filth, her final sweets and devotions.

In my own solitary and dispassionate manner, I too was devoted to her, if you can believe that I am, could ever have been capable of such a monumental selflessness. Oh, Winston, who gave you the leave, the right, to remember her, to call her back from the dead and into this fragrant spring morn? Oh self, out of the dream of her and the reverie of her plaintive, childish confessions and the nightmare of her rotted skin and trailing trampled grave clothes. I knew her and perhaps I loved her, but it is yet too early for me to decide. Give me a few more long and lonely years and I will pitifully salt your shoulder with my tears for her and our lost love which will have been created less by loss than by distance. I waver, I waffle, I loved her; I loved her not, depending on the petals of the particular flower on which I chose to count.

I readily admit that while she was among the living I was engrossed by her; by those awkward knees and jerky elbows so apparent in all her movements. There was something feverishly youthful about her, so irreplaceably graceless that without her here in front of me today, I cannot begin to qualify it. The love I had for her was more the love of a brother for a clumsy little sister, a child whose shoes are forever untied and nose perpetually dripping. I was myself a meager twenty years old at the time, and yet there I was, watching out for her, waiting for her to trip over those laces so that I might swoop down and save her. It was neither a flowery nor romantic love, and it had to do with passion only in as much as I sometimes felt the pressing desire to tuck her away into a lined inner pocket of my voluminous winter coat to keep her warm and safe and out of harm's way.

At this point you may very well begin to wonder what sort of man I am. Not simply is he youngish or elderly, fair or dark, brooding or carefree, but that most important of concerns to the newly acquainted, is he honest? But is he honest, you ponder as you sip your morning tea, is he to be trusted? I respond to you and all who care to listen that each night Prometheus-like I open my bleeding and ulcerous wounds to the vacant apathy of the carrion birds of memory only to awake whole and intact again in the morning. What sort of man does this make me? Humble or proud? Godlike? Idiotic? Cursed? Leave it only to say that I fear the desolate stretch of evening into night, for I have bad dreams.

You may wonder if I gloss over love and dwell on loss because I am not that certain sort of man, ahem, a man of the world. I can lead you on a simple tour of my life now. See, the sheets are clean and the bed made with a spinster's fastidious care. You will find no tubes of lipstick or extra toothbrush tucked away in my bathroom cabinet. I live both alone and cat-less. I can tempt you only with one torn and frayed memory which comes to me like a scene in a film shot in particularly grainy stock. It is the one time Ruth kissed me. When I recall that rapid wet little kiss, I sometimes wonder about the sort of love in which she claimed not to believe.

We sat in one of the deep back booths at work and Ruth held my hand palm up in her own small paw under the pretext of reading my fortune. With one grubby finger she traced a thin trail she called the lifeline. It crosses with the loveline she said pulling my hand closer under her scrutiny, trailing the line with her pinky, bending her head intently down to reveal to me the bare, boyishly grimy nape of her neck until out of nowhere and with a terrific smack she kissed the inside of my wrist with a good deal of tongue and slaver. She raised the moon of her face up to me and giving a riotous yelp of laughter turned and ran as though someone, some other invisible and more childish Winston was following in frenzied pursuit. I stood there in her wake watching her figure as it disappeared with the lilting jingle of a bell out the door of the coffee shop. I did not move.

No one is more harsh on myself than I. Here I set out my true failure for the world to see: I am a man who has a memory of a dead girl I cherish in private because perhaps it is easier to be with the dead than the living. I do not believe that I am alone in my fetish. We all have a dead someone to whose time-faded image we must cling; maybe yours is stashed away in a closet or a photo album, I keep mine in a white business envelope on a clip of grainy paper. Her name is spelled out, the meager, humble, conspicuously unassuming Protestantism of her name, Ruth Barbara Stevens. She is long buried and returned to the dusty ashes of the earth, and yet, I cannot give her over to nature; I cannot forget her.

I am not what you would call a happy man, but as the saying goes, I've seen something of the world in my time. I do not mean this in any crude bacheloric sense, only that for a strange and brief time in my life I believe that I was afforded a keen insight into the workings of the human heart. For the span of months when I knew Ruth, when I knew all the sundry characters to be detailed later, I was possessed of a heightened sensitivity, an exaggerated capacity to love beyond simple lust. In the end I believe I saw and ran in terror from the true brutality of mortal desires.

I am thirty years old; there is time still for all things, to start over, to forget it all, to turn my back on the past and take up a virtuous and decent life with one of the painted career girls with whom I share the elevator at work each morning. There is of course, time yet for everything. I know this because my life now is not a matter of forgetting or even wallowing, but of marking time with the humming precision of an electric clock, losing each minute to gain another hour. I don't care about the hours so much anymore, it's the minutes and the seconds, the tiny things, so much like her, so much like so many of us. The clocks I see in shop windows do not have second hands; perhaps the seconds are too small to matter. Tell me that it isn't true, tell me that the world isn't getting bigger and brighter and all the small dim ones of us left have to cling to the notion of the second hand to keep us going a little longer.

I am small and dim, not substantial enough to be called fallen or failed, and unlike yourself, gentle reader, not protected by the grace of any God, in either theory or belief. You may blame me in the end for not having done enough for her, for not having enough of the insight to which I claim I was privy. But truly, what could I have done? Me? Me, Winston H. Delacourt who never considered failure, because he never considered action until it was too late. Oh, you my judge and jury, call me guilty and I will be newly baptized; how can I separate myself from the rest of the events and the time and the youth and the love which turned to disillusionment not only with women but with the idea, romantic or altruistic, of the human heart?

Ten years plus, ten years gone and with what does one end up? When I was twenty years old I wanted to be a poet. Oh, snicker if you will, make an aside remark about my fancy prose style, but I was a child. I believed in no God, except perhaps myself as a poet, a hawker of endless words who could have created and carried a separate and better universe in a nutshell. I will not let Mnemosyne work her soporific charms forcing me with time and distance into the lie that should make me feel better, the lie that I loved Ruth. If I loved anyone it was not she. At the time the protectiveness I felt for her was mixed only with pity and disgust. I was a poet. I wanted beauty and truth and dreams and a muse like a storybook princess, and oh, you have not long to wait to understand that I had not one of those but two. Two muses, one ragged child, a thousand years ago, awkward teenage blazons, all to come to this, a heap of words on paper that will one day be as yellowed as all our obituaries.

Acquaint yourself with Ann Arbor, Michigan in the bright haze of autumn 1984. Doubtless that bustling college town with its wide tree-lined avenues has changed, not for perhaps better or worse, but simply so that it would not be the Ann Arbor of my story. You might find the places and the streets, but nothing of the life I once knew. Let it be a fiction for you, a place to be found on no road map, a place existing solely in the dark enclaves of my memory. Put everything aside now, put aside your fear of ghosts and pain and dead girls. Imagine only Ann

Arbor, her streets filled with students, her trees red and gold-leaved, her nights windy and cool, full of autumnal promise.

In the fall of my third year of studies I intended nothing more than to continue to lead a simple academic life. To this end and in actuality, this dream, I sublet a studio apartment, a dark attic with a bath and kitchenette in a house on Thayer Street. The rent was 325 dollars a month which was although tremendously reasonable for the going market, an ungodly sum for my generally empty poet's pocket. In the lingering humidity of Indian summer the heat in the attic was nothing short of oppressive, but this did not matter to me. I foresaw a winter of failed radiators, plumbing disasters, gas leaks from the archaic kitchen area; it mattered not. That small squalid flat was my dream, the one luxury I granted myself beyond cigarettes and used paperbacks. Of necessity, but quite readily, I found myself a second job to finance those peaceful hours in my cloistered cell.

The new job was not the sort of work to which I was accustomed, but it was not without a certain romantic charm. Perhaps I would not have been able to stand the drudgery of menial labor had I not still my first job, which I had begun the previous spring. I had diligently worked my way up through the ranks of the graduate library, one year in circulation, one year in rare books, until I was granted the desk position in the papryology collection on the seventh floor. I spent peaceful evenings in that large haunted room, my solitude interrupted only by the scrawling pencil or stifled cough of the occasional scholar who came to study the ancient papyrus housed there. At that time ghosts did not bother me.

I had long been more interested in the literary aspect of religion than the philosophical. I honestly admit that the true import, the laws, articles of faith, and tenets of religion were woefully lost on me. By literary perhaps I mean only the *story;* the Old Testament matriarchs appealed especially to me. I imagined those sunburnt maidens at the well; dark skin and dusty feet ready to comfort any and all travelers who passed through that land of milk and honey. I envisioned their strar͏ ͏ ͏assage and transformation into early Christianity; vov͏ ͏ ͏refusing to be broken, saints like Catherine or ͏ ͏ ͏'e in itself to pledge one's life to a C͏ ͏ ͏:h broken and bloodied nails to ͏ ͏ ͏dulgence was said to be a token of ͏ ͏ ͏nan hair, the finger of a holy man. I ͏ ͏ ͏y notion of faith, so removed from all

I was ͏ ͏ ͏ religious family. Sundays, we attended a brief service at a ͏ ͏ ͏dest Methodist Church, after which we drove in a convoy of other good folk to Bill Knapp's for lunch. It was considered rather vulgar to be too enthusiastic about God, and a reference to Mary prefaced by *virgin* was greeted with icy embarrassment. It is with the utmost chagrin that I recall my family being more ecstatic about the yankee pot roast and mashed potato special than the prospect of salvation. I am sure that somewhere back in the history of the Delacourt clan there is religion and perhaps even fervent zealotry, but by the time my father and his dutiful bride settled down in the suburbs of Detroit their fiery and more spiritual impulses had been tempered to the neatly antiseptic celebration of Christmas with a fake white pine tree hauled out of its box in the basement each year and decorated with gaudy strings of gold lights.

Unfortunately, that small and blissful papryology room had restricted hours and my financial situation warranted drastic measures. I took the job of a dishwasher at a shop on North University Street, a place called Drake's Sandwiches and

Candies. I cannot recall why or even if I applied; there had been no sign in the window. I simply went in one day for a cup of their bitter coffee and when I walked out I had a job paying four dollars and fifty cents an hour, plus the benefit of endless grilled cheese sandwiches and limeades. I had the distinction of the being the only male worker aside from the eighty-four-year-old owner who had hired me and who lived, some said, in the strangely cavernous basement of the shop.

The girls who worked at Drake's shocked me after my serene work in the library. When dealing with the papyrus which was studied under the blue glow of desk lamps, there was a blissful sense of the sacred. To those tartish college girls and vagrant dropouts there was nothing sacred left in the world, least of all femininity. Everything from the deep back booths to the grimy floor of the place was painted olive green, and the girls mimicked that mood. They were alternately depressed and indignant. One girl, Sarah, born without a certain bone in her back was no more than five feet tall and had a large tattoo fashioned after Klimt's *Kiss* which extended from her right shoulder to her sloping lower back. In the changing room she offered to show it to anyone who wanted to see.

I must admit that for a group of girls for whom rudeness was a job qualification, they took me into their ranks with something akin to genuine goodwill. Although I had no need to go in there, they let me, they invited me into that little closet of a changing room. Some girl, some Drakette, as they called themselves, would bum a cigarette from me and we'd go downstairs for a ten-minute break which would stretch into half an hour as she lighted the cigarette and started talking. That's how it started. In that dank room strewn with stockings, hidden bags of candy, and soiled smocks heavy with perfumed sweat, girls began to confide in me about their secret lives.

Consider the secret life if you will. Given the scope and list, sometimes so painfully ridiculous of our own desires and fantasies, the dreams of others should never surprise us. Oh, but how those desperate tales seemed like confessions to me, and how I savored each one like a delicate chocolate star on the tongue of one deprived of sweets. I reveled in the strangely sordid hopes of those young creatures.

In one sense, I wanted only a secret life of my own, that of dim and studious hours in my bare apartment boiling instant coffee and reading myself into better worlds. I had no desire to be a social animal, and yet I found myself mesmerized by the prospect of each ongoing life, the saga of a warm and sentient being, a fragile, wrapped parcel of neuroses and needs. I looked forward each afternoon to being told the results of Sarah's latest argument with her beau and the ordeal of poor Des who had a longtime infatuation with her psychoanalyst.

Drake's, even with its green painted floors freshly mopped and tables wiped with bleach, retained the smoky stench of burnt bacon. Fitfully, I washed when I came home from work. Like a frantic Lady Macbeth I thought the odor would never be scrubbed clean from both my soul and body. Yes, it was more than just the scent, it was what the scent symbolized—a certain moral turpitude, a rottenness to the core of everyone and thing. Terrible guilt was growing inside me; I was a solitary listener, and I did feel pity and yes, my heart bled at the utter domestic tragedy of their feminine yearnings, but somehow I enjoyed even the pain. *Yes, it is horrible,* I would agree with Sarah. *Oh, it sounds as though he has a mother complex himself,* I commiserated with the distraught Desirée as she munched on a chocolate-covered oreo.

You see, I was fairly bookish as a child. I developed my ideas about femininity from novels and embarrassingly enough, old films. The perfect woman in a poem was an elusive and beautiful creature, all the swish of silks and downcast eyes. I was in no sense prepared for Drake's, for being so surrounded by females, for being in close quarters locked in intimate discussions on the nature of love with girls clad in black stockings, their lips painted deep red and unwashed curls perfumed of patchouli.

It is true that while in high school I dated for two weeks a slightly overweight girl from my senior English class. We sat together at lunch, went, I believe, to two movies and visited a crowded science museum to gawk at the chipped remains of a tiny australopithecine female in a lighted case. In the movies she held my hand in her own large and damp one, breaking the grip only to dig into her carton of popcorn. One day we stopped sitting next to each other and our brief affair ended quietly and politely. Sadly, this was the full extent of my experience with women until my twentieth year.

I had indeed the image of the perfect woman in my head, but I had in no way thought about attaining her or even seeking her out. I do not believe that I ever wanted her to be real. She remained to me the stuff of dreams; I sought her in poems. She was, I suppose, if I try to picture her, to create one of those dreamy images on the inner projection screen of the mind's eye, somewhat Victorian, thin to the point of being willowy, even sickly, perhaps consumptive with the strange blooming color of the tubercular. Needless to say, it took me some time to adjust to the style of the contemporary gal, the Drakette, if you will.

Oh, they were pretty in a certain ratty way which just then happened to be fashionable. The deformed Sarah explained it all to me once, avid smoker that she was, endless Winstons she smoked, and laughed—*your name, my brand, our bond.* She had bright red hair which she demonstrated, by pulling out several braided strands, was not real, but hair extensions. Sometimes she wore it piled high in a beehive. She told me nothing was real anymore, that was the beauty of not being beautiful. Des had black hair cut in a Prince Valiant bob. One girl who quit when she began to appear conspicuously pregnant wore white pancake makeup and had the small delicate features of a silent movie star.

Remembering them now I am certain that we were all born in the wrong time and thrown together for a reason. Fate herself placed me there to learn something of a life in which I previously had no interest. They laughingly referred to themselves as *spunk rock chicks*. Sarah said she felt sorry for me because I had lost my childhood. She yawned knowingly, the suburbs will do that to you. My senses exploded, imploded; I noticed now, the nuance and notes of perfume, stockings, precisely clipped bangs, the delicate instep of a well-shaped foot loosed from a pair of combat boots. Oh, and when I was asked brashly by one of those hoydens to massage that heel, those five little aching digits, it was with trembling hands that I accomplished the task.

I listened to their stories with rapt attention and cooed soothing words, while inside I memorized the acts, the phraseology. I savored details and each night I went home and in the solitude of my monk's cell wrote it all down in a rather large beautiful notebook my father had given me. I abandoned poetry and filled pages with my prosaic desires. Some terrible dormant thing had been awakened in me. By day a pale dishwasher serving to carry the trash to the dumpster, by night the guardian of the sacred papers, but in my soul a sick and tormented creature, oh God, a soulless monster. Alone at night I drank bitter coffee while scribbling my torrid notes unsure whether I was asleep or awake, whether I was transcribing nothing more than my own unleashed desires.

I will to this day vehemently deny that this was simply a delayed trait of puberty. No, there was religion to my strange obsessions. The girls with whom I worked merged in a radiant blue light with the women of the Bible; they were all one. I understood this. I cast myself in the role of the confessor and created my own religion along the way. I sought in those slangy bad-mouthed girls some refuge from the present day, some reconciliation between what women seemed to be and what they were. I was afforded a strange and intimate glimpse into their feminine hearts. And yet they never faltered or held back; they did not understand or seem to realize that I was the enemy. I was not one of their own.

When Aaron Saltmarsh sat next to me in my introductory Hebrew class, I knew that he was just the sort of specimen about whom the girls told stories. Aaron Saltmarsh sat down next to me and eyed me suspiciously. There were twelve students in a room which could easily hold twice as many. I considered moving. I did not move.

"Shalom," he said to me.

I looked at him for the first time. His long brown hair was pulled back into a ponytail. His features must have endured generations of the Diaspora, so that sitting next to me in the modern language building he looked as Jacob must have when he stole the birthright from his brother.

"Shalom, I said 'sha-lom,'" he said making a peace symbol with the fingers of his right hand. "You must be one of them," he added.

"One of whom?" I asked. Of course, I knew what he meant. He meant that I wasn't one of the chosen people, that my Methodist upbringing was obvious. I longed to suddenly lie to him, to tell him that I had a Jewish great-grandparent, that there was something in me that was like him. He was staring at me with narrowed eyes. A girl sat down on the other side of me. He leaned over me to ask her, "Is your name Stacey?" She had tell-tale blonde hair dark at the roots. She giggled and said, "Nah, you must mean my roommate."

"Excuse me," I said. "What did you mean?"

"I just meant," he said now leaning back past me and winking at the girl, "that people might wonder about your motives for taking this class."

"I'm studying classical languages," I told him archly.

"Right," said Aaron.

The girl tapped me on the shoulder shyly. "Look, he doesn't mean anything by it. It's just that some people take certain classes to meet certain . . ." she paused and continued in a tactfully measured tone, "kinds of people, girl people of a certain persuasion."

"Do you dig Jewish chicks or what?" asked Aaron.

"He studies languages, he told you that about a zillion times already," the girl interceded for me.

"Because here is one who seems to groove on you."

The girl rolled her eyes in Aaron's direction. "Anyway, my name isn't Stacey. It's Robin, and if you need any help with Hebrew I'd be glad to because—"

"Hey Robin," Aaron interrupted and raised his hand midway to his chest, "when the hand goes up, the mouth goes shut."

Robin blushed with embarrassment and stared down at a blank page in her open notebook.

I turned to Aaron and asked softly, "Is that a—a Jewish thing?" "Sort of," he said with a shrug.

Aaron Saltmarsh sat beside me every day for two weeks without again deigning to speak to me. Often I studied him out of the corner of my eye. I imagined the stories he could tell, the words which could be coaxed out of him. He was tall and athletic, probably six feet tall with broad shoulders and a thick neck. He might have been a failed high school football star. His features were large and whether attractive or not, demanded attention. I noticed girls in the front row feigning a stretch as an excuse to twist and gawk at him during the lecture before turning blushingly back toward Avrim, the graduate student who instructed the class.

I was certain that the Drakettes as a collective group would have hated Aaron, but in all probability there wasn't one who wouldn't have slept with him. He was everything they had taught me to despise about my fellow men. I hated everything about him. I loathed his heavy bright rugby shirts and corduroy baseball hats. His dark hair thickly waved on his pronouncedly simian forehead. The longer I worked at Drake's and the more I heard the girls detailing their affairs of the heart and skin as it were, the more I asked myself, why? Why? Why the Aaron Saltmarshes of the world? Eventually another nagging question followed the first: Why not Winston Delacourt?

I moped. I sulked into work and emptied pails of garbage into the dumpster in the alley. Nothing cheered me. The pregnant girl left work, and we threw her a baby shower one gloomy Sunday afternoon. Two girls hired on a few days later. Tiring of my own failure, I decided to fall in love; after all, I was a male and could if necessary be as cold and heartless as seemed the prerequisite for young love. There were so many eligible girls around ready to topple into my sensitive poetic hands, and yet nothing pleased me, not one of them prodded that raw nerve of love's genius.

One bright fall morning, a morning after another night of sitting up awake writing about the hopelessness of my condition, I caught up with Aaron after class. I must have been extraordinarily, even deliriously tired to approach him. How did Balzac put it? "Late night and coffee drinking are killing me." I had remained sleepless through the entire night until at approximately 6 A.M. with the sun rising and the moon still casting a dull pearly radiance on the rundown rows of student houses outside my window, I had this revelation that it was Aaron who would help me. I did not, as I have mentioned previously, like or have any sympathy for him. He was rude and brash, but this precisely is why I could not imagine him not getting something he wanted.

As I approached him in the hallway, I noticed with a certain despairing trepidation the obvious difference in not only our dress, but in our very physiques. I am five-foot-six-and-a-half, creeping on to the rather unolympian height of five-foot-seven. He looked down at me as I reached to grab his sleeve.

"Hey, hold on," I said as he came out of the doorway. One of the girls from the front row was asking to borrow his notes. He dismissed her with a kingly wave of his large hand.

"What do you want?" he asked.

"Do you like history?"

"What?" he waited.

"What about the Bible?"

"It's my book," he said but he was starting to ease away from me toward the stairwell.

I desperately grabbed his arm. "I want to show you something. It's very important."

He took my hand off his arm with considerate authority. "Are you okay?" he asked. "Maybe you need some air?"

"I want to show you something," I repeated.

"Sure, sure," he said ushering me through the crowded hallway and down the stairs out into the light of the courtyard.

"Look," I pleaded. It was my last chance to do anything, to become anything. It all rested mystically on him, and I didn't even like him. I had to get Aaron to come with me. "It's not far. It's . . ." I pointed across North University Street toward the diag. "It's just over there."

He started to speak. I could fairly see the word forming on his lips, but he stopped and shrugged.

"Okay just calm down," he finally said as we crossed into the slowing traffic. He grasped my elbow and I did not stop him; I felt as though if he let go I would at that moment fall dizzyingly into the onrush of traffic.

"You're taking me to the library?" Aaron asked incredulously as we entered the large ornate lobby. Bright sunlight streamed through the stained glass windows. I stood in awe of it, aware of perhaps everything at that moment; aware of a God who was his, who is, reader, yours, but who would never be my own.

We rode the elevator in silence, up past the administrative offices, the special collections, up to seven east to the papryology room. Once inside it was dark and cool; light and temperature being strictly controlled to preserve the decaying papyrus. I glanced around the room in panic like a man returned to his home searching for signs of robbery, theft, pillage. The work tables stood each equipped with a little blue lamp casting a hazy glow on the shiny glass under which was preserved a faded antique document.

I took him to the first table.

"This is a fragment of the Q document, the Synoptic Sayings Source for the gospels. It's written in Aramaic. We have the second largest collection of papyrus in the country," I said.

"What's the 'Q' thing?"

"The apocrypha. Stories or sayings left out of the New Testament, but which are possibly its earliest sources, right where the Old Testament left off. "'Q' is a 'Wisdom Collection' but other documents are eschatological like the 'Assumption of Mos—'"

"Hey, slow down with the New Testament stuff," he said lightly, turning to survey the haunting quiet of the room. "What's escha-you know?"

"The study of the end, the apocalypse. It's the one thing that's constant between the Old and New Testaments . . . the signs of the end leading to the final judgement."

"You're not some kind of crazy fanatic are you? You're not trying to convert me or something, are you?" He asked warily.

"Of course not," I said annoyedly. "Don't you see? Don't you understand? Look at it all. It's all yours. That's why I had to talk to you. I want to be converted. I want to be changed. Doesn't any of this, don't these papers," I paused, held my breath and tried to collect myself. "Don't these writings make you feel awed and terrified about your history? Once you said that I was 'one of them,' but you meant that I was nothing. Really, don't you see? I'm nothing compared to this."

The silence of the room was mocking me. I was sweating into my thin shirt. "Here, look at this one," I said.

Aaron followed me over to the third row of tables to my favorite of the collection. The eerie blue light cast down on a short document in Greek. It was only a few lines long and there was a typed translation also under the glass. Next to the brief stanza was a drawing of woman, perhaps some prehistoric doodle, perhaps a goddess, the annotation suggested.

"It's a love potion," I told him. "She's interpreted as being a fertility goddess."

Aaron squinted down at the picture. The woman was naked, garlanded about the neck with flowers. Her hair hung in long dense curls and eyes sloped darkly almondine. He stood there not moving, his hand flat against the glass smudging its clear shine. He turned and quietly said to me, "I know a girl who looks just like this."

"I'd like to meet her," I said.

"The hell you would," he said looking up from the glass.

"Just to see her," I said unsure of what I meant.

"She's not your type, Buddy," he answered in a voice rich with paternal compassion; as though he knew exactly what my type was and where this gentle creature was to be found. His tone promised secret knowledge. It was a voice that had commanded a thousand head of sheep and cattle to pasture in the fertile grasses of the Tigris-Euphrates. It was the voice of Jacob cajoling his hairy older brother for a bowl of pottage. In sum, in total, Aaron Saltmarsh had all the idiocy of history on his side.

I had shown him the sacred texts of his people because I respected them. I hated him but I was in awe of everything he symbolized. I had wanted to show him the very love potions and poems that had undoubtedly brought him into existence, because I knew deep down in my hard, frozen little heart, that he could not resist a trade, justice must be done. I had given. He would reciprocate. His big kingly head and wobbly brain were ruled by the hypothalamus, that dinosaur which knows only fear, desire, and the art of the unequal bargain.

"Just tell me one thing," he asked. "You're not gay, are you? At first I thought you might be. I mean, what the hell kind of a name is Winston anyway?"

"Methodist," I said as though that would explain everything and for Aaron I know that it would.

He nodded again with that strangely sensitive insensitivity. "Never mind," he said as we headed for the door.

I felt the dust of history blowing around us. I was an apostle heady with the Word, but Aaron was like a cowboy sauntering easily toward the elevator as though into a familiar sunset.

I never told Aaron about my job as a dishwasher. I felt the need somehow to keep secrets from him, as though, foolishly, that would give me power over him. He was polite about the fact that I had to work to support myself, but I think that it confused him. He lived on the other side of town in an apartment building that had been turned into condominiums. A security guard with gold epaulets on his shoulders sat at the front desk and called ahead up to the person you said you wanted to visit. The elevators were mirrored all the way around and the halls had rich, but gaudy red velveteen papering.

Aaron, himself, did not work. His declared field of study was "premedical" but he had yet to take any classes along those lines. His father, he intimated to me, had left him a substantial inheritance after his premature death in the crash of a private airplane. Aaron had a particularly aimless quality which I had not initially detected. I grew to feel more kinship to him, but I was jealous too of the glamour of his life. My parents were solidly alive much as I tried to ignore that fact.

The first time Aaron came over to my apartment was to study for an exam. "Aleph, bet, vet," he intoned as he stretched out across my humble sofa which served as my bed at night if I had either the energy to pull it out or the fearlessness to actually sleep.

"If you want to be converted, why don't you go to a rabbi?" he asked me as I got him a beer from the refrigerator. I myself did not, still do not, partake of beer or intoxicants. I bought them because he was coming over. Gingerly, I pulled the tab.

"I don't want to be 'converted' like that," I said.

"Then what did you mean?" he asked resting his beer on the top of his Hebrew textbook.

"Oh, I suppose I meant what religion really is—or should be—mystical. I long for something mystical to happen. Actually, it would be enough to witness something mystical."

Aaron grinned at me. "You're a trip, Win," he said. "An honest-to-God trip." He took a long guzzle of his beer. "So you mean mystical like crystal balls and horoscopes?"

"No, like, like, art, when art is truly moving," I said coughing on a mouthful of beer.

Aaron was not to be put off by this talk of mysticism. "Art," he said and nodded thoughtfully. "I like that."

"Come home with me to Seven Rivers," he asked when he was on his fifth Stroh's of the six-pack. His papers littered my floor. His shoes and socks were off. He lolled on his side on the sofa toward where I sat in the window seat. "I know this girl who would be perfect for you. She's Catholic."

"For me?" My initial reaction was, of course, doubt. Had Aaron so many girls, women, concubines that he could spare one, toss her my way with the jaunty footnote that she was "perfect for me"?

"Well," he conceded brashly. "She's got a thing for me, but she's not my type. Like I said, she's—"

"Catholic?"

"Among other crazy things," he answered.

I was not drunk. In fact my stomach, so used to coffee, was churning on one beer. I felt a sickening sense of dizzy jubilation, of actual culmination. The sign I had been waiting for had come, the gift. I understood that there was some cosmic rate of exchange and if at that moment beer-sodden Aaron was offering me something I had better accept.

How lovely in itself that she was Catholic. The very word made me think of cathedrals and the hushed quiet of holy places. As Aaron collected his books and papers, I cautioned my heady dreams with historical facts: the Crusades, holy wars, the Inquisition. But what had war ever to do with women? Especially those so pure, ethereal, not of this world? They were if anything too good for this world; the wombs of Saint Anne and Mary and Elizabeth were free of sin, depicted as walnuts and fruit, universes unto themselves.

How funny it sounded when Aaron said the word "home" as though there was someone anxiously awaiting his return. It was not the way I would say home, not the place that I would have meant. He said it so casually without the disdain that thickened my voice for the mother and father who so carelessly brought me into this world. I wish above all things that they had taken more care, more caution. Perhaps, I wish that when I got into that car with Aaron on that crisp November afternoon, I too had thought ahead. People never really do think about the future or the consequences of their actions on the time line of their own being. I could not, as I say, see myself at the time moving quite certainly toward disaster.

I went into Drake's early that next Friday afternoon to do the dishes. I washed the cups and saucers, the salad plates and the greasy condiment tins with a speed that was driven by nerves. I was dumping the trash pails out back when one of the two new girls came up behind me.

"Hey Winston," she said. The wind was blowing her blousey blue smock around her thin frame. "Do you want a kitten? My cat just had kittens and I don't know what the hell to do with them." She hugged her arms around her chest in the cold wind.

I noticed long scratches on her forearms.

"Not if it's got claws like that," I said.

She laughed overly loud and hollow. "Oh this. That's not from my kitty. I did this," she said.

"You're Ruth," I said suddenly, unsure why.

"Fuck yes," she said. "Do you know where the word 'fuck' comes from? From in old times when people looked up 'fornication' in the dictionary. It said 'fornication—under carnal knowledge.' Get it? F-U-C-K?" She grinned at me expectantly and added almost wistfully, "A guy I knew told me that." Before I could respond to her strange information the girl gave her arms a little flap and ran back indoors. As she ran she called to me, "Let me know about the kitty."

She left me alone amongst the strewn orange rinds and cardboard boxes with that northerly wind blowing nothing but ill.

Aaron had a girlfriend in Seven Rivers. The problem was that this girl, Ricey, he called her, was friends with the other girl, the Catholic girl. Ah, enter Winston the cheerful deus-ex-machina to divert her attention from Aaron to myself. The thought of competing with Aaron in the eyes and amours of some young girl made me decidedly more hopeless than usual.

"That's a strange name," I said. "Ricey. Is it from somewhere?"

He thought for a moment watching the road. "I guess it's from a story she used to be crazy about when she was a little kid. The girl in the story's name was 'Berenice,' and we, that's Theresa and me, used to make fun of how Rose would say it. She'd go 'Berry-Nicey, rhymes with very spicy,'" he said and laughed. "So does Ricey, rhymes, I mean."

With one hand resting on the steering wheel and the other cradling a fountain Coke on his lap, he told me then the difference between Jewish and Catholic girls.

"Catholic girls do . . . and Jewish girls do . . ." he paused and took a long drink through the bent straw. "It's just that Jewish girls can."

I must have looked confused.

"The difference is in the guilt," he said. "Jewish girls don't feel guilty about things like that."

"How do you know?"

He sighed with a certain authoritative certainty, "I just know women, that's all.

"In fact," he went on, "Jewish chicks practically feel guilty if they don't. You know they have these ideas about men. They hate to fail men."

"What about Ricey?"

"What?"

"I mean, have you . . ." I broke off and tried to speak with the same sort of confidence Aaron had. "Have you slept with her?"

"Of course not," he said indignantly. "What are you some kind of pervert? She's just a kid."

The long-awaited Catholic girl Aaron had promised me was Theresa Martha Boughton. She joked and pronounced her name as though it was high French, the "Bout" exploding

237

from her lips as she simultaneously kissed her fingertips, *Boo-Tawnhh*. She was more striking than pretty. Like Sarah used to say, it's all about the bones. Theresa was tall, lanky I suppose, thin without being athletic in the least. Her hair was golden and it spread and splayed in bright threads clinging to the back of her cardigan sweater.

I was dazed, I must admit, at the sight of her because she was the one Aaron had offered to me. He had driven me here to give her to me and me to her. It was as though he himself was officiating the ceremony of our union. It was as much a ceremony between myself and Aaron as myself and Theresa; he told me in no uncertain terms that nothing is more bonding than the exchange of a woman between two men.

Ricey made the silent fourth to our little group that afternoon. They were a handsome couple, Ricey and Aaron. She did not shine or glow the way Theresa did, but had the slightly bovine quality of a girl who had for too long been told that she was attractive. Her pale skin had the mermaid's hint of a silvery greenish undertone. I knew from the moment I saw her that she was the girl Aaron had recognized on that tattered papyrus.

Theresa seemed to me from the first, a girl dying to escape her dreary middle-class life. I knew that the best I could offer her was the humble refuge under the wing of my art. She had dreams herself, pretensions toward the stage. I cannot say that I immediately fell in love with her. I was entranced, and yet, and yet something held me back. I wanted to know why, why Aaron had given her up so willingly. I needed to know what motives inspired his gift.

"So you got yourself a girl?" asked Ruth who was sitting on one of the high stools at the counter.

"Who told you?"

She grinned, "Word is out, mister."

She swiveled back and around the vinyl-topped stool. When she turned to the right, she dipped down and with no hands took a draught of her orangeade from a straw.

"Hey," she called after me as I headed back through the smoky restaurant to the dishroom. She slid in behind me before the door could swing shut.

The bright afternoon sun heated up the small, cluttered dishroom. It was warm and rank with the smell of rotting lemons and sugary limes stuck to the bottom of tall soda glasses.

"Well," she asked propping herself on the windowsill. She turned and laughed. "Hey look, it's Dave." She pointed out the window to the back alley were trucks made deliveries, where Dave, the owner's grandson, was selling marijuana. "Some life," she said with exaggerated sarcasm and weariness. "Some goddamn life." She scratched her cheek and looked around anxiously. "So, you know, have you two, you know, got it on?"

"I don't know what you mean," I said archly even though I had been guilty of asking Aaron the same embarrassingly adolescent question. I was getting used to Theresa and even developing some grand almost holy ideas about her cool Catholic beauty. I had this image of the pome fruit apple womb of Saint Anne sealed away from all the taint of this world. I poured the liquid detergent into a tub to presoak the greasy storage tins.

"Is she a babe?"

"She's attractive," I nodded back to her.

"I bet she's a real breeder, hunh?"

"Excuse me?"

"One of those girls who is, you know, who does whatever some guy tells her to do. They just breed and all. Not that I have anything against guys or anything. It's just . . . I don't breed. It ends with this girl," she said proudly as she tapped her chest.

She waited anxiously while I sprayed down a rack of teacups.

"Well? What do you think? Do you think I'm sick?"

"Not exactly," I said. "I'm sort of like that myself."

"No! Are you gay?" She asked leaning forward on the windowsill.

"I didn't mean like that. I meant, I don't see the point, in well, as you put it, breeding. So I suppose I don't do it."

"You don't do it, or you haven't done it? There's a humongous difference. If you haven't done it you can't say that you don't. Get it?"

She didn't wait for an answer.

"At least you're not gay. It's okay for women, but men are totally another story. Isn't that a scream, to hear me say that? Like it makes a difference to me what anybody does," she shrugged. "I guess it just seems kind of . . . gross."

Dave came in through the back door letting in fall air sweet with marijuana. He squinted at us with his bloodshot eyes.

"You," he pointed to Ruth. "Scram. Get back to work."

He winked at me as he left. "Cute little thing, hunh? I wouldn't mind getting—" I flicked the red switch on the dish machine and let the rushing *whirr* of the water drown Dave out.

When I asked the other girls about Ruth, they nodded with bright eyes. Didn't you know? Didn't anybody tell you about the two new girls? I was, it seemed, the last to learn about Ruth and Felecia. They lived together in a one bedroom apartment with their litter of kittens. It stops with this girl, she had said. Both girls were just sixteen. Ruth had dropped out of high school. Sarah said in her matter-of-fact voice, the same voice she used to tell you about the infection that followed her tattooing, that she had seen Ruth and Felecia kissing in the back booth during a break. She said it made her want to puke.

I found something romantic about their love, about their insular dedication to each other. Once I began to watch, I saw that Ruth was solicitous to her mate. She gave her sly puckish winks and talked to her in charming, low whispers. The notion that they wanted to create nothing, yet wanted to take nothing, beguiled me. They were like the same self, locked together in a rejection of a world of which I had no choice but to be a part.

Girls went in pairs, locked together, Ruth and Felecia, lip to lip; Ricey and Theresa, by linked arms. It was another world, that Seven Rivers, my weekend haunt. I paid many a solicitous visit to an aging aunt who lived in one of the city's looming, gingerbread-trimmed Victorian homes. She let me sleep in the bedroom of her son, my cousin, who had signed on with the Navy.

One day in Hebrew class Aaron informed me that he was not going home that next weekend because he had a date with a sorority girl he had met in a bar. He spoke of her with a glowing disdain. I was shocked. Aaron and I made that drive together, always the same; his car, fountain Coke, swimsuit magazines and such littering the back seat. It was with a strange sense of freedom that I realized if I wanted to go, it would have to be without him. Ricey occurred to me as an afterthought; he was lying to her and I was an accomplice to his deception.

That weekend was the first time I visited Theresa's home. She had always insisted that to save time and trouble we all converge in the spacious rather formal living room of Ricey's house. Theresa lived about a half of a mile from Rose in a modest little brick house on an avenue lined with trees. A light snow was falling as I knocked at the door.

A warmth of spices drifted out of the house, escaped into the almost-winter of the evening.

She stood for a moment before moving aside to let me pass into the doorway. "Oh, oh hello there," said the woman who shyly opened the door. She smiled and did not introduce herself. She wore a dark blue dress sprigged with flowers. It was high at the neck and as I followed her into the living room, I noticed the tiny silver buttons down the back of the frock. Theresa's mother, how calm and delicate she was, how alone in her house without a husband. Three women lived in this house which smelled of clove and apples, and they were good to weary travelers like myself. It was with blushing formality that she helped me off with my coat.

"Theresa," she called up the stairs over the polished wood of the banister. "She'll be down in a minute," she said giving me an awkward smile. Before turning to leave the room, she smoothed down an embroidered doily on the old-fashioned veneer of the phone table.

"Wait," I said and thrust out toward her the bag of candy I brought from Drake's for Theresa.

She took the red-and-white striped bag from me and peering down into it said, "Why thank you—but I'm sure this must be for Theresa."

"No," I said even though I had never before seen this creature let alone planned to greet her with sweets. "For you, for being so . . . kind . . . for letting me come here."

She blushed.

I am not the sort of person who uses the word "kind" often or even sparingly. In fact, I never use it. Looking at her smooth white hands and gentle face and her peaceful home, the word rose from somewhere in my deepest memory. Someone must have been kind to me once to force me to remember that word and apply it to that demure being. It was almost holy. She was, I had no doubt, supremely kind.

"I'll just put them in a little dish for after dinner," she said giving me again her placid, beatific smile.

"Your mother is beautiful," I told Theresa later that evening as we sat in a movie theater downtown.

"Oh Gawd," she said with an exaggerated drawl. "I hope I never end up looking like that."

Ruth looked as though the winter wind had run its icy course through her narrow frame. She came back in the dishroom often to share a cigarette with me. She was a diminutive girl, and there was always a slightly comical aspect to seeing her, grubby street urchin that she was, intent on an unfiltered Camel. Propped on the windowsill and shivering, she stared out with her cigarette clenched tightly between two fingers. Her small face reflected bluish as she pressed her cheek against the steam-dampened window and tried to see out into the slushy alley. I, with my romantic turn of mind, wondered what she saw out there day after day which was so engrossing. I saw the trash heaped high on the dumpster and strewn about the parking lot wherever the wind might care to blow it. She palmed a small circle on the steamed-over glass and pressed her eyes to it. I saw the ugliness, the coldness and desolation, the dull and obscene backside of a graying apartment building, the iced-over cars stationary in the same parking spots day after day. Ruth blessed it all with her jittery smile because she thought, and this occurred to me much later, that this was how the world was supposed to be. She was simply used to the trash and ugliness. It was the world she was born out of and into and perhaps somehow would someday replicate herself, a system of endless convoluted incest.

In the chocolate cooler in the basement Ruth confessed her secrets to me. It was there beneath the lurid glow of a bare bulb that she with one arm bracing a cardboard box and the other digging deep with a metal scoop into the maltballs said to me, "I'm just the kind of girl who's good with her hands." She shrugged and smiled. Some of the chocolates slipped from the scoop to scatter hither and fro across the concrete floor. For one desperate instant I thought that in her playful way she was trying to seduce me.

I do not believe that any sort of lust or prankish whim caused her to reveal her secrets to me, the secrets which in sum and total added up to her short, frantic life. She was unlike the other girls who wanted me, someone, anyone to listen to validate their dream lives, to be assured that the most sordid and seamy had actually happened. Ruth needed advice, but I was Winning Winston mooning over a strange new love of my own. I listened to her but it was only much later that I even thought about what she had said, what it meant to be a girl who was good with her hands.

She restocked the candy, filled the little boxes which went in the front case with creams, filberts, mints, lacy iced truffles. With her smock sleeves meant to be short, but hitting her about three-quarter length, I could see more scratches, long artful slashes, on her forearms.

"Look at this one," she said when she noticed me staring at her arms.

She pushed up further the grimy sleeve of her smock to reveal on her upper arm a raw razor wound which read "Felec."

"I was so wasted," she said with a grin in defense of the shortened epithalamium.

She mentioned drugs casually, not just the usual marijuana and cocaine, but thorazine and lithium and other prescriptions she couldn't recall. She had bloated up and shrivelled back down and now she smiled straightening a row of mints in their snug green wrappers; she was in love with Felecia. She lifted her sleeve again and pointed at the carved name to prove her everlasting commitment.

That winter was like spring. There was bloom in the stripped graying trees, life in slushy snowbanks. I smiled indulgently at the gaudy Christmas displays in store windows. In a store on Liberty Street I purchased a little wooden crèche, and set the manger scene up in my bay window where the morning sun would shine down upon those magi, that tiny hand-carved baby, and his blue-robed young mother. More than anything else I was in love simply with the idea that I had done it— I was capable of being in love. No, it was not with sad distracted little Ruth. Nor was it Theresa or even Rose or any of the black-swathed tragic chorus of Drakettes with their strophe and antistrophe of desire. I was smitten wholly heart, soul, and fevered forehead with Theresa's mother, whose Christian name I did not know.

It happened, if you can locate a time, separate a moment from the great ticking clock of the psyche, the first moment she had opened that front door to me; the cold world was suddenly all perfume. Her purity made me cringe at my own sickness; my own lurid pleasure of chronicling the stories those hoydenish Drakettes had poured out to me. I was going to throw away all my pages in the supreme act of my selfless affection for her.

But do you know what? I couldn't do it. I stood there. I had the very match, lighted and flaming in my hand. I could not do it because of my obligation to art. The stories once conceived, once written, were no longer a part of me, but belonged to the entire corpus of literature. They were not mine to destroy. Let her come and take them. Let that unseen God spirit them away to his netherworld. I left the pages hidden in the back of my binder.

Oh, I had my doubts. I had failed at the first Herculean task I had assigned myself in the name of chivalry. Those were strange days and I ignored the ill omen of my vanity. Michigan winters are humid and the snow clings to the air, hesitant to fall. In love my two lives merged into one because only now did I feel that I had a purpose; only now did I understand what it meant to have a secret life. Strange days and endless nights and I drove every weekend to see Theresa hoping only to catch a glimpse of her mother.

Allow me, if I may, to digress for a moment and simply tell you about her, about Helen Elizabeth Boughton, a name delicate and airy enough to roll around on the tongue before submitting it to its native element. She was petite, small-boned with precise features. She had the kind of beauty which is thrown into relief by plain dress. The dresses she wore were stern and formidable but rather than making her appear matronly, those dark, high-necked costumes illumined her; pale skin like lace edging the dark sleeves and proper neck. Her hair, a yellow lighter than Theresa's own, a light gold, so that *yellow* seems too garish a word for it, she wore pulled back tightly into a chignon at the nape of her neck. Loose wisps of hair escaped and caught themselves with a charming trapped sadness in the links of the gold chain on which a small cross dangled.

At the time when I met her she was thirty-seven years old. It is, oddly enough, a mere seven years added to my neatly even sum, and yet, at the time it seemed a far-off age. It is no secret to you, reader, who is clever enough to figure these things out in advance, that nothing became of my love. Oh, there was no romance with the lovely older woman, no juggling of amours between the lady and her lass to leave me exhausted, but deliriously happy. Such things do happen in the real world, do they not? Why did it not happen for me? Answer, age? Answer, foolishness? Call on fate to explain or ask the answer of your God? Would that he could stand up, prove himself by aiding me. I believe that in her own unknowing, unwitting way, she loved me. She had love, sorrowful, sad, and unconditional enough for the host of pale, lunar-antic boys who howled beleaguered under her daughter's window. Oh reader, would that your God had loved me thus!

Perhaps if I had been less honest, more devoted, I would have clung relentlessly to Theresa as a means of staying by her mother. Theresa was a mortal girl without the refinement or delicacy of her mother. She was a small-town girl who desired everything she thought was chic or dangerous, anything to relieve her relentless ennui. I tried to wile her, ply and please her with my art. I saw myself as someone who could teach her.

She had a love of the theater and a tremulous, emotive voice. She needed only a guiding hand to help her distinguish the sublime from the fraudulent. She was a brazen tactless girl, my Theresa was. I recall the sad delirious torment of my life then, trapped between Theresa and her mother. Sitting on that deep, soft sofa at Rose's house, I tried to tell Theresa about poetry. She gave my ear a tiny pinching bite and laughed, "Winston, do you know what a poem is?" I began to respond to her and she ignored, talked right over me saying loudly over and over until I was forced to get up and leave the room, "a poem is a poem is a poem . . . " I listened to Theresa with my ears; inside I hoped desperately for a snowstorm so that I might have the excuse to spend a night at her house.

Oh, something drew me to her, my bold bragging long-legged girl, but something held me back. Her hungry unrepentant kisses saddened more than tempted me. There was her mother. But what haunted me, the ignominious third reason, was Aaron. He had offered me the challenge of the gift given as a joke. I came to understand, fool that I had been, that Aaron had offered her to me as a joke. He wanted Theresa as well as Rose, but he needed to buy time. I was harmless, the proverbial eunuch in the harem. I was nothing to him. Theresa was safe with me. I very much wanted to prove Aaron wrong. I wanted to prove his entire being wrong as though he was created not out of cells, but founded on a principle which was no longer important or useful.

In February we were hit with seven inches of wet, frothy snow. It tumbled down, hurled itself from the sunless slate-gray sky with the fury of my pent-up prayers. You see, when I spent those weekends up in Seven Rivers and stayed with that convenient old auntie of mine, she lived out on an unpaved country road. I told Theresa that I couldn't make it out there in the rough weather.

"You'll have to sleep on the sofa," she said as we left Rose's house and trudged down the drive.

"Of course," I returned.

She turned to me in the strange winter afternoon light, gave me a sad little smile and kissed me full on the lips still within sight of the spacious front windows of the Simon home.

"The sofa," she repeated with her damp and snowy cheek against my face.

"Of course," I whispered back to her. At that moment I wished that I could have been in love with her. Her hair smelled of cigarettes and strawberry shampoo.

Theresa sat beside me in her cozy living room. The room was smallish and in fact everything in the house from the kitchen chairs to the narrow bookshelves seemed to have been built scaled down for a miniature, more feminine world. Framed embroideries hung on the walls: two hands clasped in prayer, the black flossed silhouette of a child. The curtains were white with no lace or frill. Theresa rested her head on my shoulder and I asked about her father.

"When did he die?" I asked.

"No," she said. "He's not dead. Last I heard he was living in Nevada. He could be anywhere. You knew that, didn't you? My parents are divorced."

"But—" I started to correct her and explain her life the way I had imagined it.

She shook her head and her hair splayed with static across my sweater. "They got divorced right after M.C. was born, but they were sort of separated before that."

"Your mother seems so . . . It must have been—was it his idea?"

"Noom," said Theresa with a mouthful of my sweater between her teeth.

"Then what?" I pursued.

"Herrmidea," she kissed my neck.

We heard light footsteps upstairs on the landing. Theresa lazily pulled away from me and yawned.

"Will you miss me?" she asked. She got up and straightened her sweater. "Don't even think about trying to sneak up into my room. Although, it would be very romantic if you did."

"Don't forget about your mother," I cautioned.

"Mother sleeps," she leaned from the waist over the banister and let her hair fall over her face, "blissfully. We should all be so lucky." She gave me a look of theatrical longing, her best Juliet.

I fell asleep under a spell, drinking in the spicy clove, lemon, and cinnamon potpourri which simmered all day on the stove. Helen hates the musty smell of this dive, Theresa said. *Helen.* Oh, what I would have done for Helen. Oh, how I loved Helena. On the verge of sleep I made promises to myself to bring her flowers and spices and figs and dates from Troy and Smyrna. I was on the warm edge of sleep. Bring her bags of licorice and sweets for her kindness. Kindness for her sweets.

As though out of my dreams, I heard her voice and saw a dim light glowing.

"Do you need another pillow?" she asked from the landing, the light from the upper stairs dull behind her.

"Mrs. Boughton?" I asked dazed. I said her name.

"Oh, don't call me that. Not now anyway. It sounds," she paused and I sat up so that I could see her standing there small and fragile on the landing, "so old."

"May I, could I ask you something?"

She took a wavering step toward me, and I thought I saw her nod.

"Who is your favorite saint?" I asked.

"What a strange boy you are," she said.

In the darkness she came to sit beside me.

"I'm not Catholic," I blurted.

"That's not so terrible," she said. "We all do the best we can."

"Are you happy?" I asked her.

There was a silence, a long and dark and lonely silence and I could feel her warm near me in the dark, thinking about her happiness and her life. It was a minute that lasted forever and I wanted her to touch me because she was good. I wondered if she was thinking about when she was a girl, a girl like Theresa with her slim young legs, a towheaded child like Mary

Clare. I wanted her to lay one cool good hand on my forehead and heal me.

"Sebastian," she said. Her voice was low and even. "You asked me which saint. I always imagined Sebastian had red hair."

"I don't love Theresa," I said quietly. I was going tell all. I was going to admit that it was she whom I adored. Snow was falling outside the window. I was going to reveal my soul to her. I was going to go on.

"It's alright," she said. "Someone else will."

She went to the window and watched the falling snow.

"Go back to sleep now, Winston," she said drawing the curtain, shutting out the night. I heard the swish of her robe and slippered feet on the wood floor. I watched as she made her ascent up the stairs. She was a point of light growing more dim with each step she took away from me.

Ruth stuck her head into the dishroom. There were dark circles under her eyes and her hair was matted in clumps.

"Winston," she said refusing to come in any farther than her head and narrow shoulders. "I think I'm losing it."

I had finished all the dishes and was sitting on the back sink smoking a cigarette, running the clock before punching out. I remembered something, one of the essential Aaron Saltmarsh lessons on women. He had said to me: Buddy, the thing to remember about women is that they have nothing to lose. He raised his eyebrows and nodded authoritatively.

"What do you have to lose?" I asked her jokingly.

"Nothing but my chains," Ruth said and gave me a mock salute. "Comrade."

I went downstairs with Ruth to the chocolate cooler. She was desperate. She wanted to tell me things, but I was in no mood to listen. I included myself, because of Theresa's damp kisses, in the realm of those talked about, not to. Ruth had a bright pleading fanatical look on her face. I sat on a stack of Hershey's boxes while she found the jar of chocolate stars for which she had been scanning the shelves.

"I never mean to do anything bad," she said.

"Well, who does?" I laughed lightly.

"Sometimes it just happens that way. I need you to help me. I need you to let me stay at your place . . . for just a couple of days, even a night would help. Sometimes I do things and I can't stop myself even though I love Felecia."

"What are you taking about?"

"It's this guy Richard, he gives me coke and stuff. He really likes me, he says. I know he doesn't really, but he says it anyway. Sometimes I can't stop myself. I just need to go where he can't find me. Please?"

I thought suddenly then of my mother not allowing me and my brother to feed a small stray kitten which had wandered onto our trim suburban lawn. It mewed outside my window for two days, begging. I gave it nothing. Ruth looked pleadingly at me. She reached into the jar, took out two chocolate stars and held them over her eyes, bobbing her head back and forth.

"Pleeeeeze?"

The kitten skulked away on the third day, gray-furred, hungry, only to be adopted by a family down the street. They called her *Bonkers* and tied a little silver bell around her neck. Alright, I told Ruth, but just for one night. She popped the chocolate stars into her mouth, spun around, reached her hand into a box of mini-jelly beans and tossed a fistful into the air. I had to laugh as they rained down on us in all the assorted flavors of the rainbow pattering on the concrete floor.

That night I waited for her. I prepared to give her the sofa bed and I would sleep in the window seat which was quite roomy although let in a chilly winter draft. I arranged the blankets, and then rearranged them. I fell asleep fully clothed sitting up waiting for her. She did not come to me.

She was not at work the next day, or after that either. I was angry at her. Yes, self-centered fool that I was, I felt that I had offered her my hospitality and she had jilted me. I imagined that she was somewhere with the mysterious Richard, the two of them laughing drunkenly at me in some dank filthy basement. I made no attempts to find her. I went again to Seven Rivers that weekend. I forgot all about Ruth.

It was becoming increasingly difficult to handle the situation with Theresa. When she kissed me I was a traitor. Her bright mouth tasted like bubble gum or flavored lip gloss, orange, wild raspberry or once even Seven-Up for which she had traded Ricey a bottle of sparkling nail polish. She liked the smells of things. She used to bury her face into my neck, whispering in her movie star drawl, "chocolatey" or "aftershavey." With each kiss I felt pangs of guilt for betraying her mother.

When Theresa wanted more than kisses, I gently admonished her. I found her forwardness disturbing, not just unfeminine, but crude. Her neediness was unattractive, her touch slightly violent with that strange mix of innocence and desperation. Once when I was pulling away from her, she suddenly grabbed my wrist and said in an odd voice, not cruel the way you might expect from the grip of her large hand, but firm, "Don't ever do that to a woman."

I longed for winter never to end. We spent endless evenings at Theresa's house. From the kitchen there was the smell of garlic and the crack of fat from the simmering meat. Mary

Clare clattered the silverware, the forks and knives like poetry as she set the table for dinner. It was all so dreamlike, and even now, I think those evenings were the most blissful moments of my life. How could I love only the mother and not the daughters too? How could I not love the small self-contained universe in each one? Oh, I knew then why Aaron had guarded his possessions, but not why he had so inexplicably given freely what could not have been taken from him. Aaron was right. He was right to want to own them, to have them, to be with them. Pome fruit all their wombs, ready to open to you, to take you in, ready and almost too ripe.

"Well aren't you sweet," said Helen when I handed her the box of pastries tied with the glittery red bow. Each time since that first meeting, I brought treats stolen from work. Ruth usually helped me, filled the bags for me with cool frosted mints and hand-dipped chocolate oreos.

"You're trying to make me fat," she exclaimed.

I took an inward joy in that fact that she had said "me," that she knew that all my gifts were for her alone.

I headed back down to Ann Arbor noticing the grayish smut of the snow on the side of the highway, the slushy telltale signs of spring. And I thought about Helen in the spring, how she would work in her garden, her fair skin protected from the sun by the wide brim of a straw hat. She was among roses and creeping ivies.

It was with complete surprise that after I made the trek up three flights of stairs to the obligatory heavy metal music of my first-floor neighbors, I spied a dark figure curled in a heap by my door.

It was Ruth. She lay wrapped in her winter coat on her side, one arm pillowing under her head, the other over it, protectively.

She did not move, and gingerly, uncertainly, I picked her up and carried her into my dark apartment. She turned her face up to me. I saw no gratitude.

"I'm going to throw up," she said.

She was weak, too sick to walk alone, and I carried her to the bathroom. I held her head as she retched unabashedly into my pristine toilet bowl. She started and stopped, started again and then rested her face on the toilet seat only to start again. I began to get worried that there would soon be nothing left of her, all the insides gone and the outside melted away.

"I'm okay, really. Can I be alone for a second?"

I was hesitant to leave her. I had an impulse to check the cabinets for razor blades or aspirin, but I left her and soon after she opened the door. How I recall her then as she stood in the doorway wearing only a clean white undershirt from my laundry basket, her underpants, and mismatched dark socks. There was a raw brittle beauty to her, not boy, not girl, a feverish little bird perched and tipping on ridiculously delicate legs.

"I'm sorry I'm late," she said sitting down next to me on the sofa and wrapping herself in a blanket.

"Late? An hour is late. Two hours is late. You are days late."

"You don't even know the shit I've been through in the past week. Shit. All shit."

"You were with *Richard,*" I said.

"Can I have some hot chocolate or something?" she asked.

"Yes," I said.

I had few comforts except those that could be mixed with water and heated over a hot plate. I opened two packets of instant cocoa and was fingering the desiccated little mini-marshmallows waiting for the water to boil when she said slowly, "Winston, he wanted me to, I almost slept with him."

"Why should that surprise me?" I said.

"Don't be mean," she said. "Not about this. I've never done it with a guy. I freaked out. He got pissed and kicked me out."

One lamp glowed idly in the corner. The kettle began its steamy insistent whine. I did not know what to say to her. I felt both cheated and cheated on. She was weak and frail, and used. That was it, the world was using her up and throwing her away so she took a kind of plaintive solace in trash and filth. She rested her head on the arm of the sofa.

"I'm tired, so goddamn tired. You talk for a while," she said. I handed her the cocoa. She held it with both hands and let it warm her ash-white face.

"I have a secret too," I told her.

"That girl you like?"

"Her mother," I found myself saying despite my promises to myself to keep my love secret.

Ruth said nothing. She blew on her cocoa and smiled thinly, almost contentedly like a child being told a bedtime story.

"She seems so *good,*" I went on. I told Ruth about Helen. I said the name lightly with the aspirated "h" soft and melodious. I told Ruth about her house and all the comfort of it with the scents and softness and the snowy boughs of trees and icy windowpanes through which I sometimes, standing in the yard outside, watched for a moment before I knocked on the front door.

"Sometimes," Ruth said, her face now flushed and sleepy, "people can be nice."

She closed her eyes. Thinking she was asleep I tucked the covers up under her pointed chin. I took the extra blanket and made ready to sleep on the window seat when I heard her tiny voice in the darkness.

"Don't go," she said. "I won't do anything. I promise."

The sofa pulled out into a rickety bed, but neither of us needed comfort that night. I rested myself at one end of the sofa and she at the other, her feet still damply stockinged pressed into the small of my back. It was not until the first pink streaks of dawn lit the room that I awoke briefly to realize that she had shifted and we lay oddly, curled together. She had wedged herself between the cushy back of the sofa and my own back. How odd it seemed, her clinging thin little body pressed against me. Her hands were balled into fists, and I could feel them too, knuckly and knobby, fighting off some intruder even in her dreams.

In the full bright 11 A.M. sun she stood still pale at the window dressed in her grubby clothes.

"You know what my problem is?" she asked.

"No," I said as I hastily collected my books for class.

"I'm just the kind of girl who's good with her hands." She smiled a cheater's grin and turned from the window to me. "You won't tell Felecia about any of this, will you?"

We walked out the door together. I noted her tiny hand with the nails bitten down and ragged on the knob of the door as she pulled it shut behind us. I felt strangely embarrassed when we parted. I did not want to touch her. I did not want to kiss her because it seemed that Ruth was too nervous to kiss. She would give you sharp biting kisses and when you later looked at your scarred skin you would see that with her little razor teeth she had tattooed her name into your flesh.

As she pulled the door shut and it clicked with a lock behind us, it was as if we were leaving behind a place of comfort, a quiet gentle place far away from Ann Arbor and our lives. It was a place to which I knew even then neither of us would return. What could I do but turn and watch her as she ambled away, hands stuck in the pockets of her jeans, her winter coat tied loosely by the sleeves around her waist. In the foreign brightness of the spring sun, I walked away from her.

The first person I expected to see and the last one I wanted to see was Aaron Saltmarsh. We were both in the second semester of Hebrew together. He sat like a trained chimpanzee in his usual seat, his thick body jammed into the little student's desk. One arm he rested elbowise on the desk, with his hand gripped under his massive mandible; his hair pushed back off his browridge of a forehead, a battle scar, though healed over, shone in the artificial light. He chewed slowly and deliberately on a wad of apple-scented gum. When I saw him like that, sitting among the other students, all of them talking or laughing or reading, he seemed so out of place. Aaron Saltmarsh, kingly and massive, should have been swinging from vines in the jungle. Yet, there he was, lording over no one, his brute frame robed in stone-washed blue jeans and a crew neck sweater. I felt a second sight come to me, full of pity, full of grace. It was no life to be Aaron Saltmarsh; the new world was built on too small a scale and there he sat squat on his broad hams waiting for someone to teach him what should have been his native tongue.

I no longer spoke to Aaron. If he went to Seven Rivers to see Ricey, which I supposed he did, he went without me. He had relinquished Theresa to me, perhaps because he had the inbred notion that he must stick to his own tribe. He had given her too me and I had all the smug pity in the world for him. I caught up with him in the hall after class.

"These are for you," I told him holding out two tickets to Theresa's play. "She wanted you to have them . . . and I do too."

"You know," he said, "you have a lot of nerve."

"What did you expect?" I blurted.

He not only did not reply, but walked right past me. I followed quickly behind him out the door and into that same courtyard that I had dragged him through in my fury and eagerness to show him my respect for his religion.

"Look, I don't blame you," he finally turned back to me and said. "I feel sorry for you because you just don't get it. She's using you . . . for a lot of things . . . but mostly to make me jealous."

"Isn't that a little self-serving?" I asked. "Maybe you just can't believe that you would ever lose out to me." I imagined that my voice rose on the word "me." It was loud and authoritative and thunderous. A flock of birds alighted from the roof of the library. The clock in the bell tower chimed with ferocity, all in echo of "me, me, me."

"Get a clue," he said shaking his head. Without another word, he crossed the street and went on walking without looking back.

I was tired. I was foolish. I rounded the corner onto North University Street and headed to Drake's. He should have acknowledged me as his equal. There were more things entangled than I had understood. It had to do with Theresa and Rose and Aaron and a childhood shared and spent together of which I would never be a part. I had entered the game late indeed. I tried to cheer myself with the thought that I really had no ties to Theresa, only to her mother. None of these other petty adolescent games had anything to do with me. Inside Drake's I looked around for Ruth, but I couldn't find her.

My head ached and I sat in Ruth's familiar window seat in the dishroom. As I lighted my cigarette and tried to feel again the warmth of the spring sun, Felecia came bustling through the swinging door with a metal tray stacked high with dirty cake plates. Instead of setting the tray on the rack and leaving, she stood there in front of me. She wiped her hands on her smock.

"It's Ruth," she said. "She's tried it again."

"It?" I asked, both surprised and taken aback. Felecia had never before spoken to me. She rarely spoke to anyone at Drake's but hovered around Ruth always listening, quietly watching.

"You're her friend, you should know. She tried to kill herself."

"When?" I asked.

"This weekend. Well, Thursday really, with pills. And then Friday she was gone again."

Felecia hoisted herself up onto the aluminum sink and sat. She was a sturdy large girl with a serious manner. She had a sort of wholesome cheerleader look to her, plain and chubby, full of all the good health Ruth was denied. She thought Ruth was seeing someone else.

"I don't know where she goes," Felecia said resting her capable hands on her knees, bare under her short denim skirt.

"I don't even know where she slept last night."

"Probably with a friend," I said.

"Oh no, it always goes like this. She starts messing around with somebody. I find out. She goes crazy and comes back to me all whacked out. This time she took some pills. They just pumped her stomach and sent her home."

"What are you going to do?"

"What do I always do? I clean her up. She takes my money. She ruins my stuff," she looked up at me bashfully under the fringe of frizzy blonde bangs. "It's not you is it? Who she's seeing?"

"No," I told her stubbing my cigarette under my shoes. I ground it down with a grim finality.

"No," she replied. "I didn't really think so. I just thought this time it might be a guy. I guess it couldn't be you. You're not like that. I can just tell."

The date of Theresa's play was drawing near. To her I suppose it meant the chance to have all eyes on her, to be truly the glittering princess in the center of the stage. I did not think the work I had done on it was my best writing. At the time I was very enamored of the work of the late Hugh Denmark. I replaced words in the script with others which I thought Theresa would like better. I used words like "lugubrious," "visage," and "verdure." I threw myself awkwardly into that play for Theresa and her mother and even for the author himself.

Hugh Denmark was another adolescent fascination which both Theresa and I shared. While I admired his work, his art, I believe she had something of a schoolgirl crush on him. Oh, wide-blue-eyed Theresa never called Terry or Tess, in the end she fooled us all. There I was loving her mother through her and fighting over her with Aaron. She was a clever girl, not unlike the girleens of the later plays. It just made sense, I suppose, that she would chose him over any of us.

"Do you like it?" Theresa asked whirling around in her golden costume.

She didn't give me time to answer.

"Maybe I should have it hemmed? And these tights, awful, really awful. And—" suddenly she pirouetted toward me, threw her arms around my neck and laughingly kissed me.

From over my shoulder I could see two faces peering at us from the doorway.

"We have company," I said softly.

"Ah, spies," she said whirling around, her hands still on my shoulders. "Come here, little spies."

Theresa's sister Mary Clare trotted dutifully over to the sofa and sat down, but Rose's sister remained in the doorway studying us with an ironic gaze. Buttercup, I think they called her. I never learned what her actual given name was.

"You look very much like your mother," I said to Mary Clare as she sat down next to me.

She shrugged her thin shoulders.

"You don't know anything," said Buttercup loudly from the doorway.

"Don't be so rude," said Theresa. "You should apologize."

"But he doesn't know anything. He thinks he knows about poetry but he doesn't."

For some reason the child had never liked me. She was allowed by her family and friends to be rude under the auspices of precocious intelligence. She had a certain allegiance to Aaron. When he was around she followed him about and mooned after him. He brought her little presents, stupid drugstore toys which threw the chubby little tyrant into ecstasies of adoration.

"Let me tell you something," I said to her. "Let me tell you—"

"Tell me about John Donne," she interrupted me.

I scanned my memory for details but drew a blank.

"Alchemy," I said to confuse her.

"You don't know anything," she said again, adamant. "Do you know about his wife? You make me sick."

"Buttercup!" exclaimed Theresa.

"Well look at him," the girl said pointing an accusatory finger at me. "Look at his stupid clothes and that *hair* and he thinks he knows something but he doesn't even know one thing."

"What's so important about some dead guy's wife?" asked Theresa.

"That's just it," Buttercup said hotly. "He doesn't know about anybody's wife. He doesn't know that John Donne's wife had about fifty kids and died in labor while her husband was writing all that junk about love."

"What does that have to do with art?" I asked her archly.

"Art?" she snorted. "I've read, I've seen your art and buddy it's just trash."

She had had her hands behind her back and now she held out my notebook to me. I believe I actually began to sweat. My hands were clammy. Oh yes, my poems were contained in that notebook, but also my tormented scribbles, transcribed stories and hopes told to me by the Drakettes. Buttercup didn't move, but made me come over and take the book from her.

"It's like the book of life," she said with a wry smile.

Mary Clare who was sitting between Theresa and I on the sofa had taken in the entire scene without saying a word. Her face lacked any trace of emotion or judgment.

"I suppose," I said setting the book on my lap, "that she has very high standards about what passes for art."

For some reason Mary Clare found this very funny and she turned away from me and buried her face into Theresa's sleeve choking with giggles.

When I saw Ruth again she had a new military haircut. I didn't necessarily try to avoid her. When she spoke to me I nodded politely at her jokes and comments. I didn't want anything to do with her; her certain kind of unstable craziness seemed infectious to me. I was, in fact, becoming impressed with the craziness of girls in general, whether it was Ruth or Buttercup.

One moment they were perfectly normal and functioning, the next they were screaming in some rage impossible to fathom. I could sense something inside myself, that same curiosity that had arisen out of the idea of the secret life, I could feel it churning deep within me, turning sour.

March came with a rain and darkness that suited my mercurial mood. I trusted no one. Helen, I thought about Theresa's mother by her Christian name although I never dared speak it aloud. Helen was a light impossibly far away, always beyond my reach. It was a rainy afternoon and Ruth sheepishly pushed in through the swinging doors of the dishroom.

"I have to talk to you," she said.

"Look, I'd really like to, but, you know, I do have my own concerns," I said. It was the first time that I refused to offer my ear to a girl who expressed need.

"Why do you hate me so much?" she asked with an uncharacteristic quiet. "I never lied to you, not about anything."

I had been standing with my back to her, pretending to be absorbed in sorting silverware. I turned toward her. She looked unspeakably awful. Her eyes were sunk into her head, circled, mooned with darkness. There was a haunted, tortured look to her thin face, and this with her shorn, almost bald head made her look like a wizened old man. I felt a sickness in my stomach at the very sight of her. I wanted to listen to her, to warm her, wrap her in blankets, feed her the chocolates and sweets that she claimed only "normal breeder girls" liked. I wanted and wanted and still she stood shivering at the tinny sound of the rain on the roof outside. I did not move.

Felecia rushed in, the doors swinging in a frenzy behind her. Her bright raincoat was streaming with water. In one hand she held an umbrella, and I thought to myself, isn't that the difference between these two? Felecia was the kind of girl who always had an umbrella with her because she understood the possibility of rain. From a pocket of her jacket she extracted a sheath of papers and waved them in Ruth's face.

"I have proof," she said. "This time you really did it, didn't you?"

"Look," she said. "Letters. And do you know what she tells him? Do you know what this lying little piece of trash bitch tells him? She says—" and Felecia paused and then resumed imitating Ruth's slangy hip drawl, "I'm thinking about you now and always. Whenever I'm with Felecia no matter what we are doing it's you that I'm dreaming about—." She broke off with a triumphant snort of disgust. Both Felecia and I stared at Ruth, who seemed to shrink, growing smaller under our combined gaze.

She said nothing. She walked out of the room alone, small and lost.

"Do you see how it is?" Felecia asked me waving those letters as some kind of cosmic proof of all the injustice in the universe. "People talk, but they never tell anything." She laughed bitterly and looked down at the letters clutched in her hand. "It all comes down to what's left on paper, doesn't it?"

The door rocked in her wake, and I could hear her calling over the din of the crowded restaurant, calling, "Ruth, Ruth."

I stood at the back window watching the rain fill the potholes in the alley, watching the waterlogged trash expand and ooze on the ground. How had it all begun? At first I had only listened. It had been so harmless. It was another thing to witness and be part of all those trials and stories. I put my hands against the window and tried to think of a saint to pray to.

The image of red-headed Saint Sebastian came into my mind and I smiled to myself, comforted.

Ruth and Felecia could, I knew, go on forever as they had been. It was just how they lived. Why couldn't all women be like Saint Anne, sealed off from all that is corrupt and tainted in this life? I knew the answer was that they reveled in the things I found most disturbing. A dog from the apartment building next door was howling in the trash in that alley. I wished my soul outside my body to howl there in the rain with him.

Ruth did another one of her disappearing acts. She was gone for three days. Every day she was gone it rained, long and cold and gray. She did not come to work. The other girls were used to this. They took over her shifts, accommodated themselves to her craziness, perhaps in hopes that she would one day reciprocate the favor. I was worried. I knew that the only one she really wanted to hurt with all her craziness was herself. But, I supposed that she was off somewhere with one of her mysterious friends in some smoky room easing her troubles with skin and sin, the best way she knew how.

I was concerned with my own problems. Ruth was on the periphery of these worries. She hovered around my mind. She represented all fear and fragility. The weekend of Theresa's play finally came; a large black "x" marked the date of the opening on my desk calender. It represented my last chance to express my feelings to Helen, but how futile that seemed! It was all so hopeless. I blamed Ruth for it all. She had infected me with her rain cloud of melancholy.

I remember the events of that night in a blur. There was the flash of a photo being taken and little Mary Clare with her serious face calling, "Say cheese!" Mr. Katz, the drama teacher patting me on shoulder and saying, "Ah, well done, boy!" in his resonant pseudo-Elizabethan accent. I recall Theresa too, on stage, fluttering in her pale yellow dress speaking words that both I and Hugh Denmark had written for her in a kind of ghostly collaboration. Her movements, her hair, it was all so golden as if she had been born from the light and was for that brief time on stage returned to it. She came right out of the light, and I was watching from the darkness of the wings.

"Tell me something nice," said Theresa as she sat at a little table backstage removing her makeup. We were interrupted every few moments as someone came up and complimented her or clasped her shoulder.

"You were wonderful," I told her. "Everything the part called for, hopeful, innocent. Good diction, fair projection."

She was staring at her face in the mirror, swabbing her pale cheeks with cold cream.

"No, nicer than that." Her voice was fast and breathy. "Why haven't you ever told me that you love me? You never say things like that."

"Why?" I asked. I did not understand how she could bring herself to discuss such an important and personal subject at that moment in the bustle of backstage.

"I want to see how it sounds is all."

"Won't your mother be coming back here any minute?" I offered weakly as an excuse not to speak intimately with her.

"And what is this thing that you have about my mother?" she asked looking at me in the mirror as I stood behind her.

"I just respect her," I said putting my hands on her shoulders. In the mirror I thought we made a handsome couple.

"It's more than that. It's weird."

"Alright," I said. "I find her presence very soothing. You might call it comforting."

Theresa snorted, wiped her face with a towel and began to work on her hair.

"Comfort is right," she nodded. "Southern Comfort."

"What?"

"You moron," she said unpinning the tight bun into which her hair had been fastened. "My mother is a lush, you know, an al-co-hol-ic." She broke the word down into syllables as though the slower she said it the more chance there was that I would believe and understand her.

"I find that extremely difficult to believe, Theresa."

"Don't you think I know my own goddamn mother? She sits in her room and she gets drunk. She isn't dangerous. She doesn't drive or anything. She just sits in her room and then if she's really loaded she wanders around the house. Up and down the stairs until she passes out on the sofa."

"Why are you saying this?"

Theresa was brushing out her hair. "Winston," her voice was firm and even. "She doesn't go to church anymore because she's too embarrassed that people will be able to tell from her face that she's a drunk."

It stabbed right through my heart. I had such pity then. I had pity for Helen whose very name suddenly seemed as though it should have been an indicator for me; it screamed of ruined virtue and lost beauty. I had pity for Ruth. I had pity for the winter which had left me with nothing but a wet hopeless spring. I had pity for myself because everything I had ever or would ever do from that point on would be futile. I should have stuck to my books and papers and never ventured out of my lonely but safe attic abode. The thought of my humble home, my own little refuge from the world, filled me with a terrible aching fatigue through me entire being. I wanted simply to go home and sleep.

"Are you coming with?" asked Theresa throwing her jacket
over her costume and shouldering her heavy bag. "The party,
you know, you said you'd go to the cast party with me."

"No," I told her. "I don't think I can do that anymore."

"I thought it might be like this," she said. She stood in
front of me shrugging her shoulders into her jacket. Her hair
was combed out long and straight. There was a glowing bare
quality to her face scrubbed free of her stage makeup.

"Maybe Aaron will go with me," she said.

"Why don't you ask your real friend. Ask Rose," I said. And
I walked away from her.

All the way on that drive downstate images of Theresa and her
mother and Aaron and Ricey tormented me. There would
always be that part of life, things between people that no one
else would understand. What was it that Felecia had said,
something about people not telling other people? It's not even
a matter of not telling, but of not knowing, not believing. I
did believe what Theresa had said. I knew, I must have always
known that her mother drank to silence the screaming of her
sadness. And my own sadness? How could I write about anything ever again when I lost myself to them, to such a strange
and split world?

When I arrived home, bleary and exhausted, I found a note
taped to my door. I had the delirious sensation that this night
would never end, that if I wanted it to continue, if only I
willed it, the night could go on forever.

I pulled the note down and read slowly its rounded girlish script— "She's tried it again. Terrible this time. Twenty-eight stitches both wrists. Screaming my name. She's in the hospital sedated. Please come see me. Felecia. 325 Maiden Lane, #11."

I went inside and collapsed onto my bed.

I had never even had one life of my own. I had been a twenty-year-old man with hair beginning to noticeably recede and a thin nose which I was often told was a sign of my puritan character. I had been used to my life, which was no life at all. Before I had to afford my apartment I was content with my quiet solemn job in the Papyrology room. And now I had two lives and three and four, lives which seemed to go on forever, multiply, complicate, be carried out in action by someone who looked like me, but was truly not me. Soon, I knew with almost relief, soon I would be alone again. I vowed that from that moment on I would avoid crowds and people and women and men. I would ever unforgiving shun the world.

I walked then to Felecia's apartment. It wasn't far and the night was mild, damp from the earlier rain. It calmed me, and I let my own troubles rest as I thought about the night Felecia must have spent. After all, there were no real threats in my life, no torment other than love, no threats of death, no deviance to my life. I stomped through a puddle, laughed aloud and called myself a great fool, a monumental fool for rejecting Theresa.

When I had handed her that final bouquet of flowers, those feverish daffodils, as the audience stood cheering, I knew that I would have to leave her. I saw something in her face that had terrified me. In the play, that silly little fairy tale, she hadn't been Theresa. She had been better than either Aaron or I had anticipated and she would not let herself be owned or dispensed. She graced the audience with her bright smiling painted face. I handed her the flowers and the look that she gave me nearly backed me out the door in fright; a look that said "yes" right down to its core. I knew what she wanted and was afraid. I was not unwilling, but unable.

Call it another one of my mistakes, a distance misjudged, an emotion mismanaged. Maybe I mistook her elation for desire, but I distinctly recall her eyes meeting mine. I wanted to be near Helen because it meant being near goodness. Poor Helen had a secret life in which her house was no longer a sanctuary filled with roseate and lovely things, but a prison in which she wandered drunk in the early hours of the morning. I felt no more love. The night was cool. I was ready to drift into anonymity.

Felecia answered the door wearing a simple white night-dress. Her hair was wet and the apartment humid and fragrant as though she had just showered.

"Is it too late to come over?" I asked her.

"Oh no," she replied. "How could I sleep?"

She ushered me into the small apartment which she and Ruth shared. I had imagined it would look like Ruth, devoid of ornament and the trappings of femininity, but this was clearly Felecia's place. A fat white cat curled on the floor. A slip was strewn over the flowered sofa. The clutter was girlish, pillows and shoes and underthings.

"Come in here," she said, leading me through the open door to the bedroom.

"It happened out there," she went on as she sat on her bed. "I can't stand to be out there. It smells like blood to me."

"What happened?"

"I came home and found her. She must have started in the bathroom and then come out there. I had to scrub the walls. Thank god it's latex paint, or I'd be out my security deposit."

I looked back and noticed wet spots on the carpet in a trail. Felecia leaned back on a heap of pillows. Her plump cheeks were waxy and clear; her eyes glittered too brightly.

"But how is Ruth?"

"*Ruth?* Oh *Ruth* is fine. She was screaming my name when the paramedics dragged her out. I think I'm going to move out of this town. My dad said he'd send me to Arizona if—"

"Did you go with her to the hospital?"

She nodded. "She should have called *him* whoever the bastard was. He should have been here to clean up the mess."

"It's been an awful night," I said.

I was sitting on a little chair by the double bed. It was a child's chair, low with a woven wicker seat that creaked under my weight. She rolled on her side on the bed. There was lace edging on the neck of her nightdress.

"You must feel awful," I said.

"I do, but I've learned. I mean, I'm learning. I can't get sucked into her freaked out world. I'm learning how it is," she repeated lightly.

She lay on her side and reached toward me, letting her hand fall on my knee and trail upward. I watched her hand as though it was some strange but harmless animal which had alighted on my person. I simply picked it up and removed it. It was easy. She didn't resist.

"What the hell is wrong with you?" I said. I wanted to shout but the night was too quiet. It was too late for shouting. I gripped her wrist in my hand and could not release it. I stood and she jerked up with me for a moment and then pulled her hand away, falling back down onto her heap of pillows.

"Ruth is in the hospital," I said. "She needs you."

"It's always Ruth, isn't it? I'm sick to death of Ruth."

More quietly this time, I asked idiotically, as though I really expected she could produce an answer, "What in the world is wrong with you?"

"Me?" she asked propping herself up on her elbows. I could see the full soft slope of her through the light nightdress. "Me? What about you? Why can't you just be *human* for once in your life?"

"I," I said with all the dignity left in my aching body, "am nothing but human. That is the problem, Felecia. I am all *too* human."

I heard her laughter behind me as I ran through the sepia halls of the apartment building. I hear her laughing still sometimes in my dreams.

What I did next amazes me yet. I went back to Thayer Street, got my car keys and drove back up to Seven Rivers. It was a three hour drive and dawn was already breaking begrudgingly over the off-ramps. I don't know what impelled me to go back. I knew there was nothing left there for me, but I wanted to explain. I was so crazed and tired that I began to see myself as a pilgrim, the wandering cowboy of my own poems. It could have been that Theresa had lied to me about her mother. I had to find out for myself. Once in Seven Rivers I pulled into the parking lot of a Burger King, lay my head against the steering wheel and fell asleep sitting up.

When I awoke it must have been midmorning. The air reeked of fried food. I was caked in sweat and the same world which the night before had seemed ominous and threatening, now smelled like a bacon double cheeseburger. I drove to Theresa's house and parked in the driveway. I didn't know who would tell me the truth I so desperately needed to hear. I stood in the driveway waiting for Theresa to emerge, and when she did not, I began to pound on the horn.

It was Mary Clare who came out. She was wearing cut-off jean shorts and an unzipped windbreaker. Her head of bright yellow hair blazed in the sun. She was the guard, the messenger. I knew that even a child had the force and will to stop me. I would never see the inside of that house again. Neither the queen or the princess would see me, not today or any other day. The message was clear. The spell was broken.

I cannot objectively say that the death of Ruth Barbara Stevens on January 18, 1993, had anything to do with my not helping her on the spring night years before. Her life and premature death seemed inevitable from the first. It is only that I wish I could have done more for her. She was the only one I truly wanted to help.

Does it make sense now? Why I no longer write poetry? Why it all seems so small and insignificant compared to the rushing, freezing waters that pulled her under their rolling sway? No, I would not even know how to begin to write a poem.

When I arrived back at my apartment that afternoon, I burned all my papers. I set aflame and afire everything, the scraps, the notes, the essays, the god-awful poems. Yes, it was romantic. Yes, it was foolish. I burned the whole bundle in the bathroom sink, scorching the ceiling with the flames. Once the words were gone the burden was lifted from me. It was as Felecia had said, writing is the only proof that anything happened.

I have nothing now that the others have. I have lamps and vases and a job at a publishing house of some repute to which I wear clean pressed white shirts. I have no contentment from meat or drink. I have only a dry aching, the endless craving for something always a little beyond my reach. For a brief moment in my life I wanted bright things, bright the way Theresa's face was bright and hard and giddy. Her face promised all the things we would do. In words, in how you place them one after another, all you are is alone. More than anything, I wanted for that strange frantic short time in my life, not to be alone.

Felecia lay across the bed and reached out toward me with her chubby child's hand. She touched my leg with a strange and awkward gentleness. She lay across the quilt in her night-dress. The windows were open and curtains fluttered white and ghostly on the breeze. All her things, her toys and tokens surrounded me. Lacy-edged valentines were taped to the mirror, love letters scattered indiscreetly across the bureau. I didn't think. I didn't have to think but my hand slapped her hand away with a short violent gesture.

When Felecia put her own good hands on me, I realized that nothing was good about any of it, not the chocolates, not the love poems, not the blandishments. I had known all along that the only good way to live was alone. I had learned that to be a girl who was good with her hands was not really good at all. All goodness was negated. They had nothing, not one of them. Having nothing, they had nothing to lose and would go around telling you this, telling you that, telling you that your own goodness wasn't really good at all.

Sometimes I don't want to be alone. I have images, clipped pictures from magazines imprinted in my psyche of bright people, of girls with thin arms and bright mouths laughing into the dull din of some anonymous party. And they are so happy. They are happy maybe because they have stolen all that is good in the world with their wondrous strong hands and hidden it away each into their own secret universe, which is dark and which is warm and in which I long to be.

Pearl

I GOT OFF THE TRAIN AT UNION STATION, slung my bag over my shoulder and looked around anxious, fearful, because I had no idea what he would look like. Anthony Christomo is the sort of person about whom you can never remember specific details. I worried that even if he was standing in front of me, I wouldn't remember him. But when I spotted him a few seconds later, the fear seemed idiotic. How could I not recognize him? We looked, sallow and skinny, dark pupils dilated as we stepped out into the bright summer afternoon, like a vampire and his girlish assistant.

He did not speak during the drive home, and I suppose I said nothing as well, falling, as I did, fallen, into his curious silence. When we got to his apartment, he unlocked the door, opened it, and made a great pretense about going in first while I waited out in the hall. He came back to me in the doorway, stuck his head out and said loudly, echoing down the empty hall, "Welcome to Wittenberg. All rooms currently available." He grinned at me, and I smiled back, less at the joke of it, but because he must have been thinking about saying it all morning. He must have been practicing it in his head as he drove, because he thought it was funny. I guess it made me sad too, how funny he thought it was.

It's hard for me to understand people and what makes them happy and sad and all that. I didn't tell my father about my deal with Martin Hamlin. To my father's mind, to the dark way he understood the world, he would have thought I had literally made a deal with the devil, but I knew that it wasn't really like that at all. But it wasn't about compromise either; it was about evolution and survival, not good and evil. My father says that people are actually worse off than apes because at least apes are still evolving and people are now actually devolving. He gave me a lot of books. It took two months, but I stayed with him and I read them all. For my birthday he gave me a typewriter and the first thing I did was sit down and write a story. I didn't show it to my father. I didn't show it to anyone, but I read it over and over and I thought it was pretty good. I told myself, sitting there in my father's guest bedroom, sweating alone in the heat of August with the space fan whirling low, dusty, and monotonous, I told myself that if I ever did show it to anyone, I would change all the names and say that none of it ever happened.

I left my father. I had to. That was, of course, part of the deal.

Denmark

Theresa,

We are yet too intimate for common salutations. Let us not set the tone of a love letter or suicide note. Leave it that what will follow is a matter of personal interest to us alone and legal matter to others involved. I saw you in one of your magazine advertisements—tanning oil, Andalusian pups, corn fritters, perhaps beer? Who can recall? You with your hair shorn call yourself Rapunzelled, sistered, a city girl graduated from the school of hard knocks with the scars, stars, and blazing six guns to prove it.

It was not easy, I think, for the rest of the world to understand us. Here I pause for a moment to set the kettle on the gas blue flame of the burner. And perhaps you did not either. So much the better, my bested child bride. The abstractions, scattered lines, bread crumb sins—do you recall the row of china kitty cats you kept above the bed on a shelf so narrow I feared they would fall and shatter on our heads as we slept? And then you took them one day and dropped them, painted with rosebuds, lilacs, cornflowers, and stripes, to watch them shatter on the pavement below. Often you left the windows open in the rain and I thought, "how theatrical of her." "I hated those hideous things," you said of the kittens. "Don't give me any more monkeys, chickens, or puppies, either," you said rejecting my foolish tokens of graceless affection. Does it surprise you so long after the fact, so deep into the winter, that I recall with absolute clarity every word you said and the particularly crisp appled midwestern inflection which added to the aura, no the cult, of your innocence? Strange now to think of you, toyless, cats out the window, bones in the bag, Hughless. But I ask you and the others (oh, Theresa, and why were there always others?) who will rifle through my papers: what man could have stood the ghost of a chance in your graveyard? As God said to Adam on one of those favonian edenic days, "Pick a bone, any bone." And here we are preparing to celebrate the birthday of our hesitant and carnation-strewn thorn capped lordling, son of a sonless father. You are no longer a girl, except perhaps to me, except in the collective memories of those who knew you. Hard luck, time is. And has. Women, I have found, prefer to be called *girls* if only for the naivete of the word, long past their natural due. Strange now to think of you and recall every word. They did not so much hang in the air (the metaphoric fault of mediocre scribblers); rather, they were bits of food, sweets, butterscotches, dry little Communion wafers, cherry tomatoes that you might have plucked from my wizened hands, pulled sun-ripe from the vines. What impressed me when I saw you at seventeen was not what others called beauty, but your relentlessness. I told myself, here is an unsentimental woman, an uncompromising woman who has never given in, even to the temptations of desire. And didn't it always have less to do with sex than symbolism? You were more like Lilith than her little sister, Eve. Do you know the story? Is it one that little girls memorize letter by letter while propped on their daddy's knee? Poor dear Lilith could have been the swollen-bellied mother of us all had only she been a little more willing to be bested. Bettered some might decline. From whence did her rebellion spring if not from her borrowed bones? Poor girl, where did she go, I wonder, leaving paradise. No mother, no daughter, left for historical outcast: grief senza torment. So many times I have heard you spoken of in crowded rooms, voices ringing, sottovoce, dolcemente, la mia sgualdrina bionda. Other women called you names and looked slyly away when you faced them. *Bitch,* they said and smiled and smiled. Prefaced, described, adjectived. *Blonde bitch, money hungry bitch, little whore.* Theresa you were anything but little and your narrow cold eyes, Teutonic-shaped, Nordic-colored, but you insisted on favoring potatoes and vinegar, that you were Irish and French. You denied your mother at every step of the game. Would Persephone have done as much? Lord, she called the devil's name in ecstasy bedded on the cracked wheat of her mother's counting house floor. *Daddy, Daddy,* you called out sometimes in your sleep.

Oh, the irony of you, my Theresa. I know you won't read my letters. I know your stubborn streak. So you, yes you, reading now trying to seem so nonchalant, you chewing with pleasure on my once fatted bones, play my Theresa. Act her part as she used to act other's, wearing the very gossamer of her soul inside out for the world to see. You will not do. Give me back my Theresa. I'll take her, bitter and hard-hearted as she is, over a hundred thousand of you warm-blooded fools.

It is inclement, dull sky, gray winter. I pour my tea. The days, I have found, go by quickly here.

Theresa, here is a question for you—what happened to my rivals? What happened to that boy you once loved and you said proclaiming like a revival preacher, one lightning rod finger in the air aimed at heaven, "This I did for you." Why? Why if you loved him so did you so eagerly abandon him? This was the question you would never answer for me. What was love to you? A traitor's childish kisses, caught again in the vines of the arbor, my Bel-Imperia, as the fleets sailed on numbering one hundred even? Strung up and dressed down by the very locks of your love? Which boy? Which ghost? Which passing shade reflected in headlights on your bedroom wall long past natural hours? You teased me with the threat of him like a father teaching his son to be his rival. It took you eight years to leave me—and I always suspected it would take you another ten to find your way back home. I no longer have the luxury of time. Strange now that I have so much of what I so lack.

Given your flights of amour-propre and indulgent reverence, I am certain it will not surprise you when I admit that
I think of you often. There could be no continuance, the
planets would not spin or circle or moon—if you did not
think about it as such. You always understood that the world
was yours—lesser individuals, fools, they never understood
what we did—that stealing was far less troublesome than
asking, borrowing, or buying.

Once a week I take my mineral bath in salts and beads of
hyacinth. My doctor insists that this has no medicinal effect,
but I disagree. Last night, there I was in the bath, naked as
Nausicca and both of us praying for an intruder, except I, of
course, had the television hooked up in the bath by a series
of rigorous and water-resistant extension cords. How odd to
have the heady scent of hyacinth in the damned dead of winter. For Christ, our lord, no flowers, ointments, or oils would
have been enough. Sinner that you were, you laughed off
your parochial girlhood, plaid frocks and buckle shoes,
telling me about the priest at your church. "What was his
name?" I asked. "Oh, I don't know. Father Friendly Hands,"
you laughed. Father of night. Father of rain. Art Father.
Further Father. You were unrepentant, a thorn of a girl,
reedy-stalked and armed to the teeth. Pick a bone, any bone,
said Father Friendly Hands, and like the magicians of old he
produced a bright bouquet of manflowers for your trouble.
In the film which I, floral-scented like second-bested Lilith,
watched there were two lovers carrying on a torrid extramar-
ital affair in their black-and-white box of a world. Across
town three little girls were playing at prank phone calls. The
phone rang interrupting the lovers' tryst so that they fearfully
break their embrace apart. Cut to the giggling bobby-soxers
who unbeknownst of the damage they do, crowd around the
phone waiting for an answer. When the hardy handsome
adulterer answers the phone, clammy in his guilty hand,
one little girl says ominously, "I know who you are and I
know what you've done." The girls cradle their phone in the

receiver, ringing off in paroxysms of laughter. What would you have done if the loaded deck was offered to you? I saw your childhood in those girls, but translated into the lurid beauty of the technicolor age. You spent your days mooning over disco tunes and hunky boys on the covers of teen mags. You read in a magazine how to give "deep, soulful kisses" and tried it out on me. "Did it work?" You asked wiping the back of your hand across your sticky mouth. You were nineteen years old.

Theresa, it is no secret that I am no longer driven. We can no longer think of better or worse; regret is the fool's luxury. I imagine you now, young, still childless, waving those thin arms of yours at some anonymous stranger in a sports car as you vamp for a camera with your black sunglasses (*shades,* Hughest, you laughingly admonished) pushed back against your tonsured hair. Every movement you made was stolen, copied, or mimicked. Your life was a tribute to the originality of your thievery.

What happened to it all? What happened to all those boys and girls who used to people your world? Seven Rivers? It's a wonder Charon himself didn't have to ferry us out of there over the Lethe with the dogs on our heels. You walked away freely. This you have admitted. What happened to the others, your playmates—the Simon sisters, dark as you were fair? Do you recall the fat little one with the James Joyce eyeglasses? The kind of child who sent participles dangling and commas splicing as she syntaxed her way into a room. She must be quite young still. How is it that you do not age while I have been old for a lifetime? Riddle me that one and I'll walk on all threes for you. What of her sister who sometimes you called friend and other times foe? The trees have lost their leaves. I would have brought you, bought you, pruned and plucked hyacinths from the queen's own garden. Would you have smiled at that? You perhaps would have thumbed your nose at me and performed a similarly lewd gesture from the Italian school. Just tell me Theresa Martha Mary Mary

Magdalene, for whom do you seek? Do you ever get the urge to pick up a telephone, dial a number at random and hope against hope that it will be me to answer when you whisper, "I know who you are and I know what you've done."

The leaves have lost their trees. How like December this December is. Bitter poetry this. I have bought a box of sugar lumps and tea bags, good thick bread, a pound of butter, tinned tuna, powdered soup like the Canaanites saltwater tears. Will this be enough, I asked myself looking over my cupboards. I shore my share of stores against the ruins of time. I saw a man say this once to a woman in a film, "From the moment I saw you, I knew if I could ever have you, I could never keep you." Bitter poetry that. All this having and getting and keeping and storing up of goods. I am, my unwitting accomplice, putting my lands in order, laying my hands on the proverbial deck, calling out for the good country doctor and the priest follows hard on his heels. Do you recall the parlor game we played, "What If?" with all those tedious friends and Romans whom we called our countrymen. "If the door is locked," you said. "I'd kick it in." And I saw the others in the circle go wide-eyed with love for you. "Of course they did," you laughed later behind our bedroom door. "What choice did they have?"

This late afternoon you would find me still hyacinth-scented, rather like flowers growing in a graveyard feeding on the meal of dry bones. This letter was to have been less of an explanation or reminiscence than a promissory note. My promise to you, purse strings unfurled, lands in order, gold tumbling among the brittle chaff. It's all yours Theresa, cattle, kit, kind, and kaboodle; legally, sound-minded and feeble-bodied, desperately, completely yours. Squander it, burn it, kick it in, roll your dollar bills into rosettes and sparrows and toss them to the boys who ice your coffee and ready themselves to do your household chores. Make them earn their wages, my love. Pay them the hard currency of perfumed kisses, a bouquet of manflowers from Potiphar's wife.

Growing was the task for another; you merely counted the quantity and fervor of the blooms. Even inside you nothing would grow. The flowers in your rooms were store-bought, exotic gifts from expectant suitors and wisemen. Your flowers, plants, vines, garlands died dry and chapped from overly much sun and paucity of water. Catch the metaphor? The bitter allusion to the sea? You favored dark men, dark-eyed, sallow-skinned sailors with eyes screaming the injustice of exile from foreign lands. I saw you eyes follow them right off the page. Recall the aging German doctor to whose arm you clung during a reading of experimental poetry by the mentally ill? "Show me," I heard you say husky and breathless as he rolled up his sleeve to reveal the concentration camp's blue-gray tattoo. You seemed so genuine then, girlish, Cain-eyed as though you knew nothing about Abel's scars.

I do not ask what has become of your work. I know the answer. I saw you grow cold to it until you sold yourself off piece by well-formed piece, the very eyes, nose, and throat of you—How could I not but approve? "Acting is far too much work," you said lazily falling picturesque across a paisley divan. Sell it, steal it, plumb the depths, check the phone booth for quarters until you find yourself a blossoming hand-ful of silver seedlings. I have also bought two lemons. They are sour and sweet. How old are you now? One has already gone bad—its insides turned to rotten froth of acid. Tell me, you haven't begun to get fat have you? What a precocious Juliet you were walking the streets of Verona like one of the chosen, still with a wafer of Christ's body hidden under the damp of your tongue, a thermometer of your Lord's devotion to you. I worry—have I made you old before your time? To whose kisses do you now cling? Remember the boy we called your fool? Your soupy poet who did the jig and lisp and amble for your affections? How does his garden grow? "Too skinny," you said carelessly dropping your words, "all bones."

I am afraid, my thorny bride, that I am spent. I am little more than a bag of bones suspending an old man's pregnant belly. Is it alive and growing in there? To end like this—mortal, foolish, afraid of the sight of my own blood, an empty head and full udders dripping with the nourishment of unborn minions. Is it awake in there? What a screaming brood of love apples they are, my demon. Those yet unborn die with me. My world and every other world dies with me. So let's not speak of old Hugh. He's a fearful old ruminant, isn't he? He gobbles at the past like a plate of limeflower biscuits

As you know, it rains in the winter here. How solemn, how sad to see the snow patterned dirty with ice and rain. The weather is banal. I am forced to count my life by the seasons. My liar, I believe that I alone truly know your sins and secrets. I take them to the grave with me; how maudlin, how banal, how bony of me, how like the weather. "Checkmate," you called out from your feverish dreams, "king me."

How delicate you were. How noble. How like a queen. Death is retrograde; it sends me and my humble chart of planets, suns, and moons, circling backward on our respective axis. Who wears the cap and bells now? Will you, do you feed my successor with your bare blood-soaked hands, the leftovers from my table. Does he handle the carving knife with a butcher's ham-fisted aplomb? I see it now, the two of you, wrenching the meat from the bones stopping never once to daub those once-clean hands against the linen. Tip for him as you did for me the tumbler free of hesitation; full to the brim with the familiar blood and ouns, the chaff and gore of your mother's corn-ripe wheat. Where I have been, others will go. It is just as well that there is no uncharted country left that a man can set out for and burn his motto into and in doing so begin to think that it belongs to he alone. Let's count ourselves lucky to have secured a few sacred hours against the enormity of what lies ahead. And perhaps you may find yourself, despite yourself, indulging in memory every time you drop a coin in the box and hear it echo ever downward, descending darkly downward. Allow me, Theresa Martha Boughton, the last dignity of paying your way, because I believe I closed my eyes and blindly chose the perfect bone.

Adieu, Denmark
December 21, 1992

Pearl

I ARRIVED SUITCASE IN ONE HAND and portable typewriter in the other. It was September and there was a chill in the air. I had grown two inches over the summer. My arms and legs were gawky, elbows exposed and jeans unrolled at the cuff. I stood in the Houghton Airport in the midst of departees and arrivals, kids heading back to school at Michigan Tech, businessmen, young mothers, ladies in brisk wool jackets, and me, standing there, clutching that typewriter like it would save me, sent to boarding school, and waiting somehow, not only for my ride, but for the realization to hit me that I was alone in the world now. My mother and stepfather had oohed and ahhed over the catalog and mailed me impressive articles about the success of the graduates of the Peninsula School. Buried away in Michigan's upper peninsula, there would be plenty of time, they assured me, for studying, for intellectual pursuits without distraction. That was funny, I was never the type of girl to get distracted. My father asked me gravely, Is this what you want? And I knew that I could renege on the deal I made with Martin Hamlin, that I was already far enough from him, but it was not his hold on me that kept me from telling my father, no, this is not what I want. There were reasons that I did not yet understand about why I had to hold up my end of the bargain. I wanted to say to my father, I don't feel comfortable with the word *want*. Martin Hamlin footed the hefty tuition bill and off I went, bags packed, skipping onto the plane, dizzy, oblivious, sweaty-palmed, happy as a lark, clutching that typewriter, burning my bridges, stringing my cliches along with the best intentioned commas.

Charlie Gumm, whose name I did not know, so that it was only later that I could see the scene and recall: Charlie Gumm was standing by the telephones, shifting from leg to leg as he scanned the thinning crowd of arrivals. His hands were jammed into the pockets of his chinos. He was a sterling boy, you could tell that about him, even from a distance you could tell; an upper classman, the kind of boy who walked teachers' dogs for them, ran errands and carried grocery bags. The work boots he wore were battered but expensive, and then, oddly incongruous, red woolen socks showed bright and new between the rolled cuffs of his trousers and his boots. He was the very picture of a boy in the school catalog. Send us your children and we will turn them into this: fine and clean and decent. He was, that day, wearing a sweatshirt with the school insignia. Hello, he said, you must be Pearl? This was the first thing he said to me. Really, he held out his hand to me and said seriously with his serious brown eyes, hello you must be, and then the inflection rose with the hint of the question, Pearl? He said my name slowly in one neat rounded syllable. He took my bag, but I held onto the typewriter. I can get that too, he said as we headed out to the parking lot. But I said it was okay, I'd hold onto it.

We drove through Calumet and he pointed out as we went all the little cities, each with its own bar and sometimes a hardware store or church; Calumet with its grand opera house, Ahmeek, Allouez, Mohawk, Phoenix, Delaware, a strip of ruined mining buildings, bricks caving in, a sign advertising mine tours 2,000 feet below the earth, closed for the season, see us next summer! All the little cities with their houses painted bright blue and green and pink and yellow, tall and narrow by the roadside. He said they were painted and tall like that so they could be seen through the snow drifts which reached upward of seven feet in the winter.

"You could get lost in the snow," he said. "And no one would find you. It happens every year. Somebody gets lost in the woods and they don't find the body until spring."

How all occasions do inform against me.

"It's true," he went on. "It happened last year. Two hunters were lost out near the Devil's Bathtub, really that's what it's called, the Devil's Bathtub. They died out there. But this girl Fawn, from school, she was lost for almost an entire day in the snow drifts, snow blind. She was lucky though. She made it back. She only lost part of her toes."

"Some."

"What?"

"You can't really lose part of your toes, can you? You lose some of them or all of them, but not part."

He paused. "Sure," he said. "I guess you must be right."

We were silent. The trees were turning orange, red, there was a browness at the edges of the day.

"That over there, that's Mandan," he said pointing out the window.

I almost missed the sign as we passed.

"Back in those woods?"

"It's a ghost town."

"And nobody lives there?"

"No," he said. "Not anymore. There's just some old mining company houses. They actually look okay when you first see them, but if you walk behind them, they have no backs. They're all rotted away. I have a book about it," he said. "You can borrow it if you want."

"Mandan," I said. But I was recalling exactly that we can never go back to Manderly, that much is certain.

I rolled down my window, but it was already long gone behind us. I saw only trees, white stippled birches, pines, the greengold of oaks and elms. We left at that moment Mandan behind with the trees and bitter wildflowers, with the list of places gone, we drove on into the suddenly darkening afternoon in silence.

"I wish I lived there," I said.

He kept his eyes on the road.

"Where are you from?" he asked.

"Flint," I said. I did not tell him about the house in Bloomfield Hills, the pirate ship, the crashing waves, my slim tan mother whose wedding ring bore the royal signet, my strong persuasive stepfather who paid for my escape. Anthony, ref: see ghost of, father.

"I'm from Pennsylvania," he said and offered me a stick of chewing gum, Juicy Fruit. "Harrisburg."

"Whenever I hear 'Pennsylvania' I think, do you know what I think? I think 'Transylvania.'"

"Ghost towns, vampires? What else?" he asked.

"Movies," I said. "That's all."

"Horror movies?"

"Have you ever seen *The Dorm That Dripped Blood?*"

"Why did you come to Peninsula?" he asked.

I had the thrilling sense that he was going to tell me secrets that would be interrupted only by the running of the opening credits. He was going to reveal that the headmaster was the devil, just like in *Satan's School for Girls* and presided over a schoolwide ring of vampires in kneesocks and cardigan sweaters; he was going to admit to me that he was, in fact, from Transylvania, but no one must know his true identity.

"I'm not trying to scare you," he said.

"Don't worry."

"I think it's the winters," he said. "That's all. It drives us all—you know, *The Shining*, have you seen *The Shining?* Alone out here. Things get—" he was growing embarrassed. He turned on the radio and began to fiddle with the dials. "Sometimes I think you could lose your mind," he said.

He tuned into a Christian station. It was some kind of call-in show for teens and the subject was temptation. He turned the radio off.

"Even worse," I said. "You could lose part of your toes."

He grinned, relieved.

"What's your name?" I asked him.

"I told you," he said. "Don't you remember? I told you back at the airport."

"You did not."

"Yes, really. It was the first thing I said to you. I said," he imitated himself stretching out his hand to me, but he did not stop there, he took my hand, held it in his for a moment. "I said, 'I'm Charlie and you must be Pearl.'"

"Really?"

He nodded. "Charles Matthew Gumm."

He held my hand and shook it. I guess it was then that there was a sudden jolt and I fell forward, bumping my head on the dashboard. He slammed on the brakes. No, it must have been the other way around. He suddenly slammed on the brakes, let go of my hand and I fell forward banging my head. I wasn't hurt, only dazed and I sat up and saw Charlie Gumm sitting completely still staring out at the road in front of us at two deer, a mother and a baby, standing still, and he as still as they were, staring back. I couldn't help staring too at the doe, waiting. The road was quiet. The sun, just past its fullest in the late afternoon was moving, dulling. Light between the leaves reflected shadows and green-tinged patterns on the road. We hadn't seen a car in miles. With the radio off and the car stopped, I heard it. *It.* I didn't even know what *it* was. It wasn't silence but it wasn't sound either. Birds, each, called out from the trees, dark-winged, to each. Charlie Gumm, his white skin, his damp eyes, his mouth slightly open and jaw tense, sat still, his hands clamped on the wheel. The doe turned face full to us, kicked up her back legs and she was gone, back into the overgrown woods. Her baby waited a moment and then followed, gone, impossibly.

I thought he would say something profound. I thought his silence meant that he would say something deep and innocent, about how it made you feel to see a deer in the road and realize that you could have killed it, how ridiculous it made you feel.

"Jeez," he said. "I almost hit him."

I didn't mean to tell a ghost story. But, I suppose, I could say it was that from the start. My father was a ghost, my mother became the ghost of her former self. We howled and haunted each other nightly in dreams and memories. I welcomed ghosts. What else did I know? Jacob Marley clattering his leg irons promising the future, Caspar, Cathy and Heathcliff, Joseph Cotten painting Jennifer Jones although she was generations dead in *Portrait of Jennie.* It was all I could do to get from one moment to the next and suddenly there was this boy, his high puritanical forehead and damp mouth talking about ghost stories, secrets, vampires, snow-blind fevers, fervors and then when he hit the brakes it was as though for a moment, time stopped. It was brief and perfect and the birds called, but it was silent, and the sun was setting but it was not moving. You could be calm and lonely and scared and peaceful in the sun like that. And if I said that I wanted to live in Mandan it was not because of horror movies. It was because of the ghosts. But now that I have been there and felt the shiver of it in the bright sun, seen the facades of the houses, the ruined root cellars like open graves, the obscene backless houses, now that I have been there, I know I will never go back. I can't bear to look at the photographs I once took. We can never go back to Mandan.

Now I've done it. I meant to be chronological here and keep you on track. That is, keep in the *time* of things so that it would seem like I was really there; play along with the game, you know, that I was writing this at sixteen not at twenty-five looking back, but I've scrambled things. I was doing a pretty good job of it for a while; I thought I was holding up my end of the bargain. I mean, you made it this far, you stuck it out with me—only to find a certain repetition of theme in place of dramatic action. A tryst, a car accident, a murder committed with the blunt sword of the present tense just dipped in poison. I meant to tell you in perfect order—I was behaving myself, no funny asides, no jokes, I kept my blouse buttoned, no tears, no hands, no embarrassing displays of self-loathing, recrimination, or regret—the way all good stories are told, *scene, summary, dialogue,* how my mother and stepfather arranged that I should attend the Peninsula School in upper Michigan and I arrived for the new school year in September while the leaves were burning on the trees and the air had that first crisp appled bite of autumn to it. My second father and only mother had graciously forwarded two trunks of belongings, and I arrived relatively unencumbered, physically, if not psychologically, carrying only one suitcase and in the other hand a typewriter. It was bright, but as we approached the school darkness crept up on us. A clean young man, who looked, I typed later that night in my journal in overwrought yet stylish prose, *like an L.L. Bean Botticelli angel, a little bit of Arthur Dimmesdale around the eyes and forehead*, picked me up at the airport and drove me to school. We saw all the funny sad lost towns from Hancock to Copper Harbor. He pointed out places like a tour guide. He had read a lot of books about the area; some of them were not really *books* he was quick to point out, but pamphlets that you could buy at tourist stops; still he was certain this did not diminish their historical veracity. He knew quirky facts like the average yearly snowfall or populations of certain towns now as compared to during the boom years of the copper industry. We were talking and not paying attention. He grabbed my hand and the car swerved. This is *summary:* We almost hit two deer. We arrived at the school and he dropped me off at the girls' dormitory and I stood there for a while, bags in hand. This is *scene:* The drive wound and twisted down a hill from darkness into darkness; the trees added shade to shade. I stood perhaps for a moment, an hour, a second, on the steps and waited for something momentous to happen. I was far from home. I could not turn around. I had no home. This paragraph ends without *dialogue*.

Scene: The girls' dormitory at the Peninsula School. There were only three buildings to the school proper: girls' dormitory, boys' dormitory, and the academic building which housed the gymnasium, dining hall, classrooms, library, and offices. Between the girls' and boys' dorms was a lone row of faculty houses one of which was in fact the art studio, and all along the way alone were pines, birch, and maples turning maple golden with sweet sweet autumnal promise. Birds lived in the trees, teachers in the houses, and out beyond the muddy playing fields there was a small stone cottage where visiting faculty stayed. Perhaps four or five miles separated the furthest points of the school, the boys' dormitory and the gatehouse. A long winding drive twisted up from the hill down to the girls' dorm and behind this building the lower fields, damp, misty overrun in the spring with geese and the fall with girls in plaid field hockey skirts. All along the terraced Japanese gardens, hidden paths, marble statues, and fountains already drained for the season, the flowers were in full narcotic bloom. This was the kingdom Charlie Gumm bestowed upon me with a sweeping gesture of his arm across the reddening horizon. He pointed to the boys' dorm, gave me his phone extension, blushed, said if I ever needed anything, just call, okay, just call, anything. And he left me.

Summary: I found my way to my room down a green painted hallway. And I passed ghostly, perhaps invisible, floated past the girls just back from a riotous summer and impossible excursions into the human heart and great tans too! I do not recall seeing any of what we used to call *adults.* The door to what was to be my room was open and on the outside was a construction paper heart, decorated with glitter and printed in blocky, girlish handwriting, *Pearl Christomo, Junior Class.* I walked in. I recall walking in the way people walk into hotels in movies. I dropped my suitcase. I looked around. I noted that there was a girl sitting at the desk, her back to me. She was staring out the window. She said, without turning (it was quite impressive how she did it really, without turning, something Robert Mitchum would have done, not girlish at all) that my view was quite possibly, quite imperceptibly, better than hers and she hated me for it. It was then that she turned and faced me.

Dialogue: "Pearl," she said. Her voice had a sullen lilt. *"Those are pearls that were his eyes."*

I watched the seams of her stockings as she paced the floor. Stockings, yes, ridiculous, black, on her slim legs. She had long brown hair that fell exactly, no more, no less, to her waist. She was eating an apple. Madam in Eden I'm. I'm sorry, I promised I wouldn't do that. Let's start over. She wore black stockings, the long length of her hair, a miniskirt, no shoes, was walking around my room sulking, eating an apple; she had said my name and did not, I am certain introduce herself the way Charlie Gumm swore he did even though moments later I could not recall this. She touched my suitcase, ran her fingers across the buttery new leather courtesy of Martin Hamlin and the Midas touch of his Gold Card. She paced the floor and I turned to face the view that she knew was better than her own even if it wasn't just so that she could suffer herself to hate me; I saw the playing fields, the fringe of wood beyond, the fresh green breast of the new world.

"Poor Earl," she said.

She meant, of course, Pearl.

But I did feel bad for Earl. Poor Earl. He never hurt nobody.

My father, the ghost, he leaned, stepped out of the doorway and smiled the way he did, regretting all he had not done or could not do for me: Welcome to Wittenberg, he said.

"I'm Walker," she said and sat on the bare mattress of my bed. The trunk that Martin Hamlin and my mother sent was open in front of her and she reached in and touched the folded row of new sheets and linens. "I don't have a nickname, so don't try to come up with one. We share a bathroom," she went on. "I'm neat. I'm telling you this so we can avoid future trouble."

"I can appreciate that," I said.

"Really," she answered casual with disinterest.

"I'm more than neat," I said. "I'm fussy."

Sometimes I could not help myself. It was something I must have inherited from my maternal grandfather, a vaudevillian sense of timing. Even if it wasn't funny you had to try to make the grand impossible gesture. You draw out *neat;* you fast clip the punch on *fussy.* I'm more than *neat,* you say, I'm *fussy.* Badompomp. Drumroll please. Only she didn't laugh.

"Whatever," she said.

Bored, I suppose, with the hand towels and pillow shams, Walker, glamorous young ingenue, a vertitable leading lady improvising her lines as the situation warranted, rose from where she sat on the bed. Her fingernails were painted black. She held in one hand the distracted globe of an apple, hemisphered by her tiny bites, turning brown, slowly by degrees becoming more an apple in the abstract than a finely waxed Jonathan red. "I'll come back for you around six thirty," she said. "For dinner."

"You don't have to."

"Yes," she said. "I do. *They* asked me."

Alas Poor Earl, I knew him.

Out she walked, legs, skirt, stockings, not through the front door with its girly pink heart of glitter, not a ventricle in sight, but through the connecting bathroom door which she shut firmly behind her. I opened my typewriter case, found the outlet, plugged in the cord and wrote that a boy named something as ridiculous as Charlie Gumm, a name that befitted either a failed vampire or a successful oral surgeon, looked like an angel of the Italian Renaissance variety. But then, although I liked the floral quality of my secret notes, I realized that I was wrong, that he looked uniquely *American;* I crossed out the line and rewrote it.

Walker, the following afternoon, dressed like some nightmare of a mobster, sullen, petulant in a tailored suit with vest, cuff links, baggy trousers, silk tie and wing tip shoes, held her fork with hands and fingers whose nails were no longer black, but pale purple. She smelled of lemons. It was better, I surmised, not to speculate on why this was. We sat together in the cafeteria. I had spent the morning meeting with counselors and cabbages and kings devising schedules mapping out the future with the thrilling speed and accuracy, the rolling indelibility of a ballpoint pen. I would be taking drawing, world civilizations, English literature, precalc, and so as not to let the body atrophy for the sake of the mind, phys-ed. Walker had chosen a table in the back away from the others, fair-haired girls with ponytails, freckles, horn-rimmed glasses; brunettes in turtleneck sweaters, their cups of herbal tea steaming hibiscus and rose hips into the September afternoon; pale redheads clutching romance novels and science textbooks. The boys wore plaid, and slammed down trays—you could hear it echo, I heard it, I swear, echoing. There were tables of boys and girls sitting together, the clatter of trays and the sudden thrilling laughter at one table or another so that everyone turned and looked, slightly envious of the new joke: girls slipped back into the cafeteria line for a second strawberry shortcake, the teachers sat together gossiping dying to get outside and smoke, and then there we were, Walker and I, sitting together, not speaking, but I didn't really mind about that. She had exquisite manners, her silver fork, her lavender-nailed pink fingers, the brilliant bright green roll of her eyes as she caught the end of someone else's conversation. And I knew too that girls from other tables turned and looked at Walker in her suit with her hair parted down the middle and fashioned into one long braid. She didn't seem to notice the stares, so I pretended that I didn't either.

"Have you meet with Mrs. Marsh yet?" Walker asked me.

"I'm going to see her this afternoon," I said.

"You'll get your job assignment from her."

"Job—"

"Mmm," she nodded.

"And—?"

"Don't you want to work together for the cause?" She collected her tray. She stood. "All for one and one for always."

"But the job?"

"Dearly innocent Earl," she said.

I followed her.

"We have to *work,* yes, that's right, as strange, as foreign and brutal and tacky and blah blah blah as that sounds, you get some little job assigned to you and you *work* and you *suffer* and you pretend not to be nauseatingly rich and you pretend," she paused, she commanded, "You will pretend that you are a better person for it."

Rich. How exquisite it all was, to be rich. All one had to do was say it, say in Walker's broad expansive theory of the leisure class, *rich,* and like magic, *magically,* one became rich. If my stepfather was rich and I sat at his table and the funeral baked meats were followed hard by the wedding cake frosting of their bedded bliss, wasn't I the princess, and wasn't Walker a princess too, and couldn't we, shouldn't we have been the happiest girly girls in the worldy world? And the world of the past was growing more tiny, inversing itself with each step I took forward, little by little, the black tights with toes darned green, the clearance racks, the face of my mother as she leaned down to make sure that the nail-polished run in her nylons didn't show beyond the hem of her skirt; piece by piece, I was selling off the past, image by memory, my past in exchange for a chance at this new life. Don't think I didn't hate myself for it. Don't think I wasn't aware that it was part and parcel the payoff of the midnight dealing done long ago, an exchange made by sleepwalkers, cheaters, double-dealers. Walker strode ahead of me, her hips straight, her shoulders regal. She had to know that everyone was watching. Out we marched, one after the other. Me, I couldn't bear to look ahead so I looked down. I followed and kept my eyes on the back of Walker's neatly heeled shoes.

Down the long wood-paneled hallway, dark while light came in through the high windows, dark, while we walked down the hallway and stopped before the door of the headmistress and stood for a moment admiring the framed photos of those serious girls who had gloriously, boldly, inscrutably gone before us.

"Are you going in now," Walker asked.

"Yes," I said. "Now," I said.

She began to back away from me down the hall.

"If she asks you, and she *will* ask you—this conversation never took place."

I thought she was being dramatic, suiting her mood to match her suit, slinking off into the shadows like George Raft or Henry James for other more private assignations. But, she stopped, she said, "If she asks you, if anyone ever asks you."

I waited. She looked both ways. She searched for spies.

"—Deny everything," she said.

The door opened before me, and I turned to call good-bye to her down the hallway, but I did not see her. She was already gone.

"I'm not native to these parts," said Mrs. Marsh who was called, both as an endearment and a slight by her girls, Marshy. "They may try to fill your head with ghost stories," she paused and folded her hands on the desk before her. "It's only natural. This region is striking and also quite desolate in the winter. But I always caution my new girls not to pay attention to local folk tales."

I sat in a leather chair across from her desk trying not to slide down, to lose myself in its slippery depth. Symbol of my moral failings: sliding, slipping, lost, losing more and more on my way down. The Puritans would have floated me in a barrel. I would have to learn how to breathe water. Mrs. Marsh, I think continued to speak at length about how rewarding my experience here would be. The thrilling possibility of falling, slipping off the chair and rolling onto the floor nearly overcame me, but I dug my fingers into the armrests.

"—the landscape is charming this time of year," she continued, her blue eyes fixed on me. Her lemony hair, bright and fine, was worn rolled and clipped into a neat chignon. On the crisp Peter Pan collar of her blouse, white, was a pin in the shape of a Huntsman's bugle. The room was warm, and the dry scent of gardenia swirled around her.

"And dear, Walker has been showing you the ropes?"

But she might have said—

"And, dear Walker, has been showing you ropes?"

To either and both questions, I answered, yes.

On the walls were pictures of hunting dogs, pointers in fields, black and white springers, golden retrievers, men in waders carrying racks of geese.

"Walker is a lovely girl, isn't she?"

Deny it.

"And what a charming family she has," Mrs. Marsh gave me, graced me with a dry bright smile. "Do you know of them?"

"She's been very helpful," I said.

She coughed, just lightly, into her delicately rolled fist.

"Well, then, so you have your schedule?"

I nodded.

"Lovely," she said. "Simply lovely."

A blazer, navy flannel, hung on a coatrack. I could not see her legs obscured by the deep red mahogany desk, but I imagined that she was wearing jodphurs and that the moment after she informed me of my top-secret assignment she might at the sound of a blaring horn in the distance leap over her desk and run out the door to find an Arabian horse saddled and ready to go while a pack of spaniels clamored in her wake. Tallyho! The hunt is on! I could hear her calling in the piney afternoon.

"We do not want to foster the attitude that children of well-off parents do not need to be acquainted with work in some form or other. Work builds spirit." She raised her eyebrows. Her fresh, flesh-colored lips were pressed together in what I think was a smile. Wasn't that my file on her desk? Didn't it say that my mother was a substitute teacher who liked to call in sick and my father was ghost whose main source of income was stealing from the rich and giving to the poor? The past was gone. It was all true. I had first taken a train and second boarded a plane and with the introduction of distance came the increase of desire. All that remained was a file that called me the daughter of a stepfather and discounted the existence, no, the persistence of that little collection of collectibles—the images of the past, the math homework I never did, my mother's face turning the key in the ignition to sheer gray soundlessness, days too cold, hours too lonely, ghosts who handed willingly over the script and said, haunt yourself, you were aways better at it than we were. Tallyho, they cried, ghostly, sheet-shrouded into the September afternoon, tallyho!

"We've found something special for you, dear. It's what we call 'faculty maintenance.' How does that sound?"

She did not wait for me to answer.

"Let me explain. We have a visiting faculty member this year. He will be teaching English, and we are delighted to have him, to have," she coughed. "Hugo Tappan," she paused for effect. "Are you familiar with his work?"

"Yes, of course," I was almost enjoying playing along with her. "I recently saw one of his plays."

"Why good for you, dear! Sometime you will have to tell me about it."

There we had been at the Star Theater in Flint, front row center to see Mr. William Shatner in the ever popular crowd pleaser, *The Plaything*, Sophie, my mother, and me, celebrating Judy's birthday with a night of "high cul-cha." We ate butter-rum Life Savers hidden in our pocketbooks and oohhed and ahhed over Shatner's rendition of Lucas, the psychotic director. Joyce Dewitt, from *Three's Company*, played the assistant who secretly loves him while witnessing him court time and again ingenues. I can't remember who played the young actress but she was pretty and Sophie had whispered suspicious comments about her being neither young nor a natural blonde.

"Mr. Tappan is here to provide us with his unique insights, his wisdom and teachings. He will require a great deal of solitude to work on his latest novel, or was it a play? I can't quite recall, dear."

"How nice," I said.

She rubbed her hands together. "Good," she said. "It's all settled. You will visit him at the gatehouse once, perhaps twice a week to do a bit of light housekeeping. He is, you know, a rather elderly gentleman."

She stopped abruptly and began writing on her notepad. She looked up, sniffed, and appeared to have forgotten who I was.

"Oh my dear, Pearl," she said. "We're all done for now. Why don't you run along and have Walker show you the library. Her family has contributed extensively to the collection, you know."

I turned. She was behind me. I was waiting. I would deny it all.

"Pearl," she said. "One last thing."

"Yes, Mrs. Marsh," I paused.

"He's something of an eccentric, a real, ahem, character. We want to make sure that everything is, that everything runs smoothly. Why don't you make an appointment with my secretary on the way out. We can get together and discuss how things are going for you and Mr. Tappan."

She smiled and waved her hand, still holding her pen, and the heady scent of gardenias, sweetened by the afternoon light, rose, warm and trapped, making the room and Mrs. Marsh herself, called Marshy by friends and foes alike, dizzying, perfumed and dry.

Scene: Walker's room, she on her bed, and I wandering, pacing the green carpet.

Summary: We will spend so many afternoons like this, a summary of the present revolves, evolves into the future. She and I, sitting or standing, pacing or scheming as the afternoon goes from light to dark and all things become by degrees more and more impossibly possible.

Dialogue: "It's strange," said Walker, "Not at all the sort of thing you'd expect for a new girl."

"So what do you do?" I asked her.

"Phone job, alumni office," she pantomimed putting a telephone to her ear, unclipped an imaginary earring. "Hellooo, Peninsula School, Alumni Relations Office, how may I be of service to you?" Her voice was suddenly charming, rich and pliable.

"So this Tappan thing is unusual?"

"To say the least."

The walls were bare, cream colored, with one poster showing the characters of "La Loteria" on her closet door. The pear, la sirena, the scorpion, *the bell,* as Walker liked to recite cryptically, *and you under it.* She knew only the grand gesture; she opened the locked door and revealed to me her collection of suits, black dresses, rich wools, and silver buttons. The scent of cinnamon and cedar lingered. She showed me photographs of her house, and these were not humble little polaroids but aerial views of the sprawling estate in, and she frowned slightly when she said it, Wisconsin. She looked closely and made me look to as well at the grainy detail and pointed out where her room was in the south wing and how at night in the darkness you could smell the orchards and pastures beyond and you slept, even with the windows wide open, heavy and without dreams.

"Why did they choose you?" she said. She snapped shut the lid to a glass-beaded box that held her treasures, photographs, jet earrings, prescription pills for headaches, an emerald pin, marbles, pirate's spoils. She held up one hand and studied her nails, lavender, perhaps deciding if they should next become pink, peach, or burnt-burnished umber to complement the season.

"I can't imagine," I said.

"Is your family important?"

From anyone else this would have been a transition to a Hallmark moment. Tears and joy, girl bonding, we would discuss how important our families were to us and how many children we each wanted and what we would name them. But this was Walker, who sat barefoot, having replaced her suit with a woolen sweater and the bottoms of an oversized pair of flannel pajamas. Important? Her rules were like the cards pulled upside down from the tarot deck, ill-aspected, read as opposite.

"At this moment they are, my mother and stepfather, either playing raquetball, dying the walls mink, or admiring my mother's perky new breasts."

"Or perhaps," said Walker, "some horrible combination of the three, say, topless raquetball."

"On an ermine-lined court."

"Are they giving the school money? Because if they were donating some idiotic amount for the continuous and idiotic renovation, it would be an easy job. My job is easy. My parents have a shitload of money and they love to use it. They're sweet like that. They paid for the new music room, and I don't have to get my hands dirty."

She opened again the lid to her treasure box and handed me a double strand of pearls. "Try these," she said, "against your teeth. They are absolutely real, full fathom five seapearls." And when I did not take them from her she rubbed the pearls lengthwise against her own perfect teeth. Seaspawned and seawracked, she cooed, she testified to their purity.

"My stepfather," I said. I held my breath. "Is Martin Hamlin."

Her face was blank. She ran the necklace around her neck over her gray sweater.

"Marvin Hamlish," she said. "He writes show tunes."

"Marvin Hamlin," I said. "He writes."

She snapped her fingers. "Holy shit, those paperbacks with his face plastered all over."

"Stepdaddy dearest."

"All that crap about love and success and learning and blah, blah, blah, isn't that his line? Learning to love?"

"Yeah."

"Well I think it sucks. People should just fuck and get it over with. *Learning to love,* how can you stand it? Loving to earn is more like it."

I wanted to confess all to her then. She alone would have believed me and the stories of Elsinore, the horror show of the rewinding movie of those days and nights when my companions had been gel-haired leading men, the bosomy yet innocent heroines of romance novels, the cast and crew of the *Poseidon Adventure* as they set sail again and again on the 4 A.M. movie marathon until finally when there was no one left and the stations had gone off the air I began constructing my own revenge tragedies. Walker, shell pink and pale, she looked as the sky darkened with her pearls and unloosened hair, less like a mermaid than the ghost of a shipwreck coming back up to the surface to pull me down with her. We would survive underwater where others had drowned before us.

"I think," I paused. "I think I'm supposed to, you know, spy, on this Mr. Hugo Tappan."

"Really," said Walker. She broke the word up into two long syllables; up on *re* and curling downward on *eally.* "This is exciting. This sounds just like something old Marshy would pull. A new girl with no friends."

"She thinks you're my friend."

"Why would she think that I would be *your* friend? She knows that I don't have any friends. Don't you get it, baby doll, don't you see little early Pearly, it's all part of the plot.

This could be the most interesting thing that's happened around here since Gretchen Deutsch dyed her hair black and stood in the courtyard," she pointed out her window, "in her Maidenform reciting 'Annabel Lee' last Devil's Night."

"Gretchen, have I seen her?"

"Probably not. She doesn't come out of her room much. She's our resident vampire, or so the story goes."

"Tell."

Walker shrugged. "Really," she said, "when we get bored we haul Gretchen out of her coffin and talk about burning her at the stake."

Postcard: Dear Pearl, we have met the wildest crowd out here (no sign of J.R. anywhere)! I refuse to ever have hair as big as the Texas ladies do! Am wearing a new blue satin blouse (gift from M. matches my eyes, he says) black skirt, and sky high heels that Sofie would call f--k me pumps, shame on her, shame on us all. Tres chic. We miss you, really! Hope to be together again soon. M. is working on the new book, but we'll be home for Thanksgiving hopefully. Study hard. Don't drink the water. Hugs and Kissengers, Judy.
Hotel Mirage, Dallas, Texas.

Grief, I believe, was the subject of the author's latest excursion into the sinewy territory of the soul. His able and ample-bodied assistant, naughty nurse Judy, had officially signed on as part of the therapy team. She said he carried a little tape recorder with him all the time, pausing to hit the record button whenever a flash of inspiration hit him, usually in public, but she thought this was cute, charming. She was proud of him, really, and it certainly must have enhanced his credibility during his seminars to have wife and helpmate right there in the front row listening too, working alongside him, committed to the problems of the common folk, sitting with her legs crossed at the ankles, wearing stylish yet feminine suits and silk blouses open at the neck revealing her plump, youthful decolletage.

Along with glossy postcards from my mother I received in my mailbox letters from Martin, the man, himself. He was formal, wrote about a bank account and trust he had set up for me, quips about his travels, local color, exotic new food he and my mother had sampled. There was never anything to imply that secret dealing that had left me in exile. Inside the envelopes there was always a crisp green fifty dollar bill. I hid them away in the bottom drawer of my desk. Not that I wanted to hoard them; no, I wanted to hand them out like Halloween candy, but there was no place to spend them, and anyway what good could that foreign currency be here in Wittenberg? Walker and I spent our days studying in the library and nights in the TV lounge on the lonely third floor of the dormitory, where no students lived, but there were faculty apartments. There was a physics teacher with red-rimmed eyes who sometimes peeked her head in the doorway, but scuttled off down the maze of hallways without speaking, and a biology teacher and his pregnant wife who was studying to be a textbook illustrator. Walker and I watched late at night foreign movies on the Canadian station. I always fell asleep, but Walker stayed awake reading the subtitles, caught up, she insisted, in complexities of plot, but she woke me, shook my shoulder whenever there was a sex scene; and I opened my eyes to the tangled confusion on the screen while Walker, damp-eyed, gripped my arm.

I did not meet the illustrious Mr. Tappan until my third week at school. But I had English and drawing class with Walker. She sat up straight in her chair in English class and scrawled dirty limericks across the clean white pages of her open notebook. Sometimes she wrote me notes. Her eyes never strayed from Mr. Spencer and she tilted her notebook toward me to reveal the lines—*He's wearing white pants? In September? Land-ho. Piña coladas on the Lido Deck. He looks like an exile from* The Love Boat. I walked the grounds alone, caught the downside, the brownside of the afternoons slipping into autumn, the faint, rich, rotten burning promise of October.

I saw Charlie Gumm in the dining hall sitting with a table of blonde girls. They were laughing, and one girl held his arm emphatically while she told a story loud enough so even I could catch pieces of it from where I sat in the corner with Walker and two other girls, Annie and Lynn. Walker claimed she didn't like them, but she put up with them whenever they felt the urge to sit with her, or rather, us. Whenever Walker swore, Annie giggled and said, "shame on you."

I looked down into my tomato soup while Lynn talked in her slow, stoner drawl about bands she had seen and places she had gone while her parents were on vacation in Mexico. Charlie Gumm, what a stupid name. How that girl took his arm. How they were all so nice and pretty and rich and clean and well-fed. I watched Charlie Gumm eat his grilled cheese sandwich and laugh so hard he practically choked. I hoped that Hamlet had spent his time well in Wittenberg. In his rooms he read by candlelight books on the origin of species, studied grammars, slept nightmares, and feared portents read in blackbirds screaming across the Western sky. Was Horatio there with him? Did they stay up all night talking of the expanding world, ghosts, future kings, the significance of flowers, signs of the zodiac, the queen who if the theory of plot was any indication would soon die of grief? He was called, summoned on a cold morning. The knock at his door. He packed hastily. Charlie Gumm wiped his mouth. Dessert was peach cobbler. He had two of them on his tray. The girl leaned over him. Her hair brushed his cheek. Hamlet rode off into the green-tinged morning with Horatio at his side. His father was dead. The girl fed Charlie Gumm a piece of peach cobbler from her own fork.

"Don't stare," said Walker.

"It's rude," said Annie.

"Who are they? Jocks or something?" I asked.

"They think they are so pop-u-lar," drawled Lynn.

"I wish," said Walker, "I could find one decent guy with those football shoulders."

"And hockey player hips." Lynn interrupted.

"I'd fuck him right now, on this table," said Walker. She punched it on now.

"That's Charlie Gumm," said Annie. "He's nice, kind of stuck-up, but cute."

"I'd fuck him," said Walker. "Would you?"

"Sure," I said. "Why the hell not?"

"Hey," said Walker. "Let's all fuck him."

Pansies, helleborus, sassafras, balsam. Hamlet and Horatio rode on silently through the morning toward their destination. Violets, prize aster, bittersweet. The king is dead. Hyacinth, peonies, honeysuckle. Long live the king. Wisteria, lavender, phlox, Queen Anne's lace.

Theresa

AARON SALTMARSH HAD A SCAR ON HIS CHEEK that went right up around his eye to his forehead from when I whacked him in the face with a hockey stick not that he wanted to anyway but his mother told him that he couldn't see me anymore or really that bitch which is what she always used to call me. She wanted to kill me but I don't I can't blame her I mean he was beautiful. You should have seen him skating that morning in the clean bright snow all glowing from the cold. I don't care what anybody says especially men, men are the absolute worst about it, if you have the choice between an older man, you know, the type who you are supposed to be able to learn from and a younger, go for the younger one. I don't regret any of it believe me that's just how it goes sometimes. It's just when you think about fairy tales the princess always goes with the prince, not the old king. It's just how it should be. And there he was and if I had known that he was skating away from me for maybe the rest of my life maybe I would have traded what passed for glamour because maybe what I thought was glamorous was just tacky, maybe, and this is the worst part, it was all just trashy dreams, the sad sorry result of my tacky upbringing, one too many beef macaroni entrees and mashed potatoes in powdery flakes from the box. When I think about it, it's not like I really lost everything—it's just like coming full circle—back to nothing—except for the money, of course. I wouldn't want to forget to mention the money. I never wrote, not really, so if you want to know why I'm starting now it's just so that someone else won't do it for me and start saying I said things I never said or felt things I didn't know how to begin so don't expect any of this to be pretty or anything like that just expect it to be true every word of it is true if you can believe that and sometimes I even convince myself it's true, hey why not, it's all true. I never wrote him letters, and I scarcely kept his, they were lost, left, tossed away. I never gave a damn and damn I still don't about words. It's all because my life never seemed real to me not even when I was little it was like I was always staring out some window or into some mirror waiting for a sign or someone or something that I had no idea would even come. It wasn't real all a bunch of coincidence things and he would have told you that they were just words. He used to give me a real migraine with his talk about how things are words and I said only when you think about them, but why did we have to think so much? It's not that I was a bad person. I mean, I even had the breaks, the good luck, and I'll be the first to admit that the looks came in handy, and more than that I like how I look, sometimes I think about looking another way, and not just the same thing but older, but totally different and I can't imagine it just like when you start thinking about how other people think and that everyone everywhere in the world right now is thinking just like you, even the stupid ones and especially the smart ones and then the sleeping ones are dreaming and I wish that I could sleep a little more. As it is now I'm going crazy and not just from lack of sleep but from the ragged dog-eared tail end of dreams that come to me when I am awake although it's never him, when I'm awake and trying to fall asleep I just imagine, I just think will he haunt me this time? But it never is and sleep maybe two hours a night and I wander, which is why I like this new apartment, with its long, narrow hallways and its windows overlooking a busy street where I can watch the people going by, and thinking and thinking and thinking about how they look, although now that I have his money plus my money I don't need much, and I don't need to work although my dear mother might say that work builds character oh god she must have said it a hundred million cazillion times winter mornings when she had to put jeans and boots on under her dress for the drive to work because the heater in the car was out and she always worried that she would get stuck roadside abandoned like mufflers and dead animals my mother would be, her fear always to be abandoned and to that end maybe her doggy dog nightmare that she dreamed so much it came true so that my father left her and me being just like him meant that I had to leave too, I knew that from the first moment I could know, I mean I was always on my way out of that rotten clean homey brick house we lived in like the three little pigs with her smells of vanilla and things always baking and her late-night crazy drunkard laughter although this I wouldn't admit to anyone but a sheet of paper, not even to Mary Clare who maybe knows her own true mother's secret and maybe not and if not I'm sure as hell not going to be the one to reveal it to her. It's like what my father used to say when he came into my room to sing me to sleep he used to say Theresa Theresa because I hid sometimes under the blankets or under the bed and sometimes too in the closet and he came in and called out always the same Theresa Theresa until I popped up because I felt safe that it was him there and not her and you may wonder how I can remember that from when I was so little from when I was maybe three years old, but I've trained myself to recall every detail, every moment of my life when my father was around. I can never recall my father being old. He was young when he left. He used to sing to me this one song—my true love came to see me/she came from the south/her back to my back/her mouth to my mouth—and the other—at a hundred degrees below zero—I lose the words but I know the tune and something about a girl who loved a sailor. What I hate is when people say things like things have a way of working themselves out, because I am certain things are always moving toward the worst because you lose one thing and something replaces it but no it is always something a little less than what you want and I lost my father young but then I got Hugh Denmark and it's funny to write the name like dirty words you should never say like a secret you shouldn't tell. So really I was still a kid when I first heard of him this Denmark guy it's funny to think about it that way. It's not like I was a real sort of bookworm reader library type girl but there were a few things, things that you pick up along the way and like lots of kids I knew then we were reading Denmark, smoking clove cigarettes and dreaming of being in the theater with our hair greasy and hey we never gave a damn then. The early plays and the two novels, they were the brilliant ones, the ones that kept you up at night when you were fifteen and alone and the words seemed to echo and cut right through your skin so you thought if you could just meet him, he would understand everything, if you could just confess everything to him you could go on living. He kept telling me he was writing me the perfect part and at that time I thought I could wait forever because when I was with him it seemed really like there was time because of the fake movie quality to it all but I don't know that he was ever really writing that thing or if he finished and the question why I stayed with him so long, well, I'll get to that just let me think about it a little let me get used to writing his name and seeing it in my handwriting and someplace other than a will or a newspaper or book cover. He was never any good with money, you know, he got it and then lost it, spent it, made more and so I wasn't surprised when I found out that the money he left me hadn't been saved up or hidden away over the years, but was the product of a recent film deal for the first book but you know with all his money that he never had a chance to waste on anything but the memory of me it's odd but it's like time came back and then left again, he bought me time, he bought me. If you know his later plays then you know what's wrong with them too and what was wrong with him still twenty, thirty years too late they were famous and all but without any guts or importance or whatever makes a thing you know good. Talent has never been my problem and sometimes I wonder if that play that part might not just have been perfect but then I know I'm fooling myself because he was a liar a filthy dirty old man and a liar and it's only that time and television make you want to feel all good and happy about how great dirty old men are at heart. I was, what did the reviewers say, transporting, elegant, mystical. It was the words that did me in in the end and the crazy thought of it, of how old he was and my god how could you introduce this 105-year-old man to people and say this is my boyfriend do you think he's cute or what? Maybe it's not important the things I wanted. I wanted two things, I wanted to be an actress and I wanted Aaron Saltmarsh. Standard. And who knows now but maybe he wanted me. I know he did when we were little right after my father left god you could say it was almost the beginning of everything because the beginning is really only where you start remembering from. My mother had this big picture of the Last Supper in her room. She had little crosses and embroidered little Bible sayings and hearts but then there was that terrible big paint-by-numbers looking picture over her bed. It was Thanksgiving I was all dressed up in this ruffly new dress, and Aaron comes

by and he knocks on the front door and his mom has made
some pumpkin cookies for my mother and he comes in and
then the next thing there is we are in my mother's bedroom.
It was a short fall afternoon and there was no snow yet. It was
dark and we didn't have the lights on and he had his hands up
under my dress but I didn't tell him to stop I must have loved
him then thinking about it sometimes I do. He gave me those
rough wet kisses insistently until I made him wipe his mouth
not for germs but the sticky boyish goo, so he gave me hard
dry kisses in the November afternoon all dark and blue light
and POW there was light when the switch flicked on in the
room and my mother started screaming bloody murder and
my aunts come running in and Aaron fast as he could went
running out but they didn't care about him it was me they
wanted and there was Jesus staring down at me with all the
saintly pity in the world. Kneel down and pray to Jesus they
said, make him forgive you, but didn't he already? Wasn't I forgiven? I didn't want his words I wanted Aaron back with me
his hands warm under my party dress. I wouldn't say anything
until my Aunt Clare grabbed me by the hair and I was screaming for forgiveness, but I never once meant it. After that we
were sneaky him and me, in his basement where we found old
copies of *Playboy* mixed in with science journals, in the garage,
anywhere and everywhere I'm sure I dreamed some of it, but
then we outgrew it funny as that sounds, and we never talked
about it, you sort of pretend that you have forgotten. I just
pretended. He was a boy, a child, and in comes Hugh Denmark with his funny ways, you could say perverted when he
took the photos first he said they were for a producer friend.
Don't be embarrassed he used to say in that paranoid way of
his and I'd say what do I have to be embarrassed of? You're the
one taking pictures of a seventeen-year-old, mister. He said I

had a dirty mouth. He said I should wash your mouth out with soap little miss Catholic girl he said oh, don't stop, he laughed. Hugh Denmark the writer the old man the miser the anarchist, wanted to overthrow the world, but at the same time he didn't want his routine changed liked his tea at a certain temperature at a certain time of the afternoon and liked expensive tinned shortbread biscuits and then he wrote those outrageous smutty plays and everybody thought it was so great because all the women are either naked or in the process of becoming naked and his big finish is always a pregnancy. Earth-shattering? Not exactly, more like the Stone Age and the critics lapped it up because it's so life-affirming. He wanted me to get pregnant. I try, call it repression, not to think about that. I mean not to even think about the things I did with him, old and filthy as he was, body and soul rotting away under my very fingers. There goes Aaron skating by again snowplow stop spraying me with powdery morning snow. Two things Hugh wanted from me, a baby, and to do his revolutionary one-woman Cleopatra show entirely nude, lounge and strut and command an army bare naked and to think that people called him a feminist simply because he liked to fuck women. The crap people will buy just because you tell them so really floors me but you could say I bought it too for a while but listen I was young and if you say that's no excuse I don't give a damn what you think and you can stop reading right now, just forget it because I don't give a fuck about you or anyone so just go pick up one of his dirty books instead I'm sure you'd get a bigger kick out of that go buy the first novel whatsit called *Sappho on the Rocks* or *Consider Venus Yearning* or whatever and let me get back to my story here I'm sure even his ghost would agree with me that he's written enough for five lifetimes and now it's my turn. I left home with him after I graduated from high school. We lived in this boxy apartment in Detroit for almost a year while he worked on his new play and then he took me to Italy and later New York and later everywhere later. He introduced me to people famous maybe not I lost track after a while and sometimes told them as a joke that I was his daughter but mostly I never saw the people again we moved fast and then stayed hidden, locked up, jammed together sleeping all day and then only getting up at night funny how I remember I began to miss daylight and wear dark sunglasses like a girl in a movie because my eyes seemed to get weak from the brightness of any kind of light but I am certain I could see in the dark see through the shadows hear beds creaking on the other side of the walls know that other people lived just as cramped up and close by but I never wondered about them, just willed it all from my mind. We spent three years like that staying in hotels and with his friends, him buying me funny little things, picture postcards, books that I left unread by the side of anonymous hotel pools. He never once said that he loved me not that that's the kind of simple reassurance a girl like me looks for not at seventeen I didn't and dead certain not at thirty. I must have been crazy then not to notice how ugly he was, not to be sickened by it. What a kid I was. We spent two years like that before he comes out with it—I want to have a baby and blah, blah, blah perpetuate the Denmark genius, he starts going on about his son, his heir and I said you know sometimes Hugh babies can be female and he just looked so horrified like the time I told him that Hamlet just seemed like a homo to me I mean what's so great about another guy who can't make up his mind? He thought it was get this, TRAGIC to bring a female into the world not because he had any pity or sympathy for women in general but because there were already too many women. See if all the women in the world had say four children instead of two then you would need only half as many women in world to produce the same amount. The true spirit of industry. But if men, or if a great enough man, wanted a son he could simply by wanting, by willing, get one—they can will and command—ahoy, inseminate now laddies, fire male, full speed ahead. After he gave me the *Hamlet* book he was quoting it all over like crazy, line after line to impress me. He said did it inspire you? Sure I said. I remember it was a dry hot day, Arizona, I think, I wanted to swim. I was wearing this shiny blue bikini standing in the doorway. Do you think you were born to play Ophelia, is that what girl actresses like yourself truly dream of? The nutty one? I asked. He cringed. Do you know what he said to me? Do you know how he tried to further my education? He said don't you find the whole notion of the bathing suit, especially the two piece, provincial? Oh how Hugh Denmark loved to educate me, ahoy, ready aim, fire. Maybe I'll go in down in history as the bitter woman who deprived the world of Hugh Denmark's litter. The first thing he did when he decided, because it was all him, that he would be my mentor, was to get me on the pill. He was a great feminist, a proponent of Freedom with a capital F for all women. When he wanted me to get pregnant he simply took me off the pill, but I just found another doctor and went back on in secret. He raged away at me why couldn't I conceive he heaved it all at me, poured into me with all the spirit his tired old flesh could muster. Zero. Oh don't get me wrong sometimes I think it would be alright to have a kid but not his not cursed with that ridiculous name and besides who could deny that I'm doing alright as is, that I'm doing alright now. Every now and then I think about trying it again about taking some part because believe me it's not like I don't get offers the whole inheritance thing really upped my status. I guess the will wasn't the biggest news in the world but it got around, made a little splash and for a while the phone rang but I never answered it that's when I moved here and then it just rang on and on hollow in the empty rooms until it stopped ringing at all and I thought about him then not just because of the money but because of death and his ghost which I wait for sleepless will he haunt me how soon I don't sleep I keep waiting. I always saw him somehow dying in a way that would tell, that would explain and dirty, ruin his sham greatness and tell the world Hugh Denmark, dead in the arms of a fourteen-year-old blind crippled girl or something, but no such luck he died alone on Christmas Eve, probably quietly, oh god, probably with a sneer on his face as he completed his favorite cocktail party question—is it the kettle that boils or the water inside? Hahaha. Probably died crying lamenting that his legacy was not carried on, legions of Denmarks saying great things, planting seeds of greatness across the globe. Once toward the end of it, and here I am even sounding like him, he always used to talk about the END as though life was a book and there was a big END printed somewhere for you—but toward the end of US, me and Hugh and our crazy run from hotel room to rented flat, US, he came to me one night late near dawn and woke me not because he was drunk or angry, but he was crying. He got into bed alongside me, pulled up my nightgown lay his face against my stomach and just kept crying. I said Hugh what's wrong? I thought somebody had died or something. He never cried he was sullen, morose I said Hugh what's happened? He just said I am going to die without leaving behind any sons. I told him, reminded him, Hugh, you have two sons in England both married and you have seven grandchildren, half of them boys. He just sighed, straightened my nightie very properly over my hips and said, don't you see it's just not the same but I didn't see and that's probably because I'm not a man or maybe because I didn't really have a father myself for so very long. I never consider it that my father left me. I think about it like he left my mother and that's just how it was it wasn't feasible for him to take me and then there was Mary Clare well he never saw her except a couple of times. How did the song go, my true love came to see me, he came in from the sun, in one hand he held a silver dagger in the other. And Aaron skated backward toward me so that he must have been facing the sun because the sun was in my eyes too. You could hear just that cold nice *whirr* of the blades on the ice. True love, there's a phrase for you alright. For a while after Aaron ended things that cold idiotic cold stupid winter I was just dead inside and then I started going to see Hugh he never laid a hand on me at first. He seemed sort of annoyed that I was interrupting him or maybe it was just an act it's hard to say with him. I wore black and was weepy my eyes were always red and I started to like how they looked that way and sometimes wore green eyeliner which is awful with blue eyes and clumpy black mascara that I borrowed from Ricey because she could wear dark like that because she was so dark in all things and ways too I think. I sat on his hard leather sofa no give to it no warmth with the chill from the window coming in behind me content just to be with him while he wrote and sometimes he would make me a cup of smoky tea. One day I was sitting there and he broke off writing, he always wrote longhand, wouldn't use typewriters, swore that nothing good ever came out of a machine, he sat down next to me and said in a calm voice that he was not a nursemaid and just what exactly did I mean coming out there to torment him? Torment? I asked. He was my idol, a symbol of everything great that I wanted, the lights, the theater, glamour, parties, oh how I dreamed of that life. I am not a baby-sitter, he lisped in that funny way he did. What should I do? I asked. Don't wear so much black, he said. It doesn't become you. Take it off directly. And well, so I did. I took off all my black and Hugh Denmark removed his worn corduroy trousers and after carefully folding them did his little bit soundlessly to me on the Indian-print rug and he said look you've bled all over my rug. He said that after, not angrily, but curiously. In some cultures, he said, you see he was always trying to teach me, to better me, best me, we would hang this rug outside as a symbol of your purity. Purity, it makes me laugh to think I ever had any of that. Your purity and our spiritual marriage. So we had a little tea, and he went back to his desk and took up his pencil and I got some cold soda water from the kitchen and a rag and scrubbed the bloodstains out of the rug. So much for my purity, the whole thing took about half an hour, scrubbing and lecture included. Mostly now I just go to the movies and I really don't stop to think about him except or really what a joke when I drop a coin in the box and I think I hear it echo all the way down to hell where he must be. Talk about a full circle like when I was a kid and I'd drag my friend Ricey to about every movie that came to town to the Capitol Theater on Pontiac Street with the balcony and red velvet seats and mirrors all the way around in the bathroom before it closed down and first she'd complain she hated this actor or that actress but we always had fun, threw popcorn at cute boys, extra butter, bought spearmint leaves and circus peanuts, cried at the end if it was at all romantic or sad, yukked it up through comedies no matter how stupid they were. Now I go alone and always to weekday matinees so that I don't have to see too many couples. Not that I spend every waking moment thinking about all this crap,

but I do live, so to speak, off his money which he probably
wouldn't have even left to me if he had just had the time, even
a couple more weeks to spend it, but sometimes a foreign
movie comes around that just makes me so furious because it
reminds me so much of how unfair the world is what with all
the pictures I see of me in other people like it was planned out
in advance the joke we are getting to the joke of it all and
young girls generally pouty-lipped foreign innocent, PURE,
learning at the feet, the easel, the pen, the pillow, of some lep-
rous old supposedly brilliant artist? Go, and I say, don't go fast
enough, out the doors girls and head for the local high school.
Find one of those bow-legged wrestling team boys, letter-
jacket, beer swigging, sweaty stupid but honest enough to
break your heart, forget about what men can teach you
because there's nothing that a man learns in his whole life that
a woman wasn't born knowing. Even before Aaron before
Hugh and the others there was never a time when I didn't
know what it would be like. Really, that morning, that February morning when I was slipping around the ice and the sun
was about to break through the clouds and I was cold but
strangely happy in a way that I would never again be in my
life, was I really older a million years older than Aaron? Maybe
when people have different gods they just think about things,
see things different so that when I knew that the world was
just how it should be that day frozen bright and him with his
dark hair and squinting eyes, when I was maybe happy for a
minute of this lousy life he had no idea because nobody had
ever made him kneel down and pray to a picture of a guy with
long blonde hair and a pretty face. If you think that everybody
knows about Jesus and how it is with him well you're dead
wrong because once when we were kids and not even that
young Aaron and Ricey came to me together he was brash and

she was shy but together it was this collective look, and they asked if it was true that Christian people prayed to a fish, I swear to god, I'm not making this up they asked me. They never saw their god they never had a picture of him but I hated them for having him together and for him being invisible and a secret and how Aaron's mother used to say with no shame at all to her voice, Theresa Theresa dear, it's time to go home and let Aaron and Ricey work on their Hebrew school homework, and there they sat at her kitchen table with their notebooks and pens and plates of cookies and funny scrawled letters not letters at all and once Ricey and I got in a fight and I threw her crazy papers in the mud and she just sat down right then and there on the sidewalk and started crying and I walked away and left her there just like that in a heap, sobbing, red-faced not smart enough to care if anybody saw her looking so stupid in the dirt. Don't get me wrong it wasn't that I was a vindictive kid, I knew that if it wasn't Ricey it would be some other girl, I know about the kind of ideas Aaron had about how people think they should stick together by kind because a lot of his family had died in the war and I never knew exactly back then which war he was talking about but I nodded, the war, the war, so I began to think that it was this war maybe still going on that kept us, that would always keep us apart and that seemed to make things more romantic but more hopeless. Even when we were just the littlest kids we were drawn to each other and we stayed so close to each other for a while but then his ideas came back to him that he had to do what everybody did and that was keep to your own in the END. People are always thinking about that end. But let me tell you from all my moviegoing experience after the projector stops, the lights go on and the END is ended. I bet Hugh Denmark went up to heaven heralded by flights of nudie girl

325

angels, and probably a couple of fat little boys too, only to have God be the image of his worst nightmare, his ex-wife, and have her hurl him down to hell where it is not all bodies writhing around in fire and brimstone doing things so nasty that that would be heaven enough for Hugh, but a place where you just stand around all day doing something boring like waiting in a line that never moves at Kmart or something. When he married her, his wife, it was because she was already three months pregnant, she was eighteen years old, a sort of middle-class girl from London, but he said she had a certain fawnlike quality, sad brown eyes, scrawny arms and legs in her schoolgirl clothes, he used to wait for her after school and they would walk to some park or other and feed the pigeons bread that he had brought. She had lank unwashed brown hair and a sad face and this appealed to him because he was in his Renaissance stage so he saw her as the image of some painting or another and obviously it went beyond the birdies in the park because she ended up pregnant and he was young and not famous so he decided that the thing to do was to do right by her and they married and moved into a little place together etc. and romantic. He was studying law at the time with not even the vaguest inclination toward writing, studying night and day and she with the baby boy, Toby or Tio or something like that, she had romantic ideas. He had hoped that she would die in labor he thought that that would be a lovely and fitting end of their relationship. But she was pregnant again within the year and getting fatter and they moved out to the countryside I don't know where you could look it up in his bio where he ignored her and practiced law and began to write, first books, and then plays. From his little study at the top of the stairs he could hear her chatting with neighbors, making excuses, Hugh isn't in now. And he would bellow down as loudly as possible—LIAR! Leaving her, you could imagine, embarrassed with her Bambi eyes tearing up. She started painting and Hugh went on with his writing while children screamed all dirty and unfed, until he left her he was glad of course, she was, he said, no longer the sweet young girl he had married. I never understood why those two boys were not enough for him. You see it seems logical to me that Hugh's worst nightmare would be a woman his own age with enough of the world to her to see that there was nothing of art to him just sickness or maybe fear. I was too young to know any better I was seventeen I mean picture me then. I was seventeen years old wore clothes my mother made for me, bought lip gloss at the drugstore I mean I had this collection of every flavor of lip gloss they made: Dr. Pepper, Raspberry, Cola. Seven Rivers wasn't such a small town I guess, it was just far away from anything big like Detroit or Chicago but close enough so that you could practically feel the excitement around you, but no, then you couldn't. I was going crazy, high school plays, Barbie dolls, JC Penney underwear in two colors, white and pink with a little mock lace elastic trim. I was born crazy is what my father used to tell me when I was a little girl he said you and me are alike and I wish that when he left he could have taken me with him. I can't take you he said, how can I be sure that you are as crazy as me? He was laughing with his strong face, what if I packed you up in my bag and then you ended up not crazy like me but sane like your good mother and then what would I do Theresa Theresa honey, send you home through the U.S. mail? He was wrong though maybe it was my mother who was crazy and me and him who were sane because we had enough sense to be crazy. My parents had me young too, when my mother was twenty, my parents in first a small apartment and then the house I grew up in. My mother, my father used to call always your good mother as though I had two but I never knew about the other the "my bad mother"—he said that she tried to get him to give up his vices, his smoking and worst of all his drinking, and for a while he did. She was a good simple girl, with decent Catholic hopes and ideas and full of charity. She believed in all the little stupid things in her life, like sewing, like praying, like making her house smell like vanilla and oranges instead of boiled beef and cigarettes. I think that she finally drove him out with all that fake sweetness, the pillow shams and doilies what kind of life was that for a man like him? He was twenty-five, full of ideas, always singing me to sleep with hilarious songs about monkeys falling out of bed and cowboys and girls shooting cheating boys, so that I knew there was a world out there full of riotous living. He stayed with her for five years, longer than he could ever imagine staying in one place, and he left too although don't compare, don't think about him in the same thought with dirty Denmark. He didn't leave her because she wasn't his gooey-eyed child bride anymore, but because he was filled with the desire to break out of that house. I'm surprised he didn't set fire to the thing, god knows I've wanted to enough times, still sometimes in my dreams or after I get those funny letters from Mary Clare. I remember the day that she was born in September probably if I tried to I could remember my own birth, I've got a mind like that, everything floats to the top that's why I was, am, such a good actress, because I don't just memorize you see, I assimilate right into the rest of it so it's all part of my life, god knows that half of the things I remember probably aren't true, are probably scenes from movies or stories other people told me, but I can't tell the difference anymore and these new memories that float to the surface are so nice and dreamy sometimes. The day Mary Clare Boughton was born my father took me to an ice cream parlor across the street from the hospital. He must have, he most certainly knew by then that he was leaving, and we sat on the wrought iron chairs probably painted white and he asked me, what flavor do you want? I wanted orange-pineapple but you see they didn't have it. He said Theresa, Theresa look at all the other flavors and I pressed my face up against the counter to stare down at the frozen rainbow of flavors, chocolaty, creamy, lime greens and pink swirls. But I was adamant. I have always been this way, I wanted what I wanted and that was all. In the end he coaxed me into a Superman sundae with little sprinkles on top, but it wasn't the same, my heart wasn't in it. With everything, with ice cream, with fathers, with boys, with acting, your heart has to be into it. Like I wanted Aaron and I couldn't have him. I wanted my father to stay and I couldn't have that. So I settled for flavor number three— SUPERMAN. Oh, I got the money from the will, but let me tell you something truly awful. How it happened was that after I graduated from high school, I told my mother that I was moving out and there was nothing she could do about it, that I was going to New York. She cried and she pleaded said that it was a terrible world out there for a young innocent girl a world of sin and salvation is a hard path to find and then when she saw that I was set on going she bought me a dozen pair of white underwear, a new toothbrush, cold cream, and a light blue vinyl suitcase from the going-out-of-business sale at the downtown Sears store. Three days later she drove me to the bus station. It was the last time I ever saw her, as I watched her from the bus window, standing there in the humid June morning wearing a cardigan sweater over a flowered summer dress and flat sensible shoes and nylons, her purse slung over her shoulder and Mary

Clare twelve years old but knobby and tall with her arm around my mother's waist. They were like a photograph of the whole world I was leaving behind and I wasn't sad at all. You could tell by their expressions that they thought that I was going away forever and I was too but at the bus station at Niles I got off and Hugh was waiting for me sitting in the station reading a soap opera magazine and giggling to himself with some crazy perverted idea or other. We went drove south and he told me that he was writing a play and that I must be patient with him and for once in my life I was. I was deliriously happy and starstruck, if only Ricey knew, if only Aaron could see me now with a real man, they had only four dull years of school to look forward to while I was going to New York to London to Paris who knew where we would go first I guess you could say that Hugh was trying to win me over, make sure that I would stay with him, trying to convince me that he needed me in the worst way and he came to my bedroom only at night with all the lights out and even the curtains drawn with no moon at all, no light at all and I was an idiot I thought that was how it was supposed to be. One night after collapsing sweaty and worn at my side he whispered to me, I need you to always be with me stay with me. Who knows now what girlish things I said back, Oh Hugh, or Sweetest, or Forever! God I could puke but then he said, do you suppose if I drew up a contract, if I gave you enough money I could buy you and keep you with me forever? I laughed and said that I believed that was slavery and slavery was illegal. He persisted, don't you own yourself, he asked? Yes, I said. Can't you sell what you own? Yes, I said. Then sell yourself to me, he pleaded, a wrinkly hand kneading my shoulder in his best attempt at tenderness. Oh, Hugh, I whispered gently, you don't have enough money for that. He pulled me to him, his big gut wet and sticky against me, he said, in the end you will be surprised at how cheaply you can be bought. THE END. Get it? In the end, his end, he fulfilled his contract, he did buy me, he did legally pay for me and I was cheap because he gave me everything after he no longer needed it. You see, that's how he thought like it was all one big practical joke he paid for me after the money was useless to him, so it was as though he never paid for me at all. Sometimes he would ask me about my little sister, that little scamp he said, that towheaded tomboy you once brought by, and how does she get along? I was with Hugh, really with him, as his protégée and ingenue and leading lady for a full six years and he asked me about Mary Clare as though she remained a child, as though he had no idea about the passage of time. But it scared me too, I was afraid he would go back for her, that he was writing some freakish new play meant to feature sisters of some sort or another not that I ever thought Mary Clare would give in to him the way I did. She was a different sort of girl, maybe because she never knew our father. Wasn't she funny that day in early June at the bus station she was wearing cut-off blue jean shorts and a sweatshirt that mother had bought for me but I wouldn't wear it because it had a teddy bear or a unicorn or something on it. It was too big and she had the sleeves pushed up, all bunched right below her elbows so her dorky stick arms hung out and before we left the house when we were standing there everybody sort of tired and nervous but mostly given up to the fact that it was going to happen, that I was leaving, she last minute runs upstairs and comes back with her hands full, with her arms full and sort of cradling against her sweatshirt all this candy, this saved-up Halloween candy that she had probably had since the last October at the least and she just sort of starts showering me with it, stuffing my pockets with Laffy Taffy,

Sprees, Mallo Cups, Mars Bars, M&M's, Sweetarts and she says shyly, you may need the sugar boost to survive out there. I ate a couple of Almond Joy bars on the bus and I was going to throw the rest away in the bathroom at the station at Niles, but I couldn't do it. I just had this image of how right she might be. You see, god knows how she got that way but Mary Clare was born a survivalist, I don't mean she had crazy ideas about guns or politics. She was a hoarder. When she was about seven I was looking for something in the laundry room and I found this little shelf low near the ground kind of hidden by rags and things, and this shelf just had row after row of canned beans, not any other kind of vegetable, just string and lima and baked and everything. When I asked my mother she had no idea, when I asked Mary Clare she said that she was just planning ahead. You never knew when beans would come in handy. And the funny thing was that she had bought them all herself, hadn't taken them from the kitchen shelves secretly can by can but bought one each week with some of her allowance money. If you ever needed anything, a couple dollars, or a spare bobby pin chances were that Mary Clare had it stashed away in some box or coffee tin and here I don't even have her letters anymore. I've moved around so much that I just misplace things, but I'm sure that she has mine and that they're someplace neat and airtight and that she knows just where to find them if ever the need arises. And I have Hugh's letters, the ahem, give a good cough, the Denmark papers as they have been called and his nutty sons calling me from overseas sputtering about the archives but what do I give a damn about them I know they just call me a slut behind my back I mean men are not very clever about these things you can just hear the clenched teeth. When I was younger it was somewhat different, say when I was seventeen and the world rose and set on Aaron Saltmarsh and his football shoulders and hockey hips I never thought anything could change that devotion. I don't know what it is with men why they loan girls out like something they own like a sweater or car keys, because they want to show that they can give but not have to give up at the same time I guess. There I was by that spring sneaking away and sleeping with the old man. So there I was seventeen like I said, the spring of seventeen, Aaron with that scar on his face coming home sometimes on weekends and holidays from college and us "just friends" and Ricey mooning around in love while Mary Clare stockpiled french cut green beans waiting for the Armageddon, and I was such a kid, all long-legged, long hair in the spring dressed in black skirts and ankle bracelets that jingled and perfume that Hugh gave me in little bottles, blue glass bottles with foreign scripted letters, borrowing Ricey's older brother's car to drive out there and meet with Hugh and sneaking away perfumed, kept. So that my old world was going away, Seven Rivers was only a name anymore, I didn't pay attention to that world do you see? I was gone long before I left. Ricey called me and she was what younger than I was so she was sixteen and very shy and she'd call me and say where have you been sneaking away to in my brother's car? She worried you know that I was stealing her boyfriend. How could I tell her that my boyfriend was some million-year-old psychopath pervert genius who would show me a world she would never understand? How could I tell her? Maybe I should have hung the rug up outside my house and said this is a symbol of my spiritual marriage, does it make sense? She would have nodded real slow and smiled sympathetically the way she did all through our shared white girl-hoods, but I always wondered about how smart she really was.

She always seemed sort of slow to me, not just plodding, not just the last picked for volleyball or dodgeball in gym class, but like in her head the world seemed to go too fast for her. She just smiled and shied it all off and was pretty enough so it never made a difference. It's hard to remember what we talked about, up all night, all hours, loves, L'AMOUR, white white girlhood in a city which claimed seven rivers in its name but really had only two and one of those not really even in our county, but beyond if you drove out further to where Aaron's cabin was on Lake Michigan, it was cold and blue and foggy but nothing like an ocean Hugh said sometimes when he drank his tea sometimes herbal he used to say and his dry cookies he could imagine jolly old England which he said he hated anyway, he said he liked to imagine just how much he hated it and his past life which meant his wife and sons and the sweet little cottage out in the country where the neighbor ladies used to call and borrow things and gossip, he detested gossip, but loved a good story and I never saw the difference. It never was fair, I mean not just that Ricey had everything, she had her little family with her dopey parents and hulking brother and freaky sister, all of them in that big old house with things, things and rugs and tables and lovely things, things I could buy now things I've always wanted and when I get over the sickness and tiredness and the bitterness I suppose I will maybe I will then. Ricey could have gone to Europe if she wanted, her family would have sent her off and bought her beautiful new leather luggage some rich brown color and smelling new and then new clothes to travel in and money to spend along the way drop out of the plane window onto the poverty-stricken saying her see-how-we-can-give-how-we-prove-our-chosenness over and over. She could have done any-thing she wanted, had whatever she wanted like the Bible story you know about David and whatshername Bathsheba, get it? Ricey took the one person I wanted but I can't even blame her, she didn't even know. She didn't even know she took him from me, in fact, she always used to say stuff like, oh, he likes you so much better than me, and do you know what? I used to really believe her. It didn't make sense to me that he could like anyone better than me because I didn't like anyone better than him. But that is how you keep the world going isn't it? I don't know even what happened to them, probably married with a hundred and one sons all dark no signs of light and her nearing thirty, no, no, twenty-seven, like me, the same but different, the same but four months older she was and her—probably fat by now, saying, Aaron don't forget to pick up the boys from Hebrew school and pick me up a gallon of ice cream while you're out and what does he think about? Me probably. Me definitely me. I don't know what happened to anyone. I could find out easy enough from M.C., but you know, I don't even want to know. They all know about me I bet because of the commercials, I even did a couple of art films, and the early things, and the photo things, the commercials which I did not do because of the money but because Hugh thought they were totally hilarious. The whole idea of television was hilarious to him. Once we were in a hotel room who can remember where anymore and he sort of sat down on the bed across from the TV and just looked at it like he had never seen one before then he said, Look, a television! Like it was the most amazing sight in the world. He said, Look, a television, I think I shall watch it! And there he sat in his ripped undershirt and boxer shorts, the heat cranked up very high, sat there sweaty and unwashed for two weeks in front of that television watching. Of course, you can guess that it was right after that when he wrote his Alice in Wonderland play with the women dressed like little girls and it was a big hit, I should know, the profits are part of the estate. See, the price that bought me? My own girlhood sold for money no longer useful to him, see the cheapness, the bargain I was, how easy it all was for him. Did he die laughing about it, mourning it, praying to God for some sexy ovulating angel to come down from heaven in one last chance to let him perpetuate the genius of his name? He said his two sons were like their mother and they have nice lives. He wanted a different sort of son, a son he could die for and dying simply turn himself inside out and become that son and go on forever getting older and turning younger and finding more doeish girls to feed off of and into until the world was populated all with himself and he could sleep with himself and his daughter and his sons and create himself everytime he impregnated himself until the day that Jesus came back down from heaven to walk the earth and who do you think he would be? Another mirror image, pockmarked and big-bellied like his own true father, Hugh Denmark. Won't it all come out in the end? Do you want to know the truth, the better than tabloid truth? I did get pregnant he must have known somehow, even though I never told him. He was different, brought me funny things, sensible things, not like chocolates and garter belts and such but once a little sewing kit in a carved wooden box and then a package of greeting cards for all occasions, like birthdays, get-well cards, sympathy notes. He was oddly too kind. I thought he was on the verge of death or some new level of senility. He patted me on the head and asked me if I was eating enough because I looked a little peaked and thin. After I had the abortion it all tapered off and things went back to normal. I had the nerve, and maybe it's true, maybe he was a genius and we're just all supposed to sit back and let him ruin our lives for the sake of his art, anyone, any girl who he sets his sights on, maybe I'll go to hell for keeping his child from the world but at the time I thought it was the right thing. The doctor, when I asked him the sex of the baby, he said, it's better that you don't know, that you forget all about it and go on. So I asked one of the nurses, a clumsy red-headed girl, she said, oh honey, it was a girl, it's better off this way it's no life out there for a poor little girl. And that was the saddest part about the whole thing. It, she, was a girl. Do you see? Since she was a girl it was like she came from me, not him, she was mine not his. But that's silly isn't it, that's all dreams, isn't it? Dreams get away from you like that, skim right up to the top. I don't know who punishes me more God or myself. It's like I did something so bad in another life that I got everything and everyone I ever wanted in this life taken away from me and then when I had the chance to make it up to have something of my own, I took it away from myself just out of spite. I lied to Ricey too out of spite and told her tossing my hair which I knew she was jealous of and laughing told her that I slept with Aaron, made her think that it was me deep down inside who he wanted and even if she slept with him, if she married him, if she had his children and was buried at his side, I was before her, and she was the second choice. I wanted it to eat away at her insides and make her as bitter as I was, know that she was always the consolation prize, second, third, fourth choice, that's why I lied to her and she probably thinks about me famous the way I am and in magazines and photographs and lets it eat away at her day by day. But what if it's true, what if they're still together, sappy pair of childhood sweethearts? And I was sold to the highest bidder for the lowest possible price. A calculated risk, I guess. We were children then. We were children and Aaron said one day he'd be so rich that he'd travel everywhere by jet and I said that I'd take a train to surprise him and he smiled straight where later it was a little crooked around the one eye where the scar was that his mother never forgave me for. He skated up fast behind me where I was walking on the ice, slipping skidding having forgotten my skates and he came up behind me hard and fast pushing me down onto the ice but twisting breaking my fall with his body until we crashed down onto the cold surface all twisted together my cheek on the snowy frozen lake, his arms holding me down and both of us laughing the whole time until not even that anymore. His breath warm, his face cold, the air frozen, listen Theresa he said to me over and over until I stopped laughing and was quiet and stopped struggling and looked up straight into his face so honest it could stop your heart. He never had cold eyes whatever else he had they were long-lashed and big and hopeful maybe girlish. Listen, he said and everything was quiet there was no one else on the lake and still a fine coat of snow broken only by our tracks and I didn't say a word then I just stared up at him like forever and ever and ever and didn't feel cold and he said, you know you're beautiful beautiful there was this pause that lasted about a hundred years as I turned my cheek full from the ice and his warm face came down to meet mine with the snow in my hair and the whole world icy and pure and frozen right to the heart of it. His face again open-eyed over mine, he said, I'm sorry but I'm sorry because. I didn't ask why or try to get up or push him off me because it would have been useless I just lay still. I did all I knew I loved him all I could all that anyone could have and I put my arms up around him and pulled him closer instead of pushing him away and he said Theresa, Theresa. He took my arms held them flat by the wrists down on the ice, but only for a minute and then pulled me up with him, but left me standing there alone while he skated away again, skated a loop around me on the ice while I just stood there dazed wondering why the ice didn't crack and pull us together inside to drown to freeze to die. I wasn't even his first choice. If he hadn't told me, if he hadn't said anything I could have been free to dream about it, to live that way and dream about him whenever I wanted instead of hating him now the way that I do and hating everyone and everything except when you forget sometimes for a week or two maybe even a whole month and then it just comes back to hit you double hard oh my god it just smacks you in the face. I wasn't even his second choice or his third, or his millionth and I was nothing. It hit me that morning that I was nothing at all and that's why it didn't matter and that's why I went to Hugh Denmark and that's why I gave up so young because I knew that I was nothing as he skated away from me, bright-sweatered, doing circles around me, spraying me with powdery snow and I walked to where he had thrown down his things not far from me and picked up his hockey stick. He didn't even seem to notice or maybe he thought I was being a sport and the next time he whizzed past me I lifted the stick closed my eyes and swung. I caught air and I spun around losing my balance and falling down on the ice and he skated up to me laughing and reached for the stick still in my hands and I didn't close my eyes this time but swung hard up at him and caught him right in the face so that he fell backward, kept falling backward away from me to crash down heavy onto the ice. Later they told me that he almost lost his eye but he told everyone at the hospital that it was an accident and we never talked about it not later when he had the scar, never said a word again about it about that day. There he was skating toward me with his face flushed warm from the cold calling I can imagine it I can hear him calling Theresa, Theresa and me with the hard cold morning light in my eyes almost too bright, almost impossible to make out his face, my true love came to see me he came in from the sun, and the thrilling bright spray of blood so warm on the ice that it steamed up for a moment until the heat vanished up toward the cloudy gray sky like an offering to that old vengeful God up there father of all fathers Hugh Denmark until it froze redpink onto the ice just like my heart which froze inside me forever.

Pearl

THE PATH TO THE GATEHOUSE was strewn with brown leaves, green redgolden on the packed dirt of the walkway. Each time after cutting through the lower fields and crossing into the woods, each time I emerged from the darkness of the maple trees into the bright garden that twisted its way until it became the gatehouse path, I was certain I had stumbled out of reality and into a movie. It reminded me of *The Enchanted Cottage* with Robert Young and Dorothy McGuire; two disfigured misfits meet and fall in love. In the summer the trellis would climb with white and yellow roses, ivy, twining morning glories, pinks and blues. I entered the cottage without knocking.

Dust swam in motes through the sunlight, swirling into the sitting room. During the night the fire had gone dead leaving the large room cold and ashy; the sun, bright the way it was, only made the cold more apparent. I checked the kindling box, found some tinder, twigs, old newspapers, and two decent logs. He kept the matches on the mantel above the fireplace mixed in, always getting lost in his collection of junk, antiques, souvenirs: a Liberty Bell plate with a fine ironic crack down the middle, a deck of playing cards, pink depression glass candlesticks patterned just faintly with scrolling roses, a hair bracelet, the box of matches, a statue of a flying fish leaping upward with a clock, long since broken, set in its belly, a child's tin airplane, apple-scented votive candles.

"Hugo," I called.

The sun from the windows, curtains open and thrown back, caught me in the eyes, and for a moment I was blinded by the brightness. I called his name again and there was no answer, but as my eyes adjusted to the light, I turned to face the corner to my right where the window met the adjacent wall, just in the very brightness, and I saw him and then I could more clearly see him sitting in the battered wing chair wearing his old dirty bathrobe, holding a glass.

"Are you drunk again?" I asked.

"Not again," he said, "still."

There was something about Hugo Tappan that made me want to use words like *cross,* and *petrol,* or *biscuits* when I really meant cookies. His accent was so strongly contagious that it was almost a parody of itself and I found myself unintentionally slipping into it at times. Other times, it seemed to me that he himself fell out of it and into a Western drawl. He was so exactly English, so Peter Rabbit, Queen Mother, and Stratford on Avon, that I wondered if it was, if he was, in fact, fake. After all, what did I, what did anyone really know about Hugo Tappan? When I arrived for tea, our first meeting, he had greeted me in his best, most beleaguered academic attire. The knees were worn thin on his corduroys and he wore a cardigan sweater with rusty leather patches on the elbows. What was left of his hair, graying yellow, straggled thin against his collar. We sipped Assam tea in the sitting room; it was more properly an afternoon room, he said. It took the better part of the morning to heat it but by afternoon, while we sat there, it was bright and pleasant. He talked at length with droll exhaustion about places he had lived and all the little houses (not unlike this one) and lanes with their quaint English names, Tristram-in-the-Woods just east of Lady

Finger Lake. I nodded and crossed my legs at the ankles with all the politeness I could muster; how lovely, I uttered. I sat on the brocade sofa, deep forest green with a swirling antique pattern of grape vines and paisley and he across from me, teacup resting on his knee, sitting on a wooden straight-back chair. It was late in the afternoon, and he had the fire going good and strong. He turned his spoon again and again swirling the heavy cream in his tea. The afternoon passed from bright to dark.

"One must always be drunk," he said lifting his glass to me, the morning sun behind him warm, his face flushed with color. "Who said that?"

"Rabelais?" I knelt by the fire stoking it up.

"Sausages and beans to that old fart. I'll give you two more tries."

"Candide?"

"Candide is not a person. Candide is a character. I do, how-ever, applaud the general Gallic drift to your line of thought."

The fire was taking, and I sat, tucking my legs under me, with my back to it. "Gerard Diepardieu?" I asked.

"Would you like a drink?" He asked reaching below his chair for the bottle.

I shook my head. "Never mix, never worry."

"Swilling gin again for breakfast over at the girls' dorm-itory, eh?"

"Always. Madame Marsh bathes us in it. She insists it does wonders for the complexion."

"Baudelaire," he said, "it was that poetic dream boy, Baudelaire, who made the cogent suggestion that one must always see the world with the intoxicated vision of a drunkard."

"Have you been up writing?"

The room was in disarray. There were papers strewn at his feet, some crumpled, some scarred with red ink. His typewriter sat on the corner library table with a sheet still rolled in its carriage.

"I have been writing execrable poesy. I want our boy, this, what have we called him—?"

"Winston?"

"Yes, that's the one, dear foppish Winston—"

"Yourself in younger days—"

"Better days," he went on. "My Winston has been awake the whole night through watching the snow fall, gently, ah, ever so gently against the glass, and writing beastly tropes of unfulfilled love. Listen to this—" He bent and shuffled through the papers below him with both hands and slippered feet. Finding the one he wanted, he raised his reading glasses, worn around his neck on a glittering chain, and read on.

"Ahem, a poem by Master Winston H. Delacourt, entitled, "We Find the Bible in the Motel Room in Ohio."

> The Lord should have taught us some things
> like how to be naked in the dark
> long past natural hours when the heat
> comes up from ourselves rather than
> the vague power of his Word.
>
> How like the weather, you say,
> how banal, how trite, a product of second-class minds
> but it's the generation who suffers, don't you agree, you say.
> And how you command the weather to thunder on—
> relying on it as though your own grave syntax.
> Storms rising in the north with rain pattering
> endlessly as spliced commas.
>
> We should have learned a few things from the Lord
> and all his frozen-hearted heated silences

saying long grave good-byes to this and to that,
as though any of it mattered as much
as the weather and the clash of hot air meeting cold
which has left us stranded somewhere in between.

We will not, I think, return here
because of a certain way that you cough when you
mention the banality of it all and the same old
tiresome jokes like the one about six hating seven.
I do not blame the weather but rather the certain
grammar of the road map which led us
from Saint Paul to Xenia
like a noun to her awaiting verb.

The weather is the Lord's adjective, you say to me,
all description, endlessly endless, usefully useless,
the downfall of better times, places, and poets than we,
and I feel so small, so naked, so lost in the darkness
that I cannot even express my fear that you are wrong.
I cannot bring myself to admit the lie,
the weather, the rain, the rising inclement fear,
a tornado never touching the same life twice—
this place where we are now will never appear on a map.

Diagram the Lord's own sentences and you will find
that we are never in the same place twice and
the weather is less an ornament to hug her noun
than an adverb to force action into our hearts
where we hide the darkness and the heat
whose pattering chronology is unspoken,
unworded, desolate.

"Well that wasn't so bad," I said.
"How you command the weather to thunder on," he boomingly
repeated pounding the upholstered arm of the chair with his
fist. "It's quite unbearable."

"What has Winston been up to lately?"

"Since last we spoke, my dear, our Winston has fallen," he placed his hands over his heart, a perfect Victorian valentine, and in doing so inadvertently spilt the remains of his glass down the front of his bathrobe, "damn it all. In love."

He rubbed at the robe, stained and spotted from other such mishaps, overturned tumblers of whiskey, gin, and beer. I caught the sweet caramel scent of whiskey and rose to get him a towel. This was the inevitable process of cleaning up after Hugo Tappan, collecting his soiled and holey socks, dirty cups, and gravy-clotted plates which had found their way mysteriously under the sofa or into the bathtub. I waited and did the vacuuming, washed the dishes and sometimes even the windows in the afternoon; it was then that I dusted and handled over and over all the objects he had collected and I wondered where they had come from and what they meant. When I could hear his heavy snoring from the next room, I sat at his writing table and read through his papers. Those handwritten notes and typewritten pages reminded me of the story of Moses and the manna in the wilderness; I never saw Hugo write and yet in the morning, there the pages were, fresh, white, and delicious.

I was caught up in the story of Winston, who, despite his obvious pretension, I found oddly endearing. Hugo was a prima donna about the new book; he kept threatening to scrap the entire thing, and it was my job not only to clean his house, but convince him to go on with the story. He told me that Winston was based on a student of his, one young Roderick Lorde *(Roderick,* just like in *The Fall of the House of Usher,* laughed Hugo, delighted) who had completed and compounded the perfect image of the distracted poet. He had taken a summer course in poetry writing while Hugo was still teaching down at Kinneret College in Ohio. All summer Roderigo wore cut-off jean shorts, black and very new, that hit right below his knee. His legs were dead white, black socks, steel toe combat boots. He wore white shirts with neat pointed collars open one button at the neck as a grim concession to the blazing heat of the Ohio Valley.

He began the term writing sonnets. The other students wrote in free verse, the usual, odes to dead grandmothers, poems in rhyme celebrating the sunrise, poems denouncing winter in favor of spring, praising baseball, asking the meaning of life in clunky-footed iambs always masculine in stress, botanical poems heady with the detailed scent of red roses. Hugo recalled that one young lady in particular had wowed the class with her "Ode to a Butterfly" which was typed in the exact shape of the fluttering creature. Roderick turned up his nose at these neophytes. He came to Hugo's office one afternoon, the dead and hottest day of summer, and breathlessly handed him a bundle of poems not in a binder or folder, but tied with a girl's hair ribbon, mauve velvet. "I want to write sestinas," he said. "I want you to teach me to write sestinas and villanelles and rondelets. I think," he paused, raising his eyes from the floor to stare steadily, unabashedly at his teacher. "I have mastered the sonnet." Often out of nowhere, when I was vacuuming or coming back into the cottage from raking the walk, Hugo would say suddenly, for no apparent reason, "I think I have mastered the sonnet." Sometimes he said it over and over, shaking his head, still incredulous, years later.

"So Winston is in love?" I asked.

I wanted Hugo to go to bed so I could find the new pages in the ongoing drama. If he stayed awake he would tell me about it, but he would never let me read the pages myself. He may have been a drunk and a mean old cynic, but I loved (although I would never admit it to him) what he did with

347

words, how he placed them one after the next, how there was no end to them.

"Is he," I continued, "finally coming out of the closet?"

"He's far too repressed for anything that extreme. It is," said Hugo raising himself, steadying himself up on the arms of the chair. "A gentle older lady. Delicate and most fortunately unattainable. He is, if nothing else, a latter day troubadour. He mutely craves but to adore."

"Who said that one, the 'mutely craves' part?"

"I said it."

"Liar." How did the girls in junior high used to say it? When you were in a fight, if you said something bad about their hair or their boyfriends: *you lie, you lie so bad.*

"Have I told you," he said stretching his arms over his head. His belly was big and fat and substantial. He stood in the sun like a cat and stretched. "My dear Pearl," he said. "Have I told you lately how I mutely adore you? You scrub and dust with the urgency of no woman I have known. Come, let's make violent love right here, right now." He made motions of unbelting his robe.

"You offend my virginity," I said punctuating the statement with three loud sneezes, one after the other. Dust swirled up against the light, making shapes in the light.

"Well then, can we at least have a spot of breakfast?" He rubbed his hands together. "I'll settle for three of your expertly basted eggs, toast, lightly browned, those charming local strawberry—"

"Is that all?"

"—And perhaps a rasher of bacon, and of course, as always, your charming company, my dear—"

"And then you'll tell me more of the love story?"

"Do you really like it? Or is this more of that American

schoolgirl friendliness about which I have so much heard?" He asked absently turning away from me to face the sun straight on. He eyed his kingdom, the stippled white birch trees, elms, roots, pines, the unweeded garden, leaves crackling in the dry sun, red, browngolden, bitter green, the pomegranate seed red of late wildflowers clustered low to the ground.

"Tell me. Please."

"Really?"

"It makes the time more easy passing," I said.

"How I adore you," he said. "Never doubt that."

I was certain then that he was not in the least bit drunk.

In the woods I meet Charlie Gumm by accident. I am crossing through from the gatehouse back to the dormitory. There is still some daylight and the cold is creeping into the air. October. It is October. Even the name adds a ripeness to things, a browness at the edges of the day. He is walking. I see him in the distance. There are ferns, wild spider plants, mosses, weeds, pines for endurance, balloon-capped mushrooms. He is walking the headmaster's retriever. The dog runs wild through the leaves, circles, runs in circles around Charlie Gumm who is walking toward me in the last light of an October afternoon. I hear every footfall and the birds go wild around me, robins, blackbirds, jays, a woodpecker rapping high in a tree. He comes toward me from the south. His path is lined with flowers. We meet each other in the woods. His face is pale and two spots of color burn high on his cheeks. The air is chill. There should be horses tethered beyond. We should be speaking of important things. We should be able to kneel in the soft dirt and call the plants by name, the herbs, ferns, and wildweed. *Saxifrage,* Hamlet says. *Bellwort,* Horatio answers.

Clematis, ivy, ginseng, dill, nightshade, ragweed, lady's slipper, senna, moss, Queen Anne's lace, delphinium, manflower, sweet william, I meet Charlie Gumm in the woods and we pass without saying a word. There are small blue flowers close to the warmth of the ground, even now, this late in the season.

"You know," said Hugo sopping his egg yolk with a slice of toast heavy with butter and jam. "You should do something about that nasty problem of yours."

"What problem?" I asked. "*Which* problem?"

"That nasty and ever-present virginity. What's the use of it? And don't, my dear, give me that sullen and dark-eyed look, for dearest, I am not suggesting that I am up to the task. You have years enough of psychotherapy ahead of you, I daresay, with that bawdy mother of yours and her second-best husband."

"I don't know," I said warily. After all, I was raised on a steady diet of daytime television, romance novels, chocolates from my mother's suitors and the dyed carnations they brought her always already wilting. "Shouldn't this be a personal decision? Shouldn't I, you know, be in love?"

"Love!" He choked on his toast. He drank a mouthful of tea. "Love, don't talk about such insipid—I know what you and my students think, what the little boys and girls think of me—that I'm a fearful old lecher, a dirty old man. No don't shake your head and deny it. He's a senile old fool with his drawers always around his ankles, but don't think that I don't know something about the way people, as you say, fall in love. Year by year," he went on, "my students have revealed and bared themselves to me, generations of third-rate lovers. *Saint Anne, Saint Anne, find me a man.* True love, romance," he coughed again. "You'll awake one morning to find yourself a modest thirty-five years old knitting tea cozies, adopting stray cats and scanning the personals for it, true love."

"Well, maybe that's my fate," I said. "Who can argue with fate?"

"I think not."

"Why should I be any different from the others?"

"Because I'm selfish, because we can't have a truly civilized discussion on any topic, mind you, from the fall of Byzantium to Princess Di's new bonnet, until you do. Something will always be missing. You will remain *uninformed*. There is no simple way to explain this. What can one say? I implore you, join us, join the living," he said this and set his cup, empty to the lees, down on the mismatched saucer.

After school I wander the aisles of the library. Walker sits nearby reading French in an overstuffed armchair. Her hair is tightly pulled back into a braid, and she holds her book close to her face. On the shelves I find *Good Morning, Midnight, Antigone,* and *Summer.* I sit on the floor in the corner and read. Walker calls to me in a whisper, come look. We go to the window and watch as Charlie Gumm crosses past the row of neat houses with their pointed roofs. He is carrying a pumpkin, orange, fat, and round in his arms. He looks, says Walker, poking me in my side, just like a boy in a movie. He missteps, almost trips, catches himself and looks around to see if anyone has noticed. Seeing no one, he walks on. Vegetable love, whispers Walker and we break into laughter until the librarian comes by asking us to be quiet please, please be quiet, please.

"Must you create that infernal racket out there," Hugo barefoot, hair tousled, said coming out of his bedroom and pulling the plug on my vacuum.

"I thought you admired my cleaning," I said.

"An enterprise more valued in spirit than in practice. How much mess, really, can one frail old man create in a week?" He ran a hand through his greasy hair. I looked at his bare feet; they were strange hideous things, the toes red and curled under.

"Just doing my job," I said. "Should I dust? That would be quieter."

"It's not your job."

"Sure it is."

"I daresay they didn't mean it so, hmm, literally. You're probably just supposed to spy on me. I have," he paused, sat in his battered wing chair, "something of a reputation."

"Really?"

"Oh, yes," he said, "I'm generally considered—"

"A bad influence?"

"—something of a bon vivant."

"I think they did want me to spy," I said.

"Well then, this is just getting jolly. Have you told them about the orgies? The nightly bacchanals and Dionysian feasts of love?"

"I told them you were a harmless old man."

"And they believed it?"

"That you were a slob who needed a lot of cleaning up after."

"Practically incontinent, hmm? How embarrassing. You've robbed me of my brute pride, my dear, left me a toothless cuckold."

"You still have your pitchfork."

"Not to mention," he stretched his arms over his head, "my minions of the undead to do my bidding."

"Why do you think I would be the one, you know, who they picked. Do I look like a spy? Do I look disloyal or something?"

"Perhaps it was luck."

"I doubt that."

"Well, then let's call it my luck, my good fortune, that you were chosen by fate to comfort me in my twilight years. I pronounce that your new job is not this prissy chargirl work, ruining and blistering your dainty little fingers. Your job is simply to converse with me."

"No vacuuming? No waxy build up? No poached eggs?"

"Eggs," he said. "Now that is another matter entirely. But let's put that aside for a moment—I have a question for you, a bit of *conversation*—"

"Alright," I said. "Let's hear it."

"We'll start with an easy one in three parts. Think about this—at one time man believed there was a chain, an order of being. There was the Lord God and then certain ranks of archangels, angels, and seraphim, cherubim and then, finally, between the apes and the angels, man."

"Go on—"

"Well, man doesn't necessarily have this faith in himself today, does he? What did it? What knocked him so far from the angels, made him lose his footing on the ladder? What three things, really, are most responsible for our loss?"

"Maybe people just got more advanced—"

"You can do better than that. I won't even count *that.*"

"It was a warm up," I said. "Not a real answer."

"By all means," he said, "think it over."

We sat in silence for a while. He studied his yellowish fingernails.

"The black plague, all that death. And no one could stop it. Didn't it kill, like, half of the world, or Europe?"

"Well, that's charming enough, but mortality rates were high anyway and the black death was simply chalked up, once again, to fate and divine will."

"Fate," I repeated. When you don't know the answer always just say *fate*.

"Number one," he said. "Galileo. The heliocentric universe. Heaven was displaced. The world did not center on, or revolve around, man."

"I can see that. Okay. So first it was the world. It would have to be right? It would have to be something terrestrial."

"Number two?" He quizzed me.

"The industrial revolution."

"You keep choosing *effects* not *causes*. Number two, Darwin."

"Lower than the angels, but not even above the apes."

"Yes," he said. "See how simple the game is if you think about it?"

"Three?"

"Psychoanalysis," he said sparing me the last guess. "Man is not the center of the universe, nor is he the inheritor of the angel's wings. Man is not even the master of his own house, his mind."

"I think there's one more," I said.

"Do go on."

"Four. Man isn't even the master of his own woman."

"Well, now here's a new bone for an old dog."

"Sure, don't you think so? The effects of gender equality?"

"*Gender equality?* You are something of a bluestocking, aren't you?"

"What do you mean?"

"You know, a women's libber."

"You mean a feminist?"

"Sisterhood, suffrage, *the cause;* the right to wear trousers and smoke cigarettes in public."

"I don't know," I said. There was something else, something missing. He wasn't getting the point of number four. What it meant—not for men to lose control over women—but for women to be free. I think I knew what it meant. I think I was born into this lost feeling.

"What?" he asked. "Do you doubt the cause?"

"It's nothing like that."

"This sounds rather intriguing and mysterious. Do go on."

"I just," I stopped. Two birds sat on the window ledge. Why would anyone be foolish enough to tell secrets to Hugo Tappan? He would only laugh and use them later against you; from his ears to his pen, that was the only progression he knew.

"You don't have to explain," he said.

"I don't?"

"It's only that you don't feel like anything, or rather like *either,* do you? Not a man or a woman?"

"Yes," I said. "That's it exactly. I never feel like either, but other girls must. I mean, they do, don't they?"

He turned to the window. "It's probably your mother's fault," he said. "It always comes back to that. All that business with the—" he gestured breasts over his own swollen belly. "—it must have been most unpleasant for a child."

It begins to rain. I am walking back to the girls' dormitory. I am thinking I am going to see him again. I hear the light, cold autumn rain, rustle of leaves. I am certain these are the footfalls of his well-worn boots. It is nothing. It is the rain, only the wind. My shoes sink in the damp earth. Plant me, plant me and I'll sleep and bloom again in the spring. Hugo told me the story of Tiresias, not man, not woman, both, throbbing between two lives. This is our fate too, he said. Because of the snakes we have separated. Blind, neither nor. The sharp and steady rain. My mother in the bathroom fingering her short, neat curls, painting her lips. The country music station plays soft on her radio. It makes you feel more feminine she says and bends to paint my face. A little mystery, she says, never hurts. I am neither nor. No one teaches you. I close my eyes blind against her. I turn my collar up. The sky darkens. A little mystery, she says and laughs, bright blue-eyed and sprays me with perfume, daubs powder on my nose. It's not one or the other; he is right. It is neither. The rain rolls under my collar, cold and bitter, down my neck. You'll see how it is, she says. You'll learn. It never stops.

"Have you given any more thought to my suggestion?" asked Hugo.

I visited Hugo now most afternoons in the school's "open time" between three and dinner at six o'clock. If I wasn't in the sunny back room of the library where there were two over-stuffed chairs, a window seat with dusty velveteen cushions and ivy creeping from pots which the librarian tended carefully so as not to water damage any of the books, then I was with Hugo.

At first I thought that Hugo wouldn't tolerate so much of my presence, that I might be nothing more than a novelty to him, a precocious child whose constant visits were a chore. Do you mind me stopping by, I had asked him. He bluntly enjoyed the privilege of being rude the way only truly tactful people do; I'll tell you when I'm quite sick of you, he said.

"Which suggestion?" I asked playing dumb. "You mean about planting tulip bulbs in the side garden?"

"It will be fun," he said. "A game to break up the tiresome monotony of this country living. Let's pick someone out for you. Set you up, as the plebs say."

"With who?"

"We have a stackful of eligible applicants—"

"Not those losers," I said watching as he shuffled through a stack of papers. "Not your students—"

"Yes, yes, what could be better? I know them quite well already. I know their little hopes and desires. It would seem that that is all they know how to write about. I'm like a doctor," he said. "It's all quite confidential."

We sat at the kitchen table. Wednesday afternoon. The warmest part of the day had just passed. The field hockey girls were out practicing, running laps, raising their sticks out on the playing fields. Hugo and I drank coffee, strong, instant, and bitter. He shuffled through his manila folder jammed full of his students' weekly poems and stories.

"By Saint Anne," he said, "let's find you a man. We'll judge the fellow by the weight of his words."

"Would you have picked Roderick if he had been in the class now?"

"Heavens no. That type is all wrong for you."

"So who's the best in the class?"

"You certainly don't want the best."

"Don't I deserve the best?"

"I'm sure your mummy and daddy have told you that kitten always *deserves* the best, but in this case it would only lead to problems. We want matter, not art. We don't want thought; we want a man of action, not intention."

"I don't like the sound of that."

357

"Let's just read on, shall we?"

He read aloud to me, his glasses on their fussy, spinsterish chain. He coughed and laughed and threw papers down muttering in disgust after only the first or second lines. He read through them all, and the afternoon lost its colors, went from brown to blue, and I knew that I should be heading back to meet Walker for dinner.

"Who is to be the lucky beau?" he asked. "What do you propose?"

"I propose to do nothing," I said and stood. I put my teacup in the sink.

"I hate that," said Hugo. "I hate letting nature take its course. I hate young love. Just promise me, if you do find him on your own, don't be coy about it, don't take his pin, don't give each other puppy dog looks, don't start staring into every mirror you pass and talking about growing out your hair."

"Would you like some more coffee before I go?"

"Just a spot," he said and held his cup out to me.

For a while I wanted nothing more than to keep on wanting.

A freshman girl knocks on my door. Pearl, she says. Her job is the front desk phone monitor. Everybody thinks she's precious, the way she answers the phone in different voices. Pearl, she says rapping lightly on my door before pushing it open. Walker, her feet in boots propped on my desk, is sitting, tilting back and forth in a straight chair. She is looking out the window. We are talking about buying goldfish and naming them for famous tragic couples. She says, Persephone and Hades. I say, Hamlet and Ophelia. Too common, she says. How about Desdemona and Othello? She goes on, we could get a Black Molly and a Calico Gold. Too crass, I say. Pearl, says the freshman, there's a boy downstairs to see you. Walker and I ignore her. She backs out of the door grinning. Jocasta and Oedipus, I say, Walker says, that's what I like about you Pearl girl, you cut right to the heart of things.

Hugo sat before his electric typewriter.

"I won't be any bother," I said lapsing, I realized, into some sort of chargirl's syntax. I almost curtseyed.

"It doesn't matter," he said. "I'm sick to death of all this morbid business anyway. Do you know what has, what is happening now?"

I shook my head.

"Winston has gone and gotten himself involved with some gaggle of teenage lesbians."

"Have you been watching *Donahue* again? Did I tell you that my stepfather was on *Donahue?*"

"It's only that," he turned away from the typewriter. "He thinks they are tragic."

"It might make for a good movie."

"Yes," he said. "Good sober fun for the entire family to enjoy, no doubt."

"Tea?"

He nodded.

"Tell me something," he called to me in the kitchen.

"Yes?"

"Do you find the quality of the tragic more appealing in a man or in a woman?"

"A woman, I guess," I said when he joined me in kitchen.

"Don't just follow me blindly," he said. "Things would—"

"I said a woman, that's my answer. Is it the right answer or the wrong answer?"

"Don't you want to know what I mean by tragic? Don't you want your terms defined before you plunge headlong into the thick of it?"

"No."

"Then please, my contrary darling, by all means, explain your answer."

He crossed his arms over his chest.

"My mother used to always talk about fate, about how meeting my stepfather was her destiny. All the women she knew, I knew, were sad, because, I don't know. You know, it's like they were all waiting for something—"

"Why do you think that was?"

"Because—"

"Because they were empty and needy? Because they were alone?"

"No, it wasn't that."

"Yes," he insisted, "it always comes down to that. What does sadness, what has sadness ever had to do with tragedy? It's about terror and pity. It's the tale of a hero's fall from a high and glorious position of favor into disgrace. I don't know that any woman could be truly tragic. I won't begrudge you the issue of sadness, but you see, it's not the same thing, not in the least."

"Women can be tragic," I said.

The kettle began to steam.

"Women can be heroic," he said. "There's no doubt about that, but they are always far too clever, too aware to be tragic. Tragic, tragedy—it's about a certain blindness of self-knowledge. Heroines never have enough bad sense, or hubris, to fall into the thick of it with their eyes wide open. It's because deep down, at the heart of it all, they consider themselves unworthy, second best. They never truly believe, as tragic heroes must, that God-given charm and warrior flair will save them from, as you and your mother put it, fate."

"Clytemnestra?"

"Pure jealousy, no fate about it. It was Achilles against whom fate conspired; Achilles who could not stop himself from bringing home Cassandra right into his wife's own Sunday parlor as a most worthwhile spoil of war."

"Jocasta?"

"What was ever tragic about a mother's love? Wasn't her son at fault for wanting too much? Anyway, it's not her story. She's incidental. She was the empty vessel of her son's desire. It's the same for Gertrude. If you seek the hero of a tragedy look to the title."

"What about," I took the cups from the dish rack, his and mine, the Dutch white and blue cups with the mismatched saucers. I poured from the carton into a little silver pitcher of milk, placed a salver with sugar cubes and tiny silver tongs down on the table. Hugo had miraculously produced these treasures from a leather satchel one afternoon saying, we have to keep civilization going. "You know, what's her name, that, with the son, Medea?"

"Haven't we covered the mother-son issue?" he said roundly.

"Antigone," I said. "It's in the title."

I poured the tea. "You would pick that one. All virgin tombs, empty wombs, and bridal shrouds. It's her father's tragedy and she comes by it secondhand. She's not a figure of tragedy, but a martyr, just as Christ himself would later be. You would have been better off choosing Cleopatra. Now there was a woman, a force with whom to be reckoned."

"Cleopatra," I said.

"It's too late now," he went on, "to say it."

"Why?"

"I'm tired of the game. It would be so nice if we had something new, something different to talk about."

"What would we talk about *then* that would be any different from now?"

"The unworded things. The difficult things. It is impossible to foresee and after it has happened it will be impossible to look back on your life in quite the same way, with the same certainty about time and events."

Sunday is the last burning day of autumn, by Monday the cold will be upon us and will remain until the thaws, the wet days of March and April. Everything is bright and golden in the last flush stages of burning, smoky, red. The sun is strong, and you can smell the dampth of the earth rising up. Charlie Gumm and I walk to the car. It is Sunday. We have packed a lunch. Last week he came by and asked, shifting from leg to leg, would you like to go see Mandan? If it's nice out, he added as an afterthought, and it's supposed to be nice out. We are going to go to Mandan. Arthur Dimmesdale said to Hester Prynne, is this not better than what we dreamed of in the forest? I'll go with you to Mandan, I said.

It is Sunday, October, the sun flickers in striations of light on light. We do not talk. We drive past the funny colored houses, bars, chimneys smoking in the morning light, children playing in the yards, washlines with the last sheets, pillowcases, bleached underthings hanging to dry, satellite dishes, dogs barking, birds overhead flying a path parallel to ours; the birds are coming with us. The blackbirds are migrating to Mandan.

We wander the one ruined street in search of artifacts, but others have been there before us. We find only dirt and weeds. In one of the houses there is graffiti scrawled on the inside wall, the floors have buckled, the stairs caved in, windows broken out; you get a chill just looking, like passing a graveyard, a chill in the bright sun. A broken child's wagon, the springs of a mattress, rags of fabric, green glass from a beer bottle.

Charlie Gumm and I eat chicken salad sandwiches and oranges. We have forgotten to bring a blanket so we sit right in the dirt and weeds. We eat and then lie back full in the sun and stare straight up into it until we see spots and shapes and blinding colors and I close my eyes. I close my eyes against the sun and feel the damp earth. The birds circle overhead in all directions, north and south and east. I close my eyes and the sun is blocked out. He is kissing me, I don't open my eyes, and he kisses me in the sun while the birds call, I am going north and south and east, I am going to meet someone who loves me and will love me forever, that is what the birds say. He says to me words that I will never repeat and asks but then kisses me before I can answer. I will never answer. The birds dark-winged call each to each, the afternoon slips away, he kisses me, and his kisses taste of oranges.

"It has to be a fair trade," I said to Hugo.

He sat at his writing desk absently scrawling Cs across his students' papers.

"What's fair?" he asked. "An eye for an eye? Apples for oranges? You of all people should know by now that there is no such thing as a fair trade."

"I'll tell you my story, and you tell me yours. So, it's not a trade then. It's only an exchange."

"It does sound intriguing," he said. "Let me think about it."

Evening is darkening all the little streets and avenues. I wake in darkness in this bed in this place and do not know where I am. There is no direction in my dreams. There is no north or south or east. I cannot sleep for my dreams. A thousand blue roses raining down from the sky. We will meet years later, by accident. He will take my arm, rest a hand on my hip. We will be older. No one will stop us. I wake to the glowing dial of my alarm clock. We saw a deer and stopped frozen together for a moment and went on in sunlight as all afternoons linger long into their evenings. I see him and can't sleep for the breath of him on my neck, sweet and salty. The birds have returned to my dreams. They flutter crossing the gray sky. Evening is invading my room through the netted lace of the curtains. There is no direction in my dreams. Time stops, has stopped, will continue always stopping now. When I wake I know where I am. I remember my name. And I hear birds in the morning fields outside my window, calling, I can hear them calling.

"You should be the first to know," said Hugo pacing the room. "It's official. I'm scrapping Winston and company. Perhaps it's finally happened; I'm too old for this make-believe nonsense."

He had taken all his papers out of his folders, his notes and drafts, and spread them with dramatic flair across the wood floor. He paced the room treading on the pages as he went.

"You can't," I said.

I removed my raincoat.

"Convince me then," he said and sat in the rocker by the grate. "Why should I keep any of it. It's a desperate bloody disaster, an old man's feeble attempt to remember the fervor of youth."

"You have to finish it," I said. "Because I want to know what's going to happen. How will I ever know if you don't bother to finish it?"

"Maybe I'll will it to you, and you can finish it."

"I don't know anything about Winston."

"It lacks something. It's not right," he said. "You can tell, can't you?"

"It's only that you don't have very much sympathy for him. Sometimes he, sometimes it's like he's only a joke."

"It's his ghost," he said. "It's the ghost of young Roderigo come back to exact his vengeance."

"He's dead? The boy is dead? In real life?"

Hugo scratched his head. He reached down and scooped up a handful of papers and then without looking at the pages, threw them back down, scattering them across the floor.

"Oh yes," he said. "He died that winter. I wouldn't have known about it, but I saw the obituary in the newspaper. It was nothing dramatic. He was knocked down by a car. He wasn't a strong person. A stronger person might have survived, but he was never a strong person."

"You see, you do have pity for him."

"That's Roderick," he said. "That's a poor dead boy who never did a thing to hurt me. That's not Winston."

"But it's the same."

He didn't answer.

"You wanted to trade," he said finally. "I'll trade then. I'm going to tell you this not because you are young and I am old, but because we understand now, both of us, how it is. It's all about pain, isn't it, in one way or another?"

I let him go on.

"There was a girl, and she was young. She came to me after he died and brought me his poems, and then I recalled the hair ribbon, the velvet ribbon with which he had so romantically bound his poems. Of course, it wasn't hers. She wasn't the type to wear ribbons. She was dressed in black, like he used to be. She gave me the poems and said he would have wanted you to have these, and this, too, something else. She handed me a package, all wrapped, a Christmas present. She said how kind he had always been, always thinking about other people."

"A gift?"

"It was quite remarkable. I can't imagine where in Ohio he could have found it, perhaps buried away at some curio shop or swap meet. It was, have you heard of them, a Victorian hair bracelet, a woven black braid as narrow as though for a child's wrist. And I said to the girl in black, why don't you take this? And she did. She put it around her wrist. Her wrists were narrow, like a child's, although she was quite a tall girl. I said, were you a very good friend of his? She laughed and said she supposed he had been in love with her, and that she didn't know anything at all about poetry only that his was a bit morbid. She turned the bracelet round and round on her wrist and said that sometimes he had made her feel as cold as the grave."

"From the story," I said. "The girl whose mother Winston falls for. That's her isn't it?"

"I don't make a practice," Hugo said, "of seducing young girls, perhaps I did when I myself was a good deal younger, but certainly not now, not then."

"You didn't—? You seduced dead Roderigo's girlfriend?" I asked incredulously. "While she was still wearing her widow's weeds?"

"Yes," he said. "I, she and I, I suppose that is, yes, exactly what we did."

It was raining. It had rained yesterday and the day before and all afternoon. The paths through the woods, the trails and walks were sodden with mud; the leaves washed bare of the trees, the limbs naked, the sky dark all day through.

"Why her?" I asked. "Was she so different?"

"From other girls? I suppose not. It was only that she was more determined to get things out of life. One couldn't escape that, her unflagging determination."

"She must have been beautiful too."

"Oh yes," he said. "Perhaps it was that at first. Later it was more. Later it is always more."

The rain was clogging things up all around us, thickening the puddles with muck, bloating the ground. Later it is always more. It was to freeze in the night and we would wake to an icy bright morning, frozen pure. The rain would turn to ice while we slept and we would wake to find the world sharp and enchanted.

"Would I have liked her? I mean, do you think I would have been friends with her?"

He laughed, hard and bitter.

"She had friends, I suppose."

"Was she your fate?"

"Yes," he said flatly.

"Was she," there are some questions we know we should not give voice to, but it was dark and gloomy, a day for ghost stories. It was getting late; it was always either getting late or just having been late, and I was young and we were talking about morbid things, death, the past, women and what they wanted, what it meant to be determined and there were things I wanted to know about men that no one had told me. "Was she at all like me?" I asked.

He frowned.

The rain fell.

"Don't be a fool," he said finally. "You are a child, nothing more than a child. She was never in her life a child. Don't be so presumptuous as to think that because you are here with me today, and she is not, that this, that any of this, has something do with you."

I was silent. I felt at that moment just like Joan Fontaine must have in *Rebecca* when she finally confesses to Maxim that she was jealous of his love for his first wife and he tells her that he hated Rebecca, and then he says to her, "It's gone forever, that funny young lost look."

"It's ridiculous to talk about these things over tea," Hugo said. "I don't mind telling you about it, and now that I've started I might as well continue. But not over tea like proper church matrons. There is nothing proper about any of this, is there? Let's you and I have a drink."

He rose and left the room, to the kitchen, returning with a clear bottle and two teacups.

"What's your poison?" He asked in a Western drawl.

"What's good?"

"None of it is, technically, good. But some of it does get the job done quite nicely."

He set the bottle and cups on the table in front of me, where I sat on the swirling brocade of the sofa.

"The trick with this is to try not to taste it," he said pouring me out a full cup of vodka. We drank in silence. I could see the lights on in the girls' dorm. Girls were doing homework. Girls were cutting ghosts out of construction paper, looping orange and black swathes of crepe, shaking glitter onto glue, gumming the glittering eyes of tracing-paper demons.

"She was, as cliche as it may seem now, an actress," he said toying with his cup. "Although I can't say she was particularly good at it. Perhaps if she had been as smart as she was ruthless, more savvy, she would have used me to get to someone who really could have helped her along. How can I explain this, she could have done great things, talent or no, great things."

"What could you have done?"

"People love illusion," he said. He looked around the room. "I teach a bit here and there. People, they remember names. They see your name in print; they remember a play they saw at a dinner theater, and they think you must be," he took a long drink, coughed, "quite rich and famous."

"Once I went into a bookstore, just one of these ones in a strip mall, before my mother married him, and I saw this big cardboard picture of him, of my stepfather."

"She stayed with me for quite a long while, longer than either of us could have anticipated."

"A child?" I said suddenly.

"Yes, a little boy."

"With her now?" I asked.

"Dead now," he said. "Quite dead."

I was quiet then. There was only the rain.

"It was inevitable. She grew to hate me, and how she let me know it every hour of the day, that she hated me, and I grew, yes, to reciprocate her hatred."

"She could have left, or you."

"She wore that damn bracelet day and night, that hair bracelet to remind me, because it hurt her, burned and left a raw bruise on her skin. Because she refused to allow anyone to hurt her as much as she could hurt herself. Did I tell you how fine her wrists were? They were like his, brittle. You have to wonder about people like them, how they survive as long as they do with barely enough skin to cover their fragile bones."

"It doesn't sound like you hated her."

"I loved her."

"Love?" I was warm from the vodka and my throat was burning. "That's the first time I've heard you use that word without—"

"Lust or disgust," he broke in. "What's the bloody difference? See, I'm a bit like Winston after all, rhyming as I go, only a third-rate scribbler who's had a little too much to drink. How ridiculous it all is; I'm going to die soon, but what difference does that make—so are you and so is that precious boy of yours."

"That's not so profound."

"Winston," he refilled my glass, "c'est moi."

I drank. I took a short sip and then a long gulp. I finished the cup in one burning shot, holding my breath. He didn't wait. He was watching. He poured out more.

"You don't give Winston enough credit," I said.

"You're a dear child," he said. "But you suffer fools too gladly."

"I wouldn't know what else to do with them."

"I was he. I wrote poor verse. I expected something in return from the world. I thought I could lie right down in fortune's lap. I met fellows in cafés and we talked about art. Someone should have shot me," he paused. "Or at least knocked me over with an auto."

"Maybe Roderick would have grown out of it."

"One never," he held up his glass. "I repeat this and hope that you write it down for future usage. I repeat, one never grows out of anything."

"I haven't learned anything," I said, drunk for the first time in my life. "From being told. Not a goddamn thing."

"No," he said, "of course you haven't. How does it feel to be more informed? We can speak so politely now. We can share a drink or two like civilized folk. You have not so much learned as discovered the truth; that you have *known* all along. Congratulations, my dear Pearl, you are now one of the living."

He toasted me. We drank.

"You, my dear, are one of us, one of the true exiles," he went on and set his empty teacup on the table. I refilled it awkwardly. The vodka overflowed spilling on the wood veneer.

"From where?"

The vodka hit me hard, light and funny, so that the rain seemed funny, and I did not know that it would turn to ice during the night. I did not know the exact and sharp ways it would freeze on the birch boughs, kill the flowers, the fruits, the tough scrub grasses, and that only the bulbs, the tulips, daffodils, and tuber roots would be safe because I had buried them in the earth. He refilled my glass.

"From where?" I heard myself repeat.

I saw the girl that was me sitting on his green brocade sofa against the backdrop of a dismal afternoon, the fire in the grate, the remains of cookies, the crusts of sandwiches, a clutter of forks and knives, my shoes by the fire, the burning flush of my face, the darkness of her eyes, the burning shape of my lips, all things I was suddenly and completely aware of, the broken clock ticking away the spent hours, the tarot cards, her hair bracelet, construction paper crowns, his scattered pages papering the floor. It seemed like hours. It seemed like days; it took him forever to answer me, and I asked one last time, a third time.

"Exiled from where?"

"From the garden," he said.

And I laughed and laughed, because I thought of him naked, fat-bellied Father Time or Lucifer with hooves and tail dancing in flowers outside the girls' dormitory, pelting the walls, splattering the clean blonde brick facade with apples, Macintosh, Jonathan, sweet, Winesap, Golden Delicious, naked and laughing, we were exiles from the garden, but we would make do here with apples, with the memory of apples, green, tart, crab apples, bruised, Sweet Sixteen, rotting, baked with cinnamon, woody, juicy, apples, bushels of them, you turned the stem to the letters of the alphabet, A, B, C, and the letter on which you broke the stem would be the initial of the boy you would marry, winterlude, Harlan, crisp, biting, poisoned, dipped in honey, sweets for the sweet, sliced, peeled in one long seamless tangle, cored, bitten, tossed away, sweet, sweet, the rain fell and fell.

Rose

I KNOW WHAT HAPPENED TO BLUEY ASTARTE, the bad painter, the loud drunk, the liar, the cheat. I know what happened to him and to all the others. I was there the day the water-sodden floor of the bathroom finally crashed down and fell in splinters, shards, an explosion of plaster right into the kitchen where two guys I did not know were drinking beer and cooking spaghetti. I was there at the beginning and at the end and I know all the details that the others have forgotten. I know what happened to Rose called Rice, who one day disappeared with Bluey Astarte in a hailstorm that was nothing short of apocalyptic. But we all lived through it, you see. We all almost all lived through it and were made stronger for it and hung plaques on our doors commemorating our genius, fortitude, and survival. In old photographs I find I cannot help but recollect the dead and imagine them to be myself. The tiny world disappeared one day.

Miss Susie had a baby. She named him Tiny Tim. She put him in the bathtub to see if he could swim. He ate up all the water. He drank up all the soap. He tried to eat the bathtub but it wouldn't go down his throat.

In the spring of 1989 I met Bluey Astarte at a party. There was, I recall, a band playing in the basement. The wallpaper in the large overcrowded living room was patterned with scenes from the Revolutionary War. I was trying to avoid a girl who had been threatening, spreading rumors around town that she was going to beat me up, for no reason, she was proud of telling people, just because. I arrived late with a certain pizza delivery guy I used to know who was also a militant something or other, maybe it was Communist. He hated the world. Frat boys ordered pizza every night and never tipped him. He was older than he pretended to be. Maybe it was Socialist. Bluey Astarte was in the kitchen arguing with the Communist about pornography. I slipped out the back door. I ran all the way home.

A sailor went to sea sea sea to see what he could see see see but all that he could see see see was the bottom of the deep blue sea sea sea.

Well it was Rose Briceland Simon. That's the whole thing, and I think it's just a little elaborate, grand, a name constructed on the MGM lot, a name that should have meant, signified a disappeared world of mint juleps, hoopskirts, nineteen-inch waists, lawn darts, and chilled lime rickeys on the veranda. It was a name that my mother dreamed up for a daughter who would be the heroine of a romance novel. A girl who would have madcap adventures and tiny feet, a girl you couldn't turn the pages quickly enough to pursue. Your name, my mother used to say, calls to mind the best sort of people. Those, she added in a distant wavering voice, who are no longer with us. I suspect these were the ghosts of her girlhood; paper doll figures whom she had drawn and scissored and creased so many times with the telling of her stories that they had ceased to be unreal. She almost believed in them herself. Hadn't there been picnics and croquet? Hadn't there been boys saying impossibly earnest nothings out of genuine boyish sweetness? Wasn't it fair to say it had all happened the way she imagined it? But Briceland was only a tarted-up version of her maiden name, Brice, and they, the Brice's, were themselves a line of dairy farmers who entered the ranks of the petit bourgeoisie by establishing a successful small ice cream company, Brice's Ices. She seemed, my mother, only too happy to be rid of her past so that she was free to remember it any way she wished. She rewrote her creamy lactose-laden youth into something else, pretty, floral, privileged, southern, when she was from the Midwest, laced with charm and suitors howling beleaguered beneath her bedroom balcony crying Rapunzel, Rapunzel, let down your long hair. One day she escaped, as all princesses do, must, will, and ran off with Arthur Simon, barely a prince, he made himself a king. Off they rode past the cows in the lower fields, past a world that was receding already from her memory, past the taste of a certain flavor of whole bean vanilla cream, past the real and into the sunset where she would remember years later to her middle child that there had been no cows, but that it had rained like a judgment from on high and yet they simply could not stop themselves.

Miss Susie had a tugboat. The tugboat had a bell. Miss Susie went to heaven, the tugboat went to hello—

My mother brushed my hair every night with a stiff wire brush whose handle was wooden and heavy, and she tore through until the curl was beaten out of it. And in the morning when the curl returned, she, at breakfast, over orange juice and toast, faced the inevitable, her private war, over sliced bananas and apple butter, so that she resorted to her last line of defense and after the dishes were washed took me out onto the back sunporch where she sat with coffee light with cream and pulled my hair into one tight braid. The pain, if this makes sense, did not hurt. Did I suffer for her? I suppose I did, because I could see through her like a ghost, silvery, an apparition who would not last long, who did not hold up under strong light, who hid her face from the sun as much to guard against wrinkles as to defend herself against time as a concept. Once only in life have I, did I see her drunk. It was after a New Year's party. She and my father returned home in the early hours of the morning. The baby-sitter, I recall, was asleep in the guest room. I slipped down the stairs. My mother's hair was black and straight. She unpinned the glossy chignon into which it was fastened. I heard her laughing, her perfume, and she was saying, I wish I was Chinese. Have I ever told you that, she asked my father or maybe was asking herself, but said it again and again until he had to carry her up the stairs, have I told you that I want to be Chinese?

The postman came on the first of May. The policeman came the very next day. Nine months later there was hell to pay; who fired the first shot, the blue or the gray?

The sun shined every day. I had a brown dress with yellow leaves on it. My best friend had a pink corduroy jumper. Her name was Theresa and she wore her hair in pigtails each tied with a pink sateen ribbon to match her dress. We were all going to be famous. We were going to sea the world. My brother was so funny he was going to be a stand-up comedian. He gathered us in the front yard, all the neighborhood kids, and told jokes he read off Dixie riddle cups, and we couldn't stop laughing even though we had heard them all before. The point was not the punch line, the point was not the newness. We did not want or need anything new. We wanted to hear the same jokes, the inevitable, what's black and white and red all over? Again and again. We wanted repetition because the flowers bloomed every year in their place in the garden and the planets spinned, spun, circled us, politely, but promptly, and we cracked up every single time we heard him ask, his eyes bright with the expectation of our laughter: why is a raven like a writing desk?

Monday I touched her ankle. Tuesday I touched her knee. Wednesday, success, I undid her dress, the rest is history!

Bluey Astarte was a fluke. He was a failure disguised as the grim reaper. And when he offered me escape I took it. Why? Because. He made sculptures out of trash. He molded tinfoil into figurines. He painted bobby pins and gave them to girls on the street. Marcel Marceau was his hero. Sometimes he did not speak for days at a stretch. I'm not exaggerating. This is Bluey Astarte we are talking about; nobody even knew if that was his real name. He was always trying to get girls to roll around on long rolls of unbleached paper, for art, he would say, it was all for the sake of art. Still, you couldn't fault him for it. He had vision. His pockets were stuffed with candy; Pop Rocks, Jolly Ranchers, gooey watermelon Now and Laters. He was generous. Care for a candy cigarette? he'd say, go ahead, keep the pack. He was thoughtful. He had sugar free coffee nips and a brand of licorice cough drops that came with sworn affidavits from Swedish fishermen on the package. But I never understood the extent of his passion, not simply for candy but for the protection of sweets and tiny things, until one day as he was tearing open the wrapper of a Snickers bar, he paused, rubbed the paper between two fingers, expectantly, or rather with a sort of tentative expectation. He asked me if I could recall the candy wrappers of childhood, the paper had been heavy, hard to rip open, and then one day it all changed, and he couldn't say what day it was exactly, when he bought a Snickers bar and found the new light wrapper that gave way easily, that put up no fight, that simply deteriorated into a shred of a material that was neither paper nor plastic but some unholy union of the two. The chocolate itself was no different, and yet, the wrapper, he was certain, caused a slight chemical aftertaste. The world was collapsing in small, impossible ways.

The day they change the Starlight Mint, he said, is the day I shoot myself. I think he meant it. He had, as anyone will tell you, vision.

Hello operator, please give me number nine, and if you disconnect me I'll kick you right behind the refrigerator, there lay a piece of glass, Miss Susie fell upon it and broke her little ask me no more questions, I'll tell you no more lies—

In the beginning there were three of us. My brother, my sister, and me. I could have escaped out the window if I had tried. My brother, Thermidor, named for my maternal great grandfather (not true) was called Teddy sometimes and Door other times, and he told funny jokes that were not funny and his mouth was generally the color of orange creamsicles. My sister, Lilith, was weighted down under the lace of her name and was not to be called Lily at any cost so we called her Butternut or Bee or sometimes if you were looking for and couldn't find her you would just close your eyes and scream at the top of your lungs, HEY KOOL-AID! And she would appear, always, through some secret trapdoor, through a mirror, from the inside of a wardrobe, with her thick glasses and raggedy hair that she cut herself, short and brutal, to spite my mother, who sometimes we forget, was also her mother. We were on order to keep scissors away from Butternut. She stole scissors from art class at school. I was the middle child. Door was big and Butternut was little and I was just right. She stole only lefties. I wanted to escape out the window. For a long time I used to go to bed early. She was not left-handed. My sister had a face like the moon.

What's worse than a truckload of dead babies? A live one at the bottom eating its way up.

For a long time I used to go to bed early, and there in the darkness I might stare at the clock, the curtains, shadows on the wallpaper, and be uncertain of which room I was in, and what the year was or the season. In the summer all attics had the same musty smell, and were unheated in the winter so in the darkness, it is understandable, isn't it, it was difficult to tell one room from the next, and one year from the previous, and the sound of someone on the stairs from the footfalls of your mother coming to tuck you in, winter, when darkness made 4 P.M. indistinguishable from midnight, only the blue and black shadows became richer, more deep, narcotic, and at that moment you knew, every time you came and come again to that moment you know exactly why it is that you went to bed early. My bedroom when I was a child had scrolling lilac paper. But I lived later in another room that had a brown floral, which I cannot quite picture. And then one day in the name of progress people began painting the attics and there was no more faded paper to be found and you had to search for rooms with that kind of charm, as they say, charm, because people began to use latex and semigloss in the name of progress and hygiene and cleanliness and there were so few rooms in attics where the walls were wainscoted with old wood and the ceiling papered with lilacs, ferns, sailing ships, Johnny Tremaine, bluebells, cornflowers, Napoleon, the Queen of Hearts, apple blossoms, and violets. In the house I lived in the summer after the summer that I left Bluey or I mean actually that he left me, there was a narrow attic stairway that led to the tiny room. It was papered with cut-out pictures from magazines, tacked and taped and glue-sticked, covering the entire low ceiling. These were the stars. These were the heavens. And when I woke in that room, or the next room, or any place years later I would open my eyes in the

379

darkness and search for those pictures, those lipsticked girls, those seascapes and school pictures of forgotten cousins without front teeth, those days, those nights, and the eyes that followed you right out of the pictures and off the pages and then to wake and say, no, and search for the lilacs and know that they too were gone, that they had been painted over in the name of progress. And I tried to recall just exactly who had left whom and when and what the season had been, and were there lilacs on the walls around us or papered Johnny Appleseed grinning Americanly as he reached to collect the forbiddenest fruit.

Ask me no more questions, I'll tell you know more lies. Miss Susie told me all of this the day before she dyed her hair purple, she dyed her hair pink, she dyed her hair polka-dot and washed it down the sink me in the ocean, sink me in the sea, sink me in the bathtub and you'll be the death of me.

Did I mention that we were all going to be famous? Yes, I thought I might have. After the beginning it was still the beginning. I do not remember anything ever stopping or starting. It was only the lack of things. The diminishing number of rooms with flowered wallpaper or packs of Blackjack gum on drugstore shelves, or for that matter, boys like Bluey, who did not hate change so much as progress. In the time after the beginning there were three of us, Aaron, Theresa, and me. Theresa wore pigtails with pink, blue, or yellow sateen ribbons, one on each side, like a little girl in the movies. My mother brushed Theresa's hair on the sunporch with the good heavy wooden brush. Theresa's hair was straight and fine. To my mother, I suspect curl held some sort of moral corruption. You see, we all have our visions of the deterioration of the world. Bluey worried about candy wrappers. My mother feared curls, despised the unruly nature of the genetic code that allowed brown to dominate blue, curly to overrun straight, in short and in point and in fact, my mother saw my father as the real contaminant, even though he was like my brother and was very funny, *hahaha,* more than *hmmm* funny, ironic. He did not so much tell jokes as do funny voices or say things we did not understand and that was funny too, *hahaha.* Aaron lived down the street. We were nice to him, I think, because he did not throw hard at us in Dodgeball games, and didn't mind if girls played along in the street, games like Bloody Mary which I cannot recollect except it involved someone screaming BLOODY MARY at the top of his or her lungs at some dark twilight hour and the rest of the group scattering and laughing and terrified. And when Aaron's father died we were all very nice to him and brought over to his house things our mothers baked, wrapped in foil or tied with ribbon. There were seed cakes and casseroles. We ate and ate. There were jars of homemade pickles, rolled blintzes, and cold egg soup. It made us sick. We ate sitting at Aaron's kitchen table after school. His mother was upstairs asleep, prescription Valium and endless days of sympathy calls taking a toll on her fresh, sweet face. She looked, Aaron's mother, almost innocent. She had a patter of speckles, a spatter of freckles, a fratter of peckles across her wide cheekbones. We liked Aaron and then later adored him and then finally could not live without him much in the same manner that we could not live without Jello Pudding Pops. He was sweet. And we were guilty. And as I think I mentioned, the sun did, in fact, shine every single damn day, rain or shine.

Remember Grant, remember Lee, to hell with them, remember me! Remember the fork, remember the spoon, remember the night in his bedroom?

This is exactly how it may or may not have happened. I was born in a summer of roses. I was wrapped in a pink blanket and brought home. A little acorn grew and grew and then one day, she said, gee ima tree. Geometry. Get it? I grew pink and pale and studied the art of invisibility. It was not easy. People said I looked like my mother. Other people said I looked like my father. I could creep through rooms without being noticed. Here is a joke about me: deep waters run still. I was more happy than not. Strike that, reverse it. I was more unhappy than not. Strike that. I was not more than unhappy. Once we spent, five Simons and three Saltmarshes, two weeks together at their cabin. Aaron's mother let me paint her nails. Her feet were small, fat, and perfect. Her hair was red. She freckled in the sun, spread white base over her brown skin and finally in an act of appalling glamour, drew a black dot on her cheek and called it a beauty mark. We wore our bathing suits and sat on the dock in the full cancerous thrill of the August sun reading *Mad* Magazine and poking each other in the ribs, asking, what me worry?

This is number one and it's only just begun. Roll me over, lay me down and do it again. Roll me over in the clover. Roll me over, lay me down and do it again. Oh, this is number two and his hand is on my shoe.

When I met Bluey Astarte I was somewhere near twenty-two years old, maybe a little more or less on either side. I was not what you would call innocent. I was living in a college town; it was, rather like myself, small and modest, and I knew Brenda whom I used to see before I knew her on Saturday mornings at the farmers' market. I spotted her at the Italian fruit counter, tiny Brenda with her straw shopping bag slung over her arm lost in the din and commotion, the colors, the overripe scents, spices, shoppers, Brenda in black tights and a minidress holding a cantaloupe in the flat open palm of her left hand with her right in a fist knocking gently on the melon. She was small and pinched and serious. Later after I knew her she introduced me to Bluey Astarte. He was or was not her cousin. But relations are not really the point. The point is that we heard those jokes over and over. And knocking on the melon never helped Brenda pick a good one. Many summers later or was it before? In that same cabin by the lake, in our seashells she sells house in a summer that wound itself into September, quite by accident, the days became all rain, and he and I, we could not stop ourselves. No, I'm sorry, I didn't mean Bluey, that would be some other time, that would be later. This was Aaron. This was in the beginning plus time, three of us, minus one Theresa, equals two, who were and was and are in some sense still, two, Rose and Aaron, divided by three.

Girls go to Mars to get more stars, boys go to Jupiter to get more stupider, girls go to college to get more knowledge, boys to Jupiter to get more stoopiter, girls go to Venus to get more—

We, the people, in order to form a more perfect union (we did. We could not stop ourselves. It was a summer of wet damp roses, petals fallen awash away, alone, along the path from the water to lake, all roses, from water to window) establish justice (we believed at the time that it was the right thing to do based on an ethos of frontier desire) ensure domestic tranquility (in point of fact, sometime earlier before the rains when the summer was bright and hot, when we had immutable faith in apple pie, in aleph, bet, vet, when we were children and we chased after the ringing bells of the Good Humor Man as though he sold salvation in the shape of red-white-and-blue bomb pops; we, he and I, at ages something less than what we are now by

383

the space of a hundred thousand years or more, discovered that uncovered his mother, who had bubble-gum-pink painted toe-nails, and my father, who did the police in different voices, had been affairing, as they say, covert, immoral, immodest, uncov-ered to the point of being discovered, as they admitted happy happy happy, could not stop themselves) provide for the com-mon defense (we armed ourselves with sticks, bottles, lipstick, dirty jokes, scissors, Champale, paper, Teaberry gum, stones, plastic cutlery, shoes with buckles, hair ribbons, bitter apples of the Dalgo Crab variety, number two pencils, rocks, marbles, dice, buttons, slingshots, cupcakes, croquet mallets), promote the general welfare and secure the blessing of liberty to our-selves and our posterity (and there would come a time in the future when I would go to bed early and grow not to think about it or him or why it was important to leave while he, Aaron, was still sleeping and what with the sun not even yet supplanting the moon of her progressive charms meaning the sun was not up and I put on his clothes and left him mine, and still he did not wake, not even when I stooped to scoop the raw, rich jingling collection of coins and paper that fell, golden, green and silver from his pockets and I left) do ordain and establish this constitution (I did not come back) for the United (we were once) States of America.

Harry gave me apples. Harry gave me pears. Harry gave me fifty cents and kissed me on the stairs. I'd rather wash the dishes. I'd rather scrub the floor. I'd rather kiss the garbage man than Harry at the door.

All the days of my childhood held either in their sway the sun, moon, or rain. I was a fool not to follow their example. And on he slept, to sleep, sleeping, on and on, so that the years would make no difference, nor impression. His mother was freckled. They had, mother and son, strange distant expressions, not as though they did not understand, but as though they were not listening to you exactly, they were always on the verge of tumbling into a bed or out of a bed or sleeping or waking and you were left with the impression that for them day was no different from night. The world could not touch the substance of their perfect, strange, blissful, heavy, unstoppable, undreamable, ten hours and counting, sleep, sleep, sleep. Did I wait? Did I agonize over the decision? Listen my children and you shall hear, no, no, a resounding three minus two, answer of no. It was the only decision that ever mattered, because it was not a decision at all, but an action. In that hazy predawn euphoria, with the foreknowledge that in all shapes, hearts, stars, and clovers it would be wrong to suddenly, silently get up and leave, that's right brothers and sisters, leave, how can I say it, how can I tell you? I had no choice. I wanted no choice. I could not, you must know the line by now, stop myself. I left and sometimes still I think it was the only moment that ever mattered in my life. Did I mention how it felt, free and awful and nauseating and wild? I met Bluey Astarte a few years later, but the point is, you see, I continued to exist. Brenda used to serve us fruit in her backyard, melon in gold metallic bowls and she talked endlessly about the value of life and we nodded and giggled but didn't really listen and then she said, have you met my cousin? And for a while I forgot all about the boy with the scar on his cheek who had once meant something and now it was actually quite difficult to recall that once dear face that had once meant nearly everything dearly once. When Bluey Astarte asked me to go with him, to light out for the territories, I did not need to think about it. I said yes. I said let's leave now, right now. Off we sailed into the wild blue yonder. Hail pelted us like enemy fire.

We were young. We were unstoppable. We were invisible to the naked eye.

Under the spreading chestnut tree I sold him and he sold me.

Theresa wore ribbons like valentine's candy, pink and velveteen. Three minus one equals two. We did our homework. She told stories she had read in romance novels as though she knew the characters personally. And after a while my mother did not like Theresa anymore, and in a way, I understood, because quite often I did not like her. She still told stories and you could not help but listen, once about this baby-sitter she knew who had been chopped to pieces by an escaped lunatic who was living hidden in between the walls of her house. It was all true. She swore by it. My mother said you could not trust her to tell the truth. When I was with Theresa I think I did not want the truth. Maybe my mother wanted only her own untruths to be believed and was suspicious of rivals to her throne. Theresa left after high school, maybe a couple of months before I did, but I did not copycat her. She had plans, blueprints, and had been mapping her escape for years, visitors brought her cakes with files baked into the creamy filling; she was going to meet a man. I ran from. She ran to. Get it? A man walks into a doctor's office, he says, doctor, doctor, I think I'm a dog. The doctor says, does it hurt?

Listen my children and you shall hear of the midnight ride of Paul Revere. He jumped in the car, stepped on the gas. The bottom fell out and he fell on his—now don't get excited, don't get alarmed, I was going to say, he fell on his arm.

Bluey Astarte and Rose Simon left the small college town in which they lived. He was a short-order cook by profession and a genius by trade. He could automatically say any word backward. He cooked hamburgers and bacon and eggs, and when he did this he wore a little white hat rather like a sailor's hat, but less jaunty. He also wore a white apron. He cooked hashbrowns, but not french fries because those were from the deep frier and handled not by the grill cook, which he was, but by the lone sadfaced boy who held hour after hour the metal basket of raw sliced potatoes and plunged them again and again into the scalding oil. Rose Simon, who was called Ricey by those whom she knew and worse names as well, worked at an antique store run by two elderly ladies, sisters, Dora and Flora or was it Daisy and Maisie? They told her, sweet as they were and scented of Avon Here's to Your Heart talc, she had a place with them whenever she came back. Rose knew that she would come back. This was not like the time she left Aaron. She knew. One always knows. And when one thinks it, and it doesn't happen, well, where's the fault in that? In our stars? In ourselves? Let's chalk it up to experience and move our little army of sentences forward. Rose and Bluey left in an unprecedented fireworks display of hail and rain and damnation. Hell opened up for a short sweet time and they rode out in glory. I could not stop them.

Oh Senior Don Gatto was a cat. On a high red roof Don Gatto sat. Oh it wasn't very merry, meow, meow, meow, going to the cemetery, meow, meow, meow, for the ending of Don Gatto.

And so it came to pass that after a time they stopped and they made camp and they lived in all manner of way plying the trade of the short-order cook across this blue blue bluest and red and white country of ours, and they sojourned in the land of Nod and they ate the fries of the land. And it came to pass that Bluey found a dog, and the dog was called Buster and they found that the dog was good. And the sun shined every day.

And one day in the course of the sun not shining, during the hours of the moon, while Rose slept, Bluey for no reason, but simply because. For no reason that anyone would ever learn, not ye nor me, took from his case, in which he kept the tools of his trade, the spatulas, graters, and whetstones, the implements of the traveling cook, a knife, and he sharpened his knife at night under the full and willing participation of the man in the moon, and he returned to the tent in which they, Rose and Bluest, found themselves habituating, and he returned and she slept on. He did not raise the knife. He waited. She did not wake. He held the knife then, against the one long rope of braid that was braided of her hair which was long and roped, and lo, the knife was sharp and he cut through the rope and cast off to sea. And she did not wake. By all accounts, she should have, but did not, could not, would never, not until morning and by then Bluey Astarte had sailed away and when she woke immediately she knew the little world would never be the same.

Hey, Miss Susie, look at Tiny Tim. He's in the bathtub learning how to swim. First he does the backstroke, then he does the crawl, now he's underwater doing nothing at all.

Did you know him? Because I did. And did you have a good life? I mean, are you enjoying yourself? Did you, do you, do you believe in progress? Here is a song Theresa sang on the swing set as the chain rattled back and forth. If all little girls were like little white rabbits, and I was a hare, I would teach them bad habits. Roll your leg over, roll your leg over, roll your leg over the man in the moon. I liked it because it was a song about bunny rabbits. But then the little acorn grew and grew and she sang the song like this: If all the young ladies were linear spaces, and I were a vector I'd intersect their bases.

Roll your leg over, roll your leg over, roll that leg over the man in moon. She sang it walking home from school as we passed the playground where the swings rattled back and forth on their chains. If two little girls were not singing this song, it would be four times as dirty and three times as long. I knew a world that never seemed to begin or end. I was, if you can believe it, a good girl once.

How do you top a car? Tep on the breaks, tupid!

I woke the morning of his leaving. I made my way to the bathroom at the state park. I looked in the mirror. I saw then. I knew. It was gone forever, that funny young lost look. I saw devastated the forbidding face of the future, stern, mean, impossible to judge. And yet, I was calm. Nothing could shatter me. I saw my face in the mirror and turned from it. I packed up what I had. I did not know north or south or east. I turned in the direction opposite the one I had been going. I moved backward. I scuttled like a crab. I did not abandon the dog. He scuttled like a dog across a sea of floors. We inched our way through the summer and made it back to the modest college town where our arrival was heralded with garlands, willow branches, baby's breath, palm fronds, the ubiquitous, the eponymous, roses, yellow, pink, red, blue, white, orange, roses, thrown from parades, from floats, from the hands of plump beauty queens, girls from all the small lost towns along the lakeshore, girls who threw lilacs, confetti, butterscotches, spearmint leaves, circus peanuts and who sang out in sweet lilting sopranos, this land is your land, this land is my land. And yes, it was all because I had returned home, swam through blue water and thunderstorms, bourne and shored up, I followed the stars, the moon, the howls of abandoned dogs in the night on the interstate who led us back, who

389

announced our arrival, who brought us to the banqueting house.

Hail Mary full of grace, bless my boyfriend's hands and face. Bless his head, full of curls, and help him stay away from other girls. Bless his arms so big and strong and keep his hands where they belong. Amen.

I made it back to the nice town, modest in size and scope. I moved into the house whose floors would one day collapse in on themselves. I lived in the attic. For a long time I used to go to bed early, summer, when it was still light and in the autumn and then the winter too. And I lived there for one year until the day I heard a knock at the front door, this was again, summer, but it was the next summer, you see, not the previous summer or any of those before when we were children in the kingdom by the sea. There was a knock at the door so early that no one else was awake, not even the guy asleep on the couch, and I opened the door and there was Bluey Astarte so pale the sun could not touch him, so tall I think he had to stoop to enter the doorway and he never apologized, in a shirt with a wide collar and snaps instead of buttons, smelling deep of sweat, his eyes the only damp thing in a disastrous drought of a summer. And I sent him away. Why? Because. Two days later during a rainstorm the house would collapse floor by floor. I sent him away and I stood on the porch watching him go. I wore exactly that day a green plaid dress and was barefoot and waited there, and then went inside where the guy sleeping on the couch spoke from a dream something cryptic which I was certain would hold the key to all our futures. But he rolled onto his side facing the wall and fell back into lumbering, slumbering faux drunken bliss. Later that day Brenda came by with a mint plant she had been promising to bring me, and she came suddenly running, she was breathless, she said, have you heard? She said, you know that Bluey Astarte is back? And before I could tell her that I knew, she went on, have you heard, she said, isn't it unreal? Bluey Astarte is back in town and was hit by a bus right at the corner of Lexington and Concord. And right then I could not remember if I had seen him yet or if it happened later, in a dream, but then I remembered the warm smell of him, and I knew it had all happened, and the sun appeared very bright, so bright as to be ridiculous, and Brenda asked me if I could hear the sirens still, and I said, yes, I supposed that I could.

The jailer gave me coffee. The jailer gave me tea. The jailer gave me all he had except the jailhouse key.

I am haunted by the past not because we were younger then, more sweet, innocent, pretty, genuine, insistent, delicate, strong, brash, not because the moon seemed more believable or everything that you wanted left in your mouth and stained your hands with the scent, the taste of licorice, but because. Because I saw myself in the mirror of the bathroom under the humming green dull din of the fluorescent bulb and I knew it would not be easy for any of us. Why trust a string of letters and call it the fate that rules your life? Later that summer Brenda broke her leg and spent her days drifting away on Demerol. You know what, she used to ask me. What? I answered. Sometimes after work I came to see her in the cramped sublet she shared with three other girls. She lay stretched out on the couch with her leg propped on the coffee table. Girls were always coming in and then departing, arriving in shorts and leaving in sheer dresses; blow-drying, lipsticking, perfuming, exfoliating, showering, combing, wringing out swimsuits and hanging strapless bras on the towel rack, leaving in their wild wake fallen change, nickels and pennies, the blistering orange scent of suntan oil, diet soda cans, princess slippers, and trails of bread crumbs. Brenda did not move. I brought her gifts, wind-up toys, candy, tabloid magazines promising to reveal the beauty secrets of the stars. You know what, she asked, grinning expectantly. I shook my head. She asked again, do, she said, do you know what? I waited. That's what. she answered in a fit of giggles until exhausted she fell back blissfully against her pillows, a chocolate bar in each hand.

And then the man says, only when I bark.

Pearl

AND SO BEGINS MY EDUCATION.

In the dining hall over a Tuesday lunch, hot dish (tater tot casserole), soup (chicken rice), vegetarian plate (cottage cheese and mandarin orange slices), dessert (pineapple upside-down cake), we sit listening to Lynn tell again the story of the night Gretchen Deutsch dyed her hair black and ran through the halls in only her bra. Walker is eating green salad, dry, no dressing. Annie says that it's bad for you like that and offers to get her a cruet of oil and vinegar. But Walker says something about December gives her the bloats, the heebie-jeebies, a cold right through the heart of her. I open the letter I have just received from my mother. Annie says it's such pretty note-paper, sky blue all patterned with pretty little delphiniums, and she almost bought some just like it at the Lord & Taylor in Chicago when she was there last year. Lynn makes a dirty joke about morning glories and Charlie blushes with his head bent low over his steaming casserole. Pearl, says Walker, you look like you've seen a ghost. It's only, I say, that my mother is going to have a baby. Wow, Annie says, that's so cool. Is it safe for her though, for an older woman? She asks with concern. But she's not, I say picking at the crust of my cake, old. She's only just turned thirty-six. Wow, says Annie again. You're going to be an aunt, says Charlie. Walker nearly chokes, but she doesn't say anything because she can't tell whether he's really stupid or really smart. The best things are tough to figure out. Do they know yet what it's going to be? asks Walker.

There's a radish speared on the end of her fork. I think it's awful, says Annie, to find out in advance. It ruins the mystery. It's going to be a boy, I say. Wow, says Annie, that's so great.

I study French, and Walker is teaching me a little Italian, the true language of tragedy, revenge, blood, and desire. She says: prego, andiamo, in che anno e nato? Uno, due, tre.

In art class we are working on self-portraits. Walker chooses charcoal, and I take pen and ink. A self-portrait is a complicated thing. Take Walker's drawing for example. We pack up our portfolios and head over to the painting studio which is in one of the little faculty houses. It is snowing out. Walker sets up her board in one room, and I go to an empty room in back where the light is good and strong. I turn on the radio. Walker doesn't like sound or distractions while she works, but I don't mind. She's neat and I'm fussy. Hello, neat and fussy, pleased to make your acquaintances. I'm listening to the Christian radio station, the teen call-in show. I sit down and dip my pen into the ink pot. I don't think. I draw this: a few lines, curls, eyes looking downward, chin, em of an upper lip, a stroke, shoulders, dip of the pen, arms at the side of, a table, dip, goldfish bowl, this is what the eyes are looking down into, the line of the fish, the pattern, light and dark of flowers on the tablecloth. I stand back. I look at it. I dip my pen again. I pattern the wallpaper behind the figure in alternation of the tablecloth. It takes less than fifteen minutes. I stand back and look.

I go and peek in on Walker a little while later and find she's roughed out a mirror image of herself on brown newsprint.

The lines are perfect. These are her eyes. She spares no senti-ment about the shallow bridge of her nose. She neither embell-ishes nor parodies her features. This is the face she sees in the mirror.

This strikes me as funny. First, I feel bad. My drawing doesn't really look like me. But, our teacher, Mrs. Moody, she told us, think about the mirror and what it shows you. Can you abide by its lines? Its truths as well as its distortions? I think she means a self-portrait is how you see yourself, and maybe not just how the mirror reflects your image. Still, it impresses me that Walker knows something about herself. She knows with her eyes closed what her face looks like. She can remember her own face. Me, I can't remember one day from the next. I rely on clocks and timepieces. Sometimes the days come all at once, like a speeded sequence in a film, all fluttering in pages off a calendar; sometimes the days don't come at all and linger in endlessness. My self-portrait is of the way I would like to look. The first lie. Pictures of the three of us. Mother and father. And child. Walker's portrait is reality, or at least repre-sentational. What the hell are you looking at, she asks all pissed off. Walkers hates to be disturbed while she is drawing. I'm looking at you, kitty cat, I tell her. Fuck off, she says and throws a pencil at me.

I go back to the other room. The sun streams in and the snow falls. I listen to the radio. There's a new caller on, a girl from Mohawk who swears that Lucifer revealed himself to her in the parking lot of the Pamida store and tempted her with cigarettes and grain alcohol. Obviously, declares the host, he was trying to lure you into a black mass. Cigarettes for the cor-rupt bread and spirits for the blood of the lamb. Tell the lis-teners what you did, says the host breathlessly, tell them how you overcame the dark legion. I said, *Be gone Satan!* says the girl. I see through your cloak of darkness and subtle guile. I said, *Get thee behind me Satan.* I said, *Praise the Lord.* I can abide by the mirror, but can it abide by me?

Saturday mornings Hugo Tappan and I drink vodka and vegetable juice because he's worried about getting scurvy. I'm a sloppy drunk. One day this will get me in trouble. I say, Hugo, I'm going to ask you a question and I don't want you to act like it's one of your bonehead students' questions. Shoot, he says, western style with his fingers making a gun. He licks lime juice from his gnarled thumb. Why do you do it? I mean, what makes you want to write? He chews at his thumbnail, pauses, and says, I get asked that one a great deal, my dear, and do you know what? Quite frankly, I usually lie. Sometimes when I feel puffed up with grand importance I say boomingly, I write because I must, because I could not live without writing. Other times I say I write the same story again and again and will stop only when I have achieved the desired effect (in that respect it's rather like drinking a nice tumbler of gin) but the truth . . . the answer is simply this; I don't know. I'm too old to remember why I started and too old to stop. But now let me turn the question on you, my young protégée, he says. When will you show me that secret manuscript you have been tap, tap, tapping away at on your little typewriter late at night? I say, showing it to you, Hugo, won't make it any better and it might even make it worse; so why show it all? Not till it's done, I say. He says, that could be years. I can wait, I say. Very wise, he says, no use revealing your scars to the world before you can do so with a bit of finesse. He says, let it age like good scotch. We clink teacups. He smiles and his teeth are brownish and rotty.

Charlie Gumm has done it with three other girls, and this he confesses to me in a fit of guilt one evening when we are alone in the boys' television room watching *Dog Day Afternoon* on the Canadian station. The first girl was named Lacey. She was his mixed doubles partner at the country club. Then there was Shannon, a distant cousin. That sounds juicy, I say. Tell me about that one. I saw an Elvis movie like that once. But he gets his serious look, and I think, this is just what he will look like when he is older and grows into his face. It is a look of stern and caring reprimand. He will grow out of the softness of his face now, the way his bottom lip droops and his cheeks flush. You can tell his forehead will be higher, his cheekbones more sharply defined. A real Arthur Dimmesdale, and miraculously enough, he claims somewhere on his family tree to be distantly related to the Mathers themselves, Cotton and Increase. I guess that means that cousin Shannon is too. When he is older he won't be so quick to talk about love. He'll spare the words. He'll be more like Hugo Tappan and Martin Hamlin and say he's not comfortable with those words because there was some shadowy girl in his past who stole the very words from him, and he was lucky that was all she took. But I'm not bragging; I'll never be that girl. I don't have that kind of ambition. I simply want to see him like this, flushed and sleepy, before the fall. To keep him in a little pint vodka bottle like in *I Dream of Jeannie*. And then he says, there was Miranda. Mims, he says, what a sweet kid she was. She was the little sister of a friend, but that was only once. It was in a car, he says with embarrassment, but you can tell he's kind of proud of it. How does that car thing work, I ask. I've always wondered about it; isn't it kind of cramped in there? The movie goes to a commercial. He puts his hand on my knee and starts trying to explain.

Hugo sings funny songs when he's drunk. He slams his fist on the oak kitchen table and likes to play Elizabethan bawdy house. Oh, the deacon went down (oh the deacon went down) to the cellar to pray (to the cellar to pray) he met a blonde (he met a blonde) and stayed all day (and stayed all day) oh the deacon went down to the cellar to pray he met a blonde and stayed all day I ain't gonna grieve my Lord no more. He sings: we're ramblers, we're gamblers, we're far away from home, if people don't like us they leave us alone, we eat when we're hungry, we drink when we're dry and if moonshine don't kill us we'll live till we die. He sings and marches in place. The grand old duke of York, he had ten thousand men, he marched them up the hill and then he marched them down again, now when you're up, you're up, and when you're down, you're down, and when you're only halfway up, you're neither up nor down.

I ain't gonna grieve my Lord no more.

I'm only just learning the words.

Hugo tells me the hard fast truth about life. He says you can read about this in any number of important and estimable sources. The great works of history and literature point out nothing so much as this truth: woman is empty. He is brightly vulgar; there is a hole, he says, a lack right through the center of her. She exists to be filled by male excess. She is forever a lady in waiting, waiting to be filled with his ideas, words, children, sex, chocolates, and promises. Her trajectory is from bed to bed, draped in a silk dressing gown, velveted, rose-petaly petaled or unclothed if you so prefer.

You lie, I say to him suspiciously, you lie so bad.

In the dining hall over a Monday lunch, hot dish (shepherd's pie), soup (turkey noodle), vegetarian plate (rice pilaf and pinto beans), dessert (sugar cookies), we sit watching the dorm council girls decorate the walls with construction paper Christmas trees, cotton ball angels, and glittery stars. Annie loves Christmas best of any holiday and can't wait to get home, hit the malls, trim the tree, sing carols, and roast chestnuts. Walker says, stop before I puke. See, says Annie, you eat too much roughage. Your body just can't digest it properly, and it makes you cranky. I'll crank you, says Walker. I have just received a letter from my stepfather. Lynn says, you sure get a lot of mail. Walker tells her that my family is postvocal and can only communicate through writing and sonar signals. This impresses Lynn and Annie. Well, read on Macduff, says Walker. Martin Hamlin says that he and my mother will be spending this upcoming holiday season in Boca with Aunt Sherry and Uncle Jay, and I am welcome to fly out and join them all. I'm stuck here over break, I conclude. How awful, cries Annie and reaches to grab my hand. You'll come home with me! No really, I say, I'm okay. I'm not a real holiday person anyway. I watch as Charlie Gumm makes his way over from the cafeteria line, his tray loaded down with two glasses of orange juice, a carton of chocolate milk, soup, shepherd's pie, and a plate of cookies. He sure eats a lot for a skinny guy, says Lynn. He's young, says Walker, but he's daily growing.

One of the songs Hugo sings goes like this: Here comes the candle to light you to bed, here comes the chopper to chop off your head. He sings it to me his breath warm close to my face. I fall asleep on the sofa. The afternoon passes, still, always, from bright to dark, sleepy and maybe drunk, just a little. I don't know the rest of the words, he says. He sits waiting for the afternoon to pass. He does not remember the worlds, um, words.

My stepfather's letter is on good heavy bond paper. He reminds me of his paternal regard for me and offers his best, most therapeutic homilies, words for the feelings and reactions of daughters when they are superseded in the family unit by newborn sons, and consequentially, brothers. He says this child will in no way infringe upon our special relationship. My mother is doing well and sends along a photograph of them at an award ceremony. She is wearing a sequined gown. His arm encircles her waist. Her breasts swell over the top of her gown. Martin Hamlin's skin glows white and eerie in the glare of the flash. Can you see yourself in the mirror, Martin Hamlin? Can you abide by the face that faces you?

The three of them, father, son, and holy ghost are going to educate me. What am I but an empty vessel waiting to be filled with words, sex, gifts, and creamy chocolates. Martin, Hugo, and Charlie. Where one leaves off, the other begins. Each has a secret vision of the order that turns the world. Let me tell you something the three of them have in common: they think we are closer to the angels than the apes. My own true father knows better, but he himself is no better than a ghost, a shrinking violet, a flower of a man. Ghost, flower, father, man. Hugo, Charlie, Martin, in no particular order. The more they teach me, the more I am determined to unlearn. Charlie, Martin, Hugo. No one teaches you anything in this life, not a goddamn thing that you don't already know. I was born whole, two weeks premature, sprung from the first prison, Elsinore, my mother's body, screaming for freedom all the way. What a fool I was then, squalling for air, bloody and triumphant. I was not trusting or trustworthy. Turn-offs: keys, maps, clocks, locks, chutes and ladders, blue hearts, green clovers, yellow diamonds. Turn-ons: scorpios, walks on the beach, vistavision. Please write or call.

My self-portrait does not realistically detail or inventory my face. I have too many times turned away from the mirror. I find myself at times when I am speaking to Hugo and looking at his rheumy eyes and rotty teeth, wondering what he sees back in my face. At these times as I grow in and out of words, I do not think of them, the three of them, only of what has come before and what is yet to come. I think it began with her and her mirrors, hand-held, cheap, gilt-plated, full-length, her naked in the dressing-room mirror looking at herself reflected from all angles while I sat waiting on the little chair, dutifully holding her purse and trying to avert my eyes, but finding this, the doubled, tripled image of her everywhere I looked in the tiny room and the overpowering sweetness of her perfume. How can all their words, rules, and stern recommendations, Martin, Charlie, and Hugo, compare with her, naked, plain, and simple?

This was me as a child, sitting on the porcelain edge of the bathtub, carefully, so as not to disturb her slips and stockings hanging to dry. She is facing herself in the mirror drawing on eyeliner. She says it's never too early to start thinking about a beauty regimen. Bottles and jars of colored oils catch the light. She says, Jesus Pearlie, with your father's face like that, with that skin and those eyes, you're going to be one hell of a knock-out someday, so you've got to learn to take care of yourself.

Her face is at times the only thing I know, the only thing I have remained certain of over the years. Her face is heart-shaped with a wide forehead that tapers down to a weak chin and this makes her large overly blue eyes look doeish, especially then, when I was a child, and she wore her eyebrows thick like Joan Crawford. I am carrying her face around with me like a wallet-size photo. I am learning as I go. She tries to paint lipstick on me. She holds my face in her hand by the chin and says, you're never too young to start a beauty routine. And as I turn and struggle, she paints on the lipstick, scented, I remember, of apricots. That's how she is, my mother, how sexy and obscure. The mascara clotted and burned my eyes, but I licked the lipstick off my mouth, scraped it against my teeth and tongue because it was like wax candy, sweet, thick, and tasting of apricots.

Was I innocent then?

Innocent, that's a big word.

He says if you seek the hero of a tragedy look to the title.

Was I innocent as I sat on the edge of the tub among the flower smells, powders, unguents, the dangling ghost feet of her nylon stockings, or had it begun long before that moment?

I've arrived, I think. Only I am not just yet certain where. I arrived on the doorstep of the Peninsula School, sat on the doorstep of sixteen with my buttery leather bags, greenish skin, my mother's promises of beauty, fortune, and riches, my father's ghost staring mournfully out of my dark eyes, my typewriter, feet size 7 and 7½ respectively in brown shoes set firmly on the packed dirt and leaves of the walkway.

I carried my bags, the typewriter, her face, the memory of her voice and how she cried that morning in the sun in her silk dress and bronzed skin and small shuddering breasts, and I do not know what will come after, later, how it will be or end;

only this, the memory of her, then at that moment, because it was the culmination of every moment that had come before. The odds and ends, now gone, lost. Clip-on earrings of cut green glass, fifty-cent beads bought at the Salvation Army, straw hats, costume wigs, the pungent acrid odor of home perm solution, all changed utterly. I do not want it back. Is this clear? I want only an exact miniature of how it was, and the words too, the stories she told me to fall asleep when nights were too hot to sleep and she placed cold towels on my forehead and we watched television all night and chewed on ice cubes. She painted me with lipstick that smelled of apricots. She held my face in her hand by the chin. It was September. And then October. Walker and I, and Annie and Lynn, some other girls too, we cut out pictures of ghosts and ghoulies and skulls. We sit on the floor of the television lounge and carve pumpkins and set candles inside. From the windows we can see the terrace, the ominous shapes of the trees, the scuffle of leaves on the path, the fat orange moon. We paint our faces with Walker's black lipstick and some fake blood from the drama club, drape sheets over our jeans and sweaters and run outside, the path, the leaves, the night, the woods, trick-or-treating, running all the way, the lone row of faculty houses where they stuff our outstretched pillow cases full of wrapped sweets, caramels, chocolate bars, Smarties, licorice, Jujubes. We take as much as they will give. Martin Hamlin stuffed her hands, her purse, her mouth, her house, full and brimming with sweets, toys, time, fortune, babies, promises, love, uncomfortable, damp and sweaty, sweet love. We run screaming across the moonlight fields, trick or treat, smell my feet, give me something good to eat. I shut my eyes and scream against the wind. Sometimes, I, the child, woke in the night in bed and caught the memory of a dream as it receded, a blackbird, sitting on the edge of my bed said to me, oh where is the man I saw come in here? I whispered, oh no, there was no man, it was only me. And the bird flew away. Sometimes I am certain that Charlie Gumm has been in my cards from the beginning. I know he is only the beginning. I know that soon I will have to try hard to recall his face, the perfect symmetry of his features. A time will come when I will not be sure that any of this ever happened. I think this even now, when I wake and sleep and dream. Other times I know that there is no such thing as fate, and that this is all my world, mine and no one else's. Charlie Gumm is a fool.

I suffer him gladly.

Charlie Gumm is bright and brown-eyed, earnest as a spaniel who might follow you home from the butcher's. He is sincere. He takes neither jokes nor kisses lightly. How does he learn the words he uses? He loves me. He loved them all, and could you darling, apple-cheeked, dearest hold that against him? He can conjugate classes and states of love to the ends and final chapters of the French grammar book. Past, future, subjunctive, passive love, conditional love, plusqueparfait, perfect love. Only why must he keep his eyes open all the time? This is not how things go in the movies. I open one eye and find this is always the case and so I say, whisper, close your eyes. Why do I ask this? Oh, please, just close your eyes.

Walker says repeat after me: Mi chiamo Pearl; chi parla piu lingue nella sua famiglia, Dove il mio angello?

I am telling my story out of order. I know I must be living in order, except when I remember, then the order is ruined, then it is all wrong. I am only learning my way through this thing. I tap on my typewriter at night, late and tinny. I want so much to keep track of the events because already I am certain that I remember the past all wrong. Was my mother really so odd, exotic, and occult? Her postcards seem normal enough. And my stepfather, surely, he had nothing more than my best interests at heart. But that is all gone. This is now. I am keeping track of events, of what happens, what has happened. Not so much because I am afraid of forgetting but because I remember it differently every time. In school I study words and numbers and formulas, equations, the meters of rhyme and angles of shapes. Walker laughs and says you speak French like an Italian, comme un'Italianne. Merci beaucoup, I say, todah rabbah, I say. I write both what I remember and what I foresee. I write blindly with both eyes closed and my hands tied behind my back. There is one detail in my favor. It is not my pretty face. Only this: I suffer fools gladly. My mother knew this, feared this, pushed my face up close to the mirror and I looked. I saw. I knew it was not going to be easy for any of us.

Over a Thursday lunch, hot dish (pasties stuffed full of rutabaga, beef, and potatoes), soup (navy bean), vegetarian plate (broccoli quiche), dessert (pumpkin pie), we listen to Walker swear a blue streak, fuck this, fuck that, fuck you and fuck them all. She's pissed off because someone stole her new tennis shoes from her gym locker. Annie coughs. She and Lynn have the flu and they are all Kleenexes and cold pills doled out in paper cups from the school nurse. Later I get sick and will blame them. Fuck this and fuck that and fuck them all because it was a long time ago. I remember being a child and being carried into my bedroom by my father. I'm wearing a little pink jacket and my mother is singing: I've already had two beers and

I'm ready for the broom, please missus Henry won't you take me to my room? I was carried in his arms and she sang and laughed: I looked at my watch, I looked at my wrist, I punched myself in the face with my fist. She bathed me and put me to bed. They talked low, I heard them, I swear I heard them, smoked cigarettes, the clock ticked out the hours as a reminder. It was three forty-five. Day was no different from night. I'll never again have the clock's hand I was dealt as a child.

I figure that's okay. I say fuck it all. I don't want the guilty pleasures of that loaded deck anyhow. The fortune-teller's promise thrills me. I'm destined for better things. I'm going to work it all backward and remember more as time passes. I'm chewing great gulping mouthfuls of the past and spitting it as I go. What's the word he uses? It's like the sounds the birds make as they fly overhead. We can never go back to Mandan. Not tomorrow or the next day. Not in the spring or summer or again and again, in the autumn. It is nothing more than a graveyard now. You'll do better to plant whole bones in your garden and hope to see them grow. Keep clear of ladders, toss salt over your shoulder, and for God's sake, show some reverence, show some caution, hold your breath when you pass a graveyard. You can lose your way in a place like Mandan, the low scrub weeds, the cans, rags, and bottles, when he asked me, will you? Will you—? His words trailed off in kisses, resumed in words and the sounds of the blackbirds all afternoon and on into evening, will you—? Can you promise me that? And I turned my blind face to the sun. Those days, those nights. Mandan. Are you still dancin' darlin'? Turn-ons: candlelight, regicide, October. There is no other way to learn but this, suffer it all. Force yourself to see her face again, the exact detail, the shades, colors, but oh, first the scents, hairspray, melon soap, the mint toothpaste, eye of newt and leg of toad, her tears, her shuddering breasts. Yes, here it is again: she takes her hands from her face, she says cold and hard, no sign of tears in her voice although they streak the opalescent sheen of her powdered face, she says over and over, it never stops. No, she says it once, and to me, I hear it again and again, because I'm afraid now, I am afraid that I understand. It never stops. She lets her head fall on top of her vanity table, her bright curls catch the light, copper and gold, gold by bronze. He stood in the doorway. The king was in his counting house. There was no metal more attractive than she, golden, copper, bronzed, and the pure sapphirine light in her eyes made more precious for each glittering tear. Turn-offs: in-jokes, uxoriousness, triple-word score, your desperate love 'em and leave 'em style.

Oh, I suffer them gladly, those hungry, unrepentant kisses of Charlie Gumm burning with puritanical desire when he talks about fucking country club girls in parked cars on summer nights. Oh Lord, it is, it was, it is all a long time ago. Trust this, even now, even the future is a long time ago. Key by key, I'm making words. This manuscript is secret. Tickety click tock, a clock, the minutes. Hey, stop peeking. This is secret. Walker sneaks looks at my papers. I pretend not to notice. It was September then. When I arrived. I know how it ends now but it is going to take some time to recall the beginning because that is far away. How did it start? Oh yes, her face. My father carrying me. I can count on this, his absence. Her presence. This is enough for now. I am sixteen years old. This is not a lot of years old to be. But it's enough. It's just deep enough and sad enough and wordy, desperate and full enough to leave me empty, to set it all in motion. Oh Lord, nothing will, can, or could stop it now, it's begun. Never bet against time, this is what I am learning, father, son, ghost, holy holy holy apes and angels, have the foresight to walk away from the cards even as they lie set against the Bohemian charm of the cloth as dealt, Celtic Cross, face down.

Hugo Tappan says that when I write a story, not those scatter-brained bits of schoolgirl crushes, but a real story with a beginning, middle, and end, he says, I daresay it will be unbearably prosy, clotted with devilishly unimportant childish nostalgias. It's all a girl can know of the world. It's all a woman ever knows. Emptiness, what she had and what she's lost, all the subsequent things she's been emptied of: the scrolling roses papering her nursery walls, tea sets, bonnets, Chinese checkers, dolls, fairy books, and princes, he says, one must never forget the princes. Or the swords, I say.

He says women cannot express themselves in any way other than absolute confusion, idiotic obfuscation. He says they have no sense of time.

I say time is what you make of it.

It is not a self-portrait. It is not a representation of reality. It is only a story. It is not even that. I ruin the order of things and this is where people most place their belief. Numbers follow one another, one, two, three, we can trust chronology, uno, due, tre. We trust the chronology of moments and know this is at least true. This is the second lie. That it all could have been different, that it was better once, that it happened just that way, it all happened just exactly as I remember it.

Charlie Gumm and I do it whenever we want and nobody, not Annie or Lynn or Mrs. Marsh or Walker or Hugo Tappan himself and no angel, can stop us. All that winter and into the spring we do it whenever we get the chance the notion the

dare. We do it without passion or expertise. We do it the way
we do our homework. We do it like Jane Eyre and St. John
Rivers before the blind eyes of Rochester. We wait for the thrill
that never comes, the thrill of getting caught. We hug our sin
in private and gloat. We catch each other's eyes across the dining hall and exchange knowing looks. We do it in the school
laundry room, the equipment closet, the kitchenette and classrooms in the long dark hours of dusk. We do it until we are
sore and bruised and sometimes bleeding and then we stop
and start again. We do it on the floor, standing up, on desks,
in the rain, out in Mandan, the grasses and wet dark earth near
the rusted barbed wire of an abandoned root cellar. Each time
it is the same. Is this a good or a bad thing? The sameness, and
to him, I always have to say, close your eyes. He has a child's
sullen mouth. Each time it is the same. When the moment
passes, the silence of the fields, the sweet questionings of birds
flying overhead, swooping down to pick scraps and crusts
from us, when the moment passes into afterthought he offers
me in boyish earnestness whatever he can find in his pockets,
a cigarette, a stick of Juicy Fruit, apples stolen from the dining
hall, butterscotch and peppermint candies wrapped in glittering cellophane.

Love is the kind of word he uses too freely. It's a word that
must indicate what it all means, what the sameness means, what
the misty fields, silence broken by the questionings of the sparrows, the blackbirds, the crows. I think I know the answer.
As well him as another, that's the line that Walker always says
with a droll lilt, her Spanish tongue, her green eyes, as well him
as another. He loves me, he swears earnestly. He loves me the
way he loves soccer, autumn, toffee, and that new car smell.
He swears endurance, and there's a certain innocent charm to
that. Me, I was never innocent. I explain to him as gently, as

obscurely as I can. I say April's green endures after the birds have gone, after the birds have tested the reality of the misty fields with their sweet questionings, then we know that April's green endures. He says that's a funny answer. He says, it doesn't make sense. After the moment passes I try to recollect it in words and there are no words. I want him to be as blind as I am, two blind mice. I close my eyes and wait for the moment to pass. Oh Pearlie, he says, why can't you just be honest with me? I'm honest, I say. He is funny like this. Innocent, even in the face of his guilt and his desire, his past, Mims in her tennis skirt under which white panties gleam, the girl in the car, although he claims as though demanding my absolution, it was only once. He is innocent because he swears that he loved them all in the moment, even if never again. Oh, Pearlie, you're better, you're different from the rest, those other girls. I can't abide by the mirror. I want him to go and struggle against the light as blindly as I; this must be the reason. This must be the explanation why I ask it so often; please, close your eyes. I suffer my way by fools and feels and motions. Oh, Pearlie, he calls my name the way the birds do, and we do it all the time.

I close my eyes and see it all the way it once was. Sometimes I can remember nothing. Only the names and nothing about how it all really was. My mother is not home. I find the door open, the lights on, scented candles burning cinnamon, all the secrets of the world laid out before me, and oh, they are no less glamorous for being revealed. No one teaches a girl anything in this life. No one can or could. I'm blind and deaf. I touch. I walk through her rooms in the blazing light and find she has marked a path for me with slips and silks, high-heel shoes, night air, camisoles, powders on her dressing table, the sponges, brushes, padded lace brassieres, the scent bottle and the empty silver picture frame, a double heart, one heart each for a picture of her two children, a son and a daughter. I appreciate the endless clutter of her rooms. I touch every surface and unstopper the bottles, almond, mandragora, tea rose, lilac, fern, vanilla, lime, talc, coffee, clove, and mint.

How lonely she must have been.

I was a child, is this any excuse?

Charlie Gumm has four brothers, Stuart, William, Thomas, and Donald. There was never a moment alone, he says in one of his bright confessional moments, a cigarette clumsy and dramatic on his lip.

I wonder what it would be like to be a family in a television movie. I will meet my mother for lunch. She looks like some forgotten film star, a floppy hat, taut skin, gloves that reach to her elbows and her arms bare to the shoulders. The restaurant is light, full of gleaming silver and waiters in white jackets who eye us appreciatively from across the room. We eat bowls of strawberries and cream and drink Perrier water from heavy crystal glasses. My couture shoes have square Cuban heels, but my mother wears white high-heel sandals with ankle straps, something like Daisy might have worn when she stood staring across from Nick's small yard at the expanse of Gatsby's well-manicured greenery, the green light, the green light. The waiters mistake us for sisters. We begin coldly. She says curtly, Pearl, you look rather well. I say, you too, mumsy, the years have been kind. But then we cannot help ourselves and by the time the melon sorbet arrives we are in tears and clasping gloved hands across the linen tablecloth, daubing our running mascara with tissues. I tell her that I understand what she meant that day when she told me why she left my father and how she wanted more. She smiles wan and winsome, oh my, I forgot all about that; I put it right out of my mind, and you should too darling. Her fingers ungloved on the silver are long and bronze and tapered. Her eyes are brilliant blue. I say what is that song you used to sing to me as a child? She smiles all misty and nostalgic and even the crusty French maître d' can barely keep back tears, while she begins to sing: if you like piña coladas and getting caught in the rain, if you're not into disco, if you have half a brain. We hug and forgive each other all past sins and transgressions, we promise to get together again real soon, and we hug one last time for effect as the final credits run. How's this for a story. A resolution between Pearl and Judy. Me and momms. Glamour girl and homely child. Or is it the other way around? Struggling mother and her daughter who had it all without knowing it and without even trying to have it. Baby, she used to say, baby, you couldn't get rid of it if you tried. It could happen, right? Who can say what will happen in the future. The future is never a lie; it's only an anticipation. The past is the real lie. The image of her at her dressing table sobbing because I was a fool, a stupid blind fool because I didn't have the sense to understand why Maxim had always hated Rebecca.

I arrived at the Peninsula School grown shabby and two full inches taller, hollow-cheeked and insistent, a head full of pronouns and no concrete images or words to back them up. The birds called out to me. I left my mother. I packed my bags. I left my father. You could say I was, I am, a fool, but I cut my losses, burnt my bridges, kissed my vanilla-scented wrist to the world and knew that with distance I would forget all about it, for a while, until the ghosts came, because the ghosts always come. She kissed me at the train station, Chicago bound, and said that all was forgiven, water under the burnt bridge, spilled milk on the kitchen counter. You will always be my baby girl, she said. I was never that. How could I have been? I don't know that I know what a good mother is, but I can't say that she was it. This doesn't make her bad as a person. I didn't understand this at first. It was only that she didn't know. How could I have been a good child? Call us sisters then. It's the easiest way. It is because, I realize, it is because I was there between them the moment she first realized that she hated him. I was there in my little pink jacket, my curls and matching cap, a dark and serious baby. I would always be part of that memory for her. The morning she stumbled in, frantic, smoky, up all night, high-heeled, asking him for a little less art and more matter, protesting too much his exquisite understanding. I shouldn't have been part of that memory for her, and yet I was, and yet I would forever be. This will be my burden. I turn my face away from the mirror ashamed at what I see.

Walker says her mother has been in psychoanalysis for four years and is getting closer with each session to the moment when she will recall her own conception.

Later my mother tells me that I was there too in Shirley's Aunt Irena's house in the living room while the cards and leaves were being read and my mother held me up to the old woman and asked her to read my fortune. Irena crossed herself and told my mother emphatically, no, no, no, it was far too early. You give the child a fate too early in life and it becomes good or bad, a destiny she will have no choice but to follow. She said the cards become a curse you must follow blindly. Whatever, said Shirl, growing bored. My mother set her smooth palm on the table. She said, well Irena what's on my horizon? I sat under the table playing with a plastic tea set, pretending to be a hostess, pretending to be Laura Ingalls Wilder, pretending to be an exiled Russian princess.

I never thought of how my mother waited for him.

Those days, ten years ago, is that all? She and Sofie (we say Zo-fee, we say Zo-fee-ahh, you look vee-lup-tu-us, deelee-shouz today . . .) are always going out, trying to meet Mr. Right, meeting men, right or wrong, coming home with flushed cheeks and phone numbers written on matchbooks, napkins, scrawled across their hands. I didn't know this was the worst kind of waiting. The men in my mother's life tell her she is pretty and feed her chocolates to please her. Men, here is what I am learning. Men think that there is an essential emptiness in women that manifests itself in a lack of morals, a fearlessness because they have nothing to lose—and it is, it must be, every man's duty and obligation, Gummy Charlie, Gooey Huey, Martin Hamlet, to fill that emptiness in one way or another. Bring on the nouns, baby, the hot glue guns, spackle, plaster of Paris. But the secret is out: a noun itself is the spirit of emptiness. A pronoun then is only a ghost, the pale shadow of emptiness.

Walker says, try saying this: L'hai augurato un buon anno?

Men don't know what to do with emptiness but to stuff it full, decorate it, love words, paintings, velvet berets, sofas, grape-fruits, bus tickets, chocolates. Fuck that. Fuck it all. Walker knows the words, fuck this and fuck them and fuck it all. It is all such a long time ago, long time to come, has been, will become, oh, whatever, just fuck it. Here is the problem with men: they want to fill without losing what they have. This is what I am learning. My mother says that no man can under-stand a woman. Momma says men want something deep and sweet and certain in a woman, everything rich and fine she can afford him and fear every moment what she will steal. What cannot be replaced. We are charmed not by what they suspect (their brave actions, their firm convictions, decisive and grimly held jaws), but by failure, their best intentions which never quite pan out. It is not necessity. It is excess. You pity them and their fears and suffer them, poor fools, gladly in your arms.

In the dining hall, a Friday lunch, hot dish (tuna casserole and french fries), soup (curry vegetable or chicken noodle), vege-tarian plate (broccoli quiche), dessert (apple cobbler), we sit and listen to Annie read her Christmas list. She's going to buy a new electric wok for her mother and a silk cravat for her father. That means tie, she enlightens us with a sniff. What do you like best about Christmas, Walker? asks Annie. That part where they put that crown of thorns on him. That's Easter, says Annie, oh Walker, you're such an incorrigible heathen. I ask Annie if she's been listening to that Christian station again. I say, *Get me behind thee Satan!* Walker says munching on the crust of her cobbler, I'm a Catholic, lapsed. It was never the same, I say, after the fall. Walker and I pretend we have sold our souls to the devil and Annie doesn't think this is very funny at all. She says it's nothing to joke about. Walker says a joke is when you laugh. And we cannot stop ourselves.

Charlie Gumm and I do it all the time. It is only that we can-not seem to stop ourselves. We do not notice the world around us. Do the days pass? Do we move from one room to the next?

What do we put on our trays in the cafeteria line? Sometimes I write things down as soon as they happen just so I will remember later. What is at the end of our forks? We are invisible. No one suspects us or knows our secret. I catch his eyes over his dish of lime Jello.

One night I am up late studying with Walker.

She says: Vuol portarmi un caffe?

I go down to the basement to the pop machine to get us a couple of cokes. We'd rather have coffee. We'd rather drink vodka like Russian expatriates. I am walking down the hall in the basement when I hear it. Yes. I stop. No. Yes, I am certain I heard it that time. There is a certain rumbling, a rustling, hushed from behind a closet door, from the darkness of the laundry room. I hear something. I stop and know suddenly that it is all around me. The school is rife and sweet with it. All through the bitter cold winter everyone else is doing it too. And no one will ever catch anyone at it because we are so deaf and dumb and snowblind. We have lost toes too numerous to count, and parts of our feet and hands are frozen numb. It is not just me and Charlie Gumm. It is everyone. You can see it in their eyes. Those blonde girls who call their parents clockwork-wound Sunday afternoon fourish, the science geeks, the prep boys, the chubby girls who try not to be noticed when they sneak back for a second dessert, the teachers, shy girls who sit alone, the lunch ladies, the dishroom guys. It is too cold for anyone to care about anything except the most base and secretive survival, warmth, mind your own fucking business. Shut the door behind you. In the spring we will dress in pastel colors, ruin our light shoes so inappropriate for the mud and rains, but that will be just like us, so wrong, so so *inappropriate,* not just liars—you know lying I can understand—but this is desperation. It will be as though this winter has never happened. I write it down as I go. I hear sounds behind doors, the hushed breath and aching rhythm as my footsteps retreat. Boys sneak into the girls' dorm through propped basement windows. They stand in the cold outside like mournful ghosts in the snow, waiting. I hear it myself. I turn. It is impossible to shut out the sound of it. In my room I turn out the lights and go to the window. Walker follows me without saying a word. I part the curtains and am certain I see someone there, a shadow in the fields, just caught, captured in the light cast on the snow, a figure in a coat and scarf waiting for some girl who has promised but never shows up to let him in because she has fallen asleep or lost her nerve or found someone else standing out there before he was. What would happen, I wonder, if I let him in and led him down the stairs to the boiler room; in the dark will it matter that he is not Charlie Gumm? I know I will never tell Charlie Gumm that I love him. Even if he comes to me one night, late, and admits to having been with some other girl, I won't hate Charlie Gumm. I won't hate him for wanting to talk about stupid people or stupid things. I watch for the lone boy in the snow. I know that he would never say a word about love. He is the one, this ghost, the one I want. I watch the boy in the snow until he turns and retreats, the snowy fields, the pearly moonlight, a shadow on the path. Maybe he was never there at all and I only made him up to make myself feel better, to justify my horrible sneaky crabby hungry wanting guilty desire for just a little tiny teensy bit more than everything on the plate. He could have been Romeo, Hamlet, Arthur Dimmesdale, Captain Kirk, Rochester, or Charlie Gumm himself meeting some other girl and greeting her with open-eyed kisses like childrens' orange aspirin; they are sweet and harmless but do nothing for the pain.

During the winter break most of the students go home, but the dorms are left open for the stragglers, the kids with families overseas, in the army, or generally unavailable. Annie and Lynn french braid each other's hair, wear earrings made of Christmas tree bulbs and sing jingle bells Batman smells/ Robin laid an egg/Batmobile lost its wheel and Joker got away. They start cracking up like crazy and then sing it all over again. Even Walker is looking forward to going home and sleeping late in her own bed, having latté in the morning, sprinkled with bitter cocoa, with her mother and sisters in the kitchen. She asks if I want to come home with her. There's plenty of room, she says, you could have a whole wing to yourself if you want. I say no, that I was never one for holidays. She says okay, but I'm going to bring you a present, a genuine Wisconsin cheese log. Holidays, what did they ever bring me as a child? Waiting for my mother to come home from some party or other and tell me about all the glittering dresses and open her purse and feed me cookies and stolen hors d'oeuvres, soggy and wrapped in paper napkins. Stories about the men she had danced with and ones who tried to look down Sofie's dress. I tell Walker that I'll be fine. All my favorites will be on TV, *Christmas in Connecticut*, *The Bells of St. Mary's*, the animated specials with Rudolf, Frosty, and the Heat Meister. We'll have fun, I tell her. Me and the girl from Sri Lanka, the twins Maggie and Monica, Bridget Davis, Gretchen Deutsch, who does not honor Judeo-Christian holidays and intends to sit in her classrooms during the proper hours. And oh, there's always Charlie Gumm.

Charlie doesn't see why we have to spend so much time with Hugo now. This should be time for us alone. What do you see in that dirty old man, he asks me, what with his creepy yellow fingernails and red eyes. And what's that smell that's always coming up off him? Sulphur, I say, and something for his arthritis. Don't think too much about him, I say, he's usually just plain drunk. Charlie has only just taken up smoking, and he doesn't approve of drinking, well, not more than a martini or two at the club, dry, the way dad drinks them and mom pours them. When Charlie's on his drinking lecture, he gets this Cotton Mather glow, all radiant and high on his forehead and long nose. Charlie and I get an ax and chop down a baby spruce and bring it to the gatehouse. We decorate it with popcorn and cut-out snowflakes, string cranberries. Hugo makes up a batch of real eggnog and slips vodka in mine and his, but leaves Charlie's, virgin, all yolk and cream. Hugo winks at me while Charlie stokes up the fire. Charlie and I run through the woods home but have to stop and walk because it's so damn cold the wind burns us, twelve below zero.

After the eggnog, the evening fires, the snow outside the windows, Charlie relents about Hugo. Even he has to admit there is a quaint Dickensian charm to the gatehouse; one tends to forget about the world outside. What can you two possibly have in common? Charlie asks me suspiciously. What do you talk about? Art, I say. Charlie nods like he's thinking about this. We run through the snow. He says let's make snow angels. I say, let's not and say we did. He pushes me into the snow and I'm freezing to death so I pull him down with me and the woods are so quiet that I'm embarrassed for any sound we make that disturbs the night. It's too cold outside just then under the moon and snow and ice and winter, too cold then even for the birds, it's too cold to do it just then, or else, I swear to God, we would have, but it's just too cold. So we brush the snow off and walk home alone together and he kisses me goodnight on the steps of the girls' dorm and I wait in the hallway with my face pressed against the window and watch him cut across to the boys' dorm until I can't see him anymore.

419

I've explained to Charlie that he should just think of Hugo more as a funny uncle than a grandfatherly type; and really, all English people are like that. He says, not Charles and Di. We are spending our winter break days so much with Hugo because of the dream world of his cottage. He feeds us treats, stuffs us full of sweetmeats like little piglets and stokes the fire up to blazing. The holiday stories he tells about London and South Wales surely must be lies, more of his rich and expert fictions; being a boy and coming home on the train from boarding school, counting the lime trees and eating plum pudding all studded with almonds and raisins and a miniature British flag stuck in the caramelized sugar of the topping, drinking brandy from his father's snifter, the acrid odor of cigars, the elaborate hats the ladies wore. He's so charming then, poised before the grate, cradling a teacup full of vodka, laying on his avuncular routine. Later Charlie says he didn't know that writers could tell such good stories. He drinks his eggnog, and I know he's sitting there thinking that he's like Tiny Tim and Hugo is the crusty but ultimately warm-hearted Scrooge and me, I guess I'm the Christmas goose. It gets late. I say I figure we better go. The snow is falling heavy and picturesque. The fire burns on. I look over at Charlie and his head is falling back against the sofa, his mouth soft, pink, and open, a sleepy flush spreads across his cheeks. Hugo sees all this too and says you two children had better stay here tonight rather than brave those woods. The path will be too icy, you musn't try to cut back through the woods in this blizzard. I hate to think of Hansel and Gretel lost in the snow with no bread crumbs.

The next morning we do it for the first time in Hugo's cottage right there in his bed. The first night we are too charmed. We giggle together and strip naked on the wrinkled sheets, whisper with laughter and say is he going to wake us in the night and spoon feed us plum pudding? Hey, Charlie says, what is plum pudding anyway? I tell him it's suet, that's all that English people eat and that's what makes their teeth so bad. He nods and pulls the sheet over his head like the ghost of Christmas future, he says, so what's suet? When we wake in the morning it is still snowing and we cannot stop ourselves. We know we should stop, but we can't. We do it before we wake or even say a word. We do it as silently as we can. We do it as quietly as we can. We feel guilty but it is not our fault; we just can't stop ourselves.

The day is cold, bright, and lazy. Hugo says there is no point in us going back to the dormitories and eating tinned meat and soup off the kitchenette hot plate. Charlie shovels the walk and chops wood for the fire. I bake cookies. Hugo naps because he has been up late writing, he says. Later when he wakes we turn on the little black-and-white television and watch *Bell, Book and Candle* with that sexy witch who falls in love with Jimmy Stewart in it. I point out that my mother is a great admirer of Kim Novak's breasts and Hugo nods with appreciative agreement. Charlie eats popcorn and bears, I think, a striking resemblance to the picture of Increase Mather in my junior high history book. The afternoon grows dark and wintery. Charlie and I sneak off to the bedroom for a nap as the snow begins to fall more heavily. I wake later in the darkness, get out of bed and find Hugo in the kitchen. I sit with him and tell him about the ghost boy I saw in the snow. We make toast and a big pot of oatmeal and drink orange juice mixed with vodka and sit talking for a long time.

Never be honest with a man, he tells me.

That's funny advice, I say, coming from a man.

He butters his toast and uses the same knife to dip into the strawberry preserves.

I'm something of a man, he says, and something of a woman.
Don't give me that Tiresias crap, I say.

Crunch, crunch. The crumbs. He smartly wipes his mouth.

I worry that he is going to unbutton his cardigan sweater,
reach into the depths of his flannel shirt over his old man's
swollen belly and reveal two perfect breasts, heady with sili-
cone, nestled like doves, exotic as ripe fruit, one in each hand
and offer them up to me, roseate aureoles, small sharp roses,
not quite woman, he will say and begin to unzip his fly.

No, instead, he only continues to wipe his mouth and says
something about old people having the dubious luxury of giving advice they never would have taken when the option was
their's. He munches his toast and watches the snow for ghost
boys and girls who might sleep on his pillows. He is certain he
has caught children's faces, frozen, chiseled in ice on his windows, stars, hearts, flowers, ghosts. He pours us more juice and
adds vodka.

Hugo? I say.

Yes.

It is quiet. Just the snow. We drink on in silence.

I say, Hugo, which is it finally—

—The chicken or the egg? he interrupts.

No.

—Descartes or the horse?

No, I say again.

Then what, child?

Which is it finally? You can tell me now, I promise I won't
tell it to anyone else. Does fate make us or do we make our
own fates?

He smiles wryly. He says, you give me too much credit. If
I knew that Pearl dear, I would be a rich old man indeed.

But you are, I say, a rich old man.

Yes, he says, and you don't think I got this way by telling all the tricks of the trade do you?

We drink.

We watch the snow.

Hugo relents.

He says, buck up little one. Let's go plug in the telly and watch that show that all you Yanks are so keen on. With the ball dropping on the drunkards in the snow.

What? I ask.

Is it too early yet? he continues. Perhaps you are right.

No, I say, I mean, what day is it?

Why it's New Year's Eve, he says.

I didn't even realize, I say.

How charming, he says, then may I have the pleasure of being the first to say it, Happy New Year.

We clink teacups like Russian expatriates.

To the year nineteen hundred and eighty-six, he says.

To fate, I say, fuck it.

To destiny, he says, defy it.

To tales, I say, tell them.

To home, he says, why how awkward, I can't think of an h-word—

To hell with it—

He nods happily.

To 1986, he says, the year One.

He pours vodka and we toast the new year, tossing out the old like so many bread crumb sins, like plum pudding speckled with almonds, like a crumbling Wisconsin cheese log in the snow for the birds to get drunk on. Happy New Year, he says, although it is a bit early for it yet. He looks at his wristwatch. It must be New Year's already some place in the world, and we, he says, you and I certainly do not discriminate on the basis of time zone.

Charlie stumbles into the kitchen rubbing his eyes. He's pink, flushed, and groggy. Hugo licks his lips. Breakfast, offers Hugo. It is past ten o'clock at night. Yes, thank you, says Charlie. He feels guilty, I can tell, about the bed we have left unmade behind us spattered with chewing-gum wrappers and shiny cellophanes of peppermint and cinnamon candies. Hugo himself cooks the eggs, makes the toast, the tea, pours the juice from the pitcher, Hugo himself, and Charlie eats every last crumb. When Hugo has stuffed him full he looks at his watch and says it is early yet, an hour left on the outgoing year. Why don't you two young creatures go at it again? Charlie nearly dies right there. His eyes blink open and shut rapidly. Me, I'm not making any bets against time. Go on, Hugo says, don't worry about the dishes. Be young, he says, go, make the best of it. He looks again at his watch. The countdown has begun. Is this quite how it happened? I realize I cannot nearly remember or is it yearly remember? Year by year I cannot dearly remember yearly enough. He looks at his clock and says, old time is fast flying. And like I said before, in the beginning, we are young and we cannot stop ourselves so we go into Hugo Tappan's bedroom, his crumpled papers littering the floor, empty gin bottles on the dresser, sheets half torn off the bed and we do it again, mechanically, earnestly, forcefully, honestly, cleverly, the way you can only when you are young and you know there is someone listening at the door.

Shakespearl

HAVE YOURSELF TWO CHILDREN. The boy will be Ophelia and the girl will be Hamlet. In the fields they share poems and crosswords, throwing kisses, each to each. No one has had to tell me of their games. She rings him in roses, dandelions, and sweet summer weeds. Ashes, ashes, we all fall down. He ropes her in roses. I have seen it all for myself.

Good Queen Gertrude sits before her looking glass in royal attire, skirts trailing, ruff on her neck, jewels, sore haunches. She unwinds her hair from the tight coils of braid. How vain is my mother about her hair which in truth is thin and brittle, but then pity her, suffer her, she was born with the look of a woman old before her time. In the firelight stroke by brush-stroke the locks shine burnished redgolden. She unfastens her bodice to warm her breasts and those nestling birds, once set free, ache upward toward the light. I hear his knock, three times, in rapid succession, upon the wooden door. She does not answer. Yes, now it all comes back to you, something of the wedding announcement, the florid hand, engraved parchment, the names, the dates, hearts and flowers, clubs and diamonds. Her second husband, our honored king, Claudius, strides about the halls in his purple finery pounding the doors, calling her name. This is his impatience; this is how he waits for her. Bring me more wine! He calls out. Quail eggs, chocolates, Rhenish wine and then, ah, honeyed Turkish coffee in tiny cups each painted with a miniature likeness of the nuptial festivities. Old Polonius shares late-night table with the king and although not himself prone to gamble deals a fair enough hand. Over plates of wine and cups of sweets, the coffee and rich liqueur, they share stories of the old wars. All the while this cannot mask his fear, this king's waiting on his queen, late, the hour is late, and she is long at her bath.

The halls echo at night with our footsteps as we search for the others. You and I, we have more care than to knock. We peek, we peer, barefoot, carrying our slippers, hushing our laughter. Together we search for Hamlet. At this point a humble attendant lord would suffice. Although we have not seen her yet, Ophelia, we know we would recognize her; the very type for tragedy, all nonsense words, fragile and drawn with a certain inhibited boldness, and oh, the flowers woven in her hair so thick, scented—nightly her hair grows with such fervor that each morning it must be cut, yards and yards of it, with pruning shears. The girls weave her hair into rugs, tapestries, linens, and cloaks for the oncoming winter. Her hair, the rich dampness of it, smells sweet and heady as flowers.

The girl will be Ophelia and the boy will be Hamlet.

I closed my eyes and followed my dreams blindly through the echoing halls. How can I any longer believe what was taught to me, what was allotted to me, meted out, expected? Here he is, ah, we have stumbled upon him at last, the prince, but hush, let's not disturb him. He shows his face only in profile, and frankly, does not seem half the man I expected a *prince* to be. High, high, boys raise the mainsail. Yo, ho, blow the man down. How thin poor Hamlet is, how delicate, how mobled, how like a queen. A mutual friend from England, who shall remain unnamed, has advance informed me of the prince's travails, his studies, late-night poems, the phone call from home, the letter never sent. Hamlet has fine wrists. He smells of tobacco and graveyards, mourns the passing of whatever has just lately gone out of passion, I mean fashion. His liege lady, he trails her plucking his lute, speaking the heresy with a troubadour's infatuation. See, peek now, quickly through this door left ajar, watch how he hesitates and wants no more than to touch the velvet hem of her dress and in doing so perhaps catch air of the almond and ginseng sachet of her swishing skirts, unbleached delicates and underthings. Gertrude, Gertrude, he can barely press his dry lips together to whistle her name in the wind. Martha, Mary, and the girls at the tomb, he prays to them with the beads and holy water: batter my heart, three-personed God. Blindly, he goes with love, blind, bound, speechless and cannot tell mother from daughter, each from each, sister from brother.

I saw her once myself, and I'll admit freely to you, yes, I too was captured by her; the cold morning, bitter gray sky, her flushed cheeks, a face on which time would make but little impression. I was once like you, righteous and God-fearing. If only she could have stayed frozen for me, at the moment of her innocence against the winter fields, if only I had not been forced to learn of her sins: vanity, overvaunting pride, sloth, greed. I go by goodness, the way of the pilgrim, and you would do well to go this way yourself, brother. Mine eyes were opened. I called on the saints, my soul, the way and found it in myself to pity her, but it was a hard road to travel; I understand the suffering and her loss of all she had once held dearly close. Time did not etch those hard lines on her face; she was born with them. I pledged myself to the cause. I sold her a shinbone of Saint Thomas himself, an unguent to quiet her night sweats, dried mandrake root, elderflowers, and a Roman coin on a glittering chain for luck with conception. Poor

Gertrude, such is the stingy hand of fate, that double-dealer, to leave this beautified woman with nothing to call her own.

Ophelia pales in comparison to the queen, oh, her downcast eyes, her conspicuous youth and somber dress. At the gaming table she seeks only to lose, but despite it all, she wins every hand she lays down. She wins, she wins, and she doesn't even know how to play. I'm sorry, she says in apology until gold coins rain from her mouth and the onlookers, we cannot help but despise her, hate the sheer luck of her draw. She trails roses, vines, and stubborn nettles. Her face is a cliche of someone else's idea of beauty. She will blush and cry, pleading for you, but her purse comes up embarrassingly rich while yours remains empty. Here, she says, coins, take them. But in your hands they crumble, turn to a brittle collection of petals, flowers, seeds, and stems. How you love to hate the ground daily she treads and rebuke her pious ministrations to the sick. Don't worry brother, they too hate her. If only she could better disguise the bloom and heady scent that heralds her arrival in their wards and locked cells. It is no wonder that when men claim to love her they love only some image of themselves reflected in her eyes. It is no wonder she falls, so often, trembling, falling. She walked right out of the mirror banked and shored sweet with weeds and willows, and we were certain that was the last of her; we were rid of her, but, oh, she returned, tossing us coins and candies and sweets with which she meant only to signify her love for us, but we in the crowd ridiculed her as the gifts pelted us and broke and bruised our skin like flint rocks, shards of glass, pebbles, clods of dirt, leaving us bloodied and broken but wanting more.

Have you seen my love? He can hunt, fish, and gamble. He comes to me from the south, with the birds, against the seasons. He can paint, sew, and spin. His back to my back, his mouth to my mouth. He can read a map, tell a tale, pull the queens from the deck with his eyes blindfolded.

One thing is clear: other women have no tolerance for Ophelia. They seek more serious diversions. Only girls and children kiss her graven image before bedtime. They trim Easter bonnets, press violets in remembrance books and soak their tiny fingers in bowls of lemon water. This is not her story. We are spies, you and I, in these damp halls at night; spies not only to their actions, secrets, trysts, and nightmares, but to their intelligence. We will go to the root, the first story, the only story. It should not be my story, Ophelia insists. Look, she's only trying to be good, to do good works. Give the story to the poor, she finally begs, the sick, the orphans, you there, take the story as your own, let it help you sleep for there is no hope for me, even in my dreams. It always comes back to Ophelia, the winning hand, the coin, truepenny, double-sided; her purse is never empty.

Listen, I wonder about guys like you. The ones who nod and seem, you know, so genuinely interested in the words of a plain-faced girl like me. No, no, don't flatter me, What can my words possibly mean to you? I wonder what it is you are thinking just now as you lean across the bar, nod gravely into my eyes and say, barkeep, set us up, me and the young lady here, with another round of Rhenish.

Every old girlfriend you can remember is either Ophelia or Gertrude. Was she clumsy, meek, harmless, childlike? Do you remember with pride her clinging admiration for you? Or was she the other? A real bitch. A walking nightmare. Hell on wheels. Did you count yourself lucky to get out of it alive and unscathed? A real piece of work, yes, she was. And yet and yet, you do recall sometimes the endless stretch of legs in high-heel shoes, the red lipstick, the tattoo with another man's name,

Daddy, in bleeding script and for you at least, Yorick, these simple heart-warming details made the pain worthwhile. They are all gone now, poor Yorick, all those girlfriends, goodnight sweet ladies, whom you remember and then get the pang in the heart, the hip, the groin—loss, money, and lust, respectively. Where are all those girls now? The men are dragging the river. Bare-chested, hardy, handsome, singing drinking songs as they go about their muddy business, the men, have as yet, found no trace of the body.

I stumble in upon Gertrude at the mirror. The girls wind and twine in loops her brittle hair. Her breasts are bare. She offers them to me, but I decline. Oh, she says, blowing hard on her hand to dry the freshly painted nails. Oh, she says, I hate a man who can't make up his mind. I do not need to remind her. I am something of a boy and something of a girl. Later she will drop the causes and effects, the clauses and appendums. Later, when I ask again while I sit at her feet and gnaw the heel of her shoe, she will just say, men, *hmmph*. I worry for her. Has she truly found love with her second husband or will she grow bored and turn for comfort once again to the grocer's assistant with his stammering dreams hopelessly phrased in list form? Men, she says, *Hmmph*. This says the queen, my mother. Not one of them will admit to this, these girls we all once knew, queens, princesses, whores and harlots, but they all believe that it is still quite possible, hush, lower your voice, but quietly, do not reveal their secret; they believe that one can spin the wheel and win, that there is a destiny that shapes the endings of romance novels.

I walk the halls listening door by door, each to each. I check behind the tapestries, the chairs, painted screens, and I am certain I heard it that time; the swish of her retreating skirts, the click and clacking of her well-heeled shoes. For whom do I search? I am lonely, and he is forever late. I am hungry. Who will love me? Who will feed me? I ask these questions while we wait for her second coat of lacquer to dry. Will it be Horatio, mother? No, the cards say that is not to be so. He is not obstinate, but firm, set in his ways; he does not, he cannot waiver. When asked to tell the tale he does so without pride, flourish, or embellishment. To him it is a tale of the hunt with winners and losers, dogs, guns, and deer. The fewer words the better. Certainly this is not enough for the ladies. We want a man who will speak the speech trippingly, that's what we want, and some chocolates and maybe flowers every once in a while. Offer the trim love words; pine is for endurance, forgive me with violets, weeds for prosperity, I long for you manflower, fennel, you are worthy of praise. Follow these rules and you will do well, boys, heed the conventions of court, know which days to sport the white rose and which the red. Delphinium, in the morning, sister, sister, you are always on my mind. Horatio does not understand the coded tropes of love, nor what it means when you get him alone, lock the door and ask as you unlace your bodice, are you my angel? Still, he has such arms and hips, a girth of neck and sinew. You'll take him in a small amount, this Horatio, this muscle-bound pragmatist and mix him with a dose of the prince, who has good prospects and a bit of money coming to him, who wears his forelock jaunty over one eye even though his arms are a bit thin, but he can ride and fence and recite with feverish sincerity the words and proofs of desire you so long to hear. Ladies, get out your mortars and pestles and grind, grind away. A pinch of Horatio, eye of newt, leg of toad, monthly blood, the romantic spirit of the prince, mandrake root, a measure of Claudius too because sometimes you like a mature man. He's a bit gray around the temples, a bit softy and swollen in the middle, a real huggy bear, a snuggly wuggly, a man you could settle down and get comfortable with, you say, because he lacks the pretensions of the prince. All that art talk bores you, and funny smoke from his French cigarettes bites your eyes. The spicy food, the bitter wine, the long words only serve to thin your blood. No, you like this Claudius sprawled out drunk on the furniture, his jacket unbraced and stomach monumental, a testament to his appetites, the balance of his vital humors, to his beer-bloated solidity, and after all, he calls you his mouse and pinches your cheek and reminds you a bit of daddy, especially when you hear him snoring at night, distant, you can hear it through the walls, the next room, the door is ajar, my mouse.

A girl like you, sister, what is it that you really want from a man? You ask this of her, of the girl sitting next to you at the bar. You've got it all going for you tonight, your drunkard's sincerity, cross-eyed desire, outlandish charm. She fidgets. It's real cute, the way she twists her straw in her teeth. Nothing, she admits shyly. But you know she's just playing. You have a sense about these things. And if it hadn't been for that last vodka gimlet, you swear, you wouldn't have said it. Nothing, you ask? She nods. Nothing, you repeat, why that's a fair thought to lie between a maid's legs. She's shocked, really, she overturns her soda and you rush to mop it up. How you apologize again and again to her. I'm sorry sister, did you think I meant country matters?

Denmark's a prison.

If I could find him now, my monkey man, lower than the angels, swinging with the gibbons, I'd run to him and never look on your sorry face again.

Denmark's a prison, I think, you'd do better to go carefully there.

This is my life: Elsinore. Who can ever escape?

These are my characters: Judith Taubman Christomo Hamlin, Polonius, Mary Sue Regan, Joan Fontaine, Aaron Saltmarsh, Sofie Kornwald, Martin Hamlin, Martha, Butternut Simon, Leonard Nimoy, Mary, Mary Clare Boughton, Hugh Denmark, Louise, Helen Boughton, Amanda Saltmarsh, Charlie Gumm, Rose Simon, Leslie Saltmarsh, Winston H. Delacourt, Rosencrantz, Roderick Lorde, Hugo Tappan, Laertes, Walker, assorted players, Osric, Annie, the girls at the tomb, Captain Kirk, Ophelia, Claudius, Earl, Thermidor Simon, Joseph Cotten, the player queen, Ruth Stevens, Linda, Yorick, Lynn, Mrs. Marsh, the grave diggers, Felicia, Mr. Sargent, Guildenstern, Nivla Strauss, Horatio, Emmie, Hecuba, Mr. Katz, Anthony Christomo, et al.

These are my places: Flint, Atlantic mine, Boston location, Baltic, Mandan, Bloomfield Hills, the law offices of Royce, Reginald and Melach, Lake Michigan, Chicago, Big Boy Restaurant, the girls' dormitory, Germany, Hart's Jewelry Store, the kitchen, the third-floor girls' bathroom at Central High, Paris, the library, the Fan Dancer Restaurant, the bedroom, Wittenberg, the Purple Flower Sushi Bar, Lake Superior, a cabin in the north woods, her dressing table, the Hyatt Regency Hotel, the gatehouse, Seven Rivers, their disheveled marriage bed.

This is my fear: Elsinore.

These are my love stories: Hamlet and Horatio, Gertrude and Claudius, Hamlet and Ophelia, Ophelia and Claudius, Osric

433

and the player queen, Claudius and Hamlet, Ophelia and Gertrude, Polonius and Claudius, Hamlet and Gertrude, Guildenstern, Yorick, and Rosencrantz, Ophelia and Laertes, oh, oh, you and I.

This is my hero: Fortinbras. I wait for him by candlelight behind the drawn curtain. It has only just begun to rain.

This is my heroine: Shakespearl.

This is her disguise: Many faces. She can wear the mask with the best of the players, jig, lisp, and amble, contort her mobile features, do the police in different voices. You are certain she has shown herself to you. Didn't you, couldn't you swear you caught sight of her in that corner? Look, over there, peek behind the arras and just catch the swish of her silks, retreating footsteps, the click of a well-turned heel, the attar of roses.

Still you cannot pick her face out of a crowd. She could be and is and was, just anyone passing by, and what's more you say, yes, you whispered it at first, but I distinctly heard it that time, what's more you say, fuck you. I've grown tired of your words and promises. And fuck them all and fuck the rest of it and fuck Elsinore where it rains and when it doesn't rain it pours. There is something secret going on. You can hear it. The vague and certain rumbling of it and so you say to yourself, fuck it all, I'm packing my bags, I'm getting out of Elsinore alive. I'm no vampire. I'm no ghost. I'm real damn it and I've got feelings too, you know? Fuck it all, let it all be gone. I'm following the birds, north and south and east. I'm going where it's warm. I'm going to meet someone who loves me and will love me forever. Fuck you, that's just how you said it. First you spit the words out, but then you got good at it and found the true tenor of your unhappiness, fuck, monotone and cold, you, it echoed down the halls, hissed through the porticoes, the columns, found its way out the windows and into the rainy night. Fuck you, I've never even been to Denmark. Fuck you and fuck it all and it was all a long time ago. I do not know these places anymore. I want the old ways. How I long for Elsinore when I was a child. How I long to inhabit that child's body like a spectre and turn my little sunflower of a face up to Gertrude who I barely recognize through the paint and hair wound rolled fancy around her jeweled crown. How I long for that child's comfort, safe in the knowledge that I was, in fact, free to go, that I could have left at any time. Oh, Elsinore, there weren't locks on the doors, sheets on the beds, everyone was beautiful and it was just like living in the movies. Fuck this world, I'll find another. I'll follow Fortinbras. I'll track his footsteps, hound his musky scent in the cold night air. He comes in a flicker of myrrh and frankincense, lighted candles. I'll follow him and not the street signs turned by the wind. I have been lost, misled, tricked that way before. I'll tread in the snow behind Fortinbras and not lose my way. Fortinbras follows the birds and heeds the auguries. He does not know me and thinks I am a pilgrim on the path. Patiently he ignores me. I'll follow him then, past the candles, past the moon, past the dawn, past the birds, past the little country churchyard where the rest are buried, until, snow on the crooked crosses, until we get to the place he has promised where there are apples and figs and bread and honey and milk and lilies and ten thousand years of peace and a warmer climate, until we reach that place and he turns finally, and I think, oh yes yes, Fortinbras, you who have never let me look upon your face, it is you, after all, who have guided me, letting me share your path with no protestations, it is you Fortinbras, strong-armed prince among men, who love, who will love me forever, who will let me walk your righteous path alongside you and I will never be alone again. You turn to me. You remove your hood, cowl, and wimple. Ah, how tired your face looks in this light, and yet, and yet, sweet, your mouth sticky as you chew on figs from the nearby fruit trees. You spit a stem on the path before you and speak to me. These are words I have so long waited to hear. What? How gentle your voice, firm, yet soft-spoken, repeat it, whisper again to me. What is it you say? I do not understand the language. It sounds like. Why will no one leave me in peace—is that it—is that what you say my sweet prince? You nod, mouth full, sticky, sweet, lasciare in pace, please, please, I will not ask again. And so I turn, you leave me no recourse but to split my path from yours. The way is lined with grape leaves, rich tobacco plants, dogs, eucalyptus trees. It is good country here. You could come with me, but no, you are receding, already a ghost, a shadow lost in the looming hills. Leave me in peace in this peaceful country. I do not know where to go. I do not know where I am. No trail, no candles, no moon, but peace, peace, small dogs and bright fruit and the silence of being completely, utterly, desperately alone and in peace, in this peaceful country to which you have led me and left me and led me alone but in peace to abandon but here, but alone.

epilogue

THAT JUNE CHARLIE GUMM GRADUATED. He went on to a good college out East, and he promised to write me, which he did; letters about the tough classes he was taking and how great the kids were, and the leaves were turning and somehow October would always remind him of me, and oh, he was rushing a fraternity and there was a girl he had just started seeing, but wasn't that the greatest thing about us, about me, that I wasn't possessive like other girls so I wouldn't mind hearing about her. He was right, I guess. I didn't mind and it all seemed, even then, far away. Hugo Tappan too left in June, on to a new school with no forwarding address except his publisher in New York. I searched the gatehouse for something he might have left behind, a token, some clue, the last final piece to his education of me, but I found nothing more than an empty gin bottle and a handful of butterscotch candies under his bed. Somehow I hoped he would leave me the girl's bracelet; I know that's foolish and perhaps even selfish of me, to want the one thing he most valued, but I was, and am, a fool for a meaningful ending. I wanted the bracelet because it would mean he had given up on her, or better yet, passed her ghost on to me. He was, I imagine, more sentimental about the past than he was willing to admit.

I didn't go home that summer. I spent the last days of June and all of July with my father drinking strong coffee and silently walking the halls of art museums. I took Walker up on her offer to spend time with her family in Wisconsin. We read best-selling novels and painted watercolors of grapes, oranges, and lemons. The house was big and old, but I slept every night deeply and without dreams, the windows open and the thick scent of the pasture, manure, wildflowers, roses in the night air. Walker's sisters were delicate beauties who swore with every other word, and their mother covered her ears protesting in Spanish their bad manners. Her sisters kissed and held my hands, one on each side of me, under the table before the main course was served at dinner. We drank red wine. The conversation veered in and out of Spanish, Italian, English, and French. We went to mass, all of us together, on Sundays.

It was while I was staying with Walker that my mother and stepfather sent word that they were going to be passing through the area on route to a seminar at a rehab clinic in Minnesota. They stayed in a nice hotel, and we had a polite dinner in the restaurant there. There was talk of baby names, the layette, the briss, and the nursery they were decorating. My mother wore a stylish maternity outfit, a modified sailor suit, white against her bronze skin. She was due in two weeks. She showed me photographs of their travels, seascapes, local celebrities whose names she had long forgotten, and then pulling out a manila envelope from her purse, she lay before me the ultrasound photo of my brother, tiny-fisted and sucking his thumb. What the photo did not reveal was the second child curled behind the first. They were to be born twins, pushing and struggling from the beginning, fighting their way into the world. I almost believed as I sat there that night that none of it had ever happened, that I had been a dreamy and troubled child, that Martin Hamlin had not dealt me the cards of my fate and demanded that I stake, bluff, or fold late at night in his kitchen over a meal of bran flakes and cold mushroom pizza. My mother laughed, drank sparkling grape juice from a wine glass and rested a hand between her breasts, above her swollen belly. I saw my stepfather's face in silhouette, a hazy glow from the bar's neon illuminating his head as he sipped brandy. He touched the edge of the photo of his yet unborn sons. A daughter would have never been enough for Martin Hamlin. I knew then that it was all true; I was the only one I could trust to remember exactly how it all had happened.

Walker and I returned to school together in the fall, shared the same suite and walked together, as another winter approached, to the dining hall in the mornings as the ground crunched away beneath us. There were no boys for us that year. We watched them from our sunny hiding place in the back of the library, those clean, sterling boys in their flannels and chinos, as they crossed the walkway in the bright autumn browness. Walker was still answering phones in the alumni office, and I was baby-sitting for Mrs. Greene, the wife of the biology teacher, who had had a baby girl in the winter. I sang and rhymed songs about blackbirds baked in a pie, the Queen of Hearts, not grieving my lord no more.

Did I miss him? Charlie Gumm, I mean. It was because I didn't miss him that I began to feel that it could have been any boy. But I was wrong. I don't know what I missed. I missed *it*. Not just sex. And not just him. But *it*. Doing *it*. How *it* was between us. And how you could never explain exactly what *it* was because there were no words for it. How he had said my name as though it was his first word and I had no choice but to believe him, how the sun shined that day just for us, he and I, our mouths sweet and guilty with oranges. There were times that next year when I woke at night with an overwhelming nausea, a seasickness of sorts, and I would rise, pull back the curtains from my window and stare out at the playing fields and the moon and the crest of woods beyond and wished I

439

could see not him, but his ghost standing there. Did I miss him? I guess I did, but I'm that kind of person. I miss everything the moment it is gone and worse, powerfully, painfully, with each passing year.

In his eighth book, *Do the Senses Make Sense?*, my stepfather discusses at great length the overattachment to the past, to objects of sentimental value and most specifically, on page 142 of the Cook House paperback edition, he describes the feeling of "oceanic nausea" that I had so often experienced. He calls it the physical manifestation of the separation anxiety; the constant punishment of the self for the foolish act of leaving the mother's body, the intentional but unconscious infliction of physical pain by the psyche meant to echo the birth pangs felt by the lost mother. The separated subject, he says, creates his own birth over and over and thus never allows himself truly to begin to live. My stepfather's solution? I never got that far. I borrowed the book from Walker's cousin Carmen that summer and read it for a while on the beach until the sun passed behind a cloud and we were caught in a brilliant downpour. The book was forgotten in our rush to pack up and head home. But, like all of my stepfather's conclusions, I suppose it was magically simple. Maybe this was the key to his long standing popularity; the subject's problem might have been unbearable, but an end to the pain was always promisingly bright and just achingly out of reach.

I still, even now, feel the pain sometimes welling up inside me, unstoppable and unexplainable for the amount of time that has passed. I find myself crying during television commercials for camera film or orange juice. Does this mean I regret leaving my mother and my childhood behind? Does it mean that I miss Charlie Gumm and his open-eyed kisses? I miss the time. Does it mean that I loved him? I'll never believe in our innocence. It was something else. Stupidity maybe, but not, but never, innocence. Love was perhaps nothing more than part of my education. I learned something from Martin Hamlin and Hugo Tappan and even memorably unmemorable Charlie about men, not just how they want and need, but how they go about getting and having until they want something new and more unattainable. In this respect men are not so different from women. But I never understood their need to love and hate at once, why the two feelings could not be separated. My mother was the opposite of that. She loved Anthony Christomo up to the exact moment when she decided she hated him, and after that she was relentless. She hated him forever and he lived like a spectre in the shadow of her hate. For my mother there was no going back. I'm afraid I suffer from a different problem altogether. I often think about that time, relive and replay it, trying to figure out how it could have been different and what I did wrong. Still, I'm not at all hopeless, nor do I believe that this is the only story I will ever tell. After all, who was right in the end, Horatio when he said "there's a destiny that shapes our ends," or Hamlet himself when leaping onto the pirate ship he came to the understanding that "the readiness is all"? You can decide that one for yourself. Me, I'm not making any bets against time. I do feel the emptiness that once set in motion, is, was, will always be unstoppable: the pronoun *it,* the sounds the birds make, apples with the sweetness of oranges, the grammar of telling a story, the unendurable nausea of giving birth to yourself again and again. This is only the first story. And even if it isn't the beginning, well, it isn't quite the ending either.